DAUGHTER OF THE VOID

DAUGHTER OF THE VOID

Chains of Fate Trilogy: Book One

H.R. Cole

Golden Scales Publishing, LLC
P.O. Box 150616
Brooklyn, NY 11215
www.goldenscalespublishing.com

Edited by Morgan Macedo, Glasswing Editing, LLC
Cover art and design by Stephanie Stott
Stock photos from Deposit Photos
Interior formatting & eBook Design by Jared Reid
Interior map art by Victoria Diaz

HC ISBN 979-8-9915303-4-7
Paperback ISBN 979-8-9915303-3-0
Ebook ISBN 979-8-9915303-5-4

This book is dedicated to my grandmother, who bought me a new book each time I visited and instilled in me a love of poetry that remains to this day.

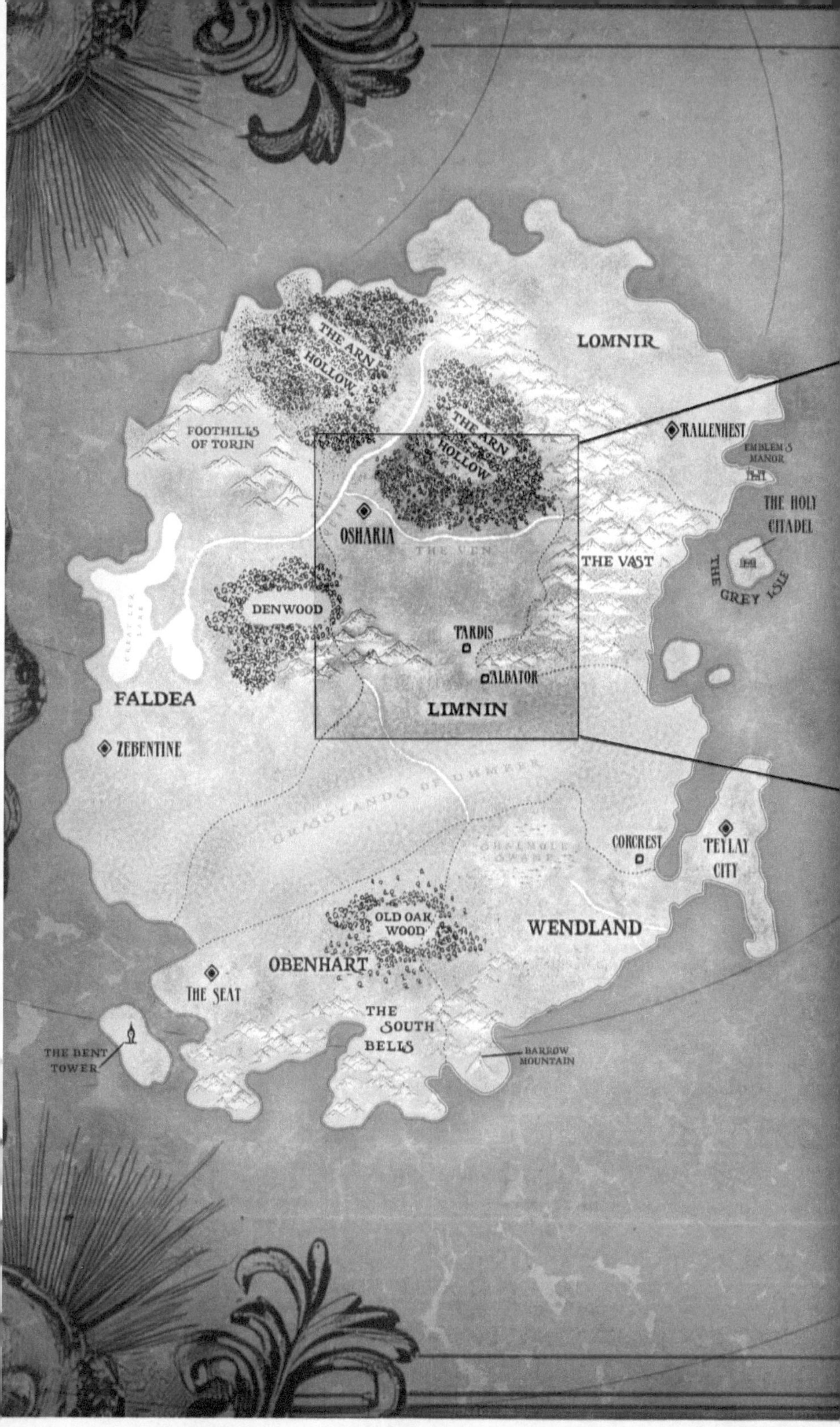

LOMNIR
THE ARN HOLLOW
THE ARN HOLLOW
FOOTHILLS OF TORIN
RALLENHEST
EMBLEM'S MANOR
THE HOLY CITADEL
OSHARIA
THE VEN
THE VAST
THE GREY ISLE
DENWOOD
GREAT ELK LAKE
TARDIS
ALBATOR
FALDEA
LIMNIN
ZEBENTINE
GRASSLANDS OF UMMER
CORCREST
TEYLAY CITY
CHALMGUT SWAMP
OLD OAK WOOD
WENDLAND
OBENHART
THE SEAT
THE SOUTH BELLS
BARROW MOUNTAIN
THE BENT TOWER

ARN
HOLLOW
TORDMEND
OSHARIA
GOLINSTONE
THE VEN
TARDIS
ALBATOR
LIMNIN
N
W
S
UHMEER

CHAPTER ONE

roplets of blood oozed from the cut on Raelyn's forearm, crimson stains fanning out across the torn fabric of her sleeve. She frowned and clasped her other hand over the wound while the cloud of dust and debris settled. *Clumsy,* she thought. How would she explain the injury when they returned to the castle?

"Rae? Are you all right?" Ellisand called down from the rock ledge above. "Are you hurt?" She peered into the shadows of the pit, glancing from her friend to a dark opening in the rocky crags nearby. "We shouldn't have come up here. Can you climb out?"

"I cut my arm," Raelyn answered, disgusted. She straightened and brushed the mud and leaves from her ripped dress, studying the steep embankments to either side. The gulch wasn't very deep—a stroke of good luck in a place riddled with yawning crevasses and bottomless pits. With how hidden the opening had been beneath thick tendrils of entwined forest undergrowth, the fall could have been much worse. She tugged her foot from the soupy mud, cold, dirty water chilling her toes and soaking the hem of her skirt. Her heart skipped a beat when her gaze fell on the cave entrance. Ellisand was right. They shouldn't have ventured out of the duchy woods and into the mountains.

The rocky peaks of the Vast, the mountain range dividing the countries of Limnin and Lomnir, were forbidden to citizens of either nation. Hostilities over who had a rightful claim to the land stretched as far back as Raelyn knew her history. The terrain was dangerous, but more than treacherous pathways plagued the foothills. Mystery wove itself quietly within the ancient trees, seeping through every hidden path, shrouding the landscape in a wildness that was well deserving of its sinister reputation.

Staring into the cave's depths, Raelyn's breath hitched as fear blossomed from thoughts beyond the impossibility of encountering dragons, griffins, or feyfolk. It was fear independent of war and creatures native to the land, borne from stories of other inhabitants lurking within the abandoned mountain passages. Frozen in place, searching the black recesses for any sign of the wretched, she wondered if one of the pale-skinned subterranean dwellers sat hidden within the shadows, watching her with similar intensity. She didn't want to find out. As the third group to lay claim to the Vast, the cursed, humanoid race of the wretched defended their territory fiercely and without mercy.

Cool, damp air wound through wisps of her loose blonde hair, and she shuddered, backing away from the opening. "I'm sure I can climb out," she muttered, striving to hide her sudden anxiety. "Can you help me out when I reach the top?"

"I'm here," Ellisand answered, offering her hand.

Grasping the roots clinging to the side of the rocks, Raelyn tentatively pulled herself off the mud floor, arm throbbing with the exertion. Her jaw clenched when fresh blood oozed through the gash, but she kept her grasp on the rough cords of vegetation and slowly progressed upward, slippery step by slippery step. Unable to pull herself over the rock lip at the top, she reached out for Ellisand's hand. Despite being slick with sweat, the grip was firm, and Ellisand used her body weight to sling Raelyn up.

"Your arm!" she exclaimed, grabbing Raelyn's wrist and examining the cut. "Your father is going to kill me!"

Raelyn inhaled sharply as pain arrowed up into her shoulder from the contact. "More likely, *your* father is going to kill *me*."

Ellisand rolled her eyes. "He only knows I exist when I'm missing. Maybe we can sneak in through the churchyard. You could change your dress. I know! You could grab a servant's shawl to hide the wound. It might buy us some time to think of an excuse."

"It's worth a try. If we can make it back before last meal, maybe no one will know we were gone."

They picked their way through the rocks and roots, quiet with urgency to return to the castle. Despite the impending punishment for sneaking out, Raelyn's heart was full; she loved being in the cool shade of the ancient trees, hidden by giant boulders and dense undergrowth. She felt more at home in the woods than she did in the confines of the stuffy castle, where she was forced to sit for hours learning skills she had no true interest in.

By the time they made it back to the uninhabited duchy chapel, the sun's last rays were casting stretched shadows behind the marble markers within the churchyard. Raelyn knew it was far past last meal, and her stomach churned with both hunger and the thought of being caught by one of her father's men. If they could make it far enough into the castle, there was a chance of avoiding punishment with a clever excuse, even if her father suspected they'd been on another outing. She looked at the red lines of sunset and sighed inwardly. The lower the sun sank into the arms of the horizon, the less likely any excuse would spare her punishment.

Hurrying through the gravesites, the pair hopped down a short set of stairs leading into the crypts beneath the western end of Castle Wedminth. Though once sealed shut, the gate now hung precariously, years of weather exposure deteriorating where the bars joined the wooden base of the door frame. With little effort, Ellisand twisted one of the rods and slid it out, opening enough space to squeeze through.

"I don't think you should come to my room," Raelyn whispered. She felt along the wall in the complete darkness, having memorized the route years ago. "It might be better for you if we split up."

"They'll be looking for both of us by now," Ellisand replied dejectedly. "I'm amazed we've made it this far. They must have every servant and soldier in the castle on alert. I don't know why I let you talk me into leaving."

Raelyn frowned but didn't reply; it was almost always Ellisand's idea to sneak out. Ever since they were children, their adventures were Ellisand's way of escaping the life of invisibility that came with being a female child and the duke's only offspring.

Raelyn instantly forgave the misplaced blame, understanding it for what it was. Ellisand was worried—and rightfully so. Months ago, when they'd been late coming home from a horseback ride, the guards had been out in full force searching the castle grounds. Based on how late they were now, making it through the main floors undiscovered would be almost impossible.

The inner entrance to the catacombs connected to the castle cellar. Opening into a large, rectangular room, the doorway was shrouded in shadow. Raelyn stepped out first, scanning the dimly lit area for signs of life. She breathed a sigh of relief when she found the cellar was empty, as usual. "I think we're safe," she whispered. "Do you think we should try the kitchen or the servants' hall?"

Ellisand placed a hand on Raelyn's shoulder and peered past her at the two stairwells climbing to the next level of the castle. "The kitchen staff will still be cleaning from last meal. If we're lucky, the other servants are out looking for us. Let's try the hall. It should be empty."

As predicted, the large room sat vacant, signs of hurriedly abandoned work littered around the benches along the wall. Remnants of bread and ale, luxuries too precious to have been left willingly, dotted the long wooden table at the room's center. Torches sputtered; it was clear no one had tended them recently. Despite the fading light, the ornate tapestries hanging overhead were vivid, their colors surprisingly vibrant for banners that received little care.

Raelyn's tension receded. If luck stayed with her, she might make it to her castle wing unnoticed. "I'll head for the stairs once we enter the east hall. Are you going to your quarters?"

"I'll go to the library. Father might believe I fell asleep there." The younger woman twirled a loose curl of her black hair. "No one ever goes to the library. I saw a maid's tryst in there once, and they weren't even trying to hide themselves."

Raelyn nodded, too distracted to ask for details, and pushed open the door.

She froze as six pairs of eyes turned to acknowledge her at the sound of the door latch.

"Emblem's Hand, Raelyn!" her father yelled, striding over to her from the group standing in the center of the hall. "What happened to you? Where's Lady Ellisand?" He grabbed her by the shoulders and looked her over.

"I'm here." Ellisand stepped through the doorway with a flare of her hands and a deep bow. She winced when her mother, the duchess, rushed from the duke's side to crush her in a fervent embrace.

Altha Wedminth, a bear of a woman by most standards, was tall and squarely built, and Raelyn had always thought her more handsome than beautiful. Her presence commanded obedience, even when she wasn't upset, and she was clearly displeased by their late arrival. The candlelight deepened the lines of her face ghoulishly, the illusion made more ferocious by her scowl.

"I'm sorry, Mother," Ellisand mumbled into the folds of Altha's dress collar. "It isn't that late, really."

"I'm all right," Raelyn assured her father. "I fell, but I'll be fine." She could only imagine what she must look like: hair unbound and tangled, yellow dress stained with blood and dirt. She was far from the image of what a woman of twenty and three should look like when receiving guests.

"How dare you drag Ellisand outside the castle walls again!" Duchess Wedminth released her daughter. She crossed the distance to Raelyn and landed a firm slap on her cheek. "Just look at you! Tonight of all nights! Commander Forthgrew, your daughter has gone too far this time. They are too old for this nonsense." She glared at Raelyn, gaze full of fury and unchecked disdain. "With all the trouble the Faldeans are causing and rumors of wretch sightings, I don't want Ellisand outside, not even in the duchy woods. You are not children anymore."

Raelyn studied her father's expression and rubbed her cheek, skin tingling from the blow. Commander Jorn Forthgrew's face remained an impeccable, emotionless mask, tempered from years of serving as commander of the guard, but Raelyn could see the irritation in his eyes. The duchess was correct. Taking Ellisand, niece of the king, out unescorted when rumors of war were growing persistent had been a dangerous idea.

"My lady, I promise you, Raelyn will be properly disciplined." He looked at his daughter. "I am sure she would never intentionally put Lady Ellisand in danger."

"We should be grateful everyone is unharmed," a man standing beside Duke Wedminth calmly remarked. "An adventurous spirit is admirable—in moderation."

Despite the late-summer humidity in the hall, the words cooled Raelyn, and she focused her attention on the tall man who'd spoken. His stance was relaxed, and he watched Ellisand intently, though not so overtly that he drew the displeasure of the duchess. Raelyn was aware of the nature behind such a stare. She frowned but said nothing, quietly assessing the strangers. One of the newcomers, a young man with a shock of black hair and dark eyes, fixed her with a piercing look, and Raelyn fought the urge to shift behind her father to escape his gaze.

Chaotic discourse erupted between Duke and Duchess Wedminth. Their voices were soon joined by the others in the party, but Raelyn couldn't focus on what was said. She did her best to remain composed and calm. She was at fault and knew there was more dignity in accepting the consequences than in pleading for mercy. As the conversation grew louder and more heated, Jorn interceded before either duke or duchess could settle on a punishment for his daughter.

"Lord Leofric, my apologies," he addressed the man who'd spoken. "Both young ladies are exhausted, and my daughter is injured. This issue will have to rest for the time being." He looked pointedly at Raelyn. "Go find Ebest and have her look at your arm."

"May Lady Ellisand come?"

"Absolutely not!" Altha held onto her daughter's shoulders. "We have much to discuss yet this evening."

With a sigh, Duke Wedminth nodded in agreement, tugging at his silver beard. "Raelyn, it is time you bid Ellisand goodnight."

Unhappy about leaving her friend to whatever fate the evening held, she glanced again at the three strangers. Lord Leofric's companion still watched her, a hint of amusement glimmering in his eyes. Unlike his lord's tempered observations, the man made no attempt to mask his focus. He remained silent while the others quibbled, one hand resting on the hilt of his sword, the other hidden beneath the flap of his violet cloak. *A personal guard?* she wondered, looking away when their eyes met briefly. Turning, she headed up the stairs and shivered, certain his gaze was still on her.

Once beyond sight, she let out a ragged breath. Getting caught had gone better than she'd hoped, but the duchess was unpredictable, especially regarding Ellisand. Raelyn would have to mind herself closely until the memory of their adventure faded, or she might face more severe punishment for a much lesser offense. Cradling her arm, she continued the long climb to the alchemist's chambers.

Ebest lived in one of the northern towers, her quarters not far from Raelyn's. The door was ajar—as usual—the older woman unconcerned with privacy. Books, stacked as high as the ceiling, some covered with a layer of dust, hid the few furnishings, while potted plants cluttered every table, shelf, and ledge, creating an atmosphere of eternal summer.

Raelyn knocked lightly on the door, walking in without invitation.

"Raelyn, what a nice surprise!" The stout woman's ruddy cheeks glistened in the lamplight. "I was just working on a new elixir. You didn't find any nettleworth on your walk today, did you?"

Despite being a master alchemist, Ebest specialized in natural medicines and used her knowledge primarily to heal the sick. The duchy didn't employ a mage to heal with magic and treated the majority of ailments and injuries with potions and poultices. While herbalism was not as efficient as supernatural healing, Ebest maintained it was necessary to encourage a working knowledge of medicine among those without magical talents.

Raelyn understood the value in approaching healing so practically. Mages who could manipulate the unseen tendrils of magic in the world were rare. Working with essence, the magic surrounding people, was strictly regulated, and mages approved to use it for healing were few and far between—and expensive. Most were Holy Knights, directly serving the Holy King, Uhmeer's spiritual leader and the voice of Emblem, God of Gods and Lord of The Circle. But sequestered away on the Grey Isle, the Knights weren't accessible to regular royalty or nobility, making available healers even rarer.

Natural medicine was far more accessible, and it was teachable. If something happened to Ebest, one of the alchemists beneath her could step in, and simple remedies could be shared for personal use, regardless of someone's station.

Still, there were drawbacks to needing ingredients. Her plants, kept in such supply to use if she needed them in an emergency, were short-lived and often used quickly, and she relied on the travels of others to get more when supplies were running short.

Biting her lower lip, Raelyn shook her head. "Things didn't go exactly as planned." She held out her arm. "I slipped. I think it will be fine, but Father insisted I come to see you."

Ebest nodded, examining the injury. "It will hurt more tomorrow after the swelling sets in. Here." She handed over a small jar of balm. "This will numb the area a bit and keep infection away. Put it on with a clean bandage before you go to bed and then again in the morning. Hopswert and firefly powder. Remember that."

"Thank you, Ebest. I'm sorry we didn't get you any herbs today."

"No worries, my dear. I'm too old to go into the Vast myself any-more, and I'm grateful that you and Lady Ellisand even think of me when you go." Her expression turned mischievous. "Speaking of our lady, that's quite the handsome troop of young men from Lomnir here tonight, isn't it?"

Raelyn raised an eyebrow. "Handsome?" She paused, reluctant to agree despite sharing the opinion. "Troublesome is more likely. You should have seen how Lord Leofric—I think that's his name—looked at her. It was like she was a prized horse."

"Bah, you're not seeing it properly, Rae. Lady Ellisand may be younger than you, but she's well beyond marriageable age. When I was her age, I had been married and in my own home for several years already."

"I don't see why she has to get married at all." At Ebest's hearty laugh, Raelyn's frown returned. "I don't think it's funny."

"It's funny, my dear, because you'll find yourself in some young man's home soon enough. Your father can only protect you for so long. With marriage for Lady Ellisand in sight, the duchess will be looking for a man for you next."

A strange pang shot through her core. The words were unsettling, and Raelyn's irritation transformed into melancholy. Twenty and three was old for a single woman of her position. As the daughter of Duke Wedminth's palace commander and of minor nobility, she had a respectable dowry, but as far as she knew, no suitors had ever come to ask for her hand. The knowledge was both relieving and upsetting at the same time. Raelyn never thought much about her appearance, but she assumed there must be something undesirable about her.

"I should go," she said. "I want to look for Hendrel again."

"That naughty wisp still hasn't returned?"

She shook her head. "He's never been gone this long. Maybe he finally got called to Emblem's Hall."

Ebest nodded thoughtfully. "If that's the case, my dear, he's the bet-ter for it. Be glad his detention on this world is through at last."

Hendrel's disappearance only added to Raelyn's gloomy mood. The will-o'-the-wisp had been with her since she was a babe, floating over her bassinet the moment the midwife placed her within the furs. He'd been a silent comfort and companion to her throughout the years, reg-ularly disappearing for a few days at a time to reappear suddenly when she missed him the most. Like other wisps, his spirit was trapped in the mortal world. Either unfinished business during life or the inability to accept death had doomed him to wander until his spirit found peace. For all Raelyn knew, her ethereal companion's purgatory might finally be finished.

"I'm going to look one more time. He's easier to see at night."

"Good luck." Ebest smiled and gave her a quick embrace. "Let me know if your arm isn't getting better."

"I will," Raelyn said, taking her leave.

Another winding staircase took her to the top aspects of Castle Wedminth. The ramparts were quiet after sundown, guarded by a skeleton crew of soldiers standing intermittently along the walk. Torches lit the way yet were unable to banish the dark entirely from the stone walls. The night was balmy and clear, and the air was still.

Raelyn looked out into the fields stretching beyond the city to the foot of the Vast. Sometimes, if she was missing Hendrel, his light appeared roaming the dark vales. Tonight, just like the last few nights before, all was complete darkness.

"Still no sign of him?"

Raelyn turned and smiled at Jackson, lieutenant in charge of the night watch. "No. For a will-o-the-wisp, he's decidedly hard to spot."

He leaned against the railing next to her. "I'm sure he's okay."

Jackson's voice lacked conviction, but Raelyn nodded. "I hope so. He's been with me for so long. I'll be sorry to see him go." She swallowed hard to clear the lump in her throat. "I won't stay. Father is angry enough with me at the moment."

"As unseemly as it is for a young woman to be out here with the men, I think your father knows we won't let any harm come your way. There's probably no safer place for you. You're basically one of us, anyway."

She sighed. His words were meant to be comforting, but she couldn't shake the grey cloud over her mood. It clung to her like the feeling of the stranger's gaze when she'd left the hall.

"Where's Lady Ellisand? She's normally with you on your nightly excursions," he asked, interrupting her thoughts.

Raelyn glanced at him, careful to keep her expression neutral. She long suspected Jackson harbored romantic feelings for their dark-haired mistress. The three of them had grown up together, though,

Jackson was a handful of years older. His question wasn't as innocent as he was making it seem.

"She's entertaining suitors, from what I gather." She saw him tense. "But apparently, I'm the only one who thinks marrying a stranger is unappealing."

He was quiet momentarily and then said, "We're all slaves to our positions, Rae. Even if Lady Ellisand found love, it would be heartache for her if the man wasn't of a high enough rank to pursue her. Maybe it is better this way."

So that's what he tells himself, she thought, looking back out toward the horizon. "Why do things have to change, Jackson? Why can't we live out our lives as we see fit?"

"Come on. You know the answer to that. You, of all people, wouldn't be happy without a bit of variety in life. Embrace change. What else can you do?" He smiled, shoving her gently like he had when they were kids.

"Go on." Raelyn shooed him away. "You have a castle to protect, and I have to go back inside."

She scanned the darkness one last time after Jackson walked away but saw no sign of Hendrel. Convinced the day had been a complete failure, she strode down the ramparts toward the warmth of the castle. The flickering torchlight of the keep tugged at her senses as the nighttime quiet enveloped her, but all thoughts of evening comforts vanished the moment she entered the watchtower.

The young man in the violet cloak blocked Raelyn's path. He leaned against the wall at the top of the stairwell, preventing her from getting downstairs without a confrontation. She stared for a long moment, too taken aback to think of anything to say. Had he followed her from their encounter in the hall? The idea felt foolish.

The man didn't acknowledge her, his face down while he cleaned a worn knife. His straight, black hair shielded his eyes. Raelyn hoped the thick fringe prevented him from seeing her. Maybe she could sneak back onto the ramparts without being noticed.

Duchess Wedminth's words echoed in her head. *You're not a child anymore.* What was she so afraid of? One yell, and twenty of her father's men would be at her side in an instant. Feeling her courage grow slightly, she cleared her throat. "Sir, would you mind if I get past you to the stairs?"

He continued to clean the blade but looked up at her. A jolt like lightning raced down her back when his dark eyes met hers.

"My name is Laris. You can use that instead of 'sir.'"

Arm throbbing within its bandage and the length of the day weighing on her like an over-laden pack, Raelyn nodded absently, ready to play along however he wanted if it meant she could get back inside. "Well met. And I'm Raelyn." She gave a quick curtsy, looking past him to the stairs. "It's late. I'll bid you goodnight."

He looked back down at the knife but made no effort to move. "You're right. It's late."

Though not easily intimidated, her heart quickened with a growing sense of unease. Danger radiated from him like heat off obsidian on a summer day. She looked from the knife in his hand to the sword at his side, customary allowances for the personal guard of a visiting dignitary. No doubt he could kill her in any number of quick, efficient ways before she could call for help, and no one would know until they stumbled over her body in the tower. Biting her lip, she took a tentative step forward.

"Don't you think it's inappropriate for the daughter of the palace commander to be strolling at night with the men?" He sheathed the knife and looked at her. "If your own reputation isn't at stake, you should consider your father's."

Caught off guard, Raelyn froze. "Excuse me?" she asked, unbelieving she heard him correctly. "Are you suggesting something was going on up here?"

"I'm not suggesting anything. I'm merely making an observation and a good point."

Her fear and uncertainty faded, replaced by indignation. Raelyn steeled herself and walked toward him, intent on making it down the stairwell, even if she had to push him down with her. He remained unmoving, and she thought he would let her by without incident until one of his arms reached out in front of her, blocking her path. She turned to retreat but found herself pinned with the wall at her back.

All her daring vanished at Laris's unbearable closeness. He smelled of wood smoke, leather, and horses. His complexion was sun-kissed and his skin clean shaven, his eyes such a dark brown they almost looked black in the dim lighting of the tower. She could feel the heat of his body bridging the gap between them and became keenly aware of the scent of lemonmint on his breath.

"I'm going to be watching you," he whispered close to her ear. "Do not cause any trouble."

Heart hammering in her chest, her eyes glossed over with frustrated tears, but she refused to let them fall. She'd been surprised by his boldness, but she was in no mood to be bullied, not within her own home with allies steps away on the castle walls. "Are you so comfortable as a guest to think nothing of threatening and insulting me?" she whispered back to him.

"Spare me your outrage," he replied flatly. "We are the ones who've been offended. I don't want any issues. You'll not interfere with Lady Ellisand and Lord Leofric. We didn't come all the way to Limnin only to sit and visit with the duke."

"Interfere? I regret the loss of my friend to marriage, but I've never intended to prevent it. I might not look like it, but I do understand how the world works."

He shifted from her side to look at her straight on, eyes narrowed in condescending doubt. "Do you? Daring words for a lady of nobility who shirks duty to play outside the castle walls."

Raelyn wished she could melt into the cold stone to put space between them. Laris's eyes unlocked from hers and moved across her face, sending lances of alarm tingling into her core. She fought to slow her thumping heart, afraid he could hear it with his closeness. Every sense on high alert, she winced when he brought a hand up and looped a stray tendril of her hair behind her ear.

He paused at the reaction, fingertips lingering on the skin of her neck. "I'm not going to harm you."

Just threaten me, she thought, swallowing hard, pulling away from his touch. Did he think she'd taken Ellisand out to deliberately avoid Lord Leofric? "I didn't know guests were expected tonight," she admitted. "We wouldn't have gone."

He was silent for a moment. "You didn't sneak her out to avoid us?"

Raelyn met his gaze. "No." She was being honest but realized there was a strong chance Ellisand had suggested the outing for that exact reason. Keeping it secret had ensured there would be no reluctance about leaving. Raelyn wasn't duty-bound by any means, but she did have the sense to know when responsibilities needed to be faced and when they could be safely ignored. Vanishing on the afternoon of a visiting lord's arrival was not something she would have agreed to. She should have known better than to unquestionably trust Ellisand's sudden urge to get out of the castle.

Laris stared at her, trying to decide if he believed her. "I want your word," he said finally. "Your promise that you'll let Lady Ellisand and Lord Leofric complete their courtship uninterrupted."

A part of Raelyn wanted to laugh at him. Between her and Ellisand, Raelyn wasn't the one he should be concerned about interrupting marriage plans. She nodded instead, the humor not enough to break through her discomfort. "You have my word."

He studied her through narrowed eyes, arms still barricading her in place. "Good."

Fresh worry gripped Raelyn when he didn't let her go, and his gaze drifted to her mouth. The atmosphere shifted; she could *feel* a change in their confrontation, though, the name of the danger replacing his ire escaped her. As he pressed slowly closer, every muscle in her body braced in panic for the unknown.

He stopped. Lips pursed, Laris squeezed his eyes shut and let out a controlled breath. He leaned back with a shake of his head. "I apol—"

Like a bird released from a snare, Raelyn sprung toward the opportunity of freedom. She ducked beneath his outstretched arm and ran down the stairs, skirts twisted into her fists so she wouldn't fall from the nervous tremors shaking her legs.

"I wish they wouldn't insist on watching us," Ellisand mumbled, glancing across the yard to the nearby tent while she pulled back her bowstring. "I haven't been able to go anywhere for the last three days without someone on my heels."

Raelyn watched her friend's arrow fly to the center of the target. Ellisand had always been an excellent shot. "If he's going to be your husband, you'd better get used to him being around," she replied sullenly. It was her turn, and she drew back, bringing the string to anchor at the corner of her mouth. Her arm ached with its injury, and the strain affected her release. The arrow landed solidly in the target but far off the mark.

"There's no formal proposal that I know of, and if there were, I don't know that I'd accept it. Lord Leofric isn't exactly what I'd want in a husband. He's so … proper. I want someone to sweep me off my feet, Rae."

"What's not to like?" Raelyn decided to be difficult. "He's young enough. He's not ugly. He seems to have some semblance of manners." They walked to the target, and she pulled her arrow, wincing at the pain in her forearm.

"Are you being serious? I thought you'd be on my side. He's hardly the rogue prince I've been waiting for. Can you imagine him singing me ballads or carrying me off for romantic, impulsive lovemaking? I can't."

Raelyn grimaced. "Please don't ask me to imagine that. You've been spying on the servants too much, I think. What will happen if you refuse his proposal?"

"There's a chance Father will push the issue and force me. I don't think he cares either way, but Mother is quite taken with Leofric. She told me our union would help unite Limnin and Lomnir again. She'd probably sell me to a potato farmer if she thought the king would praise her for it."

"She does love you, Ell. Just in her own way."

Ellisand scoffed. "Right. That's why the night we got caught was the first I've spoken to her in weeks. At least when I'm in trouble, she remembers I'm alive."

Walking back to the edge of the practice area, Raelyn glanced over at their small audience. Sitting to Leofric's right, Laris caught Raelyn's perusal and gave her a curt nod. She glared back and resisted the urge to shoot an arrow at him. Her eyes moved to her father, and he smiled, looking bored with the task of playing companion to the visitors.

"Let's go out again tonight," Ellisand said softly. "Father has been preoccupied with news of Faldean invasions to the south. He'll be distracted. It will be the perfect time to slip away. I can't take another moment of this dull marriage nonsense."

Raelyn hesitated, recalling her promise to Laris. What would he do if she accompanied Ellisand out again? What *could* he do? He wouldn't kill her. He couldn't—if he wanted to salvage Lord Leofric's marriage proposal. Ellisand wasn't always the most selfless friend, but she wouldn't marry a man who condoned Raelyn's mistreatment. An escape felt irresistible after days of castle drudgery and protocol.

"After last meal, we can leave through the bath springs," Ellisand said. Raelyn voiced her agreement, concentrating on her shot. "That might be the only place left they can't follow us." Raelyn's arrow missed the target completely, and she muttered a curse.

"Ellisand!" the duchess called from the viewing tent. "Come here for a moment, dear."

A look of exasperation passed between them, and Ellisand set down her bow and arrows. "Yes, Mother," she replied in a sing-song voice.

As her friend walked away, Raelyn smiled to herself and readied another shot. *One more*, she thought, *then I'll concede to this injury.* For a long moment, she stared down at the arrow on the bowstring, enjoying the warmth of the sun soaking in through the thin layers of her dress. A refreshing breeze chased away the heat, and she looked up—mind clear, ready to shoot.

"You'll just keep missing if you insist on shooting with your injury." Laris stepped next to her and picked up Ellisand's bow. "It's affecting your release."

He nocked an arrow and pulled back, holding his aim for a breath before letting loose. It hit the target's center, and he readied another arrow.

Her clarity vanished, and she bit back a retort and pulled her bowstring to anchor. Channeling all her willpower, she ignored the burning sensation under her bandage and made sure to keep her release fluid. The arrow soared through the air and landed next to Laris's, so close it was touching. "I'm doing just fine," she remarked.

"A competition, then, if you're so sure," he declared loudly and leaned toward her. "Best of three."

Under the viewing tent, the spectators went silent, all awaiting her reply. Searing pain in her arm screamed at her to decline the challenge. A shoot-off was foolhardy, Raelyn knew, but pride held her in place. She felt unsettled—both by her discomfort and by Laris's attention. He was testing her. He knew as well as she did that she was far from "fine."

Heart pounding, a twinge arched through her stomach when she met his smug, teasing look. "Best of three," she reluctantly agreed, trying to appear assured.

Surprise replaced that smug look in his eyes, and his expression sobered. He watched her for a long, quiet moment. Uncomfortable under his scrutiny, she grabbed an arrow and put it on the bowstring. "I'll go first," she said, drawing back. She stared at the black mark on the target's center and forced herself to hold the pull of the bow despite the pain. Sure of her aim, she let go. Another bull's eye.

No longer seeming amused, Laris nocked an arrow, pulled back, and released. His shot was quick but perfect, squeezing in between two of their previous arrows. He turned to watch her, his face unreadable.

Soldiers. Raelyn fought the urge to roll her eyes, annoyed. Laris was just as talented at hiding behind a mask as her father was. She set her second arrow and pulled back. Her arm shook, and she let down without shooting. "Just a moment," she mumbled, regaining her composure and pulling back up. She let go prematurely, but the arrow landed within the tight nest of center shots.

"Are you always this stubborn?" Laris leaned on his bow, looking out at the target.

"Are you always this confrontational?"

He frowned but didn't reply. Readying the bow, he held at aim longer than his past shots. His release was clean and deliberate. When it hit the target, the arrow split one of Raelyn's down the center.

She turned to him, mouth agape, shocked and mildly infuriated.

"Last shot," he said quietly, dark eyes locked with her blue ones.

She snatched an arrow from the bucket and nodded. *Last shot, indeed.* She would give it everything, even if her arm fell off.

Sucking in a deep breath, she held on to the air, using the pressure in her lungs to steady her position. At full draw, her entire upper body trembled with the effort of staying at anchor, and as soon as her mind recognized the shot, she let go. Not as accurate as her others, the final arrow landed low and to the right.

Heat spread through her face at the sounds of disappointment from the onlookers.

Laris wasted no time readying his final arrow. With practiced ease, he went through the motions methodically and with confidence. When he released, Raelyn knew immediately the shot wasn't headed toward center. It landed low and to the left, directly opposite hers.

They'd tied.

Cheers and applause erupted from the viewing tent. Walking next to Laris to retrieve their arrows, Raelyn couldn't shake the feeling he'd missed on purpose. She discretely flexed the fingers of her injured arm, trying to ease the tension and ache from her wound. At the target, he pulled their arrows and tossed aside the broken one. Holding hers out in offering, he looked at her expectantly.

She reached for them, but the pain made her immediately withdraw. Taking the arrows with her other hand, she looked down and curtsied. "Thank you for the challenge, Sir Laris." She emphasized his name and title slightly, remembering his words to her in the tower. Around others, he'd have to accept the proper honorific whether he wanted to or not.

He offered her a customary bow in return. "Lady Raelyn."

Lengthening her stride back toward the training grounds, she grabbed her bow and headed to the small enclosure housing the practice weapons. Hidden within the dusty plank walls, she hung the bow, put away the arrows, and looked down at her shaking arm. A garish streak of blood stood out against the pale fabric of her sleeve, and she sighed. She'd ruined another dress.

A shadow fell over her from the doorway. Raelyn hid her arm and spun around. Without pause, Laris stepped in and invaded her space, reaching around and pulling her arm from behind her back. Before she could make a sound of protest, he tugged the sleeve above her elbow and slapped a white cloth to the bleeding gash.

"I was trying to encourage you to stop shooting." He flattened his hand on the cloth, applying pressure.

Mouth suddenly dry, she swallowed and stared down at his hand. "You were trying to embarrass me."

"No," he said with an edge to his voice. "I wasn't."

She chanced a look up and felt rooted in place when he caught her stare. Heartbeat echoing in her ears, Raelyn fought for calm. Laris had spoken to her of impropriety the night they'd met, and here they were, alone again, so close she could see the dark speckles in his brown eyes. She instinctively lurched back and pulled her arm away, clamping her hand over the cloth. Too close to the back wall, she knocked into the hanging weapons and stumbled sideways.

Laris retreated a few paces. "Did I hurt you?"

She shook her head but kept her distance.

"You don't have to be afraid of me. I didn't mean to scare you that badly the other night."

She stared wide-eyed. "You threatened me but didn't mean to scare me?"

Frustration passed across his features. "Not terrify you, no." He moved closer to the doorway. "Keep the handkerchief. Something tells me this won't be the only time you reopen that cut."

She huffed in relief when he left, more shaken than she cared to admit. It wasn't fear rattling her nerves; she wasn't *afraid* of Laris harming her. He was unpredictable—a conflicting mixture of danger and thoughtfulness that kept her unsettled. Closing her eyes, she pressed the back of her hand to her forehead.

"Rae?" Ellisand stepped into the shed.

"Sorry. I'm just putting everything away."

"Mmhmm. And what was Sir Laris doing in here with you? Teaching you some of his magic?"

Raelyn rolled her eyes at the implication and her friend's teasing tone. "Offering me a handkerchief for my cut," she replied briskly. "Nothing more."

"He's handsome, isn't he?" Ellisand peered outside, scanning for eavesdroppers. "I always imagined you with someone milder, though, like a tailor or a carpenter."

"A tailor?" Raelyn lifted an eyebrow. "What do you even mean?"

"Nothing bad! Just that you're so calm and quiet all the time. I can't imagine you with a Lomnirian commander who craves blood and war. What did your father tell us? That Sir Laris has been in charge of Lord Leofric's troops in Lomnir for years now?"

"So you're saying I'm boring?"

"No! Don't be so contrary." Stepping in, she linked arms with Raelyn and pulled her toward the doorway. "I just can't picture you with a warrior, that's all, let alone an army commander and mage. He's not even *just* a mage, Rae. He's a transcendent—a mage pledged to uphold the Holy King's edicts. When was the last time you met a transcendent?"

Raelyn let herself be led into the late-day sun, thinking about Ellisand's comment. Laris's occupations were as contradictory as his personality. Reputable mages never visited her city of Albator, which was odd in its commitment to non-magical life, and Laris was the only mage she'd even heard of sworn to the Holy King as a transcendent. She didn't understand how a man could be committed to the betterment of mankind while reaping death in the service of his lord and country as an army commander.

"Don't be so sour about it." Ellisand's voice filtered in through Raelyn's thoughts. "I wasn't saying you're boring. You're the most interesting person I know."

"I'm the only person you know," Raelyn shot back with a smile. "And you're impulsive enough for the both of us. Clever," she added slowly, "not telling me about the dignitary arrival the day we snuck out."

Ellisand laughed and squeezed Raelyn's elbow as they walked up the stairs to the garden veranda. "I don't know what you're talking about. I was as surprised as you to see the courtship party."

"Your expression says otherwise, you weasel." Raelyn pulled her arm free, stopping at the door to the castle interior. "I'd best go see what dress your mother chose for my banquet outfit tonight. I'm sure it will take an hour to put on."

"An hour, if you're lucky." Ellisand waved goodbye. "Don't be late. I won't be able to relax if you're not there."

Deep shadows greeted Raelyn when she stepped inside, and her eyes fought to adjust from the bright sunlight to the dimly lit castle hallway. An unexpected shiver rolled through her, pulling out a deep breath that banished the tension tightening her shoulders and neck. She was accustomed to Ellisand's carefree comments; they rarely struck a nerve. But no matter how close their friendship, the entitlement of position eternally hung between them. Raelyn would forever be at the mercy of Ellisand's opinions, with no practical way to stand up for herself other than to match her friend's wit.

She stretched and rolled her neck while she walked, enjoying the quiet of the castle midday. The servants were busy in the lower levels preparing for last meal, their jobs in the private quarters of the castle done early in the morning.

Pushing open the door to her room, Raelyn smiled at the portrait of her mother above the fireplace and glanced over at the rose-colored dress laid out on the bed. "My punishment continues," she called to her mother's image. "The color I hate. Duchess Wedminth knows me too well." She picked up the dress and shook her head. At least there wasn't a hoop skirt.

She tossed the garment back onto the bed. The maids wouldn't arrive to dress her for another turn of the clock, long enough for her to visit the library Ellisand had touted as abandoned. She grabbed the stack of books on her nightstand and hugged them against her chest. Old and worn, they provided another means of escape, one Raelyn could embrace fully without fear of reprimand. Their worlds, the characters within, were as familiar and dear to her as close friends. She'd read all of them cover to cover more times than she cared to admit.

Heading down the hall, she kept watch for the duchess's maids, knowing they'd cause a fuss if they saw her leaving so close to preparation time. All remained quiet down the long corridor to the library, though, its archways empty and welcoming, afternoon sunlight chasing away the cold of the stone interior. The hall ended at a small anteroom with no other connecting passages—one reason the library rarely saw use. Raelyn pushed open the dark oak doors hiding the castle's treasure of books and welcomed the scent of paper and furniture polish.

She took her time putting the books away, pulling others of interest off the shelves as she went. At a row of thin, colorful covers, she paused and ran her fingers down the line of bindings. She would never be too old to appreciate the collection of funny children's stories her mother used to read to her before bed.

She slid one out carefully, its weathered, brittle binding flaked with age. The title was faded, but the pages were mostly intact. The charming rhyme told of a little boy who noticed a hole in the town dam. Realizing it would break and flood the homes if he left it to get help, he stuck his thumb in the hole and braved the cold of night to keep everyone safe. The next day, the villagers found him, and he was named a local hero.

It was one of her favorite stories and one her mother had loved, as well. She was drawn to the beautiful images in the book, the lake depicted so peacefully it pulled on her heartstrings, calling to her.

"Rae! Why, imagine finding you in here. Today is my lucky day."

Raelyn looked up as Ebest dumped an armful of books onto the table at the center of the room.

"I was just thinking about you this morning," the alchemist said. "How is your arm?"

Raelyn smiled. "Better. I did strain it a bit this morning during practice, though."

"Practice? You know better than that! Do I need to bandage it again?"

"No, no. Don't worry. I'll wrap it with the maids when I get ready for the banquet." She suddenly remembered Laris's handkerchief was still in place under her sleeve. "There's a clean cloth over it at the moment."

"Well, keep it wrapped for another day. The pressure is important, too. It helps keep swelling down. Why in the world would you insist on training today?"

"I couldn't let Ell face the Lomnirians alone." Raelyn stood and walked over to look at Ebest's pile of books. "Are these all on herbalism and alchemy?"

"Ah, yes, those handsome devils. Not all business, no. There's one or two in there that you'd approve of. I only think about my job most of the time, Rae, not all of the time." Ebest winked. "Shouldn't you be in your room? I passed the duchess's platoon of maids on my way here. I daresay they were likely heading your way."

Raelyn grimaced. "Bother. Okay. I'd better get back. The duchess already wants my head. I can't take any risks." She grabbed the few books she'd set aside and hurried to the door. "Thank you for checking on me. Here—" she made a show of setting one of the novels down "—read this next. It's my favorite."

"Ah! I will. Now, go!"

Raelyn ran down the hall back to her room, stopping the maids as they turned to leave her door. "I'm here," she said, catching her breath. "Don't go. I'm here. I'm sorry."

The women glanced at one another but nodded and followed her inside. Raelyn allowed herself a moment of relief, then she squared her shoulders. The coming hours of preparation would be worth it to earn a place back in the duchess's good favor.

CHAPTER TWO

Raelyn endured the banquet preparations without complaint. The maids weren't at fault for the amount of time it took to do her hair or secure the layers of her dress; it was the natural consequence of the duchess's complex style choices. With the final touches in place, Raelyn smiled, looking in the mirror at the end result. Even if it was part of her punishment, the rose-colored dress was more beautiful than expected.

She thanked the maids and waited for them to leave before heading to the banquet hall. Music permeated the air, sending waves of vibration through the stone of the nearby walls. After entering and greeting the duke and duchess, Raelyn accepted her carefully curated plate from the servers and watched the festivities of last meal from an alcove at the far end of the room. It was one of her favorite places. The decorative hollow was slightly elevated off the floor, and the vase within was light enough for her to push back to allow room to sit. She set her plate down, leaving large portions of the glazed boar and spiced vegetables untouched, and looked through the sea of people to find Ellisand.

She spotted Ellisand picking at the food on her plate, smiling politely while Lord Leofric talked. She looked every bit the daughter of a duke—dark curls swept atop her head, intricately wound into plaits and braids that paled in comparison to the complexity of her bejeweled, emerald-green gown. She looked like a delicate work of glass art, though Raelyn knew better. Her lifelong friend was far from fragile, nor was she as soft-spoken and reserved as she appeared to be in such company. She was the opposite of Raelyn in almost every way: confident and bold, charismatic and charming. Ellisand led, and

Raelyn followed, content to be her quiet, contemplative counterpart and the voice of reason.

On Leofric's left sat the third man from Lomnir, Tens, who seemed pleased to spend his time flirting with the servers as they refilled his cup of wine. A feeling of uneasiness settled over Raelyn when she realized Laris's seat was empty. Too late to escape, she saw him walking over to her.

Dressed in a black tailored tunic with dark eyes staring at her intently, he looked disconcertingly handsome. Memories of their previous interactions and closeness flooded her thoughts, and heat spread across her face. She was glad for the shadowed light of the hall.

"You're not sitting at the head table?" he asked her. "Worried I'll challenge you again?"

Too wary to banter, Raelyn looked away from him. "I gave up my place for you and your companions," she replied, shoving a chunk of bread from her plate into her mouth. "I prefer it here over one of the crowded tables."

"Your archery skills are impressive. Are you skilled with other weapons?"

Cautious of the casual change in topic, she shook her head. "A little, but not much, truly. Father let me have a dagger when I was little. The men humored me—taught me my forms and eventually let me practice with a wooden sword when I was old enough."

Slightly surprised by her own candidness, she looked at Laris from the corner of her eye. His disinterested expression sent a lurching sensation through her chest. *Just say "no" next time, Raelyn,* she scolded herself. *He doesn't care about your childhood.*

She turned her attention back to the dancers and picked at the remaining bread on her plate. Several lords and ladies from Albator were in attendance, and the duchess's ladies-in-waiting roamed free in their colorful dresses, searching for dance partners. By the banquet doors, Jackson stood guard, politely refusing requests as different women approached him. He shared a brief look with Raelyn from across the room, and she chuckled under her breath at his haggard expression.

"Why is it you aren't married yet?" Laris grabbed her attention back.

The words sounded more like an accusation than a question, and she couldn't help but stare at him for a moment in stunned silence. What a talent he had for keeping her constantly unsettled! Talking with him was more challenging than any sparring match she'd ever had on the training grounds, and she knew she had to be careful not to get cut. "That is none of your business."

"Chasing your suitors away with castle escapes and nighttime strolls?"

It was sarcasm but not entirely a joke. Appalled that he would speak about something so personal, Raelyn slid off the alcove lip. His blow had landed, and the cut was deep. "If you must know," she said, smoothing her dress, "no one has asked for me. Not one suitor. Not ever." She refused to look at him in the silence that followed, and they both stared at the dancers. Eventually, she took a deep breath and softly added, "I'm not your enemy. Please excuse me."

Raelyn stepped away, but he grabbed her hand. The firm, gentle contact felt almost apologetic, beseeching her to turn back and stay. Refusing to acknowledge him, she tried unsuccessfully to pull out of the grip.

"Raelyn?" Her father's voice was a welcomed sound, and the hand on hers immediately relinquished its hold.

"Will you walk with me a moment, Daughter?" Jorn asked, his gaze moving between her and Laris.

Without another glance at her unwelcomed companion, Raelyn nodded and hurried to her father's side.

"Is everything okay?" he asked, steering her out of the hall toward one of the adjacent balconies. "You seem to have caught someone's attention."

Raelyn sighed. "He's concerned I'll cause issues between Lord Leofric and Ell. Apparently, I've been labeled a troublemaker. Was our adventure outside of the castle so awful? It's not as though I kidnapped her and forced her to go."

Placing his daughter's arm through his own, Jorn patted her hand affectionately. "Lord Leofric told me he approved of your friendship with Lady Ellisand." He smiled at Raelyn's wide-eyed look. "Laris is a warrior, Rae. He's commanded Lord Leofric's forces in Lomnir since he was nineteen. His adeptness on the battlefield with stone and fire magic is legendary, and his reputation has only grown during his six years as commander." Jorn stopped and looked down at her. "Perhaps he just doesn't know how to speak with a pretty woman—or any woman, for that matter."

Dismissing her father's words, she shook her head. "Father, I already told you his interest lies in Lord Leofric and Ell. He's been nothing but rude and insulting to me during our brief interactions. I think he might actually hate me."

"And what of the fact Lord Leofric has no such reservations about you?"

"Then I'd say he was being untruthful with you."

Jorn laughed. "All right, Daughter. But if Laris seeks you out, try to remember what I've told you. Sometimes, a man who knows only killing makes for a poor conversationalist."

Raelyn frowned slightly. "And if I'm right and you're wrong?"

"Then you were kind to a cruel man, and no harm was done."

She nodded. Her father was right. Raelyn, though gifted with a quick temper, was not unkind. That she may have come off as a troublemaker, or as a willful hindrance to relationships beyond her, bothered her.

Jorn walked back toward the hall. "I'll see you in the morning, Rae. We're getting in a new group of horses. Be up early."

She smiled at his back and watched him make his way through the crowd. If her father was right, she needed to make more effort to bridge the gap between her and the Lomnirians. Laris perceived her as a threat. She didn't want that.

Walking back into the room, she located him quickly. He was reclining next to one of the giant pillars bordering the dance floor, his arms crossed over his chest as he watched Ellisand and Leofric clumsily trot around to the music. Raelyn quietly approached and eased onto the chair next to him. She felt him look at her, but she stared straight ahead, afraid to initiate conversation. After a few moments, she asked, "Do you dance?"

"Yes." He lifted his arms, clasping his hands behind his head. Before Raelyn could inquire if he would want to be her partner, he added, "But I have no plans for it this evening."

She clamped her mouth shut and choked down the rehearsed invitation. Her father had to be mistaken about Laris's intentions. Her stomach felt like it was twisting into a knot. There really must be something wrong with her. Ellisand was right; she had no business in the company of a warrior mage. It was foolish of her to think otherwise.

"Well," she mumbled, "enjoy the rest of your evening." Sliding out of the chair, she bumbled through an awkward curtsy and hurried to the opposite side of the room.

Finished dancing, Ellisand greeted her with a smile. "Are you ready, Rae? I told Mother we were taking our leave for the evening." Her smile fell a bit. "Are you all right? You look flushed."

"I'm fine." Raelyn waved away the words of concern. "Do you need to get anything from your room?"

"No. I hid some clothes for us earlier when I overheard the servants talking about a festival tonight. Oh, it will be so perfect! We couldn't have picked a better night to go into the city."

Raelyn loved city festivals. Excitement pushed away her embarrassment from moments before. "Let's hurry," she said. "The air in here tonight is suffocating."

CHAPTER THREE

ulticolored lanterns flooded the main street of Albator, its curved path wrapped protectively around the wall of Castle Wedminth. Music from the center square accented raucous laughter and shouting from hundreds of people fanned out along the roadways. Raelyn inhaled deeply. Aromas from roasting meats and spices perfumed the air, and everywhere she turned, some delicious-looking confection tempted from a storefront or vendor booth.

"Let's go dancing, Rae," Ellisand said, pulling Raelyn toward the center square.

"Someone might recognize us." She glanced at the city guards wandering through the crowd. Though less familiar with the members of the Wedminth household compared to the castle soldiers, the city guards knew Raelyn's father well. They also knew of Raelyn's and Ellisand's tendency to sneak off the castle grounds. Plain dresses and cleverly braided hair wouldn't be enough to save them from someone with a keen eye. "We can sit in the square if you like, but let's get something to eat first."

"Oh, all right," Ellisand said with a pout. "But look how much fun they're having!"

Looking out into the mob, Raelyn couldn't argue. Most of the women dancing were barefoot, with dresses cut to be revealing and skin glowing from the heat of the summer night. Every face smiled, and flowers littered the square as the women twirled to the music. It was hard to resist the urge to join in. "Do you want to find a seat while I get us something?"

Ellisand nodded, hopping in place to the music.

Across the square, one of the bakeries boasted a large display of chocolate creations. Cakes, candies, and tarts lined the tables with enough variety to satisfy any level of sweet tooth. Raelyn's mouth watered at the sight of thick chocolate cake slices spooned into wooden bowls. She selected two slices and turned around to scan the crowd for her friend. Ellisand wasn't far away, sitting on the rim of a dry fountain.

She was talking to someone Raelyn didn't recognize. While relieved to see Ellisand's companion was not one of the city guards, Raelyn's discomfort grew as she watched the pair. The older man sitting next to Ellisand spoke without looking at her, his posture guarded and rigid, out of place with his gaudy clothing and the festival atmosphere. From across the square, Raelyn noticed two more men arrive and sit at Ellisand's other side. They didn't involve themselves in the conversation, but they didn't talk amongst themselves, either, and seemed to be quietly listening. Concerned, Raelyn distractedly paid for the dessert while keeping her eyes pinned on her friend.

"Here's your chocolate, *Mary*," Raelyn said when she approached, using the name she often did for Ellisand when they were out of the castle.

"Thank you. Nort, this is my friend, Jenna." Ellisand introduced Raelyn to the man. "Jenna, Nort is here from the seaport of Corcrest. He came to trade at the festival tonight."

Raelyn smiled politely and remained standing. Festivals within the city were common and full of local goods, but they held little attraction for outside merchants. The trade shows in early fall were when the vendors and buyers came from places as far away as Corcrest.

"Your wife must miss you being gone on such a long trip," Raelyn commented, making it a point to focus on the bowl of cake rather than Nort's reaction.

"A wife probably would. My mistresses have no problem with it." His voice was deep with an unrecognizable accent, and he grinned, showing a mouthful of crooked teeth stained yellow from years of drinking low-quality ale.

Ellisand stood with a polite laugh and took a bowl of chocolate cake from Raelyn. "I suppose a woman who shares her man isn't mindful of such things. How long of a trip was it?"

"It's not important. You young ladies don't need to eat standing up. There's plenty of room here." Nort's smile didn't reach his eyes.

He patted the stone rim next to him. "There's no need to be in such a hurry."

Raelyn linked arms with Ellisand and said, "The night is young." She did her best to look apologetic. "We're meeting some friends a few blocks over, and we shouldn't be late. I'm sorry, but you'll have to excuse us. Enjoy the festival!"

The smile faded from Nort's face, the corners of his mouth falling into a flat line. "Of course. Perhaps we'll be fortunate enough to see you again, Jenna."

Pulling Ellisand away from the fountain with no more response to Nort than a slight nod, Raelyn steered them through the crowd to the other side of the square. "Keep an eye out for those men," she whispered. "I didn't like them."

Ellisand shrugged. "He was a little intense, but I don't think he meant any harm. You're as suspicious as your father, you know that?"

After an initial twinge of annoyance, Raelyn sighed, acknowledging the truth. The childhood provided to her by Jorn had been one of weapons, horses, scuffed knees, and fist fights. It was the childhood of a soldier's son. The delicacies ingrained in Ellisand from birth had been taught to Raelyn at a much later age when she could decide which beliefs she wanted to align with. Much of her disposition came from watching her father order and organize troops, not from sitting with the masters who tried to teach her the arts. It was fair to say she kept many of her father's traits. "Okay, fair enough," she admitted, "but we should probably head back all the same. Was there anything you wanted to do before we go home?"

"Yes!" The other woman's amber eyes lit up. "I want to have my fortune told, and I want you to come with me."

"No. You know I don't like the fortune tellers."

"Come on, Rae. You'll let one bad experience when you were eight ruin any fun for the rest of *my* life?"

Raelyn laughed at her friend's dramatic expression. "Yes. Go if you want to. I'll wait over here." She pointed to a bench partially hidden by flowering bushes. "But you have to promise me you won't tell me about it."

Ellisand nodded and handed Raelyn her cake bowl. "Okay. Not a word unless I find out you'll be a queen someday. Or that I'm going to marry a prince."

Watching Ellisand disappear into the street of tents, Raelyn set down the empty bowls and leaned back against the armrest of the bench, pulling her legs up onto the seat. With a handful of fallen flowers, she turned her attention to plucking the petals. Many people enjoyed having their fortunes told, and she couldn't fault Ellisand for enjoying it, too. It wasn't her friend's fault a crazed fortune teller had predicted and told, in detail, the death of Raelyn's mother when she was eight.

She paused, the memory surging to the surface of her thoughts, taking her back to the cold, rainy day when she stepped inside a ramshackle tent while her father spoke business with an informant in the alleyway. She'd been too terrified to scream when a wrinkled, bony hand clutched her forearm and dragged her into the tent interior, and she hadn't uttered a word while the old woman spit gibberish and broken sentences at her. It wasn't until the crone suddenly gained clarity and started speaking about Raelyn's mother and the fiery accident that would claim her life that Raelyn had edged out a piercing screech for her father.

Swallowing hard, she pushed the memory aside. Ellisand knew she hated Fortune Tellers' Row. At least this time, she hadn't tried her hardest to get Raelyn to join. She plucked a petal and watched it spiral to the ground, missing her mother so much it felt like a sword in her heart.

She switched her focus to the sounds of the festival saturating the night, grateful to be out of the castle and away from reminders of impending change. Ellisand would be married soon—to Leofric or a different lord. Without Ellisand to champion her, Raelyn knew the duchess would waste no time sending her away.

A pile of petals gathered at her feet while she sorted her thoughts. Halfway through the handful of flowers, Raelyn looked up when she sensed someone approach. She dropped the remaining blossoms, too surprised to speak.

Sitting next to her, Laris wiped away the dots of pink and purple strewn along the bench. "Where's Lady Ellisand?" he asked, his tone cold.

Raelyn took a deep breath before responding. "She's having her fortune read. We were just about to head back." Fear gnawed at her insides. She had pushed her luck too far. Getting caught outside the walls again was a prison sentence. The duchess might even have her whipped out in the yard. She glanced nervously at Laris.

He caught her look and turned toward her. "You're out here alone, risking your lives, to have your fortunes read?"

"We're heading back, I promise," Raelyn whispered, needing to make him understand. She could tell a layer of anger lay just beneath his composed exterior. "We've done this our whole lives. We're always safe."

He watched her without replying, and she felt color creeping into her cheeks. Something about him made her acutely aware of his every move, from the almost imperceptible narrowing of his eyes to how he shifted his weight on the bench beneath his cloak. She felt like a hare backed into a corner, wondering when the wolf would take the first bite.

"You promise?" He forced a laugh and shook his head. "Like you promised me you'd not cause any trouble? Are you always this irresponsible? I thought more of the ladies in Limnin. And you wonder why no suitors have ever come your way."

Genuinely wounded by the comment, Raelyn tried to temper the look of hurt she knew had crossed her face. She turned, pretending to scan the tents while trying to steady her breathing. It was uncommon for her to be so flustered, and the fact she was showing weakness in front of him again made her want to cry—and that infuriated her even more. When her body finally listened to her plea for calm, she turned back toward him but kept her eyes on the ground. "I'll go find Ellisand," she said softly.

He started to say something, but Raelyn was too quick. She stood and darted toward the colorful tents, leaving Laris sitting on the bench.

Fortune Tellers' Row was tidier than usual, the festival crowd an easier draw when the tents were clean and inviting. On a regular day, the fabrics were tattered and dull, prostitutes loitered in shadowed corners, and disreputable mages and nadir—followers of the chaos gods who wove essence magic for dark purposes—plied their services to the desperate. Fifteen years ago, Raelyn vowed never to walk the path of Fortune Tellers' Row ever again. Yet here she was, breaking her solemn promise to get away from Laris.

Easing her way through the festivalgoers, she spotted Ellisand's dark braid and blue dress several tents away but couldn't catch her friend's attention over the heads of the crowd. The desire to hurry and return home to avoid further punishment emboldened Raelyn, and she pushed her way along, ignoring the irritated remarks and shouts directed at her.

At the moment when she was near enough to call out, a blinding light illuminated the sky, and a thunderous boom erupted behind her in the city square. The sound rocked the city, sending a shock wave through the street. Tents ripped off poles, sweeping people into the folds of fabric and pinning them to the ground. Glass windows shattered, spraying tiny shards onto the bodies in the streets. Behind her in the square, a fireball rose upward, extended into the night air by a cloud of black smoke.

Raelyn was hurled forward, knocked off her feet. She hit the ground hard, and the breath left her lungs. Her injured arm throbbed painfully as the wound reopened. She looked up through the swirl of dust, searching for Ellisand. Amid the panicked cries and pained screams, Raelyn could hear someone calling her name.

Dazed, she pushed herself to her feet. For the second time that day, she'd been lucky; the fire wave from the blast stopped exactly where she'd been standing, but everything up to that point behind her had been turned on end and set aflame. Ears ringing, she realized it was Ellisand calling her, but the sound was not of inquiry—it was of urgency.

She spotted Ellisand fighting against the hold of two men, their faces hidden. Everything else faded away as Raelyn watched her friend being hauled away from the tent area, reaching out and yelling for help.

Ignoring the shooting pain in her arm, she stumbled forward and pulled her age-old dagger from its sheath on her calf. Fear for her friend dulled her pain, and she increased her stride, running after the abductors and leaving the bedlam behind.

Ellisand's struggling had slowed her captors enough that Raelyn caught up to them at a quiet intersection of two alleys. The chaos within the city was a dull roar in the background as she slid to a stop, facing her enemies. Ellisand continued to struggle but was unable to speak. A cloth gag tied tightly around her head muffled her cries. The men were familiar, and Nort smiled at Raelyn as they faced one another.

"Turn around and go back," he said. "Or did you want to come along?"

Breathing heavily from the pursuit and smoke in the air, Raelyn shook her head. "I'm not letting you take her anywhere. Let her go."

"Lady Ellisand is one of the reasons we're here." At Raelyn's vengeful expression, he nodded. "Yes, I knew who she was all along."

"You … Are you Faldean?"

He didn't answer her question. "It was fortuitous we found you out of the castle," Nort told her. "It makes this much easier. Now, the city can be dealt with without us having to search first."

Hope drained from Raelyn. If Albator was under attack, saving Ellisand might mean more than wresting her from a handful of bandits. The odds were already against her, and severely so. She held the dagger out and widened her stance. "I won't let you take her."

Nort laughed, and Raelyn could feel the sincerity of his amusement in the deep sound. "Very well then," he said, handing Ellisand to the other man and drawing his sword. "You probably won't be the only woman I kill today."

Despite some formal training, Raelyn had never been in a real fight. The dagger in her hand felt painfully tiny compared to her opponent's blade. Fear seized her; one poorly timed move and he'd slice off her entire hand. The reality of the situation hit with enough intensity to force her back several steps.

When Nort barreled toward her without warning, she was unprepared. Instinct and swift reflexes saved her. Pivoting to the side, she escaped the blow, and the movement allowed her to strike wildly at him while he was off balance. Her blade caught only air, and he quickly righted himself and swung at her again. Raelyn knew she lacked the strength to parry the heavy weapon and didn't trust her ability to protect her hands. Narrowly dodging the strikes with lucky footwork and growing acutely aware of her true defenselessness, she was on the verge of panic. Her worry grew when the intersection filled with men wearing unfamiliar sigils, and a figure in full plate armor stepped toward them. The man signaled to Nort, who immediately lowered his weapon.

The imposing figure walked over to her, stopping at the point of her dagger. Dressed in burnished plate metal over black linen, the man kept his face and head concealed. Only his eyes, glimpsed through the dark metal of his helmet, hinted at his humanity. He pressed his armored chest against the blade and said, "So it was you."

Before she could question him, he moved astoundingly fast, backhanding her so hard she stumbled backward against the wall of a building where she slid to the ground.

"You're the one who stifled my attack." He unsheathed his sword.

"I don't know what you're talking about," she whispered, tenderly touching her nose and bloody lip, trying to focus on him through her watery vision.

"I was wondering why the explosion was less than expected. It also explains why so little of this city side was affected. The shockwave never made it." He kicked Raelyn's dagger away and knelt. Pressing a gloved hand against her throat, he held her against the stone wall. "You dissipated it when it hit you. Had I known a warden was here, I would have killed you first."

"Warden?" Raelyn pulled at his hand. "You're mistaken."

He gripped her throat harder. "Do not insult me." His voice lowered. "I can feel my power neutralized in your proximity."

"Master Orion," Nort interrupted, "I believe this woman is Raelyn Forthgrew, daughter of the Wedminth palace commander. I have no reports on her having special abilities."

Orion ignored the other man. He stared hard at her. "Is it possible you don't know what you are?" Keeping one hand on her windpipe, he pulled off his head coverings. Blond hair, darker than Raelyn's, was pulled back from his face. The shadow of a few days' facial hair growth hugged his chiseled features. He pursed his lips, peering at her. "Do I leave you alive and bring you with us, or do I kill you and not take the risk?" His free hand stroked her bruised cheek. "Mmmm."

"Take me with you." Raelyn could barely get the words out through her strangled throat.

Orion smirked. "Clever, but foolish. Take you with us to keep you near your friend, never mind what might happen to you. A noble request and tempting, believe me. But, no, my dear, I think—even though the risk is small—that you'd be better off dead." He brought his sword to her throat.

A bright light flared between them, and Orion leaped backward, relinquishing his hold on her. The brilliant flare condensed until a flickering ball of flame hovered over Raelyn's chest.

"Hendrel!" She wished she could embrace her ethereal friend. The wisp left her and floated over to another figure entering the crossroad. Laris glanced down at Raelyn and then at Orion.

"Release Ellisand Wedminth," he commanded. "The women will be coming back with me."

"The Wedminth girl is already on her way to where she needs to be." Orion waved dismissively. Ellisand and Nort were no longer visible on the street, and Orion looked over at Raelyn, who had managed to inch her way toward Laris. "You should let me kill the warden. She affects your powers as well as mine."

"Be grateful she keeps the battleground even." Laris motioned for Raelyn to move behind him. "You and your men would die tonight if it were otherwise."

The other man laughed. "I should like to fight you, but now is not the time. I have pressing matters to see to." Orion gestured toward the castle. "I see they've set fire to the keep. Our other forces within the city will finish the job. Take my advice and abandon the woman here. Save yourself so we might meet in true battle another time." He turned his back to Laris and Raelyn, waving the men around them to move out.

Determined to go after them, Raelyn stopped short when Laris gently put a hand on her shoulder. "Pursuit is not an option right now."

"But Ell—I can't leave her!"

"She's gone, Raelyn. And I am only one man against an army. Can you get us back into the castle without being noticed? Raelyn?"

She pulled her gaze from the retreating men.

"If she's been kidnapped for her title, they won't harm her. Right now, we need to get out of the city. How did you get here from the castle?"

Concern for her father brought Raelyn's mind to focus. "There's a shrine in the city garden that connects to the bathhouse in the castle." She grabbed his hand, pulling him forward. "We aren't far away."

Hovering over their clasped hands for a moment, Hendrel darted in front of them, leading the way down a dark side street.

Once part of the private Hestor estate in the city, Albator's city garden was a sprawling landscape of flowers, hedges, and statues. Large enough to be visible from higher elevations at the city's edges, a gigantic fountain sat at its center, the artistic, architectural masterpiece a beautiful disguise for what lay beneath: a secret shrine to the chaos goddess, Delvia. After the Hestor family's worship of Delvia was discovered and their ties to the forbidden arts made known, the Holy King turned their land over to the city. The family was stripped of their nobility and confined to the Grey Isle to live under the careful watch of the Holy Citadel. The garden became a beautiful public gathering place, and the shrine below was sealed.

Or so people thought.

"There's a secret entry in the back corner of the garden," Raelyn said, pushing through thick, overgrown hedgerows. "Ellisand and I discovered it as children. It's a crack in the base of one of the statues. There's no path to it, and it's surrounded by old briar vines. Even the gardenkeepers ignore it. Here."

Along the back perimeter wall, a tall statue held vigil, the knight dressed in full battle armor, his sword held aloft in eternal challenge to some unknown foe. A thick barrier of thorn-covered vines fortified the statue's base, but without hesitation, Raelyn knelt, flattened herself into the dirt, and slid through a gap between the ground and the vines' stalks.

She waited for Laris to follow, and he did without pause, shedding his cloak before crawling beneath the vines through the opening at the statue's base. Within the small cavern of crumbled marble and dirt, Raelyn dusted off in Hendrel's light. Repositioning his cloak over his shoulders, Laris stared at her intently as she straightened, and she felt foolish when he asked, "Well?"

"Yes. Th-this way," she stammered, navigating the fallen stones that took them to the chamber floor. "There's only one tunnel from here to the shrine. From there, we can take the old aqueducts up to the castle bath springs."

At the end of the passage, Delvia's inner sanctum lay in ruin. Wooden pews in the chamber rested in splintered shards—a deliberate act when the temple was sealed—and the wood had succumbed to the slow ravages of time and moisture. Only the carved channels in the chamber floor remained as they had been, funneling water in an oval around the defunct shrine, making a symbol of The Circle in the stone.

"A shrine to the chaos goddess, Delvia, is an ill omen," Laris remarked, skirting the wooden remnants. "She's one of the three Deceivers—the goddesses who recruited mortal followers by preaching twisted variations of history." He glanced around the room, fingers on the hilt of his sword. "How far is it to the castle?"

Raelyn inclined her head toward the passage in front of them. "This way. It's a straight path. If we run, we can make it in less time than it took us to get here from the square."

He pointed at the wisp hovering by Raelyn's shoulder. "Guide, make your light useful."

Hendrel flickered and circled Raelyn, and she felt a genuine uncertainty from the spirit. "Go on," she whispered. "He just doesn't know how to ask nicely."

With a brilliant flare, Hendrel danced around Raelyn again and shot down the tunnel ahead of them, chasing away the dim shadows of Delvia's abode.

Laris grabbed Raelyn's hand before she could follow the wisp and pulled her to his side. "Stay behind me as we go," he instructed, leaning in close to her in the darkness. "You owe me for that broken promise, Raelyn." He spoke softly into her ear. "I always collect my debts."

A shiver rippled through her, and she nodded slowly, uncertain of what to say or the meaning behind his words. *Was that another threat?* She looked at the ground. She owed him her life for saving her in the city. That, alone, was an impossible debt to pay.

"Let's go before your wisp gets too far ahead." He let her go and headed down the tunnel.

Heavy swaths of smoke and the scent of burning lumber laced the air as Raelyn and Laris emerged into the castle bath chambers through an obsolete part of the aqueduct system. Despite the empty tranquility of the spring-fed bath pools, there was nothing peaceful about the atmosphere; sounds of panic and chaos echoed down from the chambers above. The oppressive environment seemed too much for Hendrel, who did a flickering lap around the bath chamber and vanished.

Fear for her father gripped Raelyn's heart, and she leaped forward, stumbling out of the aqueduct opening. She momentarily forgot Laris was with her until he grabbed her by the waist and pulled her back, holding her tightly until she stopped fighting him.

As if reading her thoughts, he said, "Your father is a warrior, Raelyn. Remember that. He will not be so easily overcome, and you'll do nothing other than distract him."

She renewed her struggle against his grip. "He may need me, and other people up there are in danger. I am not a helpless child!"

With what felt like no effort, he hauled her backward against the wall and forced her down to sit on the floor. "You may as well be a helpless child," he whispered forcefully, crouching in front of her. "You are foolhardy and impulsive, and you have no concept or control over the one skill you do possess."

She opened her mouth to protest, but he shook his head, placing a finger to her lips. "With you near me, I cannot use my powers to their full extent. You are a warden, a maker of voids in the fabric of magic. I know you do not understand, but for the sake of your father, for the sake of everyone in this castle, you must stay here. I will come back for you."

"I'm not going to stay here." She glared at him in challenge. "My father needs me."

"I don't have time for this," he replied, reaching down and grabbing the hemline of her dress. "You mistake your ignorance for admirable stubbornness." With a quick jerk, he tore off a length of fabric. "You leave me no choice."

He grabbed her wrist.

"Let go of me!" Raelyn twisted in his grasp. "What do you think you're doing?"

Laris said nothing, fending off her strikes as she kicked out with her legs and swung with her free hand. At one point, she connected with his jaw, and her closed fist made a satisfying thud with the impact. The moment of self-satisfaction was her downfall. Laris took advantage of her momentary pause and secured her other arm. Using his weight for leverage while carefully avoiding her injured forearm, he brought her arms behind her back and tied her wrists together. He reached for her feet, though she still tried to kick him, and with another strip of fabric, tied her feet and hands together.

"Laris, don't leave me," she pleaded, softly adding, "What if the enemy finds me like this?"

He stared at her for a long moment, saying nothing.

"Laris?"

"I'll come back for you." He turned, drew his sword, and headed up the stairwell.

CHAPTER FOUR

The humid air of the bath chambers pressed in on Raelyn, suffocating in its heaviness. Her clothing clung with moisture, and a steady supply of droplets from her hairline and scalp kept her eyes burning with the sting of sweat. She was thirsty and lightheaded. Her throat was sore. She had given up yelling some time ago, most likely, she guessed, around the same time the screams from the keep above diminished. For the first few hours, raw fury kept her straining against her bonds, but, eventually, she was forced into quiet submission as the skin on her wrists and ankles could take no more. She sat in silent dismay, wondering if she should inch her way back toward the aqueduct before an enemy discovered her.

Just as she decided to abandon her forced vigil, a figure stumbled down the stairwell at the far end of the bath chamber. She recognized him immediately despite the layers of blood and soot on his face.

"Jackson," she called out, her voice hoarse. "Jackson, thank Emblem!"

"Rae? Rae, is that you?" He limped over to her. "What in the world are you doing down here? Are you hurt? Your lip!" Gently taking hold of her hands, he released her bonds. "Who did this to you?"

"It's a long story. I-I'll explain later. They've taken Ell. We have to tell Duke Wedminth." Raelyn's words tumbled out faster than she could put her thoughts together. "What's going on up there? Did you see Father? Laris? Laris went to find him."

Jackson shook his head as she sputtered at him and clasped her hands in his own. "Peace, Rae. Your father was alive the last I saw him, but that was early in the attack. They came at us as the banquet waned, locking us in the hall while they slaughtered the servants. The duke and duchess were evacuated through Ebest's tower while we fought, though, I have no knowledge of the outcome of their escape."

"And Laris? Did you see him?"

"Lord Leofric's man? I did not see him." His expression shifted in thought. "Although, someone did turn the tide for us in the night." Jackson crawled to the edge of the closest bathpool and splashed his face with water. "They are not just men, Rae," he said after a moment. "There are other things in the castle. Things not made of flesh. At least, not flesh like yours or mine."

A chill raced up Raelyn's spine, and she swallowed at the surge of fear accompanying it. "What are we going to do?"

He looked back over his shoulder at her. "I'm going back up there. My duty is to my lord and lady. We crossed paths accidentally, you and I, as I sought to avoid some *thing* in the hall."

"I'm going with you," Raelyn said, pushing herself to her feet. "Please, Jackson. Don't leave me down here." She expected him to argue with her, just as Laris had, but Jackson nodded, splashing his face again with water.

"Of course. You'll be safer with me. Do you have your dagger on you?" He didn't wait for her to answer before tossing her one of his. "Here, just in case you need two."

Raelyn looked at the blade in her hand. Though no blood was visible, she could see the smears left behind from recent use. Instead of emboldening her, the weapon filled her with doubt. Laris warned her from leaving the bath chamber, but that was hours ago. What harm could there be in following her childhood friend now?

"Rae? Are you ready?" Jackson placed a hand on her shoulder. "If I fall, leave me. Get yourself to safety."

She didn't let the impact of his words sink in, though, she felt them tug at the corner of her subconscious. Without a word, she paced herself behind him, giving him enough room to maneuver as they headed up to the next level of the keep.

Raelyn wasn't sure what she expected upon entering the castle's ground level, but what she saw when exiting the stairwell etched itself into her memory, she was certain, for all eternity.

Bodies were everywhere, some familiar, others not, and where there were no bodies, there were seemingly endless streaks of blood. In the south hall, where the bath chambers linked to the main castle, servants had been cut down like stalks of corn. They lay piled together, young and old alike, and some had been ripped open from chin to groin, their entrails pooled beside them on the floor. Raelyn was no stranger to the sight of battle wounds, but the unnatural, carved-apart bodies of the men and women of the keep deeply disturbed her.

"Jackson," she whispered as they crept through the silent hall. "What manner of weapon does this to a body?"

"It's no weapon," he replied. "There are men here, yes, but with them came wretches and other creatures. Demons? Wraiths? Monsters out of nightmare? I can't say. But they strike without warning from the shadows."

"From the shadows?"

He nodded, not looking back at her. "Yes. It's almost as if they are shadows themselves. We need to make it toward Ebest's tower. Hopefully, she was able to evacuate the duke and duchess."

Raelyn never thought she would see the day when kind-hearted, grandmotherly Ebest would don the mantle of a warrior, but that was, after all, the responsibility of all those in servitude to the castle. While Ebest was not a transcendent bonded to the Holy King, she was a formidable foe by way of poisons, acids, and other concoctions. Raelyn hoped the healer was safe and Laris had been enough to end to whatever was happening in Albator.

Lost in her thoughts, she noticed Jackson had stopped on the dais leading into the northern tower. He held out a hand to still her, motioning for her to crouch down. In sync, they moved slowly up the stairs, weapons drawn, backs pressed against the wall. Something crashed loudly in a room nearby. It startled Raelyn, and she realized much of the castle was still smoldering from the initial assault. The dagger handle was slick in her hand, her grip to compensate so tight she lost feeling in her fingers. Step by slow, quiet step, they eased their way through the smoke-filled corridors.

Where is everyone? Raelyn glanced around the passage. There was not a living soul to be seen, friend or foe. She hadn't seen anyone alive since leaving the bath chambers. Was everyone dead? A dark wave of dismay washed over her. What were the chances her father was the only one who'd made it out alive?

Jackson stopped again, this time at the entrance of Ebest's quarters. Just like the last time Raelyn visited, the door was ajar, only now, no welcoming light beckoned from within. All was silent as the dim grey of dawn poured through the windows. Edging their way into the room, the pair stopped simultaneously as the scene inside revealed its bloody tale.

The piles of books Raelyn loved lay scattered and torn apart; the plants uprooted and withered; the bottles, pots, and jars of tinctures were shattered and spread in ruin along the floor. At the far corner of the room, the crumpled form of Ebest lay in a heap, her healer's robes marred with blood, her body as ravaged as those in the south hall. With a gasp, Raelyn staggered over to the body, clutching the figure to her despite its horrible gaping wound.

"No, no," she whispered, stroking the old woman's hair. "How could this happen? I'm so sorry. I'm so sorry." Raelyn looked through tear-filled eyes at Jackson, but the lieutenant didn't share her moment of mourning. Instead, he crouched at the door adjacent to Ebest's body, his ear pressed to the wood, his eyes staring at Raelyn but not seeing her.

"Jackson?"

He put a finger to his lips, silencing her. "We are not alone," he mouthed.

Gently lowering Ebest's body, Raelyn slunk over to the door. Leaning in, she could hear muffled sounds of battle.

"They must be on the ramparts." Jackson grabbed Raelyn's chin, the action more urgent than affectionate. "You either go with me now, or you run, Rae. See how far you can get. I know you have a million ways out of this place."

"I'm not leaving," she whispered forcefully. "You're all I have in the world right now, and I am not leaving your side." She glanced at Ebest and wondered how many more friends she would find in similar states.

He smiled a sad half-smile. "So be it. We do this together, no matter the outcome. It has been an honor, Raelyn Forthgrew." Jackson took a deep breath. "When I open the door, be quick. If the ramparts are clear, we won't have to worry about stealth. No one will hear us over the fighting."

She nodded.

"We should be able to see the battle before it sees us."

Dagger in hand, Raelyn readied herself and tried to control her breathing. Her heart pounded in her chest, and thoughts of being consumed by shadow beasts stole her concentration. When Jackson pushed open the door, she felt disconnected from her body, barely aware that she had made it through the doorway and was running behind him along the empty castle wall.

They made it halfway across the top of the keep when her father's shout snapped her out of her stupor. Instantly, she honed in on his figure amid a mob on one of the flat tower platforms initially designed for defense against enemies outside the castle walls.

Jorn fought ferociously alongside other Albator soldiers to hold back an advancing line of several enemy races from the keep's southern side. Pushing in on the right flank, giant creatures loomed over the soldiers just out of reach. Their forms beast-like, the mass of their bodies was concealed by a swirling and convulsing cloud of black smoke. Something was holding the creatures at bay, and as the duo closed the distance between themselves and the battle, Raelyn could see a barrier of fire—a giant wall of flame that extended along the length of the platforms on the right side. The shadowy creatures screamed with rage at their inability or unwillingness to advance, but enemy soldiers and wretched continued to pressure the Albator frontline. Raelyn paused, horrified as the unusually pale, humanoid wretches tore apart anyone unfortunate enough to get caught in their wake.

Pulling her eyes away from the scene, she turned her attention back to Jorn. "Father!" she yelled, knowing he couldn't hear her. She broke away from Jackson and sprinted toward a ladder leading onto the platform. She pulled herself up with the strength of desperation. "Father!"

At the top of the ladder, time felt like it stopped. Amidst clouds of smoke and glowing sparks, she met her father's gaze across the wooden landing. His eyes widened in surprise, reflecting anguish, not relief. Confusion dulled Raelyn's joy when she noticed Jorn's distress, and she stepped down a rung on the ladder, worried.

Loud and clear, Laris's voice rang out through the commotion. "Raelyn, no!"

Her confusion turned to terror as the fire wall holding their monstrous foes at bay vanished. Still staring into her father's eyes, Raelyn watched a creature charge toward him from the enemy line. Before she could take a single step, the life left Jorn's face as a gigantic claw pierced his chest, and blood sprayed toward her like a garden fountain.

She screamed, the sound born of utter desolation, a sound she didn't even know she was capable of making until that very moment. Blinded by emotion, she staggered forward, falling over the body of her father even as his murderer still hovered over the corpse.

Sobbing, Raelyn lay across her father, unable to move him in his heavy armor. She sensed the sinister presence looming over her and turned her face upward, in that moment, uncaring of whatever fate had in store for her. The monstrosity looked down at her, its eyes glowing red anchors in a face hidden by smoke and darkness.

She stared into the depth of the creature's gaze and was unafraid.

She was not angry.

She was … empty.

The monster raised its clawed hand, still dripping with Jorn's blood, and the edges of her vision blurred. When the razor-sharp claws swung down at her, she gave herself over to the emptiness consuming her soul.

"When death comes for you, rejoice, daughter, for in the next world, we are reborn as gods."

The words Raelyn's father had said to her when her mother died echoed in an endless loop inside her mind. She waited for the sensation of dying. Eyes clamped shut, she felt no pain of injury, but the air around her was colder than a midwinter night. The sounds of battle faded away, and all was silent.

When no enlightening moment came to explain her circumstances, she slowly opened her eyes and found herself surrounded by expected darkness.

So this is what it's like, she thought. *If I am a god, I am a god alone.*

She inhaled a deep breath and stood. She was in more than just darkness; she was in emptiness. No shapes could be seen in the black. There was no sky above and no ground below, and Raelyn could *feel* the openness around her. For a disconcerting moment, she wondered if she were floating in the night sky.

"Do not be afraid," a child's voice said behind her. "I am here to help you."

She spun around and was greeted by a familiar light, the flicker as welcome as an old friend's embrace, and warmth washed over her.

"Hendrel! You can speak!" She wrapped her arms around herself. "Where are we?"

"We are in the void. The place where all things begin and end." The wisp's shape started to expand. "It is the barrier that separates all realms and separates mortal from god and life from death."

Hendrel's flame continued to grow until the outline of a little boy stood in front of Raelyn. No distinct features were visible within the glowing silhouette, but his energy was welcoming and joyful.

"The void?" she asked. "Am I dead?"

Hendrel shook his head. "This is not the afterlife. This is the seam between the physical world and the spirit world. It is open only to those without tangible form, the gods, and—" he extended his hand toward her "—the wardens."

"I don't understand."

"I know." He giggled. "Wardens are very rare, and in our age and the age of our fathers, only three have been born. Come," he said, waving to her. "There is something up ahead."

Raelyn followed Hendrel into the darkness. While they walked, shapes materialized in the distance, and as they slowly came into focus, she realized they were the shapes of people. The body of her father was the first to catch her eye.

"You captured these souls when you entered the void," Hendrel explained, the childlike innocence fading from his voice. "They were frozen with you at the moment you left the mortal world. Unlike you, however, they cannot exist here. You must return soon, or their bodies will die as their spirits linger here."

Her eyes on the body of her father, Raelyn once again felt despair well up inside her. "My father is not alive."

"No, but you brought his energy with you, nonetheless. His spirit will pass into the next realm as it should. The others are still alive, though. In your emotional state, you pulled these people with you. They must be important to you. It is … not a thing that is done."

Looking around, Raelyn saw the figures of Jackson, Laris, and her father, all frozen in that moment from the ramparts when Raelyn thought death was imminent. Of the three, Laris, whose form was in mid-leap, held the expression with the most meaning. It was not a look of dread as on Jackson's face; Laris's look was of disappointment, and at that moment, Raelyn knew why.

"I did this, didn't I?" she asked, kneeling by the body of her father. "Laris's magic fire wall was undone because of me, wasn't it?"

Hendrel nodded, the movement barely perceptible. "You are a warden, Raelyn. Magic cannot exist in the void, and the void is a part of you. Unfortunately, you were never instructed how to control your ability."

"I should have listened to him," she whispered. "Laris warned me."

"The transcendent is powerful, but even he doesn't fully know what a warden is capable of. He knew you neutralized his power, and he knew what that made you, but beyond that, he is as uneducated as most."

"And you?" She turned her gaze to Hendrel. "Why have you never spoken to me before?"

"The void is open to us lingering souls. Though, we cannot pass through it to Emblem's Hall, where the gods reside, or to the afterlife or other spirit realms. In this place, I am not bound by the rules of the mortal world. Here, no such limitations exist." He gestured toward her companions. "I cannot explain more. If you want to save the lives of these people, your time here is at an end."

"Wait, please. How do I even leave this place? How will I find you again?"

"I will be with you as I have always been," Hendrel replied, his outline molding back into the familiar teardrop flame. "In the void, you are your own master. Envision, with intent, leaving this place, and it will be so. But know that when you open your eyes, you will return to the exact time and place you left."

"Then I'll be taking us all back to our deaths?"

Hendrel's light hovered over the forms of her companions. "Perhaps. The future is always uncertain, a tapestry of a thousand possibilities. Pictures within pictures. Should you survive, seek out the Sundered Gate. All of your roads lead you there. Go, now. Waste no more time."

With those parting words, Hendrel's light disappeared, and Raelyn was again in frigid darkness.

Envision, with intent, she coached herself. *Envision, with intent. Do not fail them a second time!* Closing her eyes, Raelyn revisited the scene of her worst nightmare. She brought to mind the smell of the burning castle, the sounds of the battle, the demon as it stared down at her, its hot breath laden with the stench of blood and decay. The intimate details of that moment mingled with the aching loss of her father's death, and Raelyn knew even before opening her eyes she had returned to the battlements.

When she forced her heavy eyelids wide, the creature was in mid-swing, its clawed hand bearing down on her. She had no time to move, and she braced for the impact, ready to meet her father in the next realm. Stars swam in her eyes, and the breath was knocked out of her lungs as she catapulted across the tower platform, not by the force of the creature's strike but by the force of Laris barreling into her. They toppled over the edge and landed hard on the catwalk below.

Unable to do anything but lie on the hard stone while air returned to her lungs, Raelyn turned her head to look over at her rescuer. Laris was also still lying on his back, though, he seemed to have fared slightly better than she, and as Raelyn watched him, he pulled himself over to her side.

"How badly are you injured?" he asked.

"I'm …" She struggled against the limited air in her lungs. "Thank you."

"Don't thank me yet. The battle is lost." Laris eased up to his knees. "Can you get up?" He leaned over her, putting one arm around the small of her back, and she gripped his shoulders for aid in sitting upright. "Raelyn?"

Her breath was back, but she couldn't voice a reply. Without meeting his stare, she nodded.

"Duke Wedminth has fallen. We need to get those remaining to safety." He shook her gently but firmly by the shoulders to demand her attention. "And it just so happens I have the castle escape artist with me."

Raelyn looked up at him as if seeing him for the first time. "What? But we're on the top of the castle walls. If a secret route exists, I don't know it."

He exhaled, picked up his sword from where it lay and looked over at her. "Come then, let us die with our comrades." He held out a hand.

Raelyn smiled weakly despite the seriousness of their situation and the tears returning to her eyes. She didn't know what to say, but she was oddly grateful for the gesture of unity. Through her blurry vision, she noticed Laris's expression wasn't one of antipathy or judgment.

He looked subdued, she decided, like a man who deeply understood what loss was and what it did to those forced to carry on.

At that moment, she knew she'd been hasty in forming her opinion of him. Even dangerous men were still men, made of flesh and bone with beating hearts. She sobered and wiped away the tears. "Let's go."

There'd been no pause in the battle after Laris and Raelyn had tumbled off the tower platform. Skirting the lower wall of the watchtower, they could hear the clash of weapons, screams, and crumbling rubble as the enemy pushed forward. A creature passed overhead, and the pair pressed against the stone wall to avoid detection. Their fall had saved Raelyn, but it had put them on the opposite side of the rampart and behind advancing enemy lines.

At the joint of the tower base and the rampart wall, a ladder led to the upper catwalk and to wooden landings where the battle raged. Without hesitation, Laris started to climb upward, sword ready in one hand, a look of determination on his face. Before he got out of reach, Raelyn grabbed his boot. "Wait," she said. "I think I do know a better way."

He looked down at her.

"It's not a secret passage." She gently patted a slender wooden door next to the ladder where she stood. "But the watchtowers were designed so the keep soldiers could move between them without disturbing the castle inhabitants. The ramparts are hollow, with just enough room for men in armor to pass through single file. We can take the passage to the far end of the battle and bring survivors in from that side."

Laris slid off the ladder and pushed the door open. Without a word, he stepped inside the passage, and Raelyn followed. She closed the door as quietly as possible, aware no one in the battle could hear the tell-tale creak, but worried, nonetheless. A brilliant orange sunrise replaced the dull pallor of dawn, and the welcome light radiated through the narrow slits along the corridor's length.

"How many towers do we pass through before we reach the far end of the castle?" Laris asked, picking up his pace.

"Two more, I think," Raelyn replied as she hurried to match his stride. "Then we will be at the—" She bumped into her companion, unprepared for his abrupt stop.

Laris held his sword out and slowly pushed back against her, forcing them to retreat the way they had come. The sound of many footsteps running from the direction they were headed made Raelyn's heart hammer in her chest, and she wished she hadn't lost both daggers in all the commotion. Braced against Laris's back, she felt helpless and knew her presence made him feel helpless in a way, as well.

Too late to turn and make a run for it, they waited to meet the unknown foe head on.

At least we can only face them one at a time, she thought, peering down the narrow passage. *We may yet make it out alive.* Though what she knew of Laris was limited, the short time they'd spent together nurtured in Raelyn a strong confidence in the mage. He was abrasive to be around, without a doubt, but he had saved her life twice already, and for no reason she could fathom other than the kindness of his own heart. In truth, she knew Laris and the rest of the soldiers would have been safer if he'd let Orion kill her. Yet he had not.

"Hold!" a familiar voice commanded from the passage ahead. "I know you. Lord Leofric's man, Laris, correct?"

A beam of morning sunlight illuminated Jackson's face as he stepped forward and held out his hand in greeting. Laris nodded. The two men clasped forearms and were about to speak, but Raelyn squeezed out from behind Laris and threw her arms around the battle-weary lieutenant.

"Raelyn?" Jackson returned her embrace, his expression one of shock. "Emblem's Hand, I thought we'd lost you."

"I have Laris to thank for it." She released Jackson and turned to her proclaimed savior. His posture was stiff, and he sheathed his sword. "Looks like she's yours again," he said to Jackson, barely acknowledging Raelyn's look. "Is Lord Leofric with you? Did he survive the final onslaught?"

Jackson nodded. "Your lord is here, though, we are twenty or so deep down this passage. He's securing our backside with the few soldiers that remain from the keep. We were lucky; as we made it into the corridors, the body of one of those foul beasts collapsed through the tower floor, sealing off the entrance and any pursuit from the enemy."

"The duchess?"

"Here," replied Jackson. "She's not holding up well, though, I dare say. Husband, daughter, and home gone in one night. Rae—" he placed a hand on her shoulder "—best steer clear of her for now."

Not understanding but having no desire to argue, Raelyn nodded. "Where are we to go?"

"Let's first get out of the castle." Jackson motioned for everyone to march onward. "We'll take the rampart corridors to the garrison and leave the city using the supply canals in there. If we're lucky, we can grab some food and weapons down below."

No one spoke as the group hurried, single file, through the utility hallways. Every so often, enemies could be heard just beyond the walls around them, the invaders sacking the rest of the castle and looting as they went. Intermittently, the screams of a discovered castle dweller tore through the night air. Raelyn prayed their deaths were swift. She knew not all would be put to the sword or given to the beasts. There were fates far worse for prisoners than death.

By nothing short of a miracle, the small troop of survivors made it down the last watchtower stairwell undiscovered. They entered the patrol garrison in the belly of the castle and found the place untouched.

"I'm not surprised," Jackson said to Laris while the group fanned out to look for supplies. "The main entrance to this garrison is actually in the city. Only two access points open within the castle, and those are in low-traffic areas. Fewer distractions for the soldiers that way."

"A small favor from The Circle," the other man replied dryly.

Raelyn grabbed what sacks of preserved fruit she could from the small pantry and turned her attention to the modest armor and weapons the garrison supplied. Most of the equipment was too large for her frame, and she doubted she could maintain the weight of a heavy plate mail, even if it did fit her. A leather cuirass, the likes she'd seen the castle archers wear, caught her eye, and she set down the bags of fruit and slid the armor piece over her head. It was a better fit than she would have guessed, but the straps along the side proved difficult to navigate on her own. She smiled in embarrassment when Jackson walked over and offered to assist her.

"It won't deflect a direct thrust with a blade," he said, securing the buckles. "It probably won't even save you from a strong slash. Like everything right now, though, it's better than nothing."

"Thank you," she mumbled, twisting the armor into the ideal position. "It's a comfort, in the very least."

He took a bite of an apple and smiled at her, patted her on the head and walked away. Raelyn continued to fuss with the cuirass, the weight and rigidity of it foreign to her. She froze when she saw Laris across the room staring at her, his look again unreadable. Too exhausted to guess what was on his mind, she refocused on adjusting her armor.

"Raelyn? Raelyn Forthgrew?"

Raelyn looked up at the woman addressing her from one of the loaded canal boats. Duchess Wedminth was almost unrecognizable. Her thick, auburn hair hung in an unbound mess, and a deep gash marred her left cheek. Her usual makeup had smeared and congealed in the lines of her face, and her banquet gown was stained with dirt and blood from weathering the attack.

It was the first time Raelyn had seen Ellisand's mother since joining Jackson's group. Before she could offer the duchess any greeting or condolence, the older woman clawed her way out of the boat, pushing through people on her way across the room.

"You!" Altha reached Raelyn and slapped her so hard the sound echoed in the small enclosure. "How *dare* you show your face here? You had one job! 'Keep her near Ellisand,' they told me, 'and she'll be safe. No mages will come for her,' they told me." She hit Raelyn again. "But you lost her! You took her out of the castle."

Hands pressed against her stinging cheeks, Raelyn shook her head. "No. I didn't know. I never meant any harm."

"And my home." Duchess Wedminth started sobbing. "My home. *Your father.* We were helpless! Helpless because of *you.*" She started pummeling Raelyn's chest, but her strikes had no more force. "Why? Why has The Circle abandoned us?"

Lord Leofric, Jackson, and several other men pulled Altha away and steered her back toward the boat. "Come, my lady," Leofric said in a soothing tone. "To the boats. We are ready to leave this place."

He cast an apologetic look back at Raelyn, who remained pressed against the wall, palms pinned to her face. The bags of dried fruit at her feet had spilled open, and she could think of nothing else to do other than lean down and pick them up. Seeing nothing through her tears, she haphazardly dumped the pieces into their bags.

Gentle hands on her shoulders stilled her labored efforts. Laris crouched beside her and helped pick up the fruit without a word. Overwhelmed with guilt, Raelyn sobbed in earnest, grateful when he pulled her to him. They said nothing while she cried, and after what felt like an eternity, Laris moved away from her.

"One boat remains," he said quietly. "We must be on it."

She looked at the canal to the solitary vessel and its two weary soldiers waiting to push off. Though her head pounded and her eyelids felt weighted down by rocks, she stood and hastily wiped her face, fighting the rush of tears that threatened to erupt again.

Laris grabbed her arm to steady her. "Listen to me," he said. "Now is not the time to cry. We are not out of danger. I'm with you, but I need you to be able to help yourself."

The words were stern but not intended to be cruel, and Raelyn knew he was right. She was truly useless if she couldn't get her emotions under control. If they were attacked while on the water, she'd need a clear mind.

"Yes, you're right." She took a deep breath and offered him a weak smile. "Now is not the time for tears."

She stepped down into the boat, and Laris pushed them adrift.

CHAPTER FIVE

arren grasslands marking the top edge of the southern regions of Uhmeer stretched across multiple nations; a strange belt of tall reeds skirted the base of Limnin. Skeletons of ancient towns and fortresses protruded from the grassy knolls, proof life once flourished in such an inhospitable place. The ruins were what had drawn Saraht to the grasslands. In such a place, she could operate close to her enemies without drawing notice. According to her reports, the attack on Albator had been a success, albeit messy, and the wheels of a plan beyond hers were well in motion. Watching the torchlight bounce off the weathered stones of her ruin stronghold, she let out a long exhale. A success, but not without new complications.

"I thought I explained the importance of a conservative approach." She shuffled through the parchments on her table. "You were only supposed to target the castle. We're trying to lure Limnin's army away from the capital, not eradicate the people here."

Standing in the center of the torch-lit room, Orion spread his arms in feigned innocence. "We encountered complications. Besides, we got the girl. That's all you cared about, isn't it?"

"Isn't it?" Saraht mocked him. She slammed her fist on the table, startling the guards at their doorway posts. "They saw your face, Orion, and you just walked away. Now Limnin knows the girl was kidnapped, not killed in the attack."

"I, too, had orders," Orion replied icily. "And you neglected to tell me there was a warden in Albator and a powerful transcendent. They almost ruined everything. We might not have secured the target if I hadn't had so many men with me. Do you think I don't know you've kept your plans from *him?* Maybe the prince would like to know the personal pursuits of one of his commanders."

Saraht sucked in a deep breath to help calm her anger. She should have known better than to show too much interest in Ellisand Wedminth. Orion was clever, brilliant. She hated recognizing those qualities in him. He'd picked up on her curiosity and assumed she was vested personally. Now, he knew he had leverage over her, though, he couldn't be sure how.

Despite Orion's intelligence, his warped sense of honor and barely concealed disdain for Saraht's command made him unpredictable. A common master had brought them together, but he was as much her enemy as he was her comrade. Everything about him disgusted her, from his greasy, pulled-back hair and roguish good looks to his sadistic mannerisms. During moments when he let arrogance fuel his decision-making, she despised him even more.

"Tell me about the warden," she said, rubbing her temples. "Such a find is unexpected."

"A beauty." Orion made a lewd gesture that made Saraht's anger boil again. "I almost brought her, too, but it's trouble enough for me to deal with one of you, let alone two. I do regret it, though. I could have used a reward for my services."

"You'll be rewarded well enough." Saraht glared at him. "Leave me. I have the pieces of your mess to pick up." She refused to let his behavior rile her further. That was his aim, she knew, and she'd already given him too much satisfaction for one evening.

"Bring me the girl," she ordered the guard at her side. "And have some food and wine brought for us. I'm sure the poor thing is famished."

While the guard left to play escort and Orion strode back out to his men, Saraht looked at a woman seated by the fireplace. "Am I being unreasonable?"

The other woman, her face partially concealed by an embroidered cowl, shook her head. "He enjoys irritating you, darling. Though, I fear the day will come when he moves against you."

Saraht waved and dismissed the remaining guards in the room, then waited until they'd left before speaking again. "Should we be rid of him now rather than later? Or does he still hold some worth for the cause?"

"He is one of Faldea's most powerful mages, well-liked by the men and held in the confidence of you-know-who. It is unwise to stir the pot just yet. Like it or not, Daughter, our world is still in the grip of male dominance. While I would well be rid of all those filthy creatures, we need them to do the things men do best, and killing is one of those things."

"Your wisdom is most valuable, as always, Mother. I'll rejoice the day you give me leave to take his head, though, mark my words."

The older woman nodded and chuckled softly. "Of course, my dear. Of course."

Both women looked over when the guard re-entered the room. Behind him staggered Ellisand, who struggled to keep up, her figure hunched over in exhaustion. Saraht looked at the young woman's bound hands, bruised face, and bloody elbows and knew the trip had been less than kind. She strode over to the guard, pulled his dagger from his belt, and slipped the blade up into his heart. It was an extreme response, but the calculated move would help her establish an atmosphere of trust. Wiping the weapon on the fallen man's pants, she leaned over and severed Ellisand's bindings.

"I'm sorry, my dear." She offered her hand. "Consider that some repayment for your suffering on the road."

Ellisand's eyes were wide, but she took the hand offered and let herself be led to a table where a servant was setting out plates.

"Please, sit. Eat." Saraht gestured toward one of the chairs and a waiting plate of dried meat with bread and cheese. "My mother, Maylam, and I welcome you as our guest. I am Saraht, and I apologize for the circumstances leading up to your arrival. No more harm will befall you." She paused abruptly and studied her ward. "No *serious* harm came to you on your journey, did it?"

Understanding the implication immediately, Ellisand shook her head.

"Good. There's no amount of death that could ever avenge such a thing."

"Men are wicked," Maylam said from her chair by the fireplace. "No doubt you still saw some of their filthy inclinations. Such basic creatures. There is a reason why women once ruled this world."

Saraht smiled and sat in her chair across from Ellisand. "Pay Mother no heed. There will be time for all that later. For now, eat and put your mind at ease. I will have a bath drawn for you. When you're clean, warm, and have a full belly, I will answer all of your questions."

Ellisand remained quiet, eyes pinned on Saraht while she ate. Distrust and wariness swam across her expression, offset by hints of loathing and anger. Such emotions were to be expected; in the hands of the enemy, feelings of uncertainty were common among captives, but what pleased Saraht was the absence of fear in the Wedminth heir.

She let her guest pick at the food in silence. Generosity and practicality would win Ellisand over in the days to come. For now, the goal was not to push her. Before she could be swayed to their cause, she had to trust her situation was safe.

A female servant took Ellisand's empty plate and bowed, arm extended toward an archway through the wall by the fireplace. Dark curls dangling in disarray around her face, Ellisand stood abruptly, her shoulders squared and head held high. She gave a slight nod of thanks to Saraht but maintained her wall of silence as she followed the servant from the room.

Alone with her mother, Saraht grinned. Ferociousness in noblewomen amused her, the trait sourced from arrogance instead of bravery, like the growl of a small dog surrounded by wolves. It was good that Ellisand wasn't afraid—but she should be. The authority of her title and position meant nothing to those who held true power in the world. When faced with survival, arrogance and entitlement became shackles, not tools of liberation.

She settled against the back of her chair and closed her eyes while she waited for Ellisand to return from her bath. Quiet moments were too few, and the darkness of her mind was the one place she could seek peace. Listening to the sounds of the fire crackle within the hearth, she focused on the breath flowing through her nostrils, meditating on the moment, allowing time and thoughts to pass without judgment.

When Ellisand was brought again into Saraht's presence, her demeanor seemed to have improved significantly. A healthy color washed her cheeks despite the bruises, and her eyes reflected wary curiosity instead of open mistrust. Dressed in a warm, modest gown of fine Orothia cotton covered by a wolf-skin shawl, she looked as comfortable as possible for having been abducted a few days before.

"Ah, now you look more like the royal young woman I expected," Saraht greeted her. "Come, let us walk together. Mother has retired for the night, and you and I have much to discuss." She linked her arm with Ellisand's. "I'm sure you have many questions."

"Where are we?" Ellisand asked with an edge of distrust. She lifted her chin defiantly. "Are you Faldean?"

"Faldean? Goodness, no, my dear. I am from Limnin, just like you." Saraht steered her captive toward a deteriorating stone stairwell. "I have no love for Faldea any more than the next." It was the truth, though, not in its entirety. Saraht's forces were indeed Faldean, but they were a means to an end, not where her loyalty lay.

"Am I here to be ransomed?"

"Though it may feel otherwise, you are not here to be a captive. I've brought you here because we are connected, you and I, and that connection has afforded you a very unique opportunity. It's why you were spared in the attack."

"Why should I believe anything you tell me?"

Saraht nodded. "I won't pretend we are allies yet, Ellisand. But now is not the time to question my kindness."

The pair stopped at the bottom of the stairwell where the fortress ruins showed heavier age, and decades of exposure had forged menacing cracks within the rocks. An ornate marble archway, the images etched into it worn beyond recognition, opened to an oval room. A white pedestal sat in the center of the space, and on it, an open book. Several women, dressed similarly to Ellisand, were painting along the span of the walls. They didn't look up as the two entered the chamber.

"This is my record room," Saraht said. "I never stay in one place long, but when I do have time, the place I stay gets painted with the same story." She walked over to the book and motioned for Ellisand to join her. "This is the Grimoire of Raloria, a forbidden text, banned in the year of King Briston the Second. It is a historical account of when women were the leaders of Uhmeer, and men were just our laborers."

She gently flipped the pages, revealing colorful images of sword-wielding goddesses and fire-breathing dragons. "Of course, during the Cataclysm, the physical strength and aggressive nature of men made rebellion inevitable, and as you know—" she closed the book "—we are now on the opposite end of the power struggle."

Saraht let her hand gently caress the grimoire, and she turned and walked over to one of the finished walls. An image of a beautiful woman sat on a throne above the bent forms of worshiping men.

"It was a golden age, Ellisand. There were no wars; there was no bloodlust. The countries of Uhmeer were united. I have these images painted when I stay in a place long enough to keep history alive. Men have long sought to change it to their favor. Maybe some young woman will find this place, and it will bring her hope in a world where the urges of men dehumanize us and devalue us."

"It's—" Ellisand looked over the painting "—beautiful. But what does this have to do with me?"

Saraht smiled, linking their arms again. "Why, it saved your life. You and I are connected, my dear," she whispered, "by blood and by fortune."

"I don't know you." Ellisand stopped and met Saraht's gaze. Doubt reflected in the younger woman eyes, her tone wary, disbelieving. And like a proper noblewoman, Ellisand's words were sewn with the thread of privilege.

Saraht smiled. "Another grave injustice," she replied, content to pander to her guest's haughtiness. "My mother was a mistress to King Rothelian during his early reign in Limnin, and though illegitimate, I am his firstborn. We are cousins, Ellisand."

"I was never told King Rothelian had a daughter." The entitlement eased from her tone, and her words belayed a hint of genuine interest.

"It's a long story, my dear," Saraht sighed. "You and I will have more time to talk in the upcoming days. To bed for now. We will share all our secrets on the morrow."

Sitting on the edge of the riverbank, Raelyn watched the stones she threw skip across the still surface of the water. It was peaceful along the gentle slope, far enough away from camp for the sounds of voices to be muffled by sounds of nature. Just a week ago, such a place would have made her endlessly happy. Shoes off, she would have been knee-deep in the water, listening to the gentle bubbling of the current as it traveled on its way. Now, the quiet only enhanced her feeling of loneliness and dragged her thoughts back to the moment she saw her father die on the ramparts. Like most from that night, the vision was crystal clear, and if she didn't curb its journey when it entered her mind, she would follow it endlessly into a pit of tears and despair.

Near her, in a thicket of young pine trees, Hendrel flickered and danced. His glow dimmed in the daylight, but he was almost at full brilliance under the shade of the trees. Several days had passed since the group's escape from the castle, and Raelyn hadn't tried to re-enter the void. Within that empty space, she felt afraid for what she might find, even if Hendrel were willing to speak with her again. Magic itself was difficult enough to comprehend, let alone dissecting the complexity behind a place where magic couldn't exist—a place that separated worlds.

At the moment, she wanted as little to do with being a warden as possible.

"Your hiding spots are decidedly out in the open," Laris said, startling her. "Rations have been prepared. Come."

"You can have mine," she said, tossing another stone into the water. "I'm not hungry."

"As you haven't been. You still need to eat. Test my patience, and I'll involve the others."

Raelyn gave a soft, derisive snort. "You'll find no aid from the duchess. Unless you mean to have her choke me with a leg of rabbit."

He leaned down so his face was close to hers. "Must I carry you over there like a child? I will discipline you like one as well if you insist. Come. Eat." The threat was softened by his hand offered to help her up.

Tempted to swat him away out of pure spite, she thought the better of it and accepted his aid. Out of everyone in the camp, Laris was the only one who regularly checked up on her, a fact that surprised and disheartened her at the same time. What she wouldn't give for some comforting words from someone who knew her better. She glanced at Jackson near the cooking fire. *He's avoiding me like I lit the castle ablaze with my own candle.* She shuddered. *I am probably no less responsible.*

Noticing she had fallen behind, lost in her thoughts, Laris reached back and grabbed her upper arm, hauling her in the way he'd become accustomed to doing over to where rations were being doled out to the other survivors. He pushed her firmly into line ahead of him. Raelyn could feel him watching her to ensure she didn't waive any portions.

"Good," he said when they both had their bowls. "Now join me so I can make sure you don't pass your meal off to someone else."

They sat down on a fallen log between the makeshift tents. The encampment was small but well-made, given the group's lack of supplies, although some in their party were wary about the chosen location. Well within the foothills of the Vast, the tents, made from the remnants of cloaks, were protected by natural rock formations and thick trees. It wasn't the threat of weather or discovery that made some survivors uneasy. During their two days at the location, strange sounds echoed down from the mountain passes, and one of the soldiers swore he saw the outline of a griffin in the distant sky.

Raelyn picked at her food, thinking. She was familiar enough with the sounds of the mountains to not be afraid. There were times on her forbidden adventures she'd seen more than the outline of a griffin. Raelyn had never told her father, but she once witnessed one of the creatures in the flesh as it feasted on an elk in a mountain clearing. The griffin had seen her; she was sure of it, but it was as unconcerned with mankind as with the field mice scurrying over the rocks.

"You actually have to eat it, not just mash it up in the bowl," Laris commented on her distracted stirring. "It's already dead, you know."

She smiled halfheartedly and put the spoon to her lips. The simple stew was thin and the ingredients sparse, but, like the camp, it was better than expected. "Your wit grows daily," she mumbled into the bowl. "To think you threatened me when we first met."

He set down his empty dish and leaned forward, elbows braced on his knees. "I assumed you were aware of your unique talent at the time and were being overprotective of Lady Ellisand. To me, you were deliberately neutralizing my powers and sneaking her out to keep her away from us."

"I thought you were just an uncouth killer."

He smirked at her admission, glancing over at her. "That I was and still am, but I was a *mistaken* uncouth killer. I'm sorry for that, Raelyn. I wouldn't have expected your ability to be kept secret from you."

She nodded, pleased and appreciative of his words but uncertain how to respond. Laris was a mystery to her, now more than ever. He was equal parts killer and savior, and those traits radiated through his words and actions. She didn't know it was possible to feel so safe in the presence of someone you also knew could—and would—take your life in an instant.

"I don't suppose the duchess will ever forgive me." She handed him the remainder of her meal. "Will any of them ever forgive me?"

Laris looked at her and shrugged. "It changes nothing if they do or don't," he said. "Lady Ellisand will still be gone, and many people will still be dead. But if they can't forgive you, they also can't forgive themselves. Remember, Raelyn, many of those closest to you knew you were a warden, but they deliberately didn't tell you. They let you grow up under the guise of a companion when you were, in truth, Ellisand's most powerful line of defense. Had you been allowed the knowledge you lacked, maybe things would be very different.

"And, if we are speaking plainly, you had her outside the castle during the worst fighting. That was perhaps the safest thing for her, and it let us put eyes on her abductors."

She sighed. "That may be true, but it doesn't make me feel better. All I keep seeing are those creatures on the ramparts. I didn't then, but now I understand I was the one who lost that battle for Albator. You can call me Rae, by the way," she said. "I think we are familiar enough now. You did save my life."

He shrugged. "I like your full name."

She let him eat the remainder of her food in silence. There was much she should ask Laris, she knew—questions about the world of magic, questions that kept bounding through her mind even though she tried to ignore them. An all-consuming numbness within made her stay quiet. Warden or not, the most important people in her life were gone, and she was just as powerless now as she was in the beginning to do anything about it. Sitting on the fallen log, listening to the sounds of the mountain and the sounds of camp, Raelyn felt disconnected from it all. *What does any of it matter now, anyway?*

"There's talk of heading west toward the capital of Osharia." Laris interrupted her inward contemplations. "I'm sure word of the attack has reached your king, but he'll want to see Duchess Wedminth in person."

"The capital?" Raelyn turned toward him. "Shouldn't we head to the fort at Mar Dereand and form a rescue party? It's only a few days from here. Osharia would take several weeks of travel."

He looked at her. His expression was sympathetic, though, she couldn't decide whether it was because of her pain or because he considered her ignorant.

"That's how these things work," he replied. "You're getting a first-hand lesson in the politics of world powers. If Lady Ellisand is a prisoner of Faldea, the act is one of war, and she will remain their captive until Limnin has their own prisoner to swap or the terms of a trade are met. It's doubtful King Rothelian would offer surrender just to spare his niece."

"What do you mean 'just to' spare Ell? She's his blood relative, and even if she wasn't, her life isn't some pawn to be moved in a giant game of conquerors."

"Raelyn, you're surprisingly ignorant for a woman raised in a castle. Lady Ellisand and all high-born children are pawns from the moment they are born. If not in war, then in marriage. Why do you think Lord Leofric and I were visiting Albator?"

She ignored his question, too unsettled by the fact a rescue mission wasn't anyone's priority but hers. "Listen to me. If we can get to Mar Dereand, we may yet catch up to her. Faldea is leagues to the west. A huntsman's party could find them."

"What seems to be going on here?" Jackson had walked over, unnoticed, during Raelyn's outburst. "Was the stew that bad?" He offered a crooked smile that faded when he saw her piercing glare.

"Is it true?" She marched over to him and stood a breath away. "You'll abandon Ell to take the duchess to the capital? The duchess is *safe*. She's with us. Ell is the one who is in danger."

Jackson peered down into her angry gaze. "Emblem's Hand, Rae, be at peace. The duchess is where my duty lies, and I must see her safely to King Rothelian."

"So it *is* true," she whispered in anger. "How can you do this, Jackson? This is Ellisand we are talking about, not someone you don't know. You love her, for Emblem's sake!" As soon as the words left her lips, Raelyn clamped her hands over her mouth. Jackson's eyes narrowed, and his lips pursed to a thin line. "I'm sorry," she said. "I had no right to say that."

He took a deep breath, glanced at Laris, then put his hands on Raelyn's shoulders and pushed her to arm's length. "That's enough." His tone was cool. "It's decided, and I'll hear no more of it." He turned to walk back toward the heart of the encampment. "Be ready to leave in the morning," he said over his shoulder.

She watched him walk away, and her outrage faded to familiar numbness. Laris remained seated. His face kept its usual unreadable mask, and he offered her no words when she walked past him back toward the river's edge. Sitting down at her spot on the grassy embankment, she stared into the bubbling current. Hendrel changed his interest from pine trees to the open water, and he flickered and blinked back and forth from ripple to ripple. His flame brought her no comfort, and she pulled absentmindedly at the grass around her. *If they won't go to Mar Dereand, I'll go on my own. No one can force me otherwise.* She tossed a handful of grass into the water. *Besides, they're better off without me.*

The main hall of Saraht's ruin stronghold remained the most intact within the old fortress. In its large fireplaces and stone coffers, oiled lumber burned without attendance for hours. Under the unsteady firelight around the room, Saraht watched her guest shovel down the food on her plate, modesty forgotten when presented with more than a soldier's rations. She picked at the roast duck and boiled potatoes, more interested in which seeds in her bed of manipulation were taking hold since their discussion the previous day.

"It is not a royal spread, for sure," she said, watching Ellisand, "but it does not want in flavor."

"The food is wonderful," the younger woman replied. "And I'm too hungry to be picky."

Saraht nodded knowingly. "You asked me before why we've never met, and I will tell you the truth now. More than thirty years ago, my mother, Maylam, became the first mistress of King Rothelian. When she found she was pregnant, and the healers told the king the child was to be a girl, he ordered Maylam to abort the baby. He wanted his first child to be a male heir, even if he was born a bastard. Mother agreed, but in secret, she conspired with the healers to spare the child—me—and sneak her out of the castle." Saraht refreshed her cup of wine. "For months, she concealed her pregnancy with clever dresses and distractions. She even went as far as hiring a beautiful young woman to temporarily snag the king's attention. But it was all for naught. King Rothelian learned of her plans and went into a terrible rage. We were banished … and at great cost." Saraht gestured to Maylam, who revealed deep burn scars behind her cowl winding down along the right side of her face and neck.

Pity in her eyes, Ellisand put her utensils down and sat back. "I'm sorry for what happened to you and your mother. I didn't know my uncle was such a cruel man."

"All men are cruel when they feel backed into a corner." Saraht sipped from her glass. "They are much like wild animals in this way. Had Mother listened to the king and terminated her pregnancy, she would have been spared his wrath and the disfiguration of her face and body." She swirled the glass in her hand. "But she will tell you it was a small price to pay for her child's life. Her suffering will be avenged one day."

Ellisand shifted uncomfortably at the other end of the table. Sensing her guest's unease, Saraht waved her hand dismissively. "Enough of my past. I'm sure you are wondering what will become of you now."

"You said I am not your captive?"

"You are not. The one I serve would be greatly displeased if he thought I was holding you against your will." Saraht smiled wryly. "I do not serve a kind master, Ellisand, but he has promised me my mother's revenge, and I am his loyal servant to that end."

"I still don't understand why you spared me," Ellisand replied. "My father won't be able to pay you if the city was destroyed as you say."

"I'm not looking for a ransom, dear girl. You are my female blood relative. I brought you here for a greater purpose—for us both." Saraht slumped down in her chair and put her feet on the table. "Besides, your father and mother are dead, Ellisand. Albator is in ruin. Even now, the dust settles on that lifeless place."

Unfazed by Ellisand's sharp gasp but noting no tears welling in her eyes, Saraht continued. "Sometimes, the truth is too terrible to hear, but terrible things are best told with frankness. I can understand if you hate me right now." She motioned for a servant to come take the plates. "And you may leave if you truly desire, but I make no promise of your safety beyond these walls. If you should stay, I promise you the opportunity of a lifetime."

"You want me to stay after you admitted to murdering my parents? I have nothing now!"

"On the contrary," Saraht interrupted, "you have more now than you've lost, but you don't know it yet. What has vanished? A life of servitude to a husband you don't love? Days trapped in etiquette classes so you can ... what? Die an early death in childbirth? Weren't your parents on the verge of selling you off?"

Ellisand sat, quiet.

"Mourn your family, Ellisand, and mourn the life you knew, but I can tell by your dry eyes the loss isn't as great as you would have it seem. I will give you a few days to make peace with your situation. If you choose to leave, you may. If you stay, I'll make more of my plans known to you."

She left Ellisand in the hall to contemplate the future and headed downstairs to the almost-finished record room. Her painters were away for a respite; Saraht was ever mindful of her lady artisans' comforts. If she wanted them to work quickly and confidently, she needed them to be happy. Running her fingertips along one of the murals, she felt the joy of her perceived schemes diminish, replaced by the heavy hatred always lurking in her heart. She stopped and scanned the dimly lit room, taking in the beauty of the images around her.

We are getting closer, she thought. *So much closer.*

The story laid out for Ellisand was true. What Ellisand didn't know was what had happened after Maylam was banished from the castle, brutally beaten, and disfigured by blade and fire. Too cruel to let his mistress slink off into obscurity, King Rothelian handed her over to the Lords of Revelry, a criminal group specializing in human trafficking and prostitution. There, she became a prisoner, and Saraht spent some of her most impressionable years witnessing the horrors her mother weathered.

It was a memory path she tried not to tread often; the images of atrocities visited upon women under the Lords were unfathomable to most folk. If she wanted to put those tales to voice, there would have been no words to describe them adequately.

I can never repay you, Mother. Saraht turned to the book at the center of the room. *You suffered so much for me. If all else fails, I will at least avenge you.* She gently flipped through the pages of the grimoire. A history book, yes, but it was so much more than that. *One way or another, we will put an end to this age of men.*

CHAPTER SIX

A heavy fog rolled through the foothills of the Vast, lit up by the first rays of dawn. Brilliant with greens and browns by day, the uneven landscape had become an ocean of silver as mist spilled down into its deep valleys and hidden caves. In the Albator survivor camp, swallowed by the pale waves, all was silent except for the sounds of waking birds, small forest creatures, and the soft rustling of a leather provisions pack.

Not wanting to take anything that would impact the group tremendously, Raelyn stuffed several apples and a handful of nuts into her satchel. As soon as the rations were secured, she ducked around the side of the tent, ever wary of the guard walking on perimeter watch. It was difficult to remain hidden in so small of a camp, but the morning fog and the old trees offered her just enough coverage to move without being noticed. Hidden for a moment, she exhaled in relief. There was one more thing nagging at her before she made off for Mar Dereand.

A weapon was paramount if Raelyn wanted to survive over the next few days, but she was reluctant to take too much away from Jackson and the others. A sword, for sure, would be missed. The escapees were lucky to have what they did, and there were already more people than weapons. She didn't want to leave the party without proper defenses if the enemy was still after Duchess Wedminth.

She glanced over toward Laris asleep on one of the open bedrolls. *Maybe, just maybe,* she thought, inching her way in his direction.

Raelyn knew the transcendent had several knives and a sword, but there was one hunting blade he often left in its sheath next to his belongings. He used this for everyday tasks such as eating and cleaning game. Raelyn felt confident it wasn't a weapon of war that would be missed. The downside to her planned thievery was that she needed to get very close to him to take the knife. If he woke, her plan to leave would be foiled.

Her suspicions were confirmed within a few steps of her target. The knife was there, and the sight of it encouraged her. Moving as quickly and as silently as she could, she slunk toward the weapon, her hand outstretched long before she was within reach. Holding her breath, she crouched and slid the dagger into her possession. Laris remained motionless. Raelyn's gaze stayed on his face while she stowed the knife in one of the slits of her cuirass.

Keeping her eyes riveted on him, she backed away slowly until she felt herself make contact with a tree. Again, she crouched to avoid detection, sliding around the trunk until she was hidden from most of the camp. In the mist, the outline of Gorin, the soldier on morning watch, wove through the trees. Raelyn held her breath and waited until he passed her hiding spot. Thankfully, he was more concerned about things outside the camp than within, and she let herself breathe again when he rounded the corner on the far side of camp.

Without a look back, she darted past the camp perimeter, running as fast as she could to ensure no one caught a glimpse of her in the twilight. For the first few minutes, she was terrified; her ears strained to hear over her footfalls for sounds of pursuit. No shouts or yells raised the alarm, and she knew the loud hammering that accompanied her running was just her heart pounding in her chest.

Fear propelled her forward until her lungs burned and her legs became heavy. The lack of food over the days prior had weakened her, forcing her to slow to a walk much sooner than preferred.

She was uncertain of exactly where she was; the rocks of the Vast were her only landmark this far from the city. In all her years, Raelyn had never ventured outside the lands under Wedminth control. She knew Mar Dereand was several days from Albator, but she had never been there. Her recollections were of the many maps in her father's planning room, not from firsthand experience.

I need to head north, she thought, hunting the horizon for a glimpse of the sunrise. *It should take me directly there if I stay in sight of the road.*

Keeping the road in her peripheral proved to be difficult. As the morning wore on, she was forced to stick to thicker cover farther away from the dusty path. Often, the bracken and rocks were impassable, and she found herself pushing forward on blind faith, grateful when she'd come to an opening and the road was still in sight. More than just secrecy compelled her to avoid the road. A wariness of strangers grew in her, strengthened with every wagon wreckage she saw melting into the ground from age. She hid as though her life depended on it when large groups of riders galloped through the area, and she wondered if they were soldiers or bandit parties. Raelyn had been raised in the shelter of castle life, but she was not a fool. She was well aware of the dangers on the road.

By the end of the first day, her bruised arms and legs ached from navigating the landscape, and when she finally slumped down to contemplate making camp, the ridiculousness of her decisions bore down on her.

Right. Good job, Rae, she chastised herself, angrily tossing sticks into a heap for a fire. *At this rate, you'll be lucky if you make it to Mar Dereand before Jackson makes it to the capital. What do you think will happen, anyway? Those soldiers take their orders from the Wedminths, not from you.*

Who the soldiers of Mar Dereand would take orders from was starting to be the least of her worries. Despite how loyal the castle guards were to the memory of Raelyn's father, their respect for her as his daughter was because they knew her. The men in the larger Albator force, part of the Limnin army, barely knew her by name, let alone by sight. She had nothing on her to prove who she was and no escorts to stand for her word. The only thing she could offer the fort's commander was a survivor's tale of an attack he would already have word of. If they were going to send a rescue party for anyone, they would have already done so as soon as word arrived.

The emptiness inside her bubbled up into anger and disgust. How could she be so stupid? She'd left the only safety available to run fool-heartedly toward the chance of a rescue operation growing less likely by the minute. Send scouts after Ellisand? All the men were probably on the alert for a grand-scale invasion.

She channeled her anger into an attempt to light a campfire, aggressively striking her knife on the flint stone she'd stolen that morning. Though confident she'd gathered the correct amount of kindling, the sparks flew everywhere but into the tinder, despite her furious efforts, and she cast the stone away in defeat.

"A fire this close to the road would only draw unwanted attention."

The unexpected voice from the forest shadows made Raelyn jump to her feet. She grabbed the hunting knife from the ground, knowing the tiny blade offered no protection against such a foe.

Laris stepped into the clearing, his hand on his sword hilt and his gaze locked on to Raelyn's. "If you intend to attack me, I'm ready to defend myself," he said. "Just know I refuse to die by the blade of my own hunting knife."

Too embarrassed and surprised to assume he was joking, Raelyn dropped the knife as if it were suddenly hot with fire. "I needed a weapon," she said weakly.

"Indeed." Laris bent over and picked up the knife, wiping the blade on his shirt sleeve. He offered the weapon back to her.

She tentatively reached out, but as her fingers closed around the handle, he grabbed her wrist and pulled her across the distance between them. His face inches away, he glared down at her, the heat of his breath raising goose bumps across her skin.

"Perhaps there will come a day when your selfishness won't rule everything you do," he growled. "To sneak away in the night from people who care about you, who have just lost their family and friends, is unspeakable and unforgivable." Raelyn tried to look away from his accusatory gaze, but he secured her jaw with his free hand and held her firm. "Do you understand that?"

She struggled in his grip but couldn't break away. "I didn't mean to upset anyone," she whispered. "I didn't think it through."

"But you knew it would upset plenty of people, Raelyn. Do you know what I had to do to keep that idiot lieutenant of yours from abandoning the group to come racing after you? I damn near had to put my sword through him."

"You're right," she said. "You're right. I just ..."

His grip relaxed, and he let the hand holding her chin fall to his side. "What is done is done," he replied quietly. "Where we go from here is up to us now. The group with the duchess will continue toward the capital. I told them I would get you somewhere safe when I found you."

"I wasn't in any danger," she mumbled, looking away. She went to step back, but the hold on her wrist tightened. Raelyn's breath caught at the look in his eyes. He held on to her for a moment longer before letting go.

"You're in constant danger," he replied and turned around to retrieve her flint. "Unless you want to sleep in the cold, let's get this campsite moved deeper into the forest."

She watched him gather up her pile of sticks and walk into the woods. Uncertain what to make of the situation, she scooped up her pack, afraid if she lagged too far behind, he'd come back and toss her over his shoulder just as he had the firewood. Part of her was relieved to have Laris's company, but part was uneasy. She'd been thrown together with him in a moment of necessary camaraderie, but they'd been at odds before that. Even though he'd admitted regret for their interactions, it was clear he wouldn't coddle her or tolerate what he felt was foolishness.

After an hour of walking beneath the gnarled trees, he stopped in a small clearing ringed by brush and rocks. In the distance, the rambling of a stream mixed with muffled sounds of crickets and creatures emboldened by growing darkness. The evening air was cool, and Raelyn shivered. Surveying the spot, she could see why Laris had picked it.

"This is a better location," he said, dumping the sticks to the ground. "The light from the fire will be hidden from the road by those boulders and our distance. If you're going to make it a habit of running away, at least listen to the things I'm telling you for next time."

She tossed down her satchel and sat down to stack the kindling. "Just because you decided to chase me doesn't mean I was running away."

"Ah, there's the attitude I've become accustomed to. I was worried it might never come back." He walked over and dropped the flint onto her lap. "Well, next time you decide to *leave*, you'll at least know not to build a signal fire right off the road."

She glared at him but said nothing, and he positioned himself across from her, back against the outcropping of rock. Raelyn focused on the flint and tinder. *Please let the fire light. Please let it light,* she prayed. She couldn't bear the thought of Laris watching her fail at a basic survival task.

She struck the flint once. Twice. Three times.

Nothing.

Sparks shot out with every effort but nothing to produce a flame.

Four times. Five times.

Nothing.

Biting her lower lip in frustration, she knew he was watching her, and she took a deep breath. "What is it I'm doing wrong?" she asked without looking up at him. To her surprise, he didn't tease her about her efforts. Instead, he moved close and took the stone from her hand.

"First," he explained, "you need to be nearer to the tinder like this." He lowered his hands over the middle of the leaf-and-grass nest. "Now strike the sharp edge of the flint—any hard stone will do—down the knife blade lightly but firmly. Doing it this way sends the sparks down, not all over."

Raelyn watched him demonstrate, and in minutes, an ember sprung to life within the pile of tinder. She nodded in understanding and sat back to help feed the infant flames. "I thought you were going to force me to go back," she said softly after watching the fire a moment, daring to glance at him.

He tossed a few larger sticks onto the flames. "It crossed my mind."

"Why didn't you?"

"I have no proof you'd be safer with them than you are right now," he said. "At the very least, I know some places where you and your wisp might find answers. And those places aren't in the capital."

Raelyn hadn't seen Hendrel since departing from the survivor camp, but he'd been known to vanish for days at a time in the past. With the revelations about being a warden, she felt as uncertain about Hendrel as she felt about Laris.

"I haven't seen him," she replied, thoughtful. "I've been a little afraid to speak with him again."

Laris reacted as if she'd slapped him. "What do you mean 'speak with him?'"

"That day on the ramparts. I blacked out. Right before you saved me and we fell." She shuddered at the memory. "I woke up in darkness, but Hendrel was there. He told me I was in the void, and that's where wardens were from and why magic can't exist around them. But I couldn't stay. I had accidentally dragged you and the others into the void, too. Hendrel told me I had to leave, or you would all die."

"You've been to the void?"

She nodded.

"Don't do that again." Laris looked at her intently. "It's too dangerous. You don't understand enough yet, and what I know is limited at best."

"I'm not looking to go back there." She shook her head. "I just want to find a way to help Ell. I don't need to be a warden to do that."

Laris's expression was somber. "I'll take you to Mar Dereand, and we'll organize travel for you there. For tonight, get some sleep." He stood and walked to the edge of the firelight. "I'll wake you up in a few hours to take a shift at watch."

Smoke from cooling cinders, mixed with the aroma of dew, greeted Raelyn's senses with her first post-slumber breath. She opened her eyes to the twilight of the morning, momentarily confused about where she was. Laris hadn't woken her for a turn at watch, and she sat up abruptly at the realization. Where was he? Had something happened to him in the middle of the night? She spun around to grab her knife but found him sitting a few feet away from her, back against the rock shielding their campsite, just as he'd been when she'd fallen asleep hours before.

"You were up all night?" she asked, pushing her tangled hair away from her face.

"Soldiers have ways around sleep," he replied. "I've spent more hours awake than this." He tossed something over to her. "Salted rabbit. Let's get moving. You can eat as we walk."

There wasn't much to pack up. Raelyn's possessions consisted of Laris's knife, the flint she'd pilfered from her former companions, and some scraps of food she'd thought would see her to the Limnin fort. She slung the sack over her shoulders and looked down at her tattered skirts. The leather archer's cuirass and tangled hair made her feel more like a bandit than anyone she'd seen on the road.

"The days have not been kind to me," she muttered. What she wouldn't give to be back in the castle, listening to the duchess chastise her and Ellisand for not having enough ribbons in their hair for a formal dinner. *How I hated it then. Now, it seems like a different life.*

"You definitely could use a bath," Laris called over, watching her self-assessment.

She scowled at him. "Not all of us can look perfect after fighting battles and becoming fugitives."

"Oh? And who is it you think looks 'perfect?'"

Blood rushed to her cheeks. Crossing her arms, she looked away. "Are you ready to go? The sun will be up soon."

He watched her for a moment, his expression amused. She waited for him to press the subject, but instead, he pushed himself away from where he was leaning and motioned for her to follow him into the forest.

During the daytime, the giant trees of Limnin's eastern woods offered a welcome envelope from the outside world. The huge limbs and gnarled, moss-covered roots created a peacefulness Raelyn likened to visiting Ebest's chambers on cold, snowy nights. The air was always heavy with earthy smells, and a fire was always ablaze within the hearth, ready to chase away the winter chill. That protective warmth wrapped around her while she and Laris picked their way under the massive canopy of leaves.

"We're traveling close to the mountains," she commented. "How do you know we're still aligned with the road?"

"The road travels parallel to the mountains for many leagues," he said. "One more day of traveling in the woods won't hurt us."

"Do you think they're still after us? The men who attacked the city?"

From behind him, she saw his shoulders heave with a deep breath. "I don't know," he replied after a moment's thought. "If they were only after Lady Ellisand, it doesn't explain why they ransacked the city. If it's ransom they're after, Duke Wedminth was their best chance. With him dead and the city destroyed, they're relying on your king's compassion, which he's not renowned for, especially after an act of war. There's also a chance now that they know what you are, they'll be searching for you, too. It's best not to take any risks."

Raelyn climbed over a large root. "I won't be much good to you if someone is on our trail. If anything, I severely handicap us."

Laris stopped, allowing her to catch up. "You would be a handicap if your abilities didn't affect all magic users. If anything, you are an equalizer," he said. "I'm no novice with my sword. Magic is not my weapon of choice."

"Would you teach me?"

"Teach you? Teach you what?"

She dug the hunting knife out of her pack. "To defend myself. I know the basic forms, but it doesn't seem like that matters much in real combat."

"First—" he frowned at the knife in her hand "—short blades are ambush and stealth weapons. They're not long enough to be used in open combat. In most situations, your enemy will have a sword, and only the most skilled knife fighters can overcome such a disadvantage. Think of that knife as your last hope."

"I don't want a last hope. Isn't there something you can teach me?"

He took the knife out of her hand but kept it sheathed. "Stand still," he said, stepping closer to her. "We don't have time for me to teach you the subtleties of battlefield combat, but I will teach you how to disable someone to buy yourself time to get away.

"Here." He held the point of the dagger on the junction of her armpit. "Sever the flesh here, and you will disable the arm." He brought the blade down to her skirt at the crease of her thigh. Looking her in the eyes, he said, "And here. This will disable a leg. A deep enough cut here will eventually be deadly." He knelt, running the covered blade across the back of her ankle and up at the back of her knee. "If you're on the ground, this will also disable your enemy.

"It's not about striking a killing blow. If you incapacitate your adversary, you're free to move on to the next. Whether he lives or dies is unimportant."

She looked down at the top of his head, unnerved by the callousness of the statement and reminded of the dangerous part of his personality she'd only glimpsed during their time together. Laris was a trained killer and a man who trained killers. "I've never thought of it that way."

He looked up at her. "My life has been different than yours. I was an orphan, and I learned early on how to deal with adversaries bigger and stronger than myself. When Lord Leofric's family took me in at their northern stronghold of Orencar, I lived a soldier's life until my talent for weaving magic emerged when I was ten-and-five years old." He dropped his gaze, his free hand resting lightly on the inside of her knee. "You're a noblewoman, Raelyn. Don't be so hard on yourself."

She muttered a sound of disapproval, and he stood.

"You will always have the typical defense targets—the eyes, nose, and groin—but know that any attacker worth the armor on his back will be prepared to protect those places." He handed the knife back to her. "Your best bet, Raelyn, is to run. Do you understand?"

She nodded slowly, not saying anything, too flustered by their interaction to absorb the full impact of what was just said. Something about him when he was close heightened her senses, raising and spreading anticipation through her that culminated in a sense of loss when he moved away. She was attracted to him, and the thought terrified her more than his infamous reputation.

As if sensing her discontent, he stepped back, his dark eyes studying her. "You're looking at me like I actually cut you with the knife."

She smiled apologetically. "I'm just thinking it all through. Thank you for showing me."

"You're uncomfortable when I get close to you," he stated, ignoring her gratitude. "I can tell. You don't need to deny it, and I don't mind. It's better than seeing you too comfortable with a stranger's touch."

Raelyn's face burned with the heat of her flush, and she pinned her eyes on the ground. "I don't mean to offend you," she mumbled.

"Far from it." He stepped across the space between them. "It's something you're going to have to get used to, though," he said quietly, hands lightly cupping the back of her elbows to keep her from moving away. "We're in this together now, and there will be times when I'll need to touch you, or you'll need to touch me. I promise I won't hurt you."

She knew he wouldn't hurt her. That was the furthest thought in her mind, but she didn't dare voice her actual fears. She swallowed hard and nodded, staring at one of the silver buttons on his black jerkin.

He squeezed her elbows lightly and stepped away. "Let's get moving. There's not much civilization between here and Mar Dereand, and we still have a long way to go."

Raelyn remained silent, lost in thought as they continued their trek. After hours of distracted trudging, the screech of a hawk filtered down through the layers of leaves, bringing her out of her trance. Beams of sunlight cut apart the forest growth to warm her face, and a loud gurgle threaded through her stomach. It was well past the lunch hour; she was hungry for the first time in days.

"It looks like there's a stream up ahead," Laris called over his shoulder. "We might be able to land some fresh fish for lunch."

Raelyn knew he had heard her traitorous stomach, though, she was secretly ready for a respite. The common shoes of a lady were no match against days of forest travel. Beneath the thin layers of material, she could feel the deceptively numb wetness of blisters and sores just waiting for the sting of open air.

After sliding on her butt down the steep embankment to the water's edge, she sat for a moment in the pile of rocks and leaves that accompanied her, surprised by the new surroundings. "What is this place?" she asked.

"An old shrine." He inclined his head toward the moss-covered remnants of a statue. "Genevive. Second Pillar of The Circle."

Brushing herself off, Raelyn walked over to the life-sized stone figure. In its glory, it must have stood on a rock ledge above the pool, but as with all things, time and neglect had crumbled the natural foundation, and now the fallen statue leaned, broken, at the water's edge. Genevive's visage was still visible beneath the layers of moss and lichen, the features intact despite nature's attempt to reclaim them. Raelyn gently ran her fingers over the curves of the goddess's face. "She's beautiful," she whispered. "Is she one of the Deceivers you mentioned before?"

"Genevive is the goddess of balance. The Deceivers were Delvia, Raloria, and Fayla, and only Raloria was among Emblem's trusted allies during the Cataclysm. Why is it you know nothing about The Circle or the chaos gods?"

"I know some," she replied. "The Wedminths revered Astor, Fifth Pillar. Most of our worship and study was of his works. I wasn't the most attentive student."

Laris made a sound of disgust. "Astor. The god of prosperity. I'm not surprised. He is well-loved by most nobility, but he's far from benevolent. Few gods are, in truth, even among The Circle. You can bathe if you want," he said, changing the subject. "The pool looks clean and the water clear. I'll search for fish downstream."

"You're sure it's safe? What if someone was following us?"

Pointing toward the cliffs around the pool, Laris shrugged. "If someone is following us, they'll have to come down the same embankment or approach us from downstream. We'll see them long before they pose a threat."

Raelyn waited for him to disappear before she started to disrobe, pulling at the bindings on the archer's mail. The weight of the armor slipped off her body, and she felt a wave of relief. By the time she stood naked on the smooth stone pebbles of the pool's edge, she was giddy with newfound weightlessness, excited to soothe her muscles and raw feet in the crisp mountain water.

Knowing better than to torture herself by wading in slowly, she dove in, submerging completely to resurface farther away from shore. The shock of the cold lasted only a few moments, outweighed by the wonderful sensation of sweat, dirt, and blood washing off her skin. In that moment, Raelyn found tranquility. She was a child again, swimming in the forest pools with Ellisand and ignorant of all the other happenings in the world. She swam out to the center, treading water and taking in the full scope of the moss-covered ruins.

Cliffs rimmed the pool, and one rocky slope plunged directly into the water, cutting off the shore of pebbles where Genevive's statue kept watch. Raelyn swam along the smooth rock wall, marveling at how deep the water was so close to the cliffside. She unwittingly rounded a bend along the perimeter and looked into a narrow opening where the cliff split in two. A few swim lengths into the crack, the pool entered a cave. She could hear the bubbling of water echo from the opening as it funneled back into a stream somewhere in the darkness.

Throughout all her childhood exploration, Raelyn had had a fondness for caves. Caves were where stories of dragons and treasure began. There wasn't a single fairy story she'd heard that had no fantastical reason for exploring a cave. Staring at the dark opening, she felt drawn to it. At the same time, she was afraid. Adventure lurked in caves, but all adventure had an element of danger.

A soft light appeared in the cave entrance, beckoning her with its familiar warmth. "Hendrel!" she exclaimed, surprised to see him materialize in such a place. "Have you found something?"

Shallow water just inside the entrance forced Raelyn to her feet. She stood at the cusp of where the water from outside flowed back into a narrow channel and then quickly cascaded down a small waterfall into a pool deeper within the cavern below. Though it wasn't a massive drop, it was too steep for her to slide down the smooth rocks, naked as she was. Thankfully, others had been there before her; a set of stairs carved into the rock along the waterfall's edge led to a landing below. With Hendrel's light illuminating the grotto, Raelyn forgot about any previous reservations. Entranced by her surroundings, the coolness that sent an involuntary shiver through her body went unnoticed.

The lower pool was shallow compared to where she'd been swimming, waist deep at the most and looked manmade. A flat deck carved out of the rock extended into the water, and on the platform, stone benches cut from the same stone sat in eternal readiness. A walkway protruded into the water, leading to a circular stage where another statue of Genevive held vigil. Unlike outside, the monument looked untouched by time. The goddess had one hand outstretched toward the benches as if beckoning while the other held a set of scales teetering on the point of a sword. Carved at the bottom of the statue was a figure of a *montigrath*, one of Limnin's fabled earth dragons.

Raelyn tiptoed along the walkway and peered at Genevive's image.

"She is the most beautiful woman I've ever seen," she whispered to Hendrel. "How did they manage to capture such kindness in her face?"

The wisp alighted on the goddess's outstretched hand, and Raelyn reached out, feeling the smooth stone against her flesh. It was ice-cold—burning in its frigidity—but before she could pull back, the darkness crashed in on her.

"I have waited long for this moment. You are so few now."

Too late, Raelyn released the statue's grip and realized she no longer stood within the grotto.

CHAPTER SEVEN

familiar sensation of emptiness assailed her senses, and Raelyn felt a wave of anxiety surge through her core. The void was as she had left it: black but not dark, empty but not without substance. Beside her, Hendrel maintained his wisp form and said nothing.

"I have waited long for this moment. You are so few now," a woman's voice carried from somewhere in the emptiness. "Too many years have gone by since I have had communion. Welcome to the seam of the worlds, Raelyn."

"Who …" Raelyn whispered. "Who are you?"

"I am the Second Pillar. The Balancer. The Sword and Shield. I am the hand that upholds Emblem's Law. I am the Lore Keeper."

"Genevive?"

"My mortal name has been lost for a long time," the voice replied. "Though, once, I was called Genevive in this place."

"How did I get here this time?" Raelyn looked at Hendrel. "I don't understand."

"You are a warden, and you touched my statue and communion altar. It is a joining place for our kind, the stone blessed with the power to connect us across the infinity of space and time. Once, there were more like you, and I was not such a stranger to the world of men." Genevive's voice echoed in the space around Raelyn's head. "Those days are better left to the past now.

"Know this, Daughter of the Void, these pathways are no longer safe for your kind. There are those of us who would harm you." Genevive's voice faded in and out as if on the wind. "There are those who would seek your domination. More than lost spirits walk the seams of the world, and wardens are more than what they were intended to be."

"What does that mean?" Raelyn shivered and wrapped her arms around her exposed chest. "Please, my lady. I feel so lost."

The goddess's voice was fainter, but she replied, "Gain the wisdom of friend over foe. Learn to read intentions within words and seek the truth in all things. You are a conduit, a link between things that should not be joined. Remember this."

"I don't understand!" Raelyn shouted into the emptiness. "Please!"

"I can tell you no more." Genevive's voice was almost inaudible. "The transcendent seeks you. He sees you are not in the pool."

Just as quickly as she'd entered the void, Raelyn was back in the grotto, her hand still clutching that of the statue. Hendrel flickered around her and up toward the stairs. She heard Laris calling her name outside.

The damp and cold finally caught up to her. Fingers numb and legs barely working, she stumbled up the stairs and splashed into the water. "I'm here!" she yelled as she emerged from the cave. "I'm here."

Atop one of the cliffs, in an effort to scan the area, Laris locked his attention on to her form swimming out of the hidden cavern. He immediately descended, angling away from the rocky slopes toward the embankment. From her position in the water, Raelyn heard him cursing to himself, her name sprinkled throughout the monologue.

She remained in the water, watching his journey, her eyes flicking from him and back to her clothes on the beach.

"Well?" he yelled at her from the pebbled shore. "Where in Emblem's name were you?"

"I found a cave," she replied, her voice shaking from the cold. "Hendrel showed it to me."

Laris lifted Raelyn's dress off the ground with the tip of his sword. "Get dressed." He glared at her. "We're camping here for the night."

She swam toward the beach, and he turned his back to her but didn't walk away. Tentatively, more out of necessity than want, she stumbled out of the water and grabbed her filthy clothes, grateful for their warmth despite their dirty state. Her teeth chattered as she slipped on the tattered dress, and though she felt the cold to her bones, she couldn't bring herself to put her shoes back on her blistered feet. The numbness of the freezing water was a blessing in some ways.

"I had a fire started before I realized you'd vanished," he said angrily. "Beyond that fallen tree, at the other end of the beach."

"Th-thank you," she stammered. "That s-sounds wonderful right now."

He glanced back at her before heading toward the area he'd picked for camp but kept silent. If Raelyn hadn't been so cold, she would have been more concerned about how furious he seemed. As it was, she was so grateful for the warmth of the fire that she hunched over the tiny flames and completely forgot about him while he gathered more wood for the night.

"Why aren't we moving on?" she asked eventually, revived as Laris's ministrations strengthened the flames. "We still have much daylight left."

"Fresh tracks," he answered. "Human and horse—and more numerous than I care to worry about."

She nodded. "Bandits? Are they always so bold? Traveling out in plain sight?"

"They weren't on the road. I came across their tracks downstream, heading in the same direction we're going. It will be best to put another half day between us."

She picked at the fish he'd cooked for her. "Laris, Hendrel showed me a communion alter."

"For Genevive?" he asked. "Is that where you were?"

"I didn't know what it was until I was in the void. The goddess—" she met his gaze across the fire "—spoke to me."

Laris let out a loud exhale. "The things you do are so dangerous, Raelyn." He leaned back as he looked at Raelyn's face and then into the flames. "What did she tell you?"

"She told me it isn't safe for me in the void. That I'm a link. A link for things that shouldn't be joined. I don't know what she meant."

"I can't be certain either," he said slowly, "but there's mention of such things in the scriptures we studied at Emblem's Manor. The great battle between Ube and his chaos gods and Ute with his god allies, the Pillars. The Cataclysm."

"What would that have to do with wardens?"

Laris shook his head, hesitating. "Wardens are tied to the gods, Raelyn. They were the gods' means of communicating with the mortal world, but beyond that, I know little. Emblem's Manor is a school for mages, and while wardens are mentioned in the histories of the world, they're only that—a mention. We were taught they became instrumental in the Cataclysm, and many were killed. The grandmasters told us not to worry about wardens, that there were so few left, we'd likely never encounter one." He smiled crookedly. "Imagine my surprise."

Raelyn shivered, a memory seeping into her consciousness. "Where is the Sundered Gate?"

"Where did you hear *that* name?"

She stared into the fire, chewing a bit of fish. "Hendrel told me to seek it. Is it a place?"

"It's a place," he answered after a moment. "That's all I can tell you."

"You mean that's all you *will* tell me," she replied sourly. "You say you don't know much, but I can hear it in your voice. You're not doing me any favors by not telling me, you know."

"You're too innocent of the world," he snapped back at her. "Things greater than us are in motion, and it's not my place to guess what it all might mean or to give you information that could put you in danger. When we get to Mar Dereand, I'll arrange for an escort to take you to Emblem's Manor. My mentor is the headmaster there. You can discuss your visions with him."

"Emblem's Manor? But that's on the opposite border of Lomnir. It will take me months to get there." The weight of his words hit her like a sack of rocks. "You're not going with me, are you?"

He stared into the fire. "My duty is to my lord. I lead armies, Raelyn. I can't abandon my post. Circumstances have allowed me to see to your safety, but our journey together is coming to a close."

It took strength she didn't know she had to stop the tears in her eyes from spilling down her cheeks, but she managed to hold the flood behind her lashes. She couldn't respond without the risk of losing her composure, so she sat still and silent, staring at her battered feet. Her father was dead, and Ellisand was beyond reach. When Laris left her, she would truly be alone.

"I'll make certain you are looked after." His tone was gentler. "You'll be safe with the master transcendents of the Manor. It would take another Cataclysm to breach their walls."

"Or a warden strolling into their midst," she said bitterly. "I can't go there. I'd single-handedly cause the most powerful school of mages in Uhmeer to become as vulnerable as babes."

Laris sighed heavily. They both knew she was right.

I was alone when I left camp. I would still be alone if Laris hadn't followed me. I have no business being upset.

The words were easier to repeat than they were to believe. While her original plan had been to get to Mar Dereand alone, she couldn't deny how comforting it was to have a companion.

"I need to find some hawksbur for my feet and arm," she mumbled. "I won't go far." She stood and dusted the loose dirt from her clothing. Stepping gingerly, she tiptoed away from the warmth of the fire. Plenty of the blue-green plants lined the bank of the stream; she'd seen them upon arrival. The greater success was not needing to conceal her emotions any longer.

Raelyn spent far longer than intended or needed, seated on the small swath of grass at the base of the cliff nearest camp. She found solace in the methodical plucking of hawksbur leaves, and their soothing liquid made a welcomed salve for her raw skin and the healing cut on her arm. Disheartened and anxious about why lay ahead, the reality of her situation also lay heavy on her heart. Without her father and the favor of Duke Wedminth, she had no promise of a future beyond what she could make for herself. While in the castle, no matter how much she tried to ignore it, the promise of an advantageous marriage was absolute. Now, she had nothing but the clothes on her back to offer the world, and her knowledge of needlepoint and the arts couldn't even earn her supper. Maybe Laris was right; she needed guidance if she had a chance of finding purpose.

A twig snapped off to her right, and Raelyn looked over her shoulder toward camp. A man walked toward them from downstream, his features difficult to make out in the long shadows of dusk, a limp keeping his steps slow and deliberate. He was tall and slight; his posture rounded. His long cloak had seen newer days and was wrapped around him like a giant blanket.

At the fire, Laris made no effort to stand up and greet the newcomer. Raelyn could see her companion's sword unsheathed next to his side, ready.

The stranger stopped short of the campfire as if its warmth drew close an impassable curtain. Without speaking, he looked at Laris and then to Raelyn, and then to the ruins of the temple in the background. From where she sat, Raelyn could sense the man's unease, and she wondered if her presence soothed him or brought further alarm. Surely, she no longer resembled a wild woman or a bandit.

"Wasn't expecting anyone here," the man finally said. "I'm not looking for trouble."

Laris motioned for him to sit. "Nor are we. We have some fish to spare if you're hungry."

The man remained where he was and looked at Raelyn again, agitated. "Only came to make some offerings to the goddess." Clearing his throat, he said, "I'll leave them here, lady, if it pleases you."

"Sir?" Raelyn questioned, pushing herself to her feet. "I'm sure the goddess is pleased wherever you see fit to leave them." She hobbled over to the fire and wiped her hands on her skirt, extending one in welcome as her father had taught her. "You've brought offerings?"

With great reluctance, he accepted her handshake, his eyes on the ground. "Yes, lady. I ... it has been so long since ... forgive my ignorance!" He crumpled to his knees and buried his face in the hem of her skirt. "You have returned to us." The fabric muffled his words. "I did not lose faith. I have kept your sanctuary holy."

Laris was suddenly at Raelyn's side. He unceremoniously grabbed the man by the scruff of his cloak and hauled him backward onto the sandy ground. "Mind yourself," Laris said harshly. He pointed his sword at the man's throat. "We have no chance to take on you."

Wide-eyed, the stranger studied the blade and the man holding it. He put up a hand in surrender. "I mean no offense. I only thought ..." he paused. "No. I was mistaken. Wishful thinking of an old prior, nothing more. I thought the lady was Genevive, come to walk her temple, and you here as her holy escort."

"Me?" Raelyn peered down at him. "You thought I was Genevive?"

The man nodded. "You bear a striking resemblance to her, lady, surely you've been told. When the temple was young, people saw her sometimes, walking the grounds in her mortal form. I thought perhaps, after all these years ..." He squinted, finally meeting her gaze. "A remarkable moment, still, as incorrect as it was."

Sword arm unwavering, Laris asked, "You were prior here once?"

"Yes. I am prior still, though, no worshipers come. I will serve the goddess until my last breath."

Raelyn knelt down and gently pushed the point of the blade off the man's throat. "Do you have a name, prior?"

"Mengat, lady. And what is the name of the woman who resembles a goddess?"

Smiling with embarrassment, Raelyn helped him sit up. "My name is Raelyn. This is Laris. We are—" she glanced at the mage "—travelers who wanted some peace from the road and a much-needed bath."

Mengat nodded, gaining his feet. "Well, the goddess will welcome you for the night. She has always blessed young love." He inclined his head toward the statue. "I'll leave my gifts and be on my way."

Raelyn was about to object to his assumption, but Laris put an arm around her waist, drawing her to his side. "We thought the Pillars might forgive us this one evening," he said. "My apologies for the caution earlier."

"No need, lad, no need," said Mengat, waving a hand in dismissal. "One can never be too careful these days. The wicked and wretched stay clear of this place, but that doesn't mean they aren't around. Came across twenty or thirty tracks on my way up the stream that could be bandits. I understand your protectiveness." He pulled several bottles and a wedge of cheese from his cloak pockets. "I'll leave these at the statue and be on my way. There's a sheltered overhang at the north end of the beach, by the way. My joints say there will be rain tonight. You might appreciate the cover."

Laris nodded, and Raelyn smiled. "Thank you," she said. "The sun will be down completely soon. Won't the night catch you on your way home?"

Mengat walked over to Genevive's statue by the pool and placed his gifts at the bottom of her pedestal. "I know these woods as well in the dark as I do the light," he replied. "My cabin is quite far, but I enjoy the walk. If you've a mind to it, stop in if you pass that way. You can't see it from the road, but if you follow the skirt of the mountains, you'll bump right into it."

"We will keep watch for it," Raelyn replied. "Is there anything we should do for the goddess before we leave?"

Mengat winked at them. "Genevive requires no offerings from her followers. I leave these as a gift. May she bless your union," he said.

"Though it was but a moment, I saw her here tonight. Thank you for that." With those words, he turned from them, limping back the way he'd come. The heavy blanket of evening covered the land in darkness, and the prior's outline vanished much sooner than Raelyn expected.

Laris released his hold on her. "We should find the shelter he was talking about. I don't feel like sitting in the rain all night."

CHAPTER EIGHT

"Let's talk about your friend." Saraht reined her horse to a halt. "What was her name again?"

"Raelyn," replied Ellisand, her dappled grey gelding rounding the top of the knoll. "Raelyn Forthgrew."

Saraht nodded and surveyed the landscape. Rolling hills of grassland stretched as far as the eye could see. If one didn't have a firm grasp of the geography of Uhmeer, it would have been easy to think it was another part of the world completely, not just a few days' ride from Albator—let alone still part of Limnin. The entire lower third of Limnin was, in fact, a great grassland until it met the sea at the Inlet of Uleam and the city of Corcrest.

A peace settled about the landscape that coincided with its emptiness. No roads cut through the vegetation, and no farmsteads revealed signs of civilization. In all her time spent in this part of the country, Saraht had only twice encountered a hermit hut or other habited dwelling nestled in the shallow valleys. Emptiness was to be expected; the grasslands were considered haunted by locals, and the remnants of the feyfolk civilizations had long been picked over for any artifacts of value.

"Would you know what I meant if I told you Raelyn was a warden?" Saraht urged her horse into a lumbering walk, motioning for Ellisand to follow.

Ellisand shook her head. "I've never heard of that before."

"The man who heads up my soldiers is named Orion. He's the unpleasant one in the bulky armor. I'm sure you know him from your journey." They trotted down a hill. "Despite his disgusting nature, Orion is a skilled warrior, partly because he is a transcendent, a mage pledged to the Holy King. Though, his vows are fairly loose these days. When he met your friend in the city, he said she neutralized his initial attack."

"I've known Raelyn my whole life," Ellisand replied snidely. "I've never heard her talk about having magic. She would have told me. She tells me everything."

"It's not magic, and most likely, she didn't know her true nature. Something I suspect was done on purpose by your families. As a friend always by your side, Raelyn would have made a convenient body-guard against magical attempts on your life. And, as a fellow warden, I would very much like to meet her." Saraht looked over and smiled at her companion. "Would you like me to send a small force to see if she survived?"

"Yes! Yes, that would be wonderful," Ellisand answered, excited. "I *feel* like she's still alive. I think I would know if she'd died. But it would be a relief to know it's not false hope."

"Good. The tide is changing, Ellisand. My master, Prince Thiir of Faldea, seeks to dispose of Limnin's corrupt and cruel King Rothelian. You are the only Wedminth child and heir to these lands and the duchy. As my blood kin, I would not part you from that right nor see it transferred to some unworthy man by way of marriage." Saraht twisted in the saddle to look at Ellisand. She dropped the reins and spread her arms wide. "This is your land. Why should some foreign lord rule in your place just because you are a woman? I dare-say we can both agree that men have no advantage over us when it comes to the critical thinking of leadership."

At Ellisand's silence, Saraht continued. "I can tell you are still uncertain, but you stayed when you could have fled, and for that, I'm grateful." Her voice lowered. "You've been told your entire life your one goal is to marry, and who am I to say otherwise?"

"I don't think I should have to marry unless I want to. Who could stand being tied to some stranger who doesn't even know the first thing about romance? I've always thought it was a terrible destiny."

"Forced husbands will no longer be a concern for you. You should hold all the power and titles you desire, even a throne if that's your wish. Should I prevail, Ellisand, you'll rule your land as you see fit and marry when or if you so choose." She shrugged. "But if I lose, you will still be able to return home, but you will forever be a pawn in the king's game of politics, used as he deems best."

Saraht knew by the thoughtful silence of her companion which future sounded more appealing. "This is why I brought you here. I would spare you the horrors that can befall all young women, married and unmarried. There is a place of power for you—with us."

"I'm not a warrior," Ellisand said. "I have no way to help."

"Ah! No need for any of that talk. Great leaders are not always skilled on the battlefield. I will teach you the nuances of what it means to rule over others, something you would have already been taught if you'd been a male heir. We won't forget your prowess with the finer arts; those things, too, have a place in the future, but you will begin more important lessons. Will you do it, then? Will you join my cause?"

There was a long pause. "You'll send out that party to find Raelyn?"

Face hidden from Ellisand as her horse pranced ahead, Saraht smiled. "Yes, my dear. I will send out a party to find Raelyn."

Raelyn opened her eyes to darkness. She rolled over, discouraged that sleep was eluding her. She lay there for long minutes, eyes closed, before acknowledging Laris wasn't beside her. The sounds of rain were gone, and it was cold. Very, very cold. She opened her eyes again and assessed the darkness, already knowing where she was.

"You're back!" Hendrel said as his light bounced around her. "It's good that you're back."

"Am I sleeping?"

"In your world, yes," he replied. "The more familiar you become with the void, the less you'll be able to distance yourself from it until your control improves. Even now, when you're asleep, it is the focus of your subconscious. You brought yourself here without even realizing it."

Raelyn sighed and sat up. "Is Genevive here?"

The wisp hovered in front of her and took a long pause before responding. "She is in her realm. The communion altar summons her to the void. She has no reason to walk the seam otherwise."

"She said I shouldn't come here anymore. Should I go?"

"Communion is dangerous. Visiting the void through your ability is less so."

"But still dangerous?"

Hendrel's light dimmed. "There is danger in all places," he finally said.

Raelyn rubbed her face, frustrated with the answer. Why was everything so cryptic? Was there no one who could offer her any guidance? "I was told you are my guide, but I've learned nothing since we last spoke. Is there anything you can tell me? Show me?"

Hendrel's candle flame morphed into the outline of the little boy. The specter sat down across from her, and though he had no features, Raelyn felt a sense of friendliness.

"I am just a child," he told her. "I know less than you about the world, but more than you about being a warden. When we first conversed, time was limited. Other souls were in the balance." He spread his arms wide. "Now we may speak more freely. I was the last warden before your generation. I lived in the Holy Citadel."

"The Holy Citadel?" Raelyn felt something in her mind start to connect. "Wait." She narrowed her eyes in concentration, the idea just out of her reach.

Hendrel nodded. "What you are thinking is correct. I was the last Holy King."

"You were a warden," she said quietly. "That's how Emblem was able to speak to the people. He used a warden."

"I was not officially the Holy King when I was murdered," he said. "I was in training. From birth, the Holy Knights tutored and molded me for that purpose. Before I could hold communion with Ute—whom you may know as Emblem—I had to have basic mastery of my abilities. Unfortunately, even among the Holy Knights, there are dark dealings. My life was cut short before I made my ten-and-first birthday."

"You speak as though you were a wise old man," Raelyn said with a sad smile. "You probably didn't get to be a child, did you?"

"I was never a child." His energy sobered. "I was born for a purpose that transcends childhood. The toys, the books, and the play of children were unfamiliar to me. My stories depicted duty; my toys were relics of my station.

"But this is not the time for a world history. While you lose no time by being in the void, the longer you stay here, the more likely you are to be noticed by other spirits and wandering gods. These sessions should be as brief as we can make them. I will give you a task. It was the first task given to me in my warden training." He stood. "The void is a part of you, Raelyn, and you can control your sphere of influence in the mortal world. Learn to feel the connection within you; you've felt it before. Once you've latched on to it—" he clasped his hands together "—imagine it as a circle around you. Then, work on controlling the size of that circle. Try drawing it in, shrinking it so you don't affect those around you. When you can successfully do that, then try to expand its size to the borders of the world if you can. In time, the circle will always exist in your subconscious and controlling it will be second nature."

"Is that why I single-handedly destroyed my home?"

He nodded. "Right now, your sphere of influence is wild. Emotion makes it expand and contract unpredictably. Had you received training, the events in Albator may have been different." He shifted back to his familiar teardrop form. "But, then again, perhaps this is how it must be."

"You are all I have left now." Raelyn wished she could embrace the light. "Please know your companionship has meant the world to me."

"And yours, mine," he said. "Now return to true sleep. Focus; find the connection to the real world in your mind. In this way, you can also return to the void when you wish."

Raelyn closed her eyes, emptying her mind of thoughts. She searched for the sounds of rain and the cold feel of stone pressed along her side while she slept. Short moments later, the sounds became real again, the cold stone unrelenting beneath her. Listening to the patter of the drops and soaking in Laris's warmth at her back, she closed her eyes and tried her best to sleep.

Dawn's beauty within the ruins was muted by a heavy rain. From within the small shelter of tumbled rock, Raelyn watched the droplets create ripples along the surface of the pool. Hendrel's light was constantly present for the first time in days, bobbing and flickering above the water, playing in the rain. She'd been lying at the entrance, head on her arm, for at least an hour, watching the darkness fade from the world outside. Behind her, Laris sat with his legs extended along her back; the nook they'd spent the night in was barely large enough for two people side by side. She knew he was awake, too, but neither of them spoke.

They were half a day behind from their original start, and with another day and night yet to be spent outside, Raelyn's mood was as grey as the rainclouds. Feeling the aches and pains of cross-country travel, the despair of her father's death, the gut-twisting worry about Ellisand's safety, and the growing responsibility of being a warden, a part of her wished the water would rise and carry her away. What did she have to live for anyway? The only option that may have offered hope was now buried beneath the truth of how vulnerable she made those around her.

"This isn't the kind of rain that will end soon, is it?" she asked Laris without looking at him.

"No. But if you're done counting raindrops, we should head out."

She felt nothing at his short reply. Even her temper had abandoned her. Besides, Raelyn knew Laris was just as weary as she, if not more so. He had the burden of maintaining watch and protecting them. She wasn't sure he'd slept at all since finding her. Pushing herself up, she rubbed her arms briskly to force out the cold seeping inward toward her bones. It was a futile task; what little warmth she generated was chased away by the damp, and once she stepped out into the downpour, no amount of friction would save her.

Laris stepped past her into the rain. "Let's get going. We'll stick to the base of the mountains to avoid the group responsible for the tracks I saw. I suspect they're traveling closer to the road to pick off travelers."

Raelyn nodded and took up the pace behind him. She knew the leather cuirass around her chest would offer some protection against the water, but she could feel the wet already working its way beneath the armor, wicking through the fibers of her dress. It would be a long day's journey to wherever they might make camp. She shivered, not having been warm to start with.

Feet wrapped in strips of cloth from her skirt, her blisters and sores were manageable, though, a dull ache nagged at her with every step. The going was much slower than before; the rocks and moss-covered tree roots became treacherous obstacles in the rain. With every slip and fall, she felt her resolve weaken, and she forged ahead to keep up with Laris, who seemed unaware or uncaring of her struggles.

Throughout the hours of trudging, Hendrel's light flickered by her shoulder. The wisp provided no real warmth, but his presence provided comfort and reminded Raelyn she wasn't alone. His purpose was still a mystery to her, but she was content just to have his familiarity and the guidance he offered. He now encouraged her, in his way, to keep going forward, even when her feet went completely out from under her, and she landed hard in a pool of rainwater trapped within a bowl of tree roots.

She sat there, rainwater pouring down her face, defeated.

"Raelyn," Laris said patiently. "Are you injured?"

She shook her head.

"Then get up. We've another half a day ahead of us." He walked over to her and offered his hand. "You've made it this far. If you were going to give up, you should have done it a long time ago."

She accepted his outstretched hand, allowing him to pull her off the ground, and they continued in the same silence they'd traveled in all morning. There was something appropriate about the lack of conversation. Though she was cold and weary and feeling the weight of invisible burdens, the forest around her reflected the quiet. The heavy rain silenced the world—from the natural sounds of the wild to her footsteps on the forest floor. There was a peace in the constant drone of the rain, as if there was nothing else in the world to do other than walk forward.

Catching up to Laris at the top of a ridge, Raelyn almost didn't believe her eyes. Like a beam of sunlight through the clouds, a small cabin interrupted the landscape of rocks and scrub trees in the valley below, the smoke from its chimney a welcome promise of warmth and respite.

"Do you think that's the prior's cabin?" she asked.

Laris nodded. "It seems a wise guess. He did say we'd run into it if we kept to the mountain base."

"Can we please take just a moment by his fire?"

"Mar Dereand is not expecting us," Laris said. "Let's not pass up the opportunity to dry off and warm up."

Suspicious at how quick he was to accept her suggestion, Raelyn wondered if he'd planned the stop all along. The realization took the edge off her mood, and she wished there was some way she could express to him how grateful she was for all he'd done for her.

"Come on," Laris called back to her, already on his way down the hill.

Humble as one might expect the cabin of an aging prior to be, the dwelling was deceptive in its plainness and boasted formidable construction. As the pair approached, Raelyn took stock of the large logs fortified with gravel mortar. A heavy cover of moss and grass stretched across the flat roof; if seen from the cliffs above, it would have appeared to be just another patch of the natural landscape. Freshly split wood sat under a lean-to adjacent to a small shed, next to which spread a sizeable garden. Though modest, the place felt well-lived and loved, and not even the steady rain could overpower the inviting smell of the warm fire within.

Laris knocked on the door. After a few moments, Raelyn noticed the curtain on the window pull aside, and she did her best to smile at Mengat when their eyes met.

"Well!" he exclaimed as the door swung open. "You two decided to stop by! And during the downpour, no less. I thought the rain might have been a convenient deterrent to stay up at the shrine another day." He winked at Raelyn. "Though, I suppose it doesn't have the most comfortable accommodations. Come in, come in."

Inside, the cabin was just as Raelyn expected it to be. Unlike Ebest's chambers with something fascinating in every corner, the prior's home was simple and bare. Beyond the necessities of a table and chairs, bed, and walk-in pantry, the space was empty of excess, except for a large fur rug by the fireplace and two bookshelves on the wall. From under the table, an orange cat watched, doubt and skepticism of the newcomers apparent in its expression.

"Don't mind Lydantus," Mengat said, ushering them to the fireplace. "He hates the rain, too, and despite his aloofness, he will expect you to pet him at some point." He looked at his guests. "Tea? Fruit? Ah, I know. How about a change of clothes while yours dry? Can you stay that long?"

"We aren't on any timeline that demands travel in the rain," Laris remarked. "If it's not inconvenient, we would like to wait out the weather."

"Certainly. Let me get you some things to change into." Mengat looked at Raelyn. "I have some of my wife's old clothing in a trunk, still, my dear. If you don't mind a mountain woman's clothes, I think they'd be a better fit for you than mine, and you'd be welcome to keep them."

"I would appreciate anything you can spare." Raelyn shivered as she said the words despite the closeness of the fire.

Mengat nodded and disappeared through a doorway at the far end of the cabin.

"Keep your senses about you," Laris whispered to her. "We know nothing about our host."

She couldn't blame his caution. She was often just as guarded when it came to strangers. But something in Mengat's demeanor was so genuine Raelyn felt guilty for thinking ill of him. "Don't assume the worst," she whispered back. "People deserve a chance to prove themselves."

Before Laris could respond, Mengat emerged from the back room, clothes draped over his arm. "Here you are," he said, tossing them over the back of a chair. "My wife was a bit taller and broader than you, lady, but nothing a belt won't fix." He sifted through the pile. "For you." He set a few articles of clothing on the table, glancing at Laris. "These should work. We are no match, now, but I once had the shoulders of a young man."

Raelyn took the clothes and headed into the pantry and drew the curtain across the doorway. Barely the size of a wash closet in the castle, the small space was stacked high with items. Trunks lined the perimeter, and drying herbs hung from the ceiling. One wall was dedicated to jars and canisters, with a salt bin for meat that made a perfect seat while she gently removed her shoes. The cloth strips pulled away, taking some of her skin with them, and she gingerly touched the open sores. *No puss. No angry redness.* The hawksbur had done a good job of soothing the skin and preventing infection. The rain, however, had done her no favors, and the little healing her skin had managed the previous night had rubbed away and then some. Her arm was less affected and well on the road to being healed.

Raelyn let her soiled dress drop to the floor and relaxed as the warm air of the cabin chased away the clammy chill from her wet clothing. She put the pants and thin shirt from Mengat on over her wet undergarments, too embarrassed by the thought of hanging them at the hearth to dry to take them off. The final piece of the ensemble was a beautiful, thick, wool shawl, and she wrapped it around her shoulders slowly in a personal celebration of warmth. By the time she emerged from the room, Laris was also freshly dressed, and he and Mengat had moved to the table, a steaming pot of tea between them, a third mug waiting for her at the empty seat.

"The clothes fit you well." The prior held his mug up in salute. "My sweet Tabitha would be pleased."

Raelyn smiled and sat down, pleasantly surprised by the sudden feel of warm fur brushing against her shins as she reached for her cup of tea. She looked down at Lydantus. "Hello. Would you like to come up here?" She patted her lap.

The cat peered up at her, its emerald eyes belying intelligence, the corners of its lips slightly curled into a smile. Without hesitation, it leaped up and rubbed against her, then flopped across Raelyn's knees.

"He's a one of the Old Guard, you know," Mengat said. "One of the last of his kind."

"The Old Guard?" Raelyn gently petted the cat. "He looks small to be a soldier."

Mengat chuckled. "The Old Guard are the divine historians of The Circle. Since the start of Emblem's rule, temples have had a feline mascot, hand-picked by the Pillar of the shrine, to keep the true record of the world's activities. You see," he explained, "humans are poor history keepers. We skew facts through our own perception, often unintentionally. The Guard, however, see all and remember all without the burden of words. Lydantus is hundreds of years old."

Raelyn's hand paused mid-pat, and she looked down at Lydantus with surprise. "Hundreds of years old? I can't even believe it! He looks in his prime. What does he do since the shrine fell into ruin and worshipers stopped attending?" Raelyn asked.

"He still keeps watch. He still remembers. Each day that goes by is still a piece in the timeline of the world, no matter how insignificant it may seem. And he will always have a home here while I am alive. In the past, the Guard served prior to prior. Now—" he shrugged "—I seem to be the last prior of the mountain shrine. I can't say what he will do when I am gone."

As if on cue, the cat hopped from Raelyn's lap onto the table and walked over to sit by Mengat's mug. "He's a fine companion," the prior said affectionately. "I am sure he will weasel his way into someone's home when the day comes."

They sat silently a few moments, sipping on tea and listening to the rain drum against the cabin walls. After a while, Raelyn asked, "What happened to the shrine? With such a dedicated master, I don't understand why it's in such a state."

"It's not a simple thing to explain." Mengat leaned back in his chair. "You see, places of worship can be in anyone's home or any town, but temples have limited placement in the world. Temples are where a god has blessed an altar site, a place where special individuals can communicate with that god. Genevive was fond of the mountains and picked this spot for one of her temples. Even then, the mountains were dangerous, and only the truly devout came to worship. When the Holy Citadel went dark, humans lost their last connection to the gods. Faith is such a fragile thing already; when the people stopped feeling heard, they felt abandoned. And, unfortunately, I am just one man and too old to stand against the will of nature."

Laris poured another mug of tea. "He is referring to the last of the true Holy Kings, Raelyn. The man currently in the citadel with that title is just a mage like any other. He is not the embodiment of Emblem the council would like you to think he is. There has been no true Holy King for decades. That's what he means when he says the Citadel went dark."

Mengat nodded. "Of course, even if it's common knowledge, saying such in the wrong company nowadays will get your head chopped off. But those of us in the worship business can't ignore the truth."

Hendrel. Raelyn sipped her tea in thought. He'd told her he was the last Holy King. What had happened to him?

As if reading her thoughts, the wisp's brightness flared at her shoulder and drew Lydantus's curiosity. The cat let out a loud meow, and Hendrel flickered around the tea kettle, enticing the feline to chase him. The two did a lap around the table before frolicking down on the floor.

Topping off his mug, Mengat chuckled, shaking his head, and both Raelyn and Laris looked at him. "Raelyn, I may be an old man, but I'm not a sheltered fool. You two are no normal travelers. I could have told you that last night. Now, here you are in my home, feet red and raw from shoes not meant for traveling and with a will-o-the-wisp attached to your soul." He fixed her with an intense stare, daring her to forego conversational pleasantries and reveal the truth. "Who are you?"

Feeling Laris's cautionary gaze on her, Raelyn adjusted the wool shawl around her shoulders and stared at the mug of tea in her hands. "We are fugitives from Albator," she said slowly, unsure how much she should share. "The city has fallen to an enemy attack."

"These are dark times, indeed," whispered the old man. "How did Faldea get a force so far into the country without notice? Such a thing is concerning."

"We don't know they were Faldean," Laris interjected. "I was there when the city fell, and I have never known Faldea to contract with the wretched or penumbra."

"Penumbra? Creatures from the Depths? The Circle save us. They haven't been seen in these lands since—"

"Since the Cataclysm. Yes, I am aware."

"Dire news, indeed, friends." Mengat frowned. "But I have trouble believing you are nothing more than survivors making your way to safety. Forgive my prying, but I have never seen someone with a wisp, and I have seen many things."

Before Raelyn could answer him, Lydantus leaped onto the table, meowing loudly. He bumped Mengat's hand with his head and jumped over to the windowsill, where he let out a low growl. The cat's tail swished wildly, and he looked back over his shoulders at the group, a long, eerie sound drawing deep from his throat.

"Something wicked approaches," Mengat whispered, on his feet so fast his chair teetered up on two legs precariously. Laris's quick reflexes saved it from clattering to the ground, and the prior looked at him, appreciative. "Quickly!" Mengat urged. "With me, to the center of the room."

The prior grabbed a bucket at the hearth and doused the fire, instantly shrouding the cabin in diluted darkness brought on by late-day rain. Hands shaking, he pulled a small box of glittering dust off the mantle and hastily sprinkled a circle on the floor.

"Stand in the middle with me." He pulled them in. "I can't do much magic, but I can weave this gemstone dust to keep us unseen. It has saved my life many times."

Raelyn's hope faded with Mengat's desperate gestures. She looked at Laris, wishing with everything she had that he would look at her and indicate all was fine, and that the magic Mengat was constructing was somehow different than other magic in the world. Instead, he met her questing gaze and shook his head.

"Something isn't right," Mengat muttered, his voice shaking like his hands. "I ... I must have gotten the patterns wrong. It's been so long."

Laris placed a hand on the prior's shoulder. "Do not waste your time," he whispered. "No magic will save us now."

Mengat looked from Laris to Raelyn, understanding blossoming in the expression across his pale face. "It cannot be."

Raelyn's heart sank. "I am so sorry. We should have told you."

Instead of outrage, the prior exhaled in relief and smiled broadly, grabbing Raelyn and embracing her. "I knew it," he whispered to her. "I knew I would live to see the day when the chosen ones returned." His expression sobered, and he stepped back. "You must go." He kicked aside the carpet on the floor, revealing a hatch in the boards. "My root cellar. At the far end, there is a brick barricade. When I dug the foundation, I accidentally broke through to an old Vast tunnel—"

A loud, piercing shriek shook the cabin. Something moved across the front of the house and blotted out the light from the windows.

Mengat heaved the hatch open. "Go! I'll close and cover the cellar door behind you. If you can get far enough, fast enough, I may be able to hold them off. If not—" he smiled "—maybe they won't search for anyone other than an old prior."

"We can't leave you." Raelyn reached for him, but Laris grabbed her and pulled her down the stairs. "Please!"

"Hush now." Mengat knelt and waved them on. "The wretched have been here before, and they haven't claimed this place yet. For my sake, Raelyn, you must go."

He didn't wait for her to respond. With a nod to Laris, Mengat grabbed the hatch handle and dropped the door shut.

If not for Hendrel, the absolute darkness of the root cellar would have been a deadly time trap. The cabin's large base above was supported by thick beams nestled in the dirt within the damp space. Even with the wisp's light, it took precious moments to identify the part of the back wall patched up with brick.

"There." Laris dragged her forward.

The patch's integrity was good, the mortar solid. Laris's weight wasn't enough to push through the barrier, and he reluctantly unsheathed his sword to pry at the bricks. Raelyn frantically searched for something else to aid them. Overhead, the cabin shuttered with a loud crash, and the vibration cast down a rain of dust and dirt from the floorboards. Spotting an old fire poker, she stumbled over to it. Without a word, she heaved the rusted metal rod across the floor to Laris, who picked it up and stabbed at where the brick met the stone wall.

A human scream made her breath catch in her throat. Something heavy moved above her. The thunderous footsteps stopped for a moment, interrupted by a deafening shriek. At the wall, Laris paused in his digging until the movement resumed. After long, agonizing moments, he motioned for Raelyn to join him.

The hole in the wall was small, but it was enough for them to squeeze by, and she pulled herself into the mountain tunnel. Hendrel's light was dim but present, his flicker conveying urgency. Laris landed next to her. He put a finger to his lips, met Raelyn's gaze, and then looked at her bare feet. Without waiting for her approval, he dropped down and pulled her onto his back. Wrapping his arms around her legs and linking her arms above his shoulders, he trotted into the darkness ahead.

CHAPTER NINE

A thick, damp chill hung in the air, the invisible blanket of moisture insistent no matter how many sconces and torches Saraht lit around her central hall. It was the curse of living in the grassland ruins; any weatherproofing was long gone with the original inhabitants, and no one in her troop had the time or the care to dedicate attention to the multitude of leaks in their temporary base. Two days of heavy rain was an annoyance, but the tiny streams underfoot were currently manageable.

"What happened?" She looked at Orion from across the planning table.

"We tracked them to a cabin at the base of the mountains. The penumbra only found one inhabitant, and it was not the warden."

Saraht rubbed her temples. "Do I have to explain this to you? The girl nullifies magic and has no control over her powers. They didn't just vanish. Clearly, the penumbra missed something. You should have gone yourself."

"I'm not your errand boy," Orion replied. "We have more important things to worry about than your side interests. We move to Pardis next, and the wretch scouts are slow to plot the course. I have men to make travel-ready."

"The warden is more than just a side interest. Now that we know of her, the master wants her dealt with." Knowing better than to push her luck with the transcendent, she asked, "Is there no one suitable you can spare? I'm sure *he* will be generous with his gratitude if the mission is a success. You can send the penumbra, but send a human, too."

Orion huffed. "Fine. I have a man who can do the job. He's not reliable if you want her alive, though."

"Whatever. Alive is preferred, but accidents happen."

Orion smirked and offered her a partial bow. "Your wish is my command, as always. I look forward to riding to Pardis together. It's about time we saw the full extent of your 'power.'"

You have no idea the full extent of my power, she thought, watching him leave. *When that day comes, you'll be the first to witness it.*

Saraht returned to the detailed map of Uhmeer spread across the table. Pardis was north of Albator by two days' ride, which meant she needed to consider a new base camp. As their small force crawled toward the capital, she needed to be within a day's travel, not just for oversight reasons, but because she was their weapon against mages. Albator was the exception; they'd had a warden and no mages, but the smaller cities within the Wedminth lands would have a more traditional defense.

"Any word on Raelyn?" Ellisand entered the hall, arm in arm with Maylam. "Was Orion successful?"

Saraht sighed but did her best to smile. "They've found tracks that might be hers. It seems she's alive, but they haven't located her just yet."

"That's wonderful news!" Ellisand exclaimed. "Rae has always been strong. Of course she would make it to safety."

"Mmhmm," was Saraht's reply, her attention back on the map. "Within the next few days, we will be moving north. Mother, are you fit for travel?"

Maylam took up her seat by the fire. "Daughter, I am always fit for travel. Does this mean you'll be riding out with the men?"

"You need not worry. I am well equipped."

"I will always worry. I am your mother. Besides, war is what we have the men for. If they are not dispensable, what are they to us?"

"You mean the soldiers?" Ellisand asked, covering Maylam in a heavy quilt.

"Yes, dear. There is a reason men fight men, and not because they are stronger than women. It is because one man's seed can create dozens of babies. One woman, however, can only carry one child. It makes women far more precious. What would have more purpose in the growth of humanity: one man and twenty women or twenty men and one woman? Do you see what I mean?"

Ellisand nodded. "I never thought about it like that before."

"Not many do. In time, I will teach you all of my wisdom, as I did my daughter. Now look at her—a force to be reckoned with," Maylam said proudly.

"All thanks to you," Saraht called from where she stood.

"My daughter did not take all of my wisdom to heart, though," Maylam leaned in close. "She chooses the sword, but I learned to fight with other skills." She stroked Ellisand's hair. "Beauty is a powerful weapon. It can disable even the most battle-hardened men. Just because you were not tutored in the ways of weaponry does not mean you are defenseless."

Though her mother spoke in hushed tones, Saraht could hear the conversation plainly. The topic didn't sit well with her, but she understood the truth in the words. If Ellisand were to be a strong ally, she would need to master all the tools she had at her disposal. The young woman was slight, unathletic, and probably had never held a sword, let alone swung one at an enemy. Battle skills were not top of the list of things she needed to learn.

"Mother speaks true, and no matter what the future holds for you, such a skill set is invaluable." Saraht looked over at them. "The time has come to start your training. We will put it to the test in Pardis. Our original plan was to use that city as another distraction point for the Limnin army, but I think there is a better way. If you can take what Mother tells you to heart and put it to practice, we may not need any bloodshed, and we may come out with important allies."

"What is it you're asking me to do?"

"Nothing that doesn't already come naturally to you," said Maylam. "You have such innate sensuality. Come. Sit. Tell me, what do you think attracts a man to a woman?"

"Well … their faces? Their looks?"

"Mmhmm. Mmhmm." Maylam nodded. "You're not wrong. Men are drawn to women's bodies, yes, but that's just surface attraction. With the right set of skills, even a woman who doesn't meet traditional beauty standards can have any man she wants by controlling this." Maylam tapped Ellisand's head.

"First," she explained, "we control their senses: a tantalizing but innocent touch, the right perfume, stain on the lips to draw attention there. Then, depending on the man, you can play to their instincts. Are they strong and honorable men who want to protect you? Oh, look, you're in a moment of vulnerability!" Maylam's eyes narrowed, and a sinister smile peeked from behind her cowl. "Are they excited by the chase? You're mysterious and disinterested, pulling your attention away just when they think they've won you."

Saraht watched Ellisand become entranced by Maylam's words. Just as she'd thought, the Wedminth heir craved both power and control, even if she didn't realize it, and had a natural curiosity about the opposite sex.

"Is the man driven by ego, or is he lacking it? Strategic compliments will win you favor. The list goes on, my dear." Maylam sighed. "That's to say nothing of the many skills for bedding a man. Those will make him crave you like he craves no other."

"Some things take sacrifice to learn," Saraht added gently. "For now, focus on learning more about these subtle skills. Bedding men isn't always necessary to get them to do what you want."

"What about women?" Ellisand asked.

Saraht and Maylam looked at one another. "Women are not immune to these tactics, but you'll find they respond less predictably. They often require a different approach." Maylam patted Ellisand's hand. "For women, we can almost always sway them with logic and reason, dear. When shown Raloria's glory, what woman could turn away?"

Saraht tuned out the rest of Maylam's lesson, mulling over Ellisand's question. It was true—women weren't as easily manipulated by physical seduction. When faced with winning another woman to their cause, Saraht always appealed first to practical necessity, and a practical need in the lives of almost every woman was autonomy. Rather than lure another woman with the promise of pleasure, Saraht exposed them to Raloria's teachings and an ideology where women weren't enslaved to men. Saraht empowered other women. She gave them the courage and desire to rise above where society told them to stay. And if that didn't work, seduction wasn't off the table. It was a much longer, slower game requiring more emotional than physical attention, but she played her part when absolutely necessary.

She fought the sudden urge to seclude herself and read her grimoire. It was a comfort and a habit during moments of intense reflection. Each line of precious prose was a reminder of the injustice Raloria suffered, how men covered over her truth and she was labeled a Deceiver. Despite siding with Emblem in the Cataclysm and being named

Seventh Pillar among his closest allies, Raloria had been shunned by the race of humanity she helped save.

Anything to preserve the patriarchy. Saraht clenched her jaw. Raloria was a champion of women, and her history was far less evil than some of the gods who sided with Emblem and sat among his chosen Pillars in The Circle. That she was considered a Deceiver was an egregious insult that made Saraht's blood boil in anger.

Next to Maylam, Ellisand was nodding enthusiastically. Saraht let her thoughts shift back into the present and willed her rage to subside. She was pleased with Ellisand's progress. Though naive, the Wedminth heir had the innate characteristics that would make her an exceptional acolyte and a formidable opponent in the battle of the sexes. By the time her training was done, there wouldn't be a man—or woman—able to resist her.

CHAPTER TEN

ravel within the mountain tunnels was slow. Laris carried Raelyn for several hours into their escape but couldn't maintain his pace indefinitely, even with strategic breaks. When he was forced to set her down, they took no rest; the tunnel behind them remained silent, but there was no way of knowing if anything still lurked in the shadows on their trail. Hendrel's light battled the absolute darkness, but his constant flicker made Raelyn's head ache. She trudged on, grateful the stone underfoot was relatively smooth.

Laris held up his hand, and they stopped. The tunnel before them split for the first time since entering the underground.

"Which way do we go?" she whispered.

He shook his head. "I don't know. If my senses are true, we've been heading steadily deeper into the mountains. At first sight, neither of these tunnels lead back west."

Raelyn knew they needed a way back above ground. They had no food or water, and even without the danger of pursuit, the tunnels could only offer them an eventual stony grave.

"If no choice is better than the other, let's just keep moving," she suggested. "We will never know, anyway, if we make the wrong decision."

Laris glanced over at her and nodded. "Grim words, but wise. Let's go left."

Hendrel floated into the chosen tunnel, Raelyn behind him, Laris bringing up the rear. She followed the wisp almost mindlessly, her thoughts elsewhere. She hoped, by some miracle, Mengat had made it out alive. She hoped Lydantus was safe with his human master up at the shrine where wicked things seemed not to go. For the first time in her life, Raelyn prayed because, despite the horrors of her current reality, for the first time in her life, she felt the gods were listening. *Genevive, please keep your servants safe from harm. Please watch over them. Please don't let their kindness have been their end.* While she walked, she searched for the presence of the void within her.

Laris's hand on her shoulder slowed her and brought her awareness back to her surroundings. He pointed up along the tunnel wall. "A ledge. We can rest up there for a bit."

The tunnels shifted from narrow and confined to cavernous and open. In some places, Raelyn couldn't see the ceiling above, deep darkness hiding the rocky crags from her sight. The ledge they rested at sat in an open expanse, the product of unstable rock tumbling to the floor below. Step-like rubble made it easy to reach, and though there was limited room at the top to stand, Raelyn was far more interested in sitting.

She collapsed onto the cold stone, finally acknowledging the burning sensation in her legs. "How long can we rest?"

Laris sat down next to her and peered at her feet. "For a bit. I'll be able to carry you again."

"No need. I'm fine."

"Your feet say otherwise."

Raelyn sprawled out and lay on her back, enjoying the momentary relief. "I don't even feel them anymore."

Laris didn't respond, dropping down to sit nearby. In companionable silence, they stared into darkness overhead, watching Hendrel's flicker lengthen the shadows, his glow too weak to reach the ceiling.

"Laris." Raelyn's eyelids grew heavy. "Why didn't Father tell me I was a warden?"

"If I had to guess, he didn't want to lose you. Wardens are rare, and people in power covet rare things. You would have been taken away, most likely to the Holy Citadel. There's a strong chance you would never have seen your father or the Wedminths ever again."

"So they let me live a lie?" She felt numb. "Now I know the real reason why the Wedminths never hired mages."

"It was selfish on all their accounts. It's not your fault, Raelyn. You didn't know."

She closed her eyes, pushing away the swell of guilt, knowing many of her decisions still contributed to their circumstances. She couldn't fault her father entirely, either. After losing her mother, he'd become extremely protective of Raelyn, and if he'd asked her about being a warden, she knew she'd have told him to do whatever was necessary to let her stay in Albator.

The thoughts became fuzzy, disconnected. With a deep breath, she relaxed against the rock at her backside, no longer wrestling with her past, focused only on the quiet slowly embracing her.

Something's not right.

The darkness behind her eyes grew blacker, and Raelyn jerked awake from her half-sleep state. She sat up and looked around, jostling Laris, who had also succumbed to the need for proper sleep. "Hendrel?" She looked around her. "Hendrel!"

The wisp's light was gone from immediate sight, but Raelyn noticed a faint glow beyond a pile of rubble at the opposite end of the ledge. She crawled over and found herself looking through a natural opening in the wall. Below, Hendrel floated in another tunnel, illuminating a chamber with square borders and high walls.

"Laris," she called over to him in a hushed voice. "Come look."

He joined her at the rock window.

"That doesn't look like a natural chamber," she whispered.

In the adjoining room, debris littered the floor. Whatever had been there was in ruin. Haphazard piles of wood and heaps of fabric were strewn throughout the space. The edges of Hendrel's light suggested there was more than met the eye, his glow illuminating the outline of storage boxes and other clutter.

"We've got to get down there." Laris studied the drop from their rock window to the space below. "There could be something useful."

Raelyn nodded. Signs of life meant much-needed supplies and a potential exit passage, and hopping into an adjacent tunnel through the small opening might delay larger creatures searching for them. For the first time in the tunnels, she felt a glimmer of hope.

"It's a drop, but I think we can make it," he whispered. "The wall is sloped. If you use it to slide down part of the way, the rest of the fall won't be difficult."

Raelyn looked at the path of descent, uncertain how her bare feet would handle any manner of fall or jump but determined not to burden him further. She watched him squeeze through the opening feet first, using his upper body to lower himself as far as possible before he released his hold. He slid most of the way down the wall and then dropped. Though far from graceful, his landing left him unharmed, and he motioned for Raelyn to start her descent.

She tentatively lowered herself the same way, silently begging her arms to hold her long enough to feel her feet find purchase on the slope. At the moment she thought her arms would give out, her toes connected with the cool stone, and she anchored herself against the side of the wall. Eyes closed, she took a deep breath and let go of the window ledge.

Raelyn knew her fall was ugly, but she was terrified to land on her feet, and she allowed her body to take the brunt of the landing. Too late, she realized Laris had intentions to catch her. In her limp state, she had no way to control her momentum, and she slammed into him with enough force to knock them both to the ground.

"You know I was going to catch you, right?" he asked with a groan.

Bruised but otherwise relieved, she couldn't help but smile. The smile turned into a laugh, and she covered her mouth to stifle the sound. She laughed even harder, watching him glare at her, covered in dust from where she'd knocked him across the floor.

"Sorry. Sorry," she said, pushing stray strands of hair from her face. "Are you all right?"

"Fine." He stood and brushed the dirt from his clothes. "For someone who just got rolled over by a human boulder."

She giggled again and had to turn away from his scowl. It felt good to laugh. "I'm glad you're not hurt. Let's see what Hendrel found."

Stretching in opposite directions from where they stood, the space sat nestled within a new section of tunnel. Chisel marks and wooden beams proved the area had been widened in the past with tools, creating a large space on each side of the passage. Remnants of shelves and their contents littered the floor. Raelyn picked through the mess, searching for anything useful.

"Here," Laris called over to her.

She looked up in time to catch an item.

"There's probably another one around if we keep digging."

She smiled at the dusty boot in her hands, never so grateful to see such a simple item in all her life. Tucking it under her arm, she hurried to where he dug and knelt to search.

Picking through odds and ends without success, Raelyn wondered if the room had once been a private trove of stolen goods rather than a storage area for useful items. She sifted through the random bits, from kitchenware and bedding to cloth and tools. Many fabric pieces were clothing, though, the piles were a hodgepodge of patterned cloth, fancy dresses, and children's attire. Few things had survived abandonment unscathed; mice and other agents of nature had worked diligently to turn the cache to dust. Discouraged that she was still without a second boot, she moved to the other side of the room to continue searching. At the very least, before they left, she could bind her bootless foot with layers of cloth.

She pushed on a wooden plank lodged in the rubble. It resisted her efforts, but determination won out, and she worked the board loose, freeing it from its stone prison. The disruption caused a cascade of debris and filled the area around Raelyn with dust. She gasped and stepped back, unprepared for what the shift in the rocks and dirt revealed.

An arm, its skin and flesh long gone, reached out from within the newly arranged pile, and in the dim light, she could make out other bones pinched between larger stones.

"I found something," she muttered loudly enough for Laris to hear. "It might be attached to another pair of boots."

He walked over and looked at her, then at the skeleton arm. "Let's dig him out. Boots might not be the only thing of value he has."

Stone by stone, they unburied the remnants of the stranger. Laris was right; the body had more to offer. A pair of knives, an empty water skein, and a scouting glass proved valuable, and much to Raelyn's relief, the skeleton still had his old pair of boots.

"It's unusually dry in this part of the tunnels," Laris said, pulling bones and deteriorated fabric out of the footwear. "Lucky for you, or these might not have held up." He handed them to her. "They've got some holes, but wrap your feet first, and you'll be fine."

She accepted them with a nod and set the pair aside to finish uncovering her discovery. Hendrel quickly passed over the remains and flitted around debris. His light shone from within the rocks by the skeleton's head, catching Raelyn's eye. She shifted her position and pulled at the loose stone.

"I've never seen a weapon like this," she said, dislodging a staff with a hooked, sword-like blade attached.

"It's a type of polearm," Laris replied. "Called a glaive."

Raelyn stood, examining the weapon. It felt balanced in her hands, and its weight was comfortable. She felt strong holding it. The long handle of smooth reddish wood with silver metalwork ended in a curved blade covered in ornate engravings. Despite having been buried in rock, no blemishes marred the weapon. When she wiped away the dust, it looked like it had just come from a forge.

"It suits you," said Laris. "It will give you reach and serve well in a number of situations." He stepped across the rocks and held his hand out in request for the weapon, and she handed it to him. "The blade is made for slicing—" he swung through a series of movements "—but the hook extending from the lower part of the blade is made for pulling. If you need to bring someone down to your level, you hook them first, and slash them afterward." He handed the weapon back to Raelyn. "It's light. It will serve you much better than my old hunting knife."

"Do you know what the marks on the blade mean?"

He shook his head. "I wouldn't worry about them. Very few weapons in the world are forged with magic, and I doubt we'd find one of those left behind under a mountain. Besides, if the blade holds power, it won't affect you, anyway." He picked up an old tunic and began tearing it into strips. "Come, wrap your feet, and let's not linger. I'll feel better if we can find something more useful, like water."

After layer upon layer of wraps, Raelyn's feet gained enough bulk to fit snugly into her new footwear. The outer casing of the boots was soft and flexible, and she bore the extra weight below her ankles gratefully. When she was done scrutinizing her feet, Laris caught her attention and inclined his head toward a tunnel exiting the chamber in the direction they'd been traveling. He waited a moment for her to join him, then they headed into the darkness.

"We have no way of knowing if this will lead us outside," he told her. "But we may as well continue in this direction so we don't double back on ourselves."

Raelyn nodded, trusting his survival senses, most of her attention on managing her gait. Within an hour, she'd adapted well to the added height and decreased sensation of walking, and she studied the glaive, intrigued by the markings.

I wonder.

She took a deep breath, searching for the connection to the void. Perhaps she could find out if the weapon possessed magic.

The void was there—a dense ball of cold within her core as if she'd swallowed a chunk of ice. Afraid she'd enter the seam of the world if she concentrated too much on the source, she relaxed her focus, following the cold into the space outside of her body. She felt it extend beyond where Laris walked in front of her. It went beyond Hendrel's light, rounding a corner of the tunnel ahead. Her senses slammed into a wall of warmth that she instinctually knew marked the end of her influence. She pulled at the warmth, trying to draw herself toward it. Her eyes closed. The barrier was so close she reached her arm out to touch it.

Lost in the process, Raelyn snapped her eyes open at Laris's touch. He shook her, hands on her shoulders.

"Raelyn. Raelyn!" His eyes narrowed in concern, and Hendrel flickered wildly around his head.

"What?" she asked, slightly dazed.

"What was happening? What were you doing?"

She blinked her eyes and swallowed, absentmindedly pushing his hands away. "I was practicing. I was trying to move my sphere of influence."

His stare pierced her. "The wisp started going crazy, and I felt magic around me again. When I looked back, you were walking with your eyes closed, reaching out to me."

"I could feel it," she said quietly. "I could feel the warmth."

"How did you know to do that?"

"Hendrel explained it. Wardens can control their power so they don't affect everyone around them."

They stared at each other for a long moment in silence.

"Listen to me." Laris's tone was quiet but commanding. "I have no desire to stop you from developing your power, but you *must* keep me informed. Do you understand?"

She nodded. His gaze held something more—a genuine concern, an unnamed emotion that sent a lance of energy through her. How much had she affected him? She realized she was studying him just as intently as he was studying her, tracing the lines of his face with her gaze, following the shadow of facial hair up to the tendrils of black hair grazing his eyebrows.

With a long blink that brought her attention to his eyes, he sighed. "If you don't want to be uncomfortably close to a man, Raelyn, you shouldn't stare like that."

"I …" She stepped back.

Laris shook his head, letting her add space between them, and turned to resume his pace. "In another place," he mumbled, "at a safer time, you'd not escape that so easily. I'll add that to your list of debts."

She frowned at his back, worried she'd upset him, hoping he knew her reaction wasn't a rejection as much as it reflected her self-doubt. Laris wasn't a sheltered lord. He was a warrior, a soldier, a man of the world. She had no doubt his life experiences included countless women skilled at satisfying a man. To think that she could compare in any way was laughable, just as Ellisand had said. Raelyn was too dull and too innocent. And she was terrified to lose her heart to a man who might tell her exactly that.

She clenched her jaw in frustration. Laris was important to her. They'd come so far in their companionship since those first threatening moments in the tower at Albator. How strange it was now to have him be the only person she could trust with her life.

"I'd like to continue practicing," she said quietly as she caught up, hoping to break the tension.

"If you can stay aware of your surroundings," he replied without glancing back. "We don't know what lies in wait for us on this path."

A while later, when he signaled for them to stop again, Raelyn felt accomplished in her mission to feel the void within and around her consistently. She found the most difficulty in maintaining her sphere of influence at its maximum expansion away from her, but when she contracted the power, pulling its perimeter closer to her core into a tighter circle, the more precisely she could control it. However, too close was almost as bad at too far. She found she lost control of the void again when the perimeter of her sphere of influence was an arm's length from her body; it was challenging to keep the cold in her core distinct from the cold outside at that range. She relaxed her concentration to take in their surroundings, trying to be present in the moment but also aware of her ability.

"More signs of life," Laris said to her. He pointed to tracks in the dirt. "These are fresh. Maybe a day or two old."

Several sets of footprints stood out against the pale clay floor. Raelyn bent over them, Hendrel at her shoulder. "Barefoot," she remarked, surprised. "And where did they come from?"

"Aye, barefoot," Laris muttered, looking at the walls around them.

"Most likely wretches. The opening must be hidden, but they dropped down from another tunnel by the look of the markings, much like we did."

Her grip on the glaive tightened. "That means we have enemies behind and in front of us."

He nodded. "Our chances are much better if you've developed some control over your ability. If we have to fight, withdraw from me as much as you can, and I will be able to protect us. Let's go. We may be nearing a break to the surface."

They crept forward, staying close to the wall, senses on alert. Raelyn's ears strained to hear the slightest sound in the darkness, but the tunnels kept their secrets in silence, the only sound made by her too-large boots scraping along the ground.

Once dry and smooth, the walls faded into jagged edges and crags. Elusive water kept the footing slick but left no accumulation to harvest to slake their thirst, and where there was once only still air, the touch of a breeze crossed her skin. She dared encourage the spark of hope that such a feeling might mean daylight. The sensation grew stronger with each step, and she peered eagerly as they crested an incline—just in time for Hendrel's light to vanish and darkness to crash in on them.

Out of instinct, she crouched, weapon protectively guarding her chest. She held her breath and waited for a command from Laris, but he, too, was still and silent. Long moments passed in the darkness. When her eyes adjusted, she saw his outline pressed against the side of the tunnel.

Legs cramping from her impromptu position, she chanced a slight shift in stance. Without the scrape of her boots, sounds echoed undisguised from the chamber ahead. Faint light from an unseen source allowed her to make out the shapes around her, barely visible though they were. She strained her eyes to see anything of concern. The source of the noise didn't seem to be advancing toward them, its commotion similar to background clatter during last meal in the castle. She felt safe enough to slowly edge her way up behind Laris.

"What's going on? Do you see anything?"

"No," he whispered. "Let's get closer to the top of the path. My guess is it opens to a room."

Creeping over the crest of the tunnel, they stopped short when it abruptly changed course, opening into a cavernous pit that plunged deep into the underground. A sharp turn to the left took the path on a spiral down along the pit perimeter, periodically widening into large outcroppings where fire pits, torches, and wooden structures squeezed into the available space to form a sprawling, multi-level, spiraling city. A multitude of tunnels and cave openings dotted the sheer walls along the path, and Raelyn could see wretches on the lower levels. Almost human in their features and form, only their translucent skin, sinewy, hunched bodies, and long limbs marked them otherwise.

"This is not good," he breathed. "We've found ourselves in a wretch lair."

"We can't go back." Raelyn scanned the expanse, hoping for an answer to present itself. "It's been ages since we've even seen a fork in the road."

"Would you stride right out amongst them?"

Only partially listening, she squinted, trying to focus her vision several levels down. Against the far wall, a glittering object sparkled in the dim light of the torches; it was moving, locked behind the bars of a narrow cage. The light stole Raelyn's breath with its beauty, like the twinkle of distant stars reflected in a pool. "There's something down there," she said. "Something is shimmering."

Laris uttered an inaudible curse. "Circle save us," he said. "They have a whyte."

"A whyte? Are you sure?"

He nodded. "Their prismatic fur creates that unmistakable shimmer. They are highly prized among those practicing forbidden magic."

"They'll kill it?" Raelyn reached up and placed her hand on Laris's forearm. "We have to set it free."

"Are you mad? That whyte would kill us just as soon as a wretch would, Raelyn. They have no love for mankind."

"Please." Her grip tightened. "We can't just leave it to be chopped up. It can do what it wants when it's free. At least we can give it a chance. And maybe it knows a way out!"

"We can't fight our way through an entire city of wretches, Raelyn. What you're proposing is suicide."

"I'm not talking about fighting. You're a transcendent, aren't you? I think I can control my power enough to give yours back to you."

"My powers aren't without limit," he responded gruffly. "What, exactly, do you want me to do? If you're looking for stealth and shadow, I'm not your best choice."

"Can you create a diversion? Maybe a few levels down to draw the wretches away from the landings?"

He surveyed the area below. "Maybe."

"Do you think that will work?"

A long silence passed before he replied. "It's not out of reason. If we can draw them away from these top levels, it would allow us to make it to one of the tunnels on the opposite side of the pit. If we need to rescue your whyte along the way, so be it."

She threw her arm around him in a quick half-embrace. "Yes! Thank you. Tell me what you need me to do."

"Fire will be the least suspicious distraction," he whispered, studying the depths of the settlement. "There." He pointed to a landing almost at the edge of Raelyn's sight, four levels below the whyte's cage. "Another supply cache, by the looks of it. One big enough to cause a large fire."

"You can do that from up here?" Raelyn asked.

Laris nodded. "It will be tricky, but there's enough fire from the torches to work with. I'll spread the blaze quickly to force the wretches into action. Make a note now of places to take cover. These upper levels might not be as empty of wretches as they seem. We'll need to be as quick and stealthy as possible."

She scanned the wretch camps. Boxes, chests, sacks, and piles of debris clogged the living spaces and created potential concealment, but no cover existed along the narrow path between those hubs of life.

"Stay put until I say," he cautioned. "If the fire fails to create enough urgency, we'll need another plan." He looked over at her. "Can you control your power?"

"I need to be farther away from you. Just a few feet. I'll go back inside the tunnel." She pushed herself away from the edge, reverse crawling until she knew she was safe to push up from her hands and knees. Back in the darkness, she pressed against the wall and focused on the ever-present cold within her core. Slowly, just as she'd practiced, she found the edges of warmth that marked her circle of influence and started to draw them toward her. She only needed to collapse her control far enough to pass Laris's position.

She stared at him intently, taking her time to withdraw her power. When the edges of her control crossed over him, Laris shuddered and extended a hand toward the pit. From her position against the rock wall, Raelyn couldn't see her companion's face, and she sat, frozen, waiting for an indication his magic was underway. Heart hammering in her chest, she clutched the glaive in both hands, ready to run as soon as he moved.

New sounds echoed up from the wretch lair in waves, sounds of fear and confusion growing louder and more congested as the moments crept by. The smell of smoke assailed Raelyn's nostrils, carrying in on the gentle draft she'd appreciated earlier. Not long after, she saw a great black cloud climbing out of the center of the pit.

Laris gained his feet. He motioned for her to follow but didn't wait before darting down the path. Raelyn sprinted forward, careful to remain close, but not too close, in the event he needed access to his magic again.

They ran down the spiraling path at full speed, unprotected and vulnerable. Legs weighted down by her oversized boots, Raelyn struggled, helplessly slow and exposed. She waited to hear the hiss of arrows soaring toward them, to feel the impact of a wretch's bone spear as it found its mark within her clumsy body. To her great surprise and relief, neither happened, and she slid behind a stack of boxes on the first campsite landing, across from Laris. He looked at her and gave a nod. She knew they needed to keep moving. The fire on the levels below raged, and now, mixed with the early sounds of alarm, there were shrieks of anger and confusion.

Free of inhabitants, the first landing provided a clear view of the pit and its other encampments. A tattered trio of tents protruded from within the crates and sacks, and liquid boiled over in a pot hung above a bed of hot coals. Just as Laris left the cover to race farther down the path, Raelyn spotted something she couldn't pass up: a full water skein. She lunged over to the tent where it was tied and severed the cord with her weapon. With the precious bag nestled in the crook of her arm, she hopped over several sacks and ran in the only direction she knew Laris could have gone.

The next tier was also empty, but to Raelyn's dismay, she didn't see Laris. She spent panicked moments looking for him among the towers of debris at the landing's edge before she decided to move on. A whole level stood between her and the whyte's cage, and she knew the distraction of the fire couldn't keep her enemies busy forever. She had to keep moving. Laris was ahead of her; if he'd made it through already, she just had to catch up to him as fast as possible.

Another long stretch of path separated the landing she'd left from the adjacent camp, and she ran as fast as she could, her legs burning from the weight on her feet and the lack of energy in her body. She gritted her teeth and ignored the persistent aches, running past the third camp and heading to the fourth. *Halfway there,* she thought. *Just keep running!*

Despite her stubbornness, nature eventually took over, and Raelyn's tired legs gave out just past the fifth and final camp on the second level. She stumbled hard to her knees. The water skein plopped to the ground, and the glaive flew out of her grip and skidded down the path. A familiar sensation of warmth spread across her knees, and she knew without looking she'd torn through both her pants and flesh. *Where is he?* She crawled toward her weapon. *Why didn't he wait for me?*

Footsteps running behind her brought instant comfort, and Raelyn realized she must have passed Laris on accident. She grabbed the glaive and turned around with a sigh of relief.

Instinct saved her from the crushing blow of a studded club. Her senses recognized the threat well before her eyes acknowledged the wretch bearing down on her, and she managed to roll toward the inner wall as the club swung down. Immediately, she gained a crouched position and brought the glaive up in time to stop her adversary's charge. He paused just shy of her blade and lowered his club, circling while she kept him out at range.

Urgency pressed heavily on her as she stared into the eyes of the wretch and tried to inch her way slowly down the path. He was tall, his pale skin almost transparent. Long hair on his head encapsulated his shoulders in a thick mantle, and unlike the stories she'd been told, he was fully clothed, not naked and beast-like, and not dressed in metal armor like the wretches she'd seen in Albator. His eyes, dark with heavy lashes, belied an intelligence she also hadn't expected, and that revelation added fear to her sense of urgency.

"Stay back," she mumbled. "Stay away from me."

His eyes narrowed at her words, but he didn't respond. Raelyn wasn't confident he knew any of her language. He was examining her, she knew, calculating the threat she posed. His eyes flitted from her face to her weapon to the giant boots on her feet. He stared longest at the polearm, and Raelyn wondered if he'd seen it before.

Without warning, he jumped toward her, deflecting her blade to the side with one swift blow. She spun away from his attack and struck him across the back with the shaft of her weapon. The movement felt uncannily natural, but Raelyn had little time to marvel at her prowess before instinct took over again.

Doubled over from the impact, the wretch stumbled forward, and Raelyn brought the butt of the glaive up to strike him in the head. Hurt but not disabled from the initial blow, he leaned out of harm's way just in time. He regained his stance and pushed toward her, swinging the club back and forth in an impenetrable arc.

No match for his brute force, Raelyn was forced to retreat until she felt the wall at her back. Out of options, she dove under one of his swings and whipped her weapon as hard as she could at her attacker's legs. The wretch lifted one foot, but not the other, and the glaive pole slammed into his ankle. He cried out and toppled to the ground, immediately clawing at Raelyn as she pushed herself to her feet. For the briefest of moments, she hesitated, aware that what she was about to do was irreversible, but as the wretch's fingers dug into her calf, she knew there was no other way. With clear intent, she brought down her blade and plunged it into her enemy's back.

The finality of delivering the killing blow sent Raelyn staggering back. She let go of the glaive and left it to sit in the body of her enemy, the pole wobbling back and forth at her release. She hadn't expected to *feel* the blade sink into the wretch's flesh, to feel the shudder of his body as his heart beat its last, to see in his eyes a web of confusion, pain, and anger. The moment had been intimate, and it shocked Raelyn with its impact.

Shouts from the levels below drew her out of her stupor. The black plume of smoke in the center of the pit had dissipated, replaced by a less threatening cloud of dark grey. She knew time was running out to get to safety. She spun around, afraid more wretches had seen the brawl and arrived, but the pathway above and below was empty. Near the landings of the third level, another half loop around the pit would see her to the whyte. She steeled her mind against thoughts of what she'd just done and pulled her weapon free, grabbed the water skein, and ran down the path as fast as she could.

Determined to rush straight to her goal, Raelyn almost missed the signs of battle at the third level's first camp. Like the rest of the wretches' setups, tents of random shapes and sizes dotted the outcropping of rock, spaced chaotically apart and separated by all manner of storage bins. Unlike the empty areas above, not all the occupants had left, and while the sight of their bodies was sobering, it was also a sign Laris had been there before her. She took a moment to glance at the four wretches where they'd fallen.

Commotion across the pit snagged her attention, and she darted back onto the path. Two campsites away, Laris was battling on the whyte's landing, engaged in combat with the wretch guarding the cage. As she ran, her gaze fell on another wretch dressed differently from the others, standing apart at the opposite end of the platform. A mage. Hair a brilliant white, second only to the iridescent robe he wore, the creature raised his arms. Raelyn begged her legs to go faster. *He'll alert the entire place!*

At first, she hadn't understood why Laris seemed reluctant to use his transcendent powers to get them through the lair, but now she saw the value in remaining unnoticed for as long as possible. From what her father had told her and what she'd seen in Albator, she'd convinced herself Laris was the most powerful mage in existence—but she didn't know the extent of his powers. She knew he, like all mages, was limited to whatever specific patterns of magic he'd studied. He was not indestructible, and he was not without weakness. In enemy territory, with enemy mages, stealth was prudent.

He was in the heat of battle when she reached him. "Stay back," he yelled to her, parrying a wretch's slash. "There are only three of them!"

But he was wrong. Raelyn barreled past him, ignoring his shouts to her, and angled toward the mage she knew was lurking near the small fire just beyond the whyte's enclosure. She leaped over a pile of animal carcasses, focused on the wretch about to use his magic. Startled at Raelyn's arrival, the creature stepped back from what he was doing and brandished a curved blade. He made no attempt to strike and instead thrust out his opposite arm, palm open.

Without thought, Raelyn focused everything she had on his hand and pushed her sphere of influence outward just as the spell manifested. The magic attack dissipated, and a look of shock passed across the wretch's features. His surprise quickly morphed into rage, and he screeched like an animal, advancing toward Raelyn with the knife.

Ready to meet her new foe, she widened her stance and wiped the sweat from her hands. She adjusted her grip on the glaive and stepped forward, hesitating when a shadow fell over her from behind. Lifting her chin up to see, her eyes met those of a piercing blue surrounded by glimmering white fur, and she suddenly felt the weapon plucked from her grasp.

Before Raelyn could acknowledge what was happening, the whyte lunged and twirled with deadly finesse, swinging the polearm as if it were an extension of its own body. In the blink of an eye, the wretch mage lay dead on the stone ground, body cleaved completely in half. The whyte knelt by the corpse, tenderly touching the white robe, now stained with blood. The creature whispered something and bowed its head, eyes closed. Raelyn felt such a profound sadness in the action that she could easily guess where the robe had come from.

"I am so sorry," she breathed, not intending to say the words out loud.

The whyte looked over at her and they stared at one another. Its delicate features and form appeared feminine, and long fur around its face, neck, and legs accented the short white fur over the rest of its body. Pink skin peaked out on the palms of its hands, and brilliant, deep-blue eyes bore into Raelyn. It slowly stood and walked over to her and held out the glaive.

Tentatively, Raelyn accepted the weapon back.

"You," the creature said in a heavily accented female voice. It reached out and gently pressed a finger to Raelyn's chest above her heart. "Breaker of magic locks. Dar'Liha is grateful."

Raelyn looked at the remnants of the cage lock, realizing her sphere of influence must have nullified the magic holding it together.

"Raelyn!" Laris approached, stopping next to the open cage. "Raelyn, slowly step toward me," he said, his voice low, his gaze locked on Dar'Liha. "You don't know what that creature can do."

The whyte moved between them, issuing a strange growl, and Raelyn watched in awe as the fur on it shifted. The once airy and soft hairs went rigid and laid flat. In moments, Dar'Liha was covered in plate armor made from her coat. She extended her hand back toward Raelyn, wordlessly requesting the glaive.

Instead of handing the weapon over, Raelyn put her hand in Dar'Liha's grasp. "We are all friends," she said and looked at Laris. "We don't have time for this. We need to go."

Until then, Raelyn hadn't realized just how true those words were. No more smoke filled the cavern, and the sounds of desperate toil below steadily faded. It wouldn't be long before the wretches returned and saw the bodies of their comrades. The trio needed to put as much distance between them and the lair as soon as possible.

"Do you know of a way back to the surface?" she asked the whyte.

Dar'Liha nodded. "Show you. Come." She took off in a relaxed lope down the right side of the spiral path and headed to the nearest tunnel entrance.

The brief moments of stillness left Raelyn's muscles in knots, but she forced herself into a clumsy jog. Laris fell into stride beside her, and she could feel his gaze on her, assessing her torn and bloody clothes.

"Are you hurt?" he finally asked.

"Not really," she replied. "I encountered some trouble along the way here, that's all."

"Me, too. I thought you were right behind me."

"Me, too."

He let out a humorless chuckle. "You're going to be the death of me."

"This way, Men," Dar'Liha said, motioning for them to follow her into the tunnel entrance. "Come. Hurry."

CHAPTER ELEVEN

A fierce wind bore down on the wooded hills of eastern Limnin. Within her large canvas war tent, Saraht tried to ignore the relentless flapping of fabric caused by the gale, but the sound was so loud she found it difficult to focus on much else.

"Forgive me." She closed her eyes and pressed her fingers against the lids. "What is your man's name?"

"This is Ezramoris," Orion repeated. "He's the one you asked for."

"I thought you'd sent him out already." Saraht moved her fingertips to her temples. "Why is he still here?"

"He just returned from other errands. Like you and me, he sometimes answers to a higher power."

Another of His servants. She studied the man kneeling before her. *Can I trust one of Orion's lackeys?*

Ezramoris remained motionless beneath Saraht's scrutiny. Covered head to toe in black leathers, he wore the garments of someone who valued stealth and movement over physical protection. Head bowed, naught beyond his eyes showed of his hair or features, and his eyes told her enough about the character of the man. Green and piercing, they were cold eyes, intelligent eyes. They spoke to her of tenaciousness, obsession, and cruelty. Just by looking at his eyes, she knew the man before her would pursue his quarry to the ends of the world. He would not waiver from his direction. To do so would mean breaking whatever twisted, internal code of honor he adhered to.

"I need you to find someone," she said. "On your feet. Look at me."

He did as she ordered, as stone-still on foot as on his knees.

"There is a woman by the name of Raelyn Forthgrew. I need you to bring her to me. Alive is best, but dead is acceptable." She glanced at Orion. "We will show you where she was last seen and allocate whatever reinforcements you require."

"I need nothing, my lady," Ezramoris replied, his voice surprisingly deep and rich.

Saraht nodded distractedly. "Be that as it may, I'll send a penumbra with you. You must not underestimate this woman, and there is a chance she travels with a transcendent."

"Even transcendents are made of flesh and bone," he replied, bowing. "But send who or what you will. It matters not."

Smaller than Albator, what Pardis lacked in territory, it made up for in population. Buildings lined every street, reaching several stories above the cobblestone roads. A network of rope bridges and ladders laced overhead connecting the blocks, and at the center of it all stood Montigrath Castle—a curious, solid stone structure once assumed to be an abandoned *montigrath* aerie. With lush gardens and decadent landscaping, the castle grounds were fenced off from public access.

Sliding off her mount, Saraht handed the reins to a waiting stable boy and strode over to where Ellisand and Maylam were dismounting. "Welcome, my dears, to Montigrath Castle. Home of Baron Audolon and his brother, Sir Djuron." She linked arms with the other women and headed through the garden gate and up the castle stairs. "Baron Audolon has long been a sympathizer to Faldea, and tonight, we secure his support. They are expecting us. Prince Thiir has arranged it."

"Are there no women we can speak to?" Maylam muttered. "It's as if the whole female race has up and vanished from nobility."

"I know, Mother. That will change soon. Why, Ellisand is the very reason we were granted this audience. If that's not promising enough, you'll have to wait to see your pupil showcase her skills."

Maylam nodded but said nothing more, and Ellisand smiled in reassurance from Saraht's opposite side.

Originally, Saraht planned on taking Pardis in the same way she'd taken Albator, moving her specialized forces up the eastern edge of Limnin to pull more of the nation's army away from the capital. With

Ellisand slowly converting to their cause, however, Saraht now had a recognized member of Limnin's royal family in her ranks, and there were places, like Pardis, where other strategies might be more beneficial. Ellisand, as the heir to the Wedminth duchy, was above Baron Audolon in rank. His lands were within her domain, and by law, what she declared was to be taken as if the king had made the decree. Thiir preferred diplomacy to bloodshed, and he hadn't questioned Saraht when she'd requested to set up an audience in Pardis. Once the lines of communication with Baron Audolon had been opened by Thiir, the pompous Limnin noble had been all too willing to let Saraht in with Ellisand in tow.

Through life experience, Saraht knew the order of a girl just ten-and-eight years of age held little weight in a political world dominated by men. They would have to play the game tonight. And play they would; no one was more skilled at the game than Maylam.

Saraht looked at Ellisand as the giant doors of the castle swung open. "Take this day to rest and prepare for tonight. Bathe and let the servants do your hair. I'll come to you before we dine. Stay in your room. Do not let anyone see you before our audience."

Ellisand nodded. "I understand."

Saraht gave the young woman's arm an appreciative squeeze. Truthfully, there was little harm in letting her explore, but something about Ellisand still made Saraht wary. Ellisand was always amiable and seemed to genuinely sympathize with Saraht's cause. She spoke little and smiled often, yet there was a sharpness to her, conveyed by her quick learning and keen eye. The thought that she could be devising a plan to escape seemed unlikely, but Saraht hadn't made it to where she was by taking chances. Until the girl proved her loyalty tonight, Saraht would keep an eye on her.

"Welcome, honored guests," said a well-dressed woman standing in the center of the vestibule. She issued a deep courtesy. "I am Mrs. Greshmore, Housekeeper of Montigrath."

"We are pleased to be under your care," Saraht replied. "We are the emissaries Baron Audolon is expecting."

Mrs. Greshmore folded her hands at her front. "We were told to watch for your arrival. Please allow my girls to see you to your rooms." Three servants curtsied and stepped forward, one to each guest. "The grounds are yours to walk as you like," the housekeeper continued while the maids ushered Saraht and company up the stairs. "Last meal is promptly at the seventh hour. We will send escorts to your quarters ten minutes beforehand."

As suspected, they were all housed on the same floor. Saraht made a mental note of Ellisand and Maylam entering their respective rooms before she stepped through the doorway into hers. Once inside, she waved the servant away and bolted the door behind her.

For all the grandness of the gardens and the interesting history of the castle, the guest room was disappointingly lackluster. Dark and dreary, the only natural light came from a too-small window on the far wall, and the deep fireplace prevented the light within from escaping. A strategically placed lamp and handful of candles brightened up the space enough to see the modest furnishings, but the bed looked as if it hadn't been used in years, and Saraht knew it was optimistic to think the linens were fresh. She briefly wondered if all dignitaries were given such substandard accommodations or if this was seen as adequate for an unassuming noble girl and her two common companions.

Reluctant to sit on the bed and end up in a dust cloud, she took a seat next to the fire. Closing her eyes, she clutched a silver pendant at her neck and slid apart the medallion to reveal its contents. Inside the casing, her finger grazed the shard of marble that served as a proxy altar. Like jumping into a black pit, she let her body pitch forward into the darkness, indifferent to the sensation of falling that used to terrify her as a child. A rush of air surrounded her, and with a deep exhale, she knew she'd successfully entered the void.

"I'm in Pardis," she declared to the emptiness. Acting as an anchor, the marble stone made sure she was in the right location, even though she seemed to be alone. "If all goes well, no lives will be lost, and we'll be able to resupply."

A dim point of light emerged from the darkness. It made its way over to her slowly, dipping low while it floated as if it barely had the strength to carry its nonexistent weight.

She watched the struggle, contemplating the unknown soul being controlled with essence magic to act as a connection to Prince Thiir. Somewhere, in some dark, oppressive place, a host body lay deteriorating on a makeshift altar of marble as its life energy was used to relay messages about military and political schemes.

"That is well," replied a raspy voice as the flickering light hovered near her. "You move slowly, Saraht."

"I am deliberate." She resented the shiver that raced up her spine at the criticism. "We are on track, Master."

"Rumors abound. The other warden eludes you. I am watching, Saraht. Long have I let you move forward freely. Do not mistake my generosity for ignorance."

"Never, Master. I am committed to our cause. I do not waiver."

"You are committed to *your* cause," the voice corrected. "But your thirst for revenge is absolute, and in that, I know you do not waiver. To that end, you will be loyal. Continue as you must, but when we next speak, I expect you to be in the capital."

She bowed her head, and the pathetic light vanished. Alone, she stood in the void, embracing the solitude. It brought her no joy to work with a nadir who had mastered essence magic. Saraht was a killer, it was true. She'd taken countless lives. But she would never be able to condone the use of essence magic for anything other than healing. The manipulation of the magic energy of living beings for personal gain was a dark art, a forbidden art. It was at the heart of the wardens' creation story. Prince Thiir wasn't just a mage who dabbled in the dark arts; he was a nadir, sworn to serve Ube, the Nameless God.

She closed her eyes and pushed away thoughts of morality. She couldn't allow anything to stand in the way of her progress. If one life was the cost of Faldea's support, so be it.

She took a hot bath after returning from the void. The steaming water did more than cleanse her from time on the road; it did wonders to relieve some of the tension she felt after exiting the cold, lifeless seam between the worlds. Speaking with the master always taxed her. She worried he knew more than she wanted him to know, and deep within her heart, she was certain he missed nothing and saw through all her schemes. Knowing she was likely just a pawn made her feel helpless and incompetent, but he was right; in the end, her thirst for revenge trumped all other things. Pawn or not, she would be the last thing King Rothelian saw before he died. What happened after was of lesser consequence.

Climbing out of the water, she toweled off and slipped on the dress her mother had made for such occasions. Crimson and trimmed with gold, it was lovely for something lacking the beads and jewels most women of nobility wore. Maylam's talents as a seamstress were just as impressive as her other skill sets. It was a dress that, in its plainness, put many fancier dresses to shame.

She swept up her long brown hair and secured it in a crown around her head. She was no longer a young maid or looking for a husband. She certainly was not out to impress and had no desire to fuss with ornate decorations. Too much attention to her appearance would be considered improper when Ellisand was the star of the show tonight.

Satisfied with the final result, she left her room and headed down the hall to Ellisand's chamber. After a soft knock, she heard a welcome and went inside.

"Saraht, you look lovely," Ellisand said from where she sat, a maid weaving blue ribbon into her hair. "Maylam makes the most beautiful dresses."

From her spot in a cushioned chair by the far window, Maylam waved her hand in pleased dismissal.

"That she does. The blue suits you, and I don't know where she found the silver lace for the berthe, but it is exceptional. Are you ready for tonight?"

"I am ready," the younger woman said confidently and without hesitation, attention on her reflection in the mirror.

While studying Ellisand's face for signs of apprehension, Saraht was pleased and surprised to find none. *There is a hidden strength to her,* she mused. *I was not so calm the first time I had to embrace my femininity as a tool.* To Ellisand, she replied, "Good. You will find once you've dealt with one man, you've dealt with them all."

The maid holding Ellisand's hair paused briefly at those words before continuing with her work, but Saraht didn't miss the hesitation.

"These words are for you, too, my dear," she said to the servant. "In the war of inequality, there are no stations. You are a woman, and you are with allies. If you ever have a need, remember you are not alone."

The girl blushed and quickly nodded, eyes pinned on her work.

"Why must we wait for last meal before gaining an audience?" asked Ellisand. "We could have left hours ago."

"So eager to be back on the dusty road again, I see. Don't worry. There will be plenty of time for that." Saraht picked at a cluster of grapes. "This is simply how these things work. The weak find comfort in ceremony, you know. It stops them from having to make decisions or think for themselves. You'll find old men such as Audolon and Djuron are slaves to such things. They wouldn't know what to do if the breakfast tray didn't arrive at the same time every day."

"They beat us if that happens," the maid said quietly without looking up from the elaborate swirls in Ellisand's hair. "They had my friend Marchelle whipped out in the yard one morning. She was late because she'd been ill."

Ellisand reached up and placed a hand on the girl's arm in sympathy.

"You see?" Saraht sighed. "Creatures of habit and routine. Do not expect to have much unscheduled conversation."

"What happened to Marchelle?"

At Ellisand's question, the maid's ministrations ceased, and she stood quietly for a long moment. "She was too sick, and the lashing did her in. We're not allowed to talk about it," she whispered.

Saraht stood and walked over, offering a partial embrace. "These walls tell no secrets," she said. "Nor do we. Did you know Lady Ellisand here is far more powerful than either master of this castle? She's the king's niece, and she will save us all."

The maid smiled and looked back at her work, securing the final ribbon in place. With a deep curtsy, she excused herself, and Ellisand got up to examine her reflection in the mirror. "My mother would have been pleased with this," she said softly with a light touch to her hair.

"The loss of a mother is always hard, child," Maylam commented. "She would have been proud of you."

Ellisand smirked, still studying her appearance. "Mother was never proud or content with anything." Her voice held an edge. "Dresses and hair she knew, but she wasn't much of a mother. She couldn't wait to get rid of me."

Saraht and Maylam shared a surreptitious glance.

"Women of station become locked in a cycle." Maylam nodded to herself knowingly. "Born a woman, groomed to bear children, sold to marriage. Then they pass on that cycle to their daughters."

"You must have been close to your father, then?" Saraht tested the tension of the familial ties, starting to understand why the deaths of Ellisand's parents hadn't impacted her much.

"Father was kind but didn't know what to do with me."

"Well—" Saraht walked over and put an arm around Ellisand's shoulders "—now you can decide what to do with yourself. It's almost time. Shall we make our way down to the banquet hall?"

Ellisand tugged at her bodice and nodded. "Let's go meet our hosts."

"I do hope the food is at least edible," Maylam said, watching them head out the door. "I'll keep the fire going for when you return."

Saraht blew her mother a kiss and closed the door behind them.

Trumpets heralded entry into the banquet hall—a large, oval room with irregular pillars. Like many parts of Montigrath Castle, there were no windows, and though occupants might have a sense of the time when they arrived, it was easy to lose hold of such senses in the eternally candlelit space. Long tables for parties were undressed with wood exposed, unlike the smaller head table used for more intimate gatherings. Covered with a delicate cloth and well-thought-out place settings, it featured game pies and fruits stacked amongst the dinner plates. Several large, silver serving platters overflowed with cheeses and dried meats. Tall candlesticks illuminated the seating arrangement, adding an eerie glow to the glazed pies.

Upon first sight, Saraht considered the dining arrangement charming—with the exception of the two large, flamboyantly dressed men who didn't bother to stand when she entered the room. Her irritation increased when the lack of courtly courtesy extended to Ellisand. Even an infant male announced as the Wedminth heir would have received a standing welcome. She bit her tongue. She was nothing to these men other than Ellisand's attendant; everything now rested on the young woman's shoulders.

"Ah! Welcome! Welcome!" Cajoled Audolon from his seat at the table. He waved a grease-covered hand, sending bits of chicken flying through the air. "I hope you don't mind we started without you. We aren't in the habit of letting good food sit for very long."

"I understand, my lord," Ellisand replied politely, ignoring his lack of manners. "I would not wish for you to go hungry."

The cloaked insult to both men's weight landed lightly but was still felt, and Audolon paused his gluttony for a moment to watch Ellisand take a seat at the other end of the table. Saraht stood at her back. "Indeed," he muttered and grasped his wine glass, watching the two women with new interest.

"Well, there's no reason to make small talk." At the head of the table, Djuron motioned for one of the servants to refill his cup. His short grey beard did little to hide the pock-marked, red skin of his face, and even though the evening was cool, droplets of sweat lingered at the hairline of his brow. His eyes, the color of steel, held no warmth, and he said, "We've heard rumors, of course. You don't look like you're being held against your will by Faldeans, child."

"I was not kidnapped so much as saved." Ellisand flashed a disarming smile. "And while I have mourned the loss of my family deeply, I believe these things have happened for a reason."

"Oh?" Audolon snorted. "You believe the hands of fate flattened Albator to the ground? That destiny has some ultimate design for you? I say, that is a bold assertion from one so wet behind the ears. Albator is now a mass gravesite, and you think you've walked out the other side bright as a new copper coin?" He chuckled and looked at his brother. "Our new Lady Wedminth has much to learn."

"The King moves even as we speak," Djuron added. "We hear word he's bolstered the capital's defenses. And suddenly, here you are, not much the worse for your ordeal, seeking audience with us. We are not so foolish to think you are a refugee requiring asylum. That much is clear."

From her spot across the table, Saraht was careful not to fidget or speak and draw attention. She was there to observe only, and what she saw was of great interest. Heading into dinner, she'd assumed Audolon, as lord of Montigrath, was the brains behind the brothers' operations. Now, listening to Djuron and noting his calculating mind, she realized she'd been mistaken. Within the man's body, now soft from age and lifestyle, was the spirit of one who once led others. He was the one they needed to target, not Audolon. Saraht hoped Ellisand had discerned as much, as well.

Then, as though the hands of fate were involved, a gentle draft fluttered the candlelight across Ellisand's face, and the young woman laughed. The sound was melodic and entrancing, and with the candlelight still dancing off her features, she pushed back her chair and stood. Raising her cup of wine, she beamed a smile at their hosts. "My good lords, you are just as winsome as I'd been told, and I daresay much more intuitive."

The compliment was given so sincerely that both men at the table shifted uncomfortably, but they were clearly pleased with the acknowledgment from the beautiful young woman before them.

"If I may," Ellisand continued, "I would not insult you with indirect conversation. I'll speak plainly because I respect you and look for your wisdom of experience." She walked over and sat on the table's edge next to Djuron.

Saraht knew, because this was how the game was played, that the lilac perfume Ellisand wore was now filling the space around their hosts, pulling at thoughts that had less to do with politics and more to do with primal instincts.

"I am here because I believe we are of like minds," Ellisand said softly. "For years, I saw my father beset by the demands of the capital. He bore it all in silence since the king was his brother-in-law, but I knew even our city could barely pay the tax rates. I admit I was ignorant of my uncle's nature, but now I have been informed there are many reasons he is not a fair and just king." She placed a hand on Djuron's shoulder. "I can only imagine the difficulties your city has suffered. And you have suffered."

He looked up at her, and she smiled, a knowing look in her eyes.

"The king showed favor to Albator," Audolon said. "Here, the poor starve in the streets, and we were beset with plague last season when the bodies got beyond control." He leaned in toward Ellisand. "We couldn't leave the castle," he whispered. "Nasty mess."

"You know, I hear they haven't had issues with the plague in Faldea for years now."

From across the table, Saraht carefully watched the dance. She wasn't genuinely interested in the steps themselves; it was an old dance, a predictable dance. She'd been the lead with many other partners long before. What she was interested in was Ellisand. The young woman had taken Maylam's teachings to heart and then some. She was like an artist, slowly crafting something of intricate beauty, its final form hidden from everyone except the one holding the paintbrush.

"I think we have much in common, my lords," Ellisand was saying, now standing between where the two sat. As she spoke, she strategically touched a shoulder or an arm, laughing and leaning in close, tempting eyes, ears, noses, and touch.

"Well, we can't openly oppose the king," Audolon said cautiously. "But if there were to be a positive shift in leadership in Limnin—and I'm not saying the throne, mind you—we would certainly consider lending our support to such a change."

"I, too, desire to see Limnin thriving. And I'd like to set that as my aim: to make a *positive* difference in the capital." Ellisand let the words hang in the air, and the lords looked at one another.

"A partnership, then." Djuron boldly laid his hand over Ellisand's. "For political reform in the kingdom. Such alliances are usually sealed with a token of goodwill. We've hosted you graciously and with the utmost discretion. I trust you have something worthwhile to offer us in return."

The next part will matter most, Saraht thought, curious to see how well the Wedminth heir kept her composure. It was one thing to flirt and tempt a man's fancy, but it was another to secure his steadfast loyalty and support. Such great prizes came with much higher prices, and all women knew the cost without being told. Ellisand was young and inexperienced. She was the perfect temptation for an aging lord with lukewarm principles and high ambitions. She wouldn't know what it meant to bed a man, but that was part of the appeal.

An unpleasant experience, to be sure, but Saraht felt no remorse for the task she'd set Ellisand to perform. The girl was a means to an end, a convenient ally. Saraht would use her to spearhead her way to the king. And if the journey didn't destroy Ellisand, she'd likely become a steadfast vassal in the times to come.

King Rothelian, after all, was the main goal … but also just the beginning.

The clink of wine glasses brought her focus back to the forefront of the table. Ellisand and Djuron glanced in her direction, smiling and speaking too softly to be heard. Patting the steel-eyed man's arm, Ellisand walked back to where Saraht stood.

"I'll be retiring now," she said, her tone every bit that of a noblewoman used to giving commands. Saraht gave a slight, customary bow of her head and went to follow, only to be stopped short by Ellisand's hand on her shoulder.

"No," the young woman said evenly. "Not you. You have other duties to attend to tonight." She looked over her shoulder and smiled at the brothers. "Shall we speak again on the morrow?"

Audolon raised his glass to her. "We shall, Lady Wedminth. If my brother finds your offer satisfactory, we'll have much to discuss."

"Oh, I'm sure he will," Ellisand replied pleasantly. She looked at Saraht. "I'm sure he'll be more than satisfied."

CHAPTER TWELVE

The pace Dar'Liha kept was unforgiving. Several times, Raelyn stumbled as she ran behind the whyte, her over-sized boots more of a hindrance in escape than the blessing they'd been during her and Laris's trek. As they hurried away from the smoke and distraction of the wretch encampment, the mountain tunnels grew narrower, less uniform, and more cave-like. The footing was uneven and slippery, and pools of crystal-clear water dotted each passage they turned down.

Running with the glaive added awkwardness to Raelyn's already erratic gait. She adjusted her grip, keeping the blade pointed behind her as a basic precaution should she fall. The strategy did nothing for ease of travel, and she struggled to keep up with her companions as they forged ahead.

"Let me carry that." Laris slowed and held out his hand. "Focus on your footing."

Practicality won out over stubbornness, and she handed it to him without argument. Letting go of the weapon, she felt a wave of regret. In Hendrel's dim light, she could see weariness written across Laris's features. His dark eyes lacked their usual sharpness, and lines of dirt and sweat on his unshaven face aged him a handful of years.

I'm sorry, Laris, she thought, unable to speak the words at that moment. *This is all because of me. All because of my selfishness.*

They were moving again, but Raelyn couldn't quiet the torrent of guilty thoughts. Even though she knew being a warden wasn't her fault or her choice, she acknowledged how her recent decisions had affected those around her. If she hadn't left the castle baths, left the survivor camp, asked to visit with the prior, and insisted on rescuing a creature they knew nothing about, their situation would likely be very different. She would be in the capital under lock and key, and Laris would be headed back to Lomnir with his lord.

He had used magic for her, too, despite the hardships he'd endured and their days without enough food or water. Raelyn had no real depth of understanding when it came to magic, but she knew it was punishing to those with a talent for it. To be able to see a substance invisible to most in the world and then to be able to learn how to manipulate it like threads on a spool was something that took years to learn and decades to master, depending on a mage's area of focus. It was why employing a castle mage was so costly. Being able to see magic wasn't enough. Using it effectively required stalwart dedication, and what price could be put on a lifetime of knowledge?

Trudging along at the back of their group, Raelyn let her eyes follow Laris as he jogged ahead. She would find a way to repay him someday. Even if all she could do was make wiser decisions in the future.

"Men rest," Dar'Liha said, pointing to a dry shelf of rock along the passage floor. "Must climb soon."

"Climb?" Raelyn scanned the walls around them. Slick like the ground underfoot, they were coated with an unfamiliar yellow mineral that looked like it had melted over the top of the natural stone.

The whyte nodded, her blue eyes brilliantly bright even in the dim lighting. "Pale Men coming. Must climb."

"Pale men," Laris said thoughtfully. "I guess they do resemble humans enough."

"They were men once, weren't they?" Raelyn asked. "Before the Cataclysm?"

He nodded, stretching out on the dry rock. "Forever cursed by Emblem for siding with his brother, the Nameless God."

Only a minute passed before Dar'Liha said, "Come. Climb. Pale Men soon."

Uncertain but without other options, Raelyn stood shakily from the too-brief respite and walked over to Dar'Liha. The whyte pointed to an area of the passage ahead where the yellow mineral created a step-like formation that disappeared into a black crack in the rock overhead.

"Small Man first." Dar'Liha urged her forward. "Dar'Liha last."

Steps in appearance only, the intermittent mineral notches were slippery and cold as ice. Raelyn pressed her entire body against the wet surface and painstakingly inched upward, afraid one misstep would see her back at the bottom in an injured heap. Fingertips gripping far beyond their ability, she ignored the pinpricks of pain taking root and forced her hands into anchors to bear her weight. Step by slow step, she navigated the rock wall with Hendrel flickering next to her to light the way.

She couldn't feel her fingers when she reached the top of the climb, which she knew was a blessing. Hoisting herself over the last ledge, she crawled forward enough to make room for the others before rolling onto her back and breathing a sigh of relief. When she opened her eyes, she was surprised to see the night sky. It was far away, tucked within the cracks of the ceiling above, but her eyes instantly found the light of stars. They were radiant, tiny beacons in a world of grey and black.

"Thank Emblem," she whispered, soaking in the image. "Laris, there are stars." She felt every bit a child as she pointed up at the sky, hoping the sight would bring him the same relief it brought her.

He emerged from his climb in time to catch her words and moved next to where she lay. He gazed in the direction of her outstretched arm, staring at the sky for a long moment before looking down and offering a hand to help her to her feet. He flinched slightly at her grip—as did she—and she knew his hands were as battered as hers from the climb.

"Come." Dar'Liha beckoned them toward a small opening in the rocks. "Almost there."

Almost there must have meant something different to whytes, Raelyn later decided, as their journey continued for hours. She'd lost all sense of time while under the mountains, but the aches and pains in her body kept time in their own way. The longer they bumped around in the dark, the more her fatigue and discomfort grew. When the single-person passage finally opened up to their destination, she wasn't sure which part of her body hurt the most.

The gentle touch of a breeze carried her complaints away with it. They'd entered a sinkhole—a great cavern in the cave system with a collapsed roof. Above, the sky was fully visible with no barrier of rocks obscuring the starry cascades and full moon hanging the blue-black of night. Though the walls around were high, Raelyn noted a few places where fallen rocks were piled into promising points of ascension.

She took in the view, astonished to have stepped from within the mountain into a scene of soft moss and delicate grass. All around her grew a lush garden of wildflowers, some drinking in the moonlight, others shut away while awaiting the sun. Though no herbalist, she knew a few by sight. She'd gathered them often in a life that now felt like it had been a dream. Bright moonlight bathed the landscape, and she could see the entirety of the space stretched as wide as a castle courtyard.

Dar'Liha flopped down near a ring of upright stones that marked the sinkhole's center. Too large to have been picked up by human strength alone, the uniform obelisks were speckled grey-green, covered in lichen, and marked by time. Within their midst, a stone bowl of equal age and appearance held solitary vigil. Oversized like the leaning stones around it, the bowl was filled with water as clear as what they'd passed in the tunnels. The sight of the shimmering water amplified the dryness in Raelyn's parched throat, and she swallowed in anticipation.

Before addressing her thirst, she shed her boots and pulled off what remained of her cloth bindings underneath. Unlike her arm, her feet were slow to heal, but that was expected. She hadn't given them any rest or treated them since her time at Genevive's shrine. The cool, soft touch of the grass was pure bliss, and she took her time walking over to investigate the stone circle and the water within.

She looked for Laris and spotted him walking along the perimeter. Checking for a way up or for hidden ways in, she assumed. Dar'Liha had spoken of safety and showed no inclination to leave, but that didn't mean danger wouldn't find them.

"A shrine?" she asked the whyte as she approached the bowl. She ran her hand along the rim while peering at the still pool within. Dipping her dirty hands into the crystalline liquid for a drink felt disrespectful.

"Moon water."

"Moon water. For?"

"For seeing."

"Don't drink it. There's a spring over there along the cliff that should be safe. This water is for scrying, I believe," Laris said as he joined them, passing a handful of berries to each. Raelyn immediately stuffed them into her mouth, their sweet juice a divine burst of flavor against her tongue. Laris sat down with his back against one of the stones and looked out the way they'd come. "An unfounded practice, but some believe you can see the future by interpreting waves in the magic around the moon, reflected in the water."

"Incredible." Raelyn looked at the silver orb in the sky above them. "I'm not surprised the moon has magic."

"Everything has magic. Even a blade of grass."

"Even me?"

He met her gaze. "In your own way, though, it's difficult to describe. You have essence magic, like everyone, but it's—" he paused "—different." He plucked a blade of grass and held it up between two fingers. "Everything you see has a magic counterpart, like a shadow. For those of us who can see it, it looks like fine threads loosely bundled together. They resemble the object but lack its detail and substance. By learning to pull those threads and weave them into something else, we can affect what's in the tangible world.

"You don't have essence magic like us, exactly," he said, staring intently at her. "There's something else around you. Not threads; it's more like mist. I can't explain beyond that."

Raelyn's stomach issued a long, low growl at the introduction of the berries, the first food she'd had in some time. Looking down at her reflection in the scrying pool, she barely recognized herself. Like Laris, she wore a heavy mask of grime, and the hollows of her cheekbones had become more pronounced. Another growl from her stomach was echoed by a surge of thirst, and she headed toward the mossy spring Laris had found along the nearby cliff. She took her time drinking in the cold water; it took several moments for enough to fill her hand, and one palmful was not nearly enough to quench her thirst.

"Where's your guide?" Laris asked when she returned, bringing her back from thoughts of warm baths and hot meals.

Hendrel was nowhere to be seen. "I wonder …" she replied softly, more to herself than to him. "I should ask him next time where he goes when I can't see him."

"You've been visiting the void, then?"

"Not often, don't worry. But it seems like the only place where I can find any answers, even though they rarely make sense."

The slight downward curve of his mouth hinted at his disapproval, but he nodded. In the moonlight, his black hair stood stark against his other features, with straight locks covering his forehead and obscuring his eyes. It reminded her of the first time she'd seen him up close in the castle tower.

"You should get some sleep," she said abruptly. "I can't remember the last time you slept."

"I told you—soldiers are trained for such times."

Dar'Liha sat up. "Safe here," she said. "No Pale Men. We sleep."

"See? No excuses." Raelyn made her way over to him. "Sleep. I'll even stay up as lookout if it eases your mind." She reached for her glaive at his side.

He grabbed her wrist and pulled her off balance so she stumbled down next to him. "*You* are going to sleep," he said, not letting go. His face close to hers, he added quietly, "You don't have to be tough, Raelyn." The words were stern but not chastising. "Stop punishing yourself."

"If I fall asleep, I know you won't, and you need it more than I do," she said stubbornly, unable to meet his eyes and unwilling to acknowledge the truth of his words.

The hold on her wrist eased, but he didn't let go. His eyes swept her face, and she felt caught between the urge to flee and whatever part of her was relishing the warmth of his closeness. "Are you that afraid of me still?" he asked, amused.

Her eyes snapped to his of their own accord. "Of course not!"

"What did I tell you about getting used to my touch? We'll both be warmer if you stay close."

It was the lightness of his touch, Raelyn decided, that made it white-hot and all-encompassing. No one in her whole life had so freely touched her so often. He awaited her answer, but she wasn't sure she knew it.

Laris reached up with his free hand and brushed aside a strand of her hair, letting his fingertips linger on her skin. She froze. She wasn't sure if she was breathing. She knew she wasn't. His eyes searched for something in hers, but at her shocked expression, his gaze softened. His touch left her, taking all the warmth of the night with it.

"I'll sleep, Raelyn," he said, turning away from her with a crooked smile. "You will, too, though."

Who could sleep now? she thought, heart thudding in her chest. She stayed next to him, discretely putting a handspan between them before she lay down, her back toward his back.

"You've been practicing," Hendrel said, pleased. "It's not so difficult once you get used to the feeling, is it?"

Raelyn nodded. She'd only just entered the void, but her thoughts were already straying away from mastering warden abilities to other, more human concerns.

"Good. Now that you can move your sphere of influence, the next step is to learn to compartmentalize it."

"Hendrel, what's the point to all of this?" she asked moodily. "We're not at war with mages. Am I destined to be some safeguard tucked away in a nobleman's castle?"

"Perhaps," his child's voice replied. "But the truth is we are always at war. There will always be those who seek to use magic to dominate and control, to take away the free will of others. There will always be the nadir. You will have no shortage of honorable causes to fight for, Raelyn."

She sighed. He was right. And she was going to start by rescuing Ellisand.

"Now, you must work to control your sphere of influence on a more finite level. Compartmentalization is learning to negate magic in one person while allowing its freedom in someone else—while being close to both.

"Start by focusing on your inner sense of the void and splitting it in half, trying as best you can to make two distinct sensations within. Then, when those compartments of power are clearly defined, try sending them out separately. Be mindful not to let them collide and combine again."

Hendrel seemed like he wanted to say more, but he paused. For a long moment, he didn't speak, and his light, which always had an unpredictable flicker even in its human silhouette, seemed frozen, unwavering.

"Hendrel?" she called to him. "Are you alright?"

Like her voice had broken a spell, he flickered back into motion. "There is something searching for you here," he said. "It is close. You must go."

"Wait! Tell me, should I go to the capital? Should I go to Emblem's Manor with the transcendents? Hendrel?"

"You must seek the Sundered Gate, Raelyn. Now go! Do not return here, even if the need is dire. Wait for my signal in the other realm." He vanished, not lingering long enough to transition back to wisp form. Without his light, the void felt darker than usual, and the atmosphere became ominous. Oppressive warmth quickly replaced the familiar cold, and an orange hue tinged the nothingness.

Something *was* coming, and it was coming for her. Raelyn shut her eyes and thought of Laris, latching on to his presence as a lifeboat in the sea of her subconscious.

She sat up with a gasp, startling her companions awake. She apologetically waved off their confused looks. "Nightmare," she muttered, offering a half-hearted smile.

Next to her, Laris's expression was full of doubt. "Now is not the time to keep secrets," he warned. "Tell us what's really going on."

Why could he read her so well? She lay back down, looking at the dawn sky painted pink and blue, fading into the edge of night.

"Something was searching for me," she said at last. "In the void. Hendrel told me not to return." She looked around for the wisp's light but found him absent in the material world. "I don't know what it was, but it felt powerful and ... I don't know ... ancient?" She shook her head. "It was like nothing I've ever felt."

Dar'Liha stretched and stood. "Come. Moon Mother will help. Not far."

"Your people?" asked Laris.

The whyte nodded. "My people."

"We should go," he said, looking over his shoulder at Raelyn. "I don't know where we are in the mountains or what path would be the safest out. They're our best chance."

She reached for her boots, the sight of them no longer relieving. Her feet ached at the thought of imprisonment within the sweaty layers of ill-fitting cloth. What choice did she have? It was pain either way. At least the boots would spare her from more serious injuries as they journeyed on.

She tore off what remained of her lower pant legs to rewrap her feet. *I'm sorry I didn't take better care of these clothes for you, Mengat. I couldn't have done without them.*

As the first rays of morning sun touched her face, she hoped somewhere, against all odds, Lydantus and his master were warm and safe in a soft bed, still enjoying the blessed peace of daybreak slumber.

CHAPTER THIRTEEN

Within the heart of the Vast, mountains rolled like white-capped waves into more mountains as far as the eyes could see. The air was cool, sometimes even cold, in the small pockets hidden away under the trees and rocks of the valley. Looking at the giant peaks surrounding her, Raelyn felt a comforting insignificance, as if the world would be just fine without all of them and had always been so.

Their pace was steady but not rushed through the forest, and after some time, she realized they were following a well-concealed trail. Dar'Liha led them along without speaking, but the silence was companionable and far from quiet. The land was alive and thriving, filled with birds, squirrels, and other small wildlife. Briefly, Raelyn thought she saw a mountain stag, but the creature was too stealthy for her to be convinced it had been there at all.

As she suspected, the whyte's depiction of "not far" was unreliable. Since climbing out of the sinkhole, they'd traveled at least half a day.

"We should rest and eat," Laris called out, stopping as if reading her mind.

Dar'Liha looked back and waved them on. "Not far."

"We were 'not far' ten miles ago," Raelyn whispered, approaching him.

He nodded. "We'll rest for a bit. The forest has plenty to offer." Shaking his head at their frontrunner, he pointed into the trees. "A short break and some food."

The whyte turned back to join them, seemingly unbothered by the decision. She crouched and stared at Raelyn while Laris disappeared into the tree line.

"Sorry," Raelyn told her. "We haven't had a proper meal in days, and I'm not as used to this type of travel as you two."

"Small Man rest. Moon Mother will help."

"I don't know if anyone can help." She attempted a smile. "Is the Moon Mother your leader?

"Moon Mother is Moon Mother." The whyte gestured for Raelyn to hand over her glaive, which Raelyn did. Dar'Liha looked at the weapon, inquisitive, and gently touched the markings on the metal. "Famine," she said.

"Is that its name?"

The whyte nodded and handed the polearm back.

"Dar'Liha," Raelyn began hesitantly, "the whyte fur mantle worn by the wretch in the caves … that was someone dear to you, wasn't it?"

A veil of sorrow drew across Dar'Liha's features. "Life mate. Pale Men capture two moons ago. She hunter for village. Never come home."

"I am so sorry. I wish we could have arrived sooner to save her."

"Pale Men pay," Dar'Liha said, resolute. "Dar'Liha not rest until dead."

Raelyn reached over and placed a hand in comfort on the whyte's forearm.

They sat quietly together until Laris returned, his arms cradling what he'd foraged like a precious treasure. Gently dropping the pile down in their midst, he divvied it out, handing off various nuts, berries, and unfamiliar tuber roots that reminded Raelyn of potatoes. They were bitter uncooked but not unbearable, and she ate them gratefully without a word of complaint. Too soon, the food was gone, and a dull ache replaced the hunger in her stomach with a mixture of satiety and sickness at the food's unfamiliarity.

"We'll see if Dar'Liha's people can steer us toward Osharia," Laris told her. "As much as I think Lomnir's masters in Emblem's Manor would be helpful, I don't know if it's wise to bring you into a foreign country and away from the protection of your king." He looked pointedly at her. "And," he added, "maybe it's time to take you to the Sundered Gate."

"You're going to take me there? When you wouldn't even speak of it before?" She stared back in disbelief. "What about all that talk of fate and things beyond our control?"

"We were still strangers then, Raelyn. You have to understand there was information I withheld for our safety and the safety of the people around us. I had to be certain of your character."

"Come," Dar'Liha stood. "Talk on way. Not far."

They collectively stood, but Raelyn grabbed Laris's arm as he went to follow their guide, turning him back to face her. She almost recoiled from the warmth in the contact. Having initiated it, she was caught off guard by the familiarity of the gesture, and her fingers tensed from the thrum of the sensation. Her anger made her hold firm. He glanced down at her hand and then to her face, his expression amused but also anticipatory. He looked at her as though she'd asked him to a battle he knew he'd win.

"You've let me fumble through the darkness this whole time?" she asked. "Just how much do you know?"

"I know nothing that can tell you how to be a warden, so temper your anger. All I know is a history lesson, at best, about the Gate and its location. We've got a long journey ahead to get out of the mountains. There is plenty of time to talk about it."

His answer wasn't satisfactory. She was frustrated and a little frightened after what had happened in the void. Even though she was learning what she could do as a warden, she still had very little knowledge about wardens or their role in the world of magic. That Laris knew details and couldn't be bothered to tell her turned her frustration into anger.

"We're going to talk about this sooner, not later," she replied, letting go of his arm and stomping off in Dar'Liha's direction.

Powered by her emotions and a belly of wild tubers, Raelyn forged ahead. She took the middle position, leaving Laris at the rear, and pushed herself to stay closer to the whyte than to the man behind her.

She was surprised when, not too long after leaving their resting place, they crested a ridge and saw the outline of stone structures tucked between the boulders of a deep ravine. Like any village, the place thrummed with activity. Fires burned in outside hearths; the sounds of children laughing bubbled up from the streets; a handful of whytes tended gardens, greeting each other in passing.

Raelyn and Laris followed Dar'Liha down the steep path to the village, hopeful not to draw too much attention. But soon, everyone within sight stopped to marvel at the strangers entering their midst.

Raelyn tentatively lifted a hand in greeting, but her sentiment wasn't returned.

"Follow," Dar'Liha instructed them, taking a dirt path along the outskirts of the buildings. "First, meet Dom'Olo. Village chief."

The chief's house was stone like all the buildings in the village, but unlike the others, its rock walls were smooth and dark. At each corner grew a gnarled tree with branches so reaching and spindly they intertwined with one another just below the roof's peak. The canopy created a natural veranda at the entryway. Colorful flowers contained by a vine fence peaked out from behind the home.

Dar'Liha knocked on the wooden door, and after a few moments, they heard rustling from within. A gravelly, deep voice said something in a language Raelyn had never heard, and Dar'Liha answered in kind. The back-and-forth continued until, voices escalating, the latch on the door made a resounding click. A white-furred face appeared in the dark crack that opened, ice-blue eyes peering out at them.

Dom'Olo looked the travelers up and down. His wrinkled face reminded Raelyn of the ancient scholars in Albator, their white beards so long they may as well have been a fur cloak. The chief's white coat was thinner and patchier than Dar'Liha's, and he wore a pair of oddly shaped spectacles across the bridge of his nose. He spoke again, motioning for them to enter.

Inside, the house was not at all what Raelyn expected. As it was made of stone, she assumed the inside would be cold and dark, even with its windows. She was wrong. The interior was covered in wood planking, giving the space a warm, rustic feel. Furs lined the floor, and lanterns gave off a welcoming glow with their ample light.

"Chief say wait here for Moon Mother. Eat. Must wait for dark."

Despite her tiredness, Raelyn wasn't in the mood to sit. She examined the room briefly before asking, "Is there a bath?"

"Spring. Follow path."

"You're not going through a feyfolk village unescorted." Laris interjected, moving to sit at the dining table. "Just because one whyte is in our debt doesn't mean the others will be friendly toward you."

She knew he was right, but she wouldn't give him the satisfaction of agreeing with his good sense. "I'd like to be alone for a bit."

"No. We didn't make it this far to take risks like that. I'm coming with you. I won't watch you ... at least not the whole time."

A jolt shot into her core at the deep turn in his tone, but she refused to be swayed. "Dar'Liha? Can you accompany me?" she asked the waiting whyte.

"That's not a suitable alternative." Laris frowned. "We shouldn't separate, and you know that."

"Both come," Dar'Liha said. "Will wait by spring rocks."

Raelyn breathed a sigh of defeat and huffed her agreement, striding intently out the doorway and turning down the narrow path without waiting for Laris and Dar'Liha to catch up. She wasn't sure why she was so angry. Laris was right; there was plenty of time to discuss the Sundered Gate. They had to get out of the Vast first, and his not being open about what he knew was a minor affront compared to all he'd done to aid her.

Winding away from the chief's house, the path meandered through a landscape of rocks and trees on the outskirts of the village. Raelyn met no other whytes on the path, and those close enough to see her from the edges of their yards offered a passing glance and not much else. Dark recesses of the forest around her contrasted deeply with bright patches of sunlight that gave the shadows depth and substance. Before long, the stone buildings were lost from sight, and the sound of churning water met her ears. The path ended at a series of steam-enveloped pools, and the gravel beneath her feet faded into the natural rock at the water's edge. Currents welled up from within the water's depths, creating a steady churn that rimmed the perimeter with frothy bubbles.

"Will wait there," Dar'Liha told Raelyn when the whyte and Laris arrived a few moments later. She pointed to a cluster of boulders nestled off the path within the trees. "Will watch Tall Man for you."

Bending down and tentatively touching the water, Raelyn smiled at its warmth. "Thank you." She didn't look at Laris. "Keep a close eye on him for me."

Laris didn't respond, and but his annoyance was palpable, and Raelyn only glanced up when she heard their footsteps move away and grow faint.

After quickly checking her surroundings to ensure they were out of direct sight, she stripped down and stepped carefully into the pool.

The heat was soothing and scathing to her battered feet, and a dull sting across the surface of her healing sores confirmed the pools were salt water. The more of her body she submerged, the more the pain in her feet became an afterthought. She hadn't had a hot bath since the night Albator was attacked. Her enjoyment was indescribable; she didn't know such happiness could come from something so commonplace.

After dunking fully, she lounged up to her chin in the water, studying the world around her and letting the sounds of nature heal her mind as the water healed her body. Nearby, a pair of birds hopped playfully up and down the branches of a small bush. They tussled and chirped and tussled again. Raelyn began to think about what Hendrel told her in the void.

Could she use the birds for practice? Would it harm them? She watched them thoughtfully. She didn't think they were in any danger. Even if they used magic in some unknown, animal way, affecting that magic momentarily wouldn't have much of an impact, would it?

She decided to try it, confident she could pull her sphere of influence back if something went awry. Turning her focus inward, she found the cold, compressed ball that was the void and visualized it splitting into two separate spheres. After several tries, she briefly felt the separation and realized visualizing it wasn't enough. She had to *feel* the individual orbs of the void, a task that proved more difficult than she'd expected.

So lost she was in concentration she didn't notice when Dar'Liha entered the clearing, holding an armful of clothes.

"Small Man," the whyte yelled to get Raelyn's attention. "Too long for hot water. Time to dress."

Raelyn looked around, suddenly aware of how far the sun had moved overhead and the new angle of the shadows around her. "How long have I been here?" She looked up at Dar'Liha. "I feel like I just sat down."

"Long. Tall Man try to come. I tell him no. He wait up path."

"Well, thank you for that. Are those clothes for me?"

Laying the items across a log near the pools, Dar'Liha nodded. "Menfolk visit sometimes. Leave items here. Dom'Olo brought for you."

"Menfolk? You mean humans like us?" Raelyn was intrigued. Did that mean there was a human settlement nearby?

"No," her companion replied. "Menfolk."

She smiled politely and nodded, knowing it would get her nowhere to ask more. As skilled as Dar'Liha was in the common tongue, it seemed not everything had a direct translation. "Thank you for the clothes. I'll be out in a moment." She submerged herself one final time, relishing the water's warmth as it closed around her.

By the time they returned to Dom'Olo's, the whyte village was well within the grip of evening. Though the sun hadn't finished setting, the height of the mountains shut out its final rays and cast the valleys into a premature twilight.

Raelyn's mood had greatly improved. Her new clothes were light and comfortable. Most importantly, the footwear Dar'Liha left her was like nothing she'd ever worn. Tall, reaching almost to her knees, the boots were made from soft, delicate hide and were padded on the inside. The flexible soles allowed her to achieve a good fit once she secured the laces. Hair pulled back into a long braid, she felt restored to her old self.

Laris sat at the table after they entered the stone home. He'd changed into a new shirt and brown jerkin brought down by Dom'Olo while she was bathing, and the youthfulness of his face was renewed by the fresh shave he'd managed at the small stream fed by the spring. She stared at him, and he returned her scrutiny.

"You're not forgiven yet," she told him, lifting her chin stubbornly. "But I *guess* there'll be plenty of time to talk about it. We can start right now."

He smiled broadly, possibly the biggest smile Raelyn had ever seen from him, and he bowed his head slightly to show his defeat. "Do you feel better now, lady?"

"I do," she replied, walking over to sit across from him. "I never knew a hot soak could be so enjoyable."

He nodded slowly. "It is a simple pleasure cherished by most who've endured hardships. Even the most hardened soldiers are keen for a hot soak after long nights of death, darkness, and terror on a battlefield."

He traced the lines of the wood with his finger. She wondered how many battles he'd seen, how many lives he'd taken. That circumstances existed capable of terrifying someone so strong was beyond her comprehension. She suddenly felt very, very naïve and sheltered.

"Was it peaceful in the springs?" he asked.

Raelyn nodded. "Aside from some birds, all was quiet. It was much needed."

"You'd been soaking for so long we were wondering if you'd run away again."

"Oh, 'we' were wondering that, were 'we'? I didn't know Dar'Liha was so familiar with my past escape attempts."

"Very," he said, looking up at her. "She sang my praises for saving you from certain death."

Raelyn snuffed in amusement. "I see you're feeling refreshed from our journey, too, *my lord.*" As she said the words, they hitched in her throat, and her heart felt like it skipped a beat. Calling him her lord, even in jest, felt awkward, not because he wasn't a lord, but because it was a title reserved for her future husband.

He didn't let on if he noticed the soft interruption in her voice. "We seem safe for now. That alone is a relief. We should learn what we can from their Moon Mother tonight and take a few days to recover fully."

She locked eyes with him. "Tell me," she said softly. "Now is as good a time as any."

"The Gate? It's not such a secret, Raelyn." He frowned. "It's a shrine for all the Pillars and Emblem, and it once housed altars for the Nameless God and chaos gods, too. It was sealed away by mages after the Cataclysm. No one other than the Holy King knows its true location, though, we know the capital city was built on the site."

"Why wasn't it just destroyed?"

He shrugged. "The world may need it again someday."

The last glimpses of daylight slipped through the window at Laris's back. *Why am I being sent to an altar site?* she wondered. *Does one of the gods have something to tell the world?* Resting her head on her arms folded on the table, she inhaled deeply, savoring the feeling of being warm, clean, and momentarily safe. The lids of her eyes grew heavy while she stared out the window, watching dusk turn into darkness.

How long into nightfall do we have to wait? Raelyn wondered. *Is the Moon Mother a priestess? A prophet?* She closed her eyes. They'd received no clues.

A firm touch on her shoulder woke Raelyn from a dreamless sleep at the table. Laris stood next to her, while Dar'Liha and Dom'Olo waited in the doorway.

"It's time," Laris said. "They're ready for us."

"Come." Dar'Liha turned to leave. "Moon Mother awake."

"Awake?" Raelyn whispered to Laris as they followed the whytes out of the house. He shook his head, no more aware of what they were heading into than she was.

Illuminated by lanterns along the ground, the path circled the chief's house and journeyed through the garden at its back. Even in the dark of night, the meticulously cared for and strategically placed plants encouraged a sense of serenity and calm. The garden continued down along steep hillsides on either side and out of sight, and Raelyn realized it wasn't so much a garden as it was an elaborate entryway.

As the path ended, the plants on each side circled out and rejoined, creating an oval space ringed by flowers of all sizes and colors. Two benches spaced equally apart along the perimeter divided the space, and a decorative rock formation twice the height of a man rose toward the night sky at the center of the natural enclosure. At its top, a large, leafy plant with wide, silver-blue flowers soaked in the moonlight. Tendrils and vines spilled down the rocks but didn't extend beyond the stone tower.

Dar'Liha motioned for them to stop, and Dom'Olo entered the clearing alone. He went to the base of the rocks and knelt, bowing so low his forehead touched the ground. Speaking soft words in the whyte language, his voice carried to Raelyn's ears on a newly stirred breeze.

Any light in the garden pulled inward and condensed around the blue flower as Dom'Olo spoke. It flickered and shifted, reminding Raelyn of Hendrel's much-missed light. While she watched, the flower began to grow and change shape. The petals folded and stretched into delicate limbs and a body, human in shape but not in detail. Tendrils rose to create a crown of hair and wove elaborate vine patterns around the developing figure.

The Moon Mother's features were delicate, her eyes glowing white orbs that seemed to swirl with moonlight. Around her, the vines and leaves of her plant base created a high-backed chair where she sat with an air of otherworldly nobility.

Dom'Olo motioned them forward, and Raelyn clutched the cold of the void within her core, terrified she'd accidentally banish the forest spirit from their presence.

"Do not worry, Raelyn." The Moon Mother's voice was whispery, melodic, and rich. "I am a being of substance in this world, as are you. My life does not depend on magic."

Uncertain how to respond or if she was expected to speak freely, Raelyn bowed in gratitude but remained quiet. The Moon Mother turned her attention to Laris. She studied him a moment, something in her expression amused.

"And so, the world begins anew," she said, her gaze shifting back to Raelyn. "To think so much time has passed already. Tell me, what is it you wish to ask of me?"

"Direction," Laris replied. "We seek to leave the mountains."

The Moon Mother shook her head. "The *gonsidhe* can instruct you." She pointed at Dar'Liha and Dom'Olo. "Ask me what you truly need to know."

"The *gonsidhe*?" Raelyn looked over at their hosts.

"Yes. That is what they call themselves. But like all feyfolk, they are known by other names in the land of Men." The Moon Mother beckoned Raelyn closer. "You are here because you are lost, and not because you are lost in the mountains."

"I ..." she faltered, looking away from the nymph-like creature toward the ground. "You're right. I've spent my entire life living a lie, and I still don't know what to do, where to go, or how to help the one person who needs me."

"You do know where to go," the Moon Mother replied calmly. "You have been set upon a path, but you're torn between loyalty and destiny. Do you choose the life of your friend or the lives of the many? Even now, you're being hunted and searched for. There are beings on your trail, both mortal and immortal."

"Immortal?" Raelyn hesitated, thinking back to the attack at Mengat's cabin. If what the Moon Mother said was true, the penumbra was likely still on their trail—if not something more sinister in its place. She hadn't been able to save Mengat. She doubted she could save Ellisand. "If I can't even save my friends, how can I possibly save others? Am I supposed to leave Ell, then?"

The Moon Mother paused for a long moment before answering. "There is no right or wrong way, only the way you choose. The world will reshape itself regardless."

"I don't even have my guide anymore," Raelyn said bitterly. "Do you know of Hendrel? Is he safe?"

"I am not formless. The world's seam is closed to me. But those who frequent such places are not so easily dispatched. He will come to you when the time is right."

"I'll take Raelyn to the Sundered Gate." Laris's declaration echoed through the garden. "I will see her safely there, but we must leave the Vast and, by the sounds of it, soon."

"The way is dangerous. You are not as welcome in many hidden places of the world as you are here with the *gonsidhe*. They were once allies of Men, but many other feyfolk would do you harm, and you must pass through their domains on your journey. Here, in my valley, I welcome the *gonsidhe* and all peaceful beings. That is why they tend my gardens and shelter me while I slumber in daylight."

"Are there no allies you have to call on?" he asked her. "No way to speed our travels? We've seen glimpses of what's coming, and I think it's wise for everyone if you set us on the most direct path."

"There is a way," she answered. "With my blessing—my mark of keeping—many of the feyfolk will let you pass. But there is a price to be paid for it."

"Name it," Laris said without hesitation.

"To the west of this village, there is a shadowed grove. Beneath it, a tomb. It is the dwelling place of Mondek. Once a lord amongst fey-folk, he has become corrupt and mad from his bloodlust of the pale ones beneath the mountains. His hatred has bent his mind and made him unable to tell friend from foe. He now slays all within his forest domain. I would have you end his reign of destruction in exchange for my blessing. That is my request."

"He's beyond the power of you and your kind?" Laris asked.

"We have some who could ease him from suffering in this world." She folded her hands across her lap. "But that is not the natural order of our kind. We do not interfere with one another."

Laris squared his shoulders. "And yet you would send me to kill him?"

"Yes," she said with a note of sadness. "I, who have loved Mondek over centuries and will for centuries more, would have you do this kindness that I cannot do myself."

A hush fell over them all at her words, and Raelyn swallowed the lump that suddenly formed in her throat. It was no small thing the Moon Mother was asking of them. She wanted them to deliver mercy at the cost of someone she held dear. Because she loved Mondek, she didn't want him to continue to suffer.

"I'll do it," Laris agreed solemnly, running a hand through his hair. He let out a deep breath. "Is there aught we should know?"

"Mondek is no longer a lord. He is no longer one of the feyfolk," the Moon Mother cautioned. "He is a monster. Do not expect to recognize what he has become. He will be deadly by both tooth and claw but also by magic. As a former lord, his powers are strong, but they are now guided by his twisted heart and mind."

Laris glanced at Raelyn, nodding slowly. "Very well. I'll see it done."

"A gift," the Moon Mother added, "to aid you." She waved her hand, and an opening appeared in the stone beneath where she sat. From within, she pulled out a blade longer than a dagger but not quite the length of a sword. Its hilt was blue and silver, the blade made from dark metal with silver etching.

A vine wrapped around the weapon and stretched to where Laris stood. He took it carefully, testing the weight and balance in his hand.

"Its name is Blue Deimos. From a time when gods warred for control of this realm." She looked at Raelyn. "You have found Famine. Both weapons were forged in feyfolk fires long ago and are especially deadly to the feyfolk—the nonhuman races—due to the way our blood reacts to alloyed metal."

"You made weapons to use against one another?" Raelyn asked, surprised.

"The way we are now is not how we were always. Both time and experience are cruel teachers." The Moon Mother looked up into the night sky. "Mondek is summoned by the moon, as am I. You will find him reluctant to face the sun, hunkered within his underground tomb during the day. I know not which you prefer, the confines of the ground or the openness of the grove, but use that information as you will."

Laris bowed his head respectfully. "We'll take our leave in the morning."

"Raelyn." The nymph-like creature stood and floated down to them on a current of vines. "The last Holy King guides you, and things in the world are shifting. Old powers are stirring. Their movements are just ripples and undercurrents now, but there will come a time when we must survive their waves or be swept away. Do not fear what you don't know. You were born to this gift, and it is yours to control."

She extended a limb and touched Raelyn's face. The caress was cool to the touch but comforting, and Raelyn met it with a timid smile. "Thank you," she said softly. "I will do my best."

CHAPTER FOURTEEN

Staring into the fire dying in the hearth, Saraht wiped the blood from her hands with a silk cloth. Methodically, she went along the edges of her fingernails first, down to the creases of her knuckles and onward, until each finger regained its usual appearance. She used water only, leaving the smell of blood as her token of another night of successful negotiating.

Across the room, features obscured with shadows from the fading firelight, Djuron hunched, unmoving. Tied to his chair, he was alive but barely, his shallow, raspy breaths letting her know he wasn't gone just yet. Nor did she want him to be.

Next to him, his brother sat in similar restraints, though, no harm had come to Lord Audolon other than the wound to his pride. Unlike his brother, he was alert and upright, drenched in sweat and urine. Bound and gagged but not blindfolded, he was there to watch.

Saraht took a sip of wine from her glass at the fireside table. It was a shame they'd ended up doing things the hard way, but Ellisand's devious, brazen ploy had forced Saraht's hand. In a small way, she was impressed with the Wedminth heir's cunning and boldness, but at the same time, such independent thinking was inconvenient.

It had nothing to do with Saraht feeling forced into unwanted intimacy. As if she'd have gone through with playing sexual placater to these horrid men. She'd taken on that role too many times before realizing men were just as much flesh and bone as any creature. They were far less capable than most wild animals at defending themselves, especially indulgent lords who wore their swords for decoration. Men like these, she'd learned, were just as swayed by fear as they were by carnal desire. And fear was far more powerful for long-term control.

Men were more cooperative if they had something to lose. Seduction had never been her preferred path, and she was no longer an innocent young girl without other talents. With torture, she never had to give up a part of herself.

She wasn't sure how many more days she'd draw out the torment. Baron Audolon appeared adequately distraught. He'd been compliant with what she'd asked and had nodded enthusiastically when she'd peppered him with demands. Still, she needed more time to think before she moved on with her mother and Ellisand.

The girl had thought quick on her feet and saved her skin—and virginity—and perhaps that was best. If Saraht's master wanted Ellisand's loyalty and wished to put her on the throne instead of King Rothelian, her virtue could become another bargaining tool down the road.

As much as she didn't want to admit it, trying to have Ellisand seduce the Pardis lords had been a poor decision. The future queen of Limnin shouldn't be sullied by those so unworthy.

At least she'd gotten to witness the power of simple flirting. And she did take quickly to our narrative of male inferiority. Perhaps we are still aligned.

There was more work to do before Ellisand would be told her true purpose. Saraht had to be assured of her loyalty, which required more reinforcement of Raloria's teachings. Thankfully, Pardis had a thriving trafficking business. Not only were the poor plentiful to pick from, there were enough middle- and upper-class nobles to make such endeavors profitable. Without a doubt, the Lords of Revelry had a presence somewhere in the city.

Tomorrow, she'd seek them out, but for a much different purpose than that of their usual clientele.

"You're not upset with me?" Ellisand asked, skeptical.

Sitting across from her for the first time in a handful of days, Saraht shook her head and took a polite sip of tea. "I know why you did it, and I adapted as I always do. You did catch me off guard, I will admit." She looked darkly at Ellisand. "I would think twice before using that trick again, however. At least not without my knowledge."

Smiling unexpectedly, she raised her teacup in salute. "To the late Sir Djuron. Who would have thought a man's heart could give out so unexpectedly?"

"Indeed," Ellisand muttered, swirling her tea. "How very unexpected."

"Today, we must visit the market. I need supplies before we take our leave, and Orion has requested some large deliveries to his encampment at the edge of the territory."

"Shall I get Maylam?"

"Mother will need her rest before we make for the road once again. Let her enjoy the luxuries afforded to us here. You and I can go. It will be good to get some fresh air. These stone walls are stifling."

They finished their tea and assorted pastries in relative silence. A few comments on the food and drink passed between them, but an air of awkwardness persisted. Saraht was doing her best to appear unaffected by Ellisand's actions from the other night, but Ellisand didn't seem to believe she'd been forgiven so easily.

In truth, Saraht couldn't convince herself the other woman's unexpected ruse was simply a brilliant last-ditch effort to save herself. What had happened felt like it was more than that. It felt like a calculated attempt at … what? She couldn't put her finger on it, but she knew it was worth watching.

Before taking their leave of the servants, Saraht asked the housekeeping staff to deliver a message to Baron Audolon as a way of feigning innocence of his whereabouts. Free from Montigrath oversight as the servants hurried away, Saraht and Ellisand strode off the grounds and into the noble district of Pardis.

Clean, well-maintained roads stretched out in all directions. The cobblestones were swept, and manicured hedges followed the lines of the streets. Shops were contained within buildings with colorful signs and decorative glass windows. They were welcoming and, Saraht guessed, prepared to charge exorbitant fees for the friendly accommodations.

"We'll carry on a bit," she said when Ellisand stopped at one of the shops' windows. "We can get the same goods in a less expensive part of town."

Ellisand turned away to follow. She looked distracted, and Saraht wondered if she was reminiscing about her home. No doubt Ellisand was used to visiting such high-end merchants. She probably had no true grasp of how important money was for people of lesser circumstances.

Passing through an open cast-iron gateway, they stepped from the noble district into the city commons. Here, there were no manicured hedges, no streetsweepers. Refuse lined the edges of the roads, dumped into clogged ditches from above, the small channels originally designed to carry the waste into the city sewers. If shops were in standalone buildings, they were hidden by layer after layer of street vendor tents. Saraht kept a close hold on her sphere of influence. No doubt there were nadir lurking in the dark alleys, and she saw no reason to draw unwanted attention.

Along the way, they stopped and spoke in hushed tones with several vendors. What she'd said was true; they needed to resupply. Moving an enemy force around unnoticed was no small thing, and it was only a matter of time before the bulk of Limnin's army became a threat. Their only saving grace was that King Rothelian didn't know where they were headed. He would have to chase them from the starting point of Albator, and as long as she didn't remain anywhere too long, her smaller force should continue to outpace the Limnin army. Rothelian would have no idea they'd even visited Paris since no forceful takeover had been necessary.

A swinging black paper lantern caught Saraht's eye from a side street to their left. *Finally*, she thought, steering Ellisand toward the telltale symbol marking the Lords of Revelry territory. Unlike red-light districts, also known for satisfying the pleasures of the flesh, the black-light district was for specific clientele only and dealt in perversions rather than pleasures.

Saraht kept a hand on the sword beneath her cloak. Part of her welcomed conflict here; she craved it. She wanted nothing more than to slash her way from one end of the street to the other, emerging at its end covered in the blood of those seeking enjoyment from the suffering of others. But today was not the day to slake her righteous thirst for blood—at least not until the opportunity presented itself. For now, she just needed to let the black-light district make an impression.

"I was told to look for a man in this location," she lied, glancing over her shoulder at Ellisand. "This doesn't seem right, though. This is where the Lords of Revelry do business."

The shadows along the street held horrors that Saraht made sure the girl witnessed. Broken bodies—some alive and others dead long enough to let rot set in—lay curled in discarded heaps. Battered, bloodied, and mutilated, they'd been tossed into the street after they'd been used. Once a week, the Lords paid a cleanup service to come and clear them out. Some were still being abused; their patrons hunkered over them, identities hidden behind dark hoods and black masks.

Behind her, she heard Ellisand retch.

"Come, let's get off the street for a moment." The redirection was deliberate. She'd reached the place she'd been searching for. True to all black-light districts, one building was reserved for the highest-paying customers. Large golden doors identified it at the front, each painted with an image of a black dragon. Without hesitation, she pushed one of the doors open and stepped inside.

There were no guards to stop them. The Lords of Revelry didn't need armed protection. No one would get past the magic curtains protecting the entry vestibule unless they knew the password. *Or if they're a warden.* She smiled smugly. But Saraht wouldn't use her abilities to get access into the manor. Doing that would alarm the entire place, and that would accomplish nothing. Luckily for her, a childhood spent in the black-light district afforded her the knowledge of every password and secret code used by the criminal elite.

She turned to a young woman standing behind a counter—the only piece of furniture within the small ingress. *"Igsalmian Denavvo,"* she said. The girl made no reply; it was possible she couldn't. Removing tongues was an easy way to keep workers from telling secrets. Soon after, the curtains made of magic pulled aside. Of course, the old code was still being used. It was uncommon, but not so uncommon that it would be out of place.

To Ellisand, it would have sounded like the name of the man they were meeting, perhaps, but to those who knew, it was a moniker used by one of the Lords' founders. To invoke it meant you'd already paid in full, and almost no doors were closed to you except those on the ground level, which were reserved for nobles of the highest rank.

Saraht didn't want to spend too much time in the manor, but she wanted to ensure Ellisand learned the true nature of Limnin's nobility. Pardis wasn't unique; what she was about to see happened in every city, every town, even if there was no black-light district to provide commercial release.

After walking through a long hallway decorated with extravagant trappings and paintings, they entered an open parlor filled with plush couches and colorful pillows. Fruits of all kinds overflowed from artfully crafted display tables, and servants walked around with bottles of wine in hand as if they were working a royal banquet. A grand staircase led upward to the next level at the opposite end of the room. Its carpeted steps were black as night.

As expected, the parlor held more than just servants. Down almost every line of sight was a naked body. Some were young, some old, all slick with sweat and red from clumsy grabbing and prodding. From what she could see, Saraht was disappointed. The activities in the parlor were reasonably tame. Usually, patrons who chose to enjoy the public areas of the manor were exhibitionists, thriving off the shock value brought to others in the room. She'd been hoping to show Ellisand more than just common rough sex. *We'll have to go straight to him.* She sighed inwardly. *Hopefully, he doesn't mess this up.*

Ground-level rooms were off-limits to them, but she doubted anyone was in them, regardless. Only visiting royalty or high-ranking nobility would be put on the ground level where access to the tunnels leading out of the black-light district was quickest. Their target would be on the second level. He was still a very important man, after all.

Without a word to Ellisand, Saraht strode confidently through the room to the stairs, climbing up the middle of the carpeted steps like she owned the building. In a way, she did. In her mind, anything she could take by force could be considered hers, and the magical defenses of the Lords' manor were as meaningless to her as the strands of a spider web.

Walking along the second-floor balcony, she watched each door they passed until she saw the mark she was looking for. Discrete, placed there for her eyes only, it looked like nothing more than a smudge of dirt against the red of the ornate oak. "Let's try this one," she said quietly, as if to herself, knowing Ellisand could hear her. She knocked twice and turned the handle.

The scene before them was as disturbing as she'd hoped. Lord Audolon, naked as the day he'd been born, was splayed out across the garishly decorated bed. Around him, small, frail slaves—both male and female—sat quietly, chains at their necks securing them to the unusually thick bedposts. One sat by Audolon's head, feeding him bits of fruit from a large platter. At the end of the room opposite the bed, a young man hung by his arms from a wooden frame. His eyes were closed, and his skin was raw from whatever instrument had been used to beat him. It was a powerful visual that Saraht didn't feel was necessary, but she'd been vague about her instructions.

"What is the meaning of this?" She drew her sword, feigning outrage. "You abandon your host duties to Wedminth's heir in favor of torturing slaves?"

Lord Audolon didn't attempt to rise, and Saraht wondered if it was fear weakening his legs or embarrassment. She'd been clear on what would happen if he didn't participate in her plan in the black-light district, and with the death of his brother so fresh, it was natural for the sight of her to be jarring.

"Go mind your business," he finally ground out, his voice hoarse. "I paid my dues. Just the same as every noble here."

"Disgusting." Saraht spit on the floor. "How dare you call yourself a noble? There's nothing honorable in this … this … depravity."

Audolon propped himself onto his side, not bothering to cover his lower half. "Every noble in the country has been a guest of the Lords of Revelry at least once." He gestured to Ellisand. "Her father included."

"That's not true!" Ellisand stepped forward, and Saraht held out an arm to stop her. "My father—"

"Your father liked them even younger," the naked Audolon spoke over her. "He was no better than any of us and worse than some of us. Don't be a fool."

"Enough." Saraht let her sphere of influence expand, breaking the magic locks on the slaves' bindings. "We're taking them and all of the slaves here. And my master—your future lord—*will* hear about this."

A warden's ability was invisible to those without magic, but the Lords' manor was built with layer upon layer of magical construction and fortifications. Nadir had incorporated magic into everything from the soundproofing in the walls to the intricate locking mechanisms on various confinement devices. Because of that, the entire building shuddered when Saraht extended her arms and expanded her power as far out as the street. Doors flung open, chains shattered, and barriers restricting the movement of servant and patron alike, vanished.

"Ellisand, gather the workers. I'll join you in the hall after I speak with our good Lord Audolon."

"Here, come here." Ellisand motioned for the terrified men and women to join her. "You're safe now, we won't harm you." She ushered them toward the door, looking over her shoulder at Audolon on the bed. "My father would never have come to a place like this," she said matter-of-factly before hurrying through the doorway with a swirl of her skirts.

Alone with the Pardis baron, Saraht smiled and lowered her weapon. She knew better than to say anything out loud; the soundproofing in the walls was gone. She wasn't about to risk Ellisand inadvertently hearing about her scheme. Instead, she nodded and bowed, letting him know she considered her favor honored. She'd leave him in peace, albeit on her leash. He was hers now, another tool in her growing arsenal.

The manor's downfall was just the start. Saraht reconsidered her blind eye toward the rest of the black-light district. If they were liberating slaves, she would liberate them all. Then, she would feed them and clothe them, and they would spread word of her benevolent deeds wherever they went.

CHAPTER
FIFTEEN

A day and a half, the Moon Mother said their journey would take. The distance wasn't far, but the terrain was harsh—a landscape of deep ravines and fragmented rock faces. Laris and Raelyn had to make it past an area the *gonsidhe* called the Shattered Pass, and sliding down the side of a moss-covered rock just to be faced with another to climb over, Raelyn felt it had been aptly named.

Giant shards of stone embedded in the ground rose around them, standing on end. Smaller chunks filled the gaps and created uneven steps between each rock wedge. Looking at the sheer cliffs off to either side of them, she wondered how frequently pieces of the mountains plummeted down to have covered the ground so completely.

She almost ran into Laris's outstretched hand, waiting to assist her over a high stepping stone. Placing her hand in his, she found what purchase she could with her feet on the rock and let him haul her upward.

"We should be almost clear of this area by sundown," he said as he scanned the horizon of protruding rock splinters. "But I don't think we can avoid making camp in the pass."

"How often do you think the rocks fall?" she asked, voicing her concern.

Laris frowned. "Too often for my liking."

They stood there together, taking in the view. The first leg of their journey had been quiet. Raelyn wasn't surprised; Laris was always quiet, especially when marching through the wilderness. Still, she sensed something was on his mind. He wasn't brooding or angry; he still watched over her as he always did, yet his look was distant in the moments he helped her climb rocks or navigate unsure footing. *Maybe he's thinking about the battle to come.* She stole a glance at him, wondering if he was afraid.

"I can see you looking at me, Raelyn," he said, keeping his own eyes forward.

She smiled and playfully bumped him with her shoulder, in good spirits after the days of rest with the *gonsidhe*. "You seem lost in your thoughts," she said gently at his returned half-smile. "Is it the battle we're to face?"

He hopped down from the rock and looked up at her. "Perhaps some. I've never fought a feyfolk lord before, let alone a corrupted one. It wouldn't be wise to go into it overconfident."

"And that's it?" she prodded, ignoring his gesture for her to jump down.

"That's it."

The slight hesitation before he answered her was telling. "You're a horrible liar, you know," she admonished. "After all this time together, I know you better than that."

"Are you going to jump down, or do I have to come up there to get you?"

"It does no good keeping it inside." She pressed her hand over her chest theatrically. "*A joy shared is a joy doubled; a sorrow shared is a sorrow halved*, as I've been told." She had been told many, many times. The image of Ebest's mangled form flashed through her thoughts, and her boldness momentarily faltered.

Laris wordlessly shrugged off his pack and set it on the ground. With a deep breath, he hoisted himself back onto the rock almost effortlessly, much to Raelyn's surprise. "I warned you," he said ominously into her ear.

He'd carried her before, but this was different. Instead of a careful connection borne from life-or-death circumstances, this was a deliberate, claiming hold. He wrapped his arm firmly around her waist and pulled her against him, chest to chest. Stunned, it took her a second to react, but she did so by planting her hands against his chest and pushing away as hard as she could. "What are you—"

He held her tighter, using his other arm to lock her into place. "Stop fighting me, or we're both going to fall," he growled.

"Laris!" she protested, twisting in his arms, trying to escape. During a brief pause in her thrashing, he dropped down to a crouch and shifted his arms to below her buttocks. In one fluid movement, he stood and slung her over his shoulder.

Acutely aware of the feel of his fingers adjusting their position on the back of her thigh and uncomfortable with his shoulder in her stomach, Raelyn stopped resisting. It only took a moment for him to hop down to the ground, but it felt like an eternity for her.

She remained still just long enough for her feet to touch the ground, and then, with an enormous effort, she leaped away—or tried to. The slick moss beneath her feet had other plans. Her foot slipped to the side as she tried to propel away. She lost her balance, toppling into the very person she was trying to get away from.

Laris caught her but couldn't stay upright, and he fell back with her sprawled over the top of him. She lay there for a long moment, defeated and afraid to meet his gaze. "I am so sorry," she mumbled, trying to push herself up. "I didn't—"

Putting his hand on the small of her back, he shifted his weight forward without warning, forcing her onto her backside. Ignoring her gasp of surprise, and without a word, he straddled her upper legs, staring down at her on the ground. He was heavy; he wasn't sparing her his weight. He swatted away her attempt to leverage out from beneath him.

"You didn't tell me your guide was the last Holy King," he finally declared, his voice low.

Wide-eyed, she looked up at him.

Laris placed a hand on either side of her shoulders and leaned closer. "Are there any other details I'm missing?"

Heart pounding, she shook her head. Her chest felt like a giant hand was pressing down on her. She knew he wasn't angry, but she felt nervous just the same. This. *This* was the great equalizer between wardens and mages. For all her strength to shut magic out of the world, she was as vulnerable to physical injury as anyone else. Even more so, because she lacked any realistic martial training, she was at his mercy.

"Good." His gaze swept over her face, lingering on her mouth. "No more secrets."

"Why ..." Her voice came out as a broken whisper. He was so close it was the only amount of sound she could put between them. "Why does that matter?"

Laris's eyes flicked up to hers. "You don't think it's important that the last Holy King, the direct conduit to Emblem, has been your guiding light since birth?"

She parted her lips to defend herself, but he gently clamped a hand over her mouth. "No," he cautioned her, "just listen. I know now, without a doubt, you're on a fated path. Lives will be at stake. Ours and many others. You're destined for something, Raelyn, and it's my duty as a transcendent of the Holy King to see you to it." He was almost nose to nose with her, the breath of his words skirting across her face. At that moment, she swore she could feel his heartbeat pounding as fiercely as hers.

She stared into his eyes, absorbing what he'd said but distracted by what she saw in his gaze. There was softness there but also something intense, hungry. His hand over her mouth was firm but not crushing, his skin warm. She could feel its roughness brush her lips—the hand of a warrior.

She wasn't sure how long they'd been staring at one another when he closed his eyes with a long blink and turned his head. "Tell me to get off of you," he said, gravel to his voice. "Do it. Say the words." He moved his hand away from her mouth.

Bewildered at the sudden change in him, she didn't say anything at first, only then realizing more of the length of his body had pressed against her during his speech. She drew in an unsteady breath.

"Get ... off?" The words were so soft and hesitant they were more of a breathy question than a command.

He turned his face back to hers, their eyes briefly meeting before his dropped to her lips again. "Emblem's Hand, what's the matter with you?" he muttered. "That's not how you should say it in the least."

He kissed her then, hungrily at first and then gently at the sounds of surprise she made against his mouth.

Raelyn had never been kissed, but she knew the moment their lips touched, she wanted Laris to kiss her. She followed his lead, vaguely aware of his hand in her hair at the back of her head, his other hand cupping her cheek. She held on to his arms, unsure what to do with her hands. Feeling the need to shift her position off the uneven rocks at her back, she scooted her hips slightly and felt his whole body go stone-still.

He held her face in his hands and pressed his forehead to hers, his eyes closed. "Don't do that," he told her. "I'll get up now."

"But I didn't—"

He nodded and kissed her forehead. "I know. Just trust me." He pushed away from her and gained his feet.

She sat up, feeling flushed and lightheaded. She was embarrassed but also giddy. Laris offered his hand and helped her up. Before she could turn away, he captured her chin between his fingers and made her look up.

"Don't dismiss my intentions," he said firmly. "That wasn't a mistake or some passing fancy. I don't intend on returning to how things were between us before." More gently, he added, "Don't be embarrassed. I've wanted to do that for a long time, and I plan on doing it again."

Heart skipping in her chest like a stone across water, she nodded, unable to translate her thoughts into words while he stared at her. With a brief caress of her cheek, Laris let her go and turned to resume their trek. She waited long enough for him to be out of earshot before letting out a long exhale. *He plans on doing it again.* She touched her lips. *How in the world am I supposed to prepare for that?* Grumbling to herself, she broke free of her trance and jogged to catch up.

They cleared the Shattered Pass just as darkness blanketed the mountains. On Dar'Liha's advice, they kept no fire. The *gonsidhe* had warned them it wouldn't be wise to attract unexpected enemies on their way to Mondek's lair.

Bedroll open and rations in hand, Raelyn sat at the base of one of the last cliff shards at the end of the pass. She stared up at the night sky, searching for stars, but the curtain of sunset was slow to draw back, and only a few pinpoints of light were bright enough to stand out.

The events of the day felt surreal as they played in a loop within her mind. She glanced over at Laris as he did inventory on his pack. Had what happened between them been real? Had she dreamed it? After all they'd been through together, she had to finally face why her heart raced in his presence. She wondered when his deeper feelings for her had developed. Was it the same as for her—that moment he'd walked over to her at the Wedminth banquet?

Despite still feeling self-conscious about their interaction, Raelyn was relieved he showed no hint of regret or disappointment. He'd behaved just as he always had; he'd spoken to her just as he always had.

The only difference now was that he'd taken her hand freely several times as they'd climbed up and down the rocks rather than waiting for her to accept his offers of help.

"We should talk about our battle strategy," he said, walking over to sit beside her. "We'll get there midday tomorrow, which leaves us to fight in the confines of the tomb or wait to draw him out into the grove at dusk."

"Maybe you'll have a better sense of which when we get there." Raelyn offered him a bit of her bread. "What is it you want me to do?"

"You're going to stay out of sight and definitely out of harm's way," he replied, taking the ration. "I'm going to need you to neutralize our magic. I'll stand a better chance if he and I are both limited to our physical strength."

"Are you certain? Wouldn't it be easier to use your magic to bury him before he comes outside?"

"I'm skilled in weaving stone magic, yes, but I doubt it would be so easy to kill one of the feyfolk. We can't risk it. And to use fire magic, I'd need you to tend a flame. If it went out, I'd have nothing to pull from."

She frowned, picking at the remaining bread in her hand.

"You don't have to worry, Raelyn. I wouldn't have accepted this task if I didn't think I could. I've won against worse odds."

She sat silently, thinking about what he'd said. "Is it hard?" She flicked a few crumbs to the ground. "To constantly face death in battle?"

He didn't reply right away. "It gets easier," he finally said. "At first, when you're just a foot soldier, you live in constant fear. With time, some battle hardening, and some victories, the fear isn't as pressing. You come to accept death as the price all warriors pay. It's either your day or it isn't."

She looked at him with disbelief. "Tell me you don't believe that. What about things like honor and conviction and righteousness? All those things that are supposed to help a warrior be free of fear?"

He snorted at the forcefulness of her words. "Fairy stories paint an unrealistic picture of heroes. Fear isn't something to be cast out completely. It keeps us alert and alive. It helps us appreciate our blessings and opportunities."

She bit her lip and looked up at the new wash of stars across the sky. She was afraid and spent a lot of time trying to get rid of her fear. Maybe he was right. Perhaps she needed to accept that sometimes she just had to do things while afraid.

"Do you remember the night we met face to face in the watch tower?"

His question effectively snapped her attention back. "How could I forget? I thought you were going to kill me."

"I was trying to figure you out. I knew you were a warden right away, and I needed to know if you were working for the Wedminths or against them. We should have been informed about you since I was a mage in the Lomnir party. No one said anything before our arrival or after, so I couldn't be certain you weren't a spy from another country."

"That's why you threatened me?"

"*Warned.* I warned you. I didn't threaten you."

She rolled her eyes at him. "You had a dagger in your hand. You pinned me against the wall!"

There was a hint of a grin on his face. "There were other reasons I did that."

Heat rolled through her body at his words and the memory of his closeness that night. "You were not kind to me at all," she said matter-of-factly, raising an eyebrow at his feigned innocence. "You even denied my attempt to get you to dance during the banquet. It was supposed to be a peace offering."

"I was doing my best to keep you away," he replied, "even though I was the one who kept seeking you out."

Shaking her head with a shy smile, she had to look away from him. The blink of a small light caught her eye, and Raelyn realized the air was twinkling with lightning bugs. Pointing them out, she excitedly tugged on Laris's arm. "Oh, look! Look how they've filled our camp."

He let her hang on to him and stared at the small area with their supplies and bedrolls. "I think they're saying it's time we turn in. We can discuss more of the plan in the morning."

She nodded, reluctant to move away from his warmth but still too uncertain about their bond to push for staying close. "To bed, then," she said, standing. "Let me take a turn at watch so you can rest?"

"Just this once." He pointed to her bedroll. "You sleep first. I'll wake you."

Some time later, he did wake her, much to her surprise, but she was grateful. She wanted to be useful, not just some helpless fool who'd spent her life protected behind castle walls. That he was trusting her so he could get some sleep made her extremely happy.

"Don't try anything brave," he whispered to her. "If you see something suspicious, wake me up immediately."

"Of course." She picked up Famine. "I promise."

He stared at her accusingly, and she shooed him away. "I promise. I promise. Go to sleep."

Raelyn watched Laris settle into his bedroll under a rock outcropping across the camp from where she sat. Her vantage point provided a clear view of their surroundings, though, she couldn't make out much in the near-complete darkness. The moon was now obscured by clouds, and there was a faint earthy smell in the air foretelling of rain. It was chilly.

How nice it would be to see Hendrel's light, she thought, scanning the darkness. She was worried about him, though, the Moon Mother's words had lifted her spirits some. Until Laris pointed it out, she hadn't focused on the fact Hendrel was the last true Holy King. Since he'd always been with her, it was easy to forget that spirit guides weren't common. To think it was random circumstance that brought them together, given what she was, made her realize her naïveté.

She let her gaze wander along the edges of what she could make out in the darkness, mindlessly tracing the almost invisible silhouettes of rocks and scraggy undergrowth by their camp. Every so often, when the moon broke through the clouds, she could see farther up the open valley in the direction they were headed. It was a few hours before her prediction proved true, and the first tiny droplets of rain peppered her face, carried in by a sudden gust of wind.

Laris was mostly protected from the change in the weather, but Raelyn watched his form closely for any signs of waking. It would be just her luck for him to miss out on sleep due to rain when he'd finally agreed to let her take a turn at watch. She slid off her rock perch and quietly crossed the camp, scooping up her bedroll, now damp from the spitting precipitation. Walking over to where Laris lay, she opened up the blanket and draped it over the edge of the outcropping, wedging it into cracks in the rock and securing it as best she could in the darkness. Satisfied it would help shield him at least a little, she turned around to go back to her post.

She froze mid-step. Fifty paces from her, near where she'd been sitting watch, was a large, irregular mass. Its shifting form was darker than the night around it, but it blended in with the darkness so well Raelyn couldn't be sure of its actual size. It was moving, gliding, almost slithering, it seemed, along the ground by the rock, as if looking for her. In a passing moment of moonlight, she saw it rise, a nightmarish twist of flesh, branches, bones, and tattered robes towering at least three heights of a man.

It couldn't see her, she suspected, or they'd have been dead already. Stepping backward with a slow, deliberate movement, she kept her eyes locked on the creature for any indication it was aware of her. It gave none, but with the moon again hidden behind the gathering rainclouds, Raelyn didn't trust her senses. She inched her way back toward Laris, hoping she could wake him without giving them both away as the rain picked up, careening down from the sky in thick sheets.

Her hand brushed the wet fabric of the makeshift weather flap, and she eased down to a crouch, still watching the inky spot across the camp that marked the creature's whereabouts. She could no longer tell what it was doing, but it didn't seem to be approaching yet. With painstaking care, she pushed the bedroll fabric aside, praying it didn't dislodge from the rock. Shifting into the shallow area with Laris, she let the weather flap fall silently back into place.

Being unable to see whatever was lurking outside was terrifying. Raelyn acted quickly, pressing her hand across Laris's mouth in one fluid movement as she half crouched, half sprawled next to him. His hand covered hers immediately, and she realized he'd already been awake. There was no need for words, which were too risky, even if whispered. She knew Laris sensed her fear and urgency.

He carefully moved her hand away and eased her back against the rock, indicating he wanted her to stay there. She felt him moving, searching for the hilt of one of his weapons, and he shifted to his knees. He reached for the end of the hanging bedroll and moved it just enough to see out into the night.

She cried out, startled, as the weather flap was ripped aside, and Laris was taken with it as the creature dragged him from their cover. Before Raelyn even knew what was happening, he was gone. Rain pelted her face, forcing her eyes shut, and she heard him shout something indecipherable. Desperate, she wiped her face to disrupt the veil of rainwater obscuring her sight and peeled her eyes open against the sting of the water. She strained to hear his voice again and hunted for him through her blurry vision.

A soft, blue light arced through the darkness, providing just enough brightness for Raelyn to see the outlines of Laris and the creature in the camp clearing. The transcendent, free from his attacker's hold, had drawn Blue Deimos. The blade's glow was more a part of the strange metal than a source of illumination, and it cast a faint aura across Laris's arm, barely brighter than a flickering candle. In the depths of the night, however, it was the only light standing between them and the unseen.

The creature loomed over Laris as if studying him. Though its features were lost in shadows created by the sword's light mixing with the dark of night, Raelyn could see a crown of bones and twisted branches poking out from beneath the remnants of a hooded cloak. As it leaned in, the light caught its eyes, revealing the translucent, sightless orbs of a creature accustomed to dwelling in complete darkness.

It's blind, she realized. That's why it couldn't find her after she'd left her post.

Laris was on one knee, holding Blue Deimos out as a guard. He was injured, she could tell, and was waiting for his opponent to force a move. Remembering what they'd spoken about the day before, Raelyn felt for the void. Was this Mondek? It had to be. But there'd been no signs of magic yet. If she expanded her sphere of influence for a creature without magic, she might take away Laris's best chance of defense.

A vibration in the air around her banished any doubts. The vibration thrummed throughout the camp, raising rocks and chunks of soil with it. The creature extended its arm and pointed a gnarled finger, and the debris in the air stilled just long enough for Laris to protect himself before it turned into a storm of projectiles.

Arms outstretched, hands and fingers working, shaping a force invisible to Raelyn, he hastily threw up shields of rock, pulling them with a sweeping gesture from the ground in thick sections. It saved him from the barrage but not from his opponent's swing, which shattered the rocky barriers as if they were made of glass.

Raelyn hesitated no longer. She let the void expand around them. It was a faster expansion than she'd practiced, less controlled but still within her power to call back. When it reached the two combatants, she *felt* their magic absorb into her invisible wave.

A piercing shriek erupted from the creature's throat. It turned toward her, aware of her now that she'd touched it with her power. She dove for her glaive and Laris's other sword as the monstrosity bore down, galloping across the distance between them on all fours.

Touching the sword scabbard at the moment its bony hand grabbed her around the waist, she screamed at the feel of its fingers digging into her abdomen. Its rotting flesh came away in handfuls as she desperately pulled at it, her other arm jabbing ineffectively with the sword still in its scabbard. The creature pressed her into the ground, leaning its weight into the hold it had on her. The scent of decay, earth, and old parchment flooded Raelyn's senses. She cried out in agony.

It abruptly let her go, issuing a cry of its own as Blue Deimos found purchase in the flesh of its back. Laris mercilessly ripped the short sword out, plunging the weapon into his adversary again to capitalize on the weakness. Mondek let the strike land on his forearm. He used their closeness as an opportunity to slash down with both clawed hands, Blue Deimos still embedded in his body. Laris let go of the weapon but couldn't get clear in time to avoid the attack. A deep gash opened across his chest, the force of the hit knocking him onto his back.

Raelyn lay belly down in the dirt, watching through blurred vision. She was bleeding, the warm creep of blood fanning out on the ground beneath her. Her pain changed from lancing licks of white-hot fire to a growing smolder, present and consuming but not maddening. She wondered if she was dying. Amidst her swimming vision, she noticed the first edges of dawn creeping up over the mountain peaks.

A strange headiness overcame her. She felt separated from her body, watching as Mondek slithered over to where Laris was trying and failing to get back onto his feet. The monster was wounded. Shimmering, wet streaks of telling of blood on its body glistened in the growing twilight of dawn.

Two spheres of void pulsated within her core, cold and heavy. She could feel them as distinctly as if they were held in her hands. They were expanded out into the camp, masquerading as one sphere of influence, but she could see the divide. She could see infinite divides. Slowly, like separating strands of hair from a knot, she pulled them apart from one another, keeping them touching, careful not to pull back and inadvertently restore Mondek's powers. When a clear line of division formed, she tried to withdraw the side locking out Laris's abilities.

It wouldn't come. Both spheres shrank inward, and she quickly extended them again. Her focus was wavering. Still on her belly, she thrust her arms out and spread her fingers wide on each hand. On Laris's side, she visualized pulling the void as she closed her fingers; on Mondek's side, she pushed outward with a flat palm. The physical aid gave her the advantage she needed, and she felt her influence over Laris seep back. He'd cautioned her about returning his abilities to him without warning, but she had no choice. She wasn't sure she had the strength to call out to him.

When she knew he was free, she worked on maintaining her control over their enemy.

The rain stopped. At some unknown moment, a fog had settled around them. *Why isn't he moving?* Raelyn watched the scene unfolding with desperation. Why wasn't Laris attacking? Didn't he know he had his powers back? Tears rolled down her face as Mondek hoisted him into the air by one of his arms.

The sound of breaking rock echoed around them, so thunderous that Raelyn thought a piece of the mountain was tumbling down. The ground at Mondek's feet split open, pushed aside by a giant stone hand on an arm of bedrock. It punched out of the ground, holding Blue Deimos in its clenched grasp, the blade no more than a kitchen knife in the giant grip. It burst forth, impaling the corrupted feyfolk lord straight through his chest, the shining blue of the blade erupting through bone and rotting flesh, held aloft against the last glimpses of the night sky.

Laris dropped to the ground where he lay, unmoving but breathing.

Raelyn let go of the last thread of strength she'd been clinging to. It was over. She could finally close her eyes.

CHAPTER
SIXTEEN

Towns grew frequent the closer Saraht's party got to the capital, some blending together through a string of farms unclaimed by any formal community. Unlike the grasslands, the northern region of Limnin was fertile and rich. Crops grew fruitfully without much tending; rain was regular but not hindering, and sunlight was commonplace more days than naught.

As much as she loved the mystery of Uhmeer's grasslands, Saraht deeply appreciated the tall, majestic trees of the north. When clustered together, they made dark, foreboding forests that protected from wind and weather, and when solitary on a distant hill, they reminded her of giant sentinels standing watch against some ancient doom.

Her horse stumbled, struggling out of a deep wagon mark on the muddy road recently soaked by early morning rain. She glanced over at Ellisand riding tall on a dappled gelding, the young woman quieter since their time spent in Pardis. Behind them, seated on the back of a barrel-bellied mare, Maylam dozed in and out, rocking with the sway of the plucky bay beneath her.

They hadn't talked much about the events in Pardis or about their liberation of black-light districts in several other towns along the way, but Saraht wasn't worried by the lack of conversation. She felt assured Ellisand now realized she wasn't someone to underestimate or manipulate. The deception at the dinner party was a one-time success, and only because Saraht had allowed it to be so. She knew the Wedminth heir was warring with the carefully crafted revelation about her father while still coping with feelings about his untimely death. Deny the allegations as she might, Ellisand wouldn't be able to unhear them or disprove them. Like a slowly gathering rainstorm, the cloud over her father's integrity would build until it released a rain of resentment. It didn't matter that the claims made by Audolon against the duke had been false. Ellisand's emotional detachment from her parents was fertile soil for the seed of doubt about her father. By the time she realized the deception—if she ever did—it would be too late to change anything.

Saraht decided she would share her ultimate plan with her soon. Even if Ellisand wasn't fully won to their cause, the choice between Saraht's righteous aim and a stagnant station under King Rothelian's thumb seemed easy, especially with the duke's muddied reputation.

"We'll be coming up on Golinstone soon," she announced. "We'll stay at the inn for a few nights while my men catch up and make camp along the Ven."

Ellisand nodded, pointing toward a dark line of trees in the distance. "Is that the Arn Hollow? The Ven runs along its edge, does it not?"

"The cursed forest itself. They say one of the mad mages from the Cataclysm still walks its borders. A perfect place for Orion to make camp, I daresay."

The road worsened right before entry into Golinstone, chewed into a thick slop by travelers, wagons, and horses converging. They passed under a tall archway where the town's faded banner flapped lazily in the breeze. It was so deteriorated from exposure to the elements the insignia was barely visible, colors washed to a dingy grey.

Saraht was Limninian, even though she served Faldea, and the Inn at Golinstone Fork was known to her. Years ago, when she was just a child, the innkeeper and his wife sheltered her and Maylam after they'd escaped from the capital. Saraht remembered being terrified of the tall, burly man and his equally masculine partner when they'd discovered her and her mother hiding in the stables. Rather than cast them out, Jormand and Penelope had fed them, clothed them, and let them stay in one of the inn's largest rooms while they regained some strength of mind and body.

She'd been a faithful patron ever since.

"Here we are," she said, dismounting at the front of the building. She handed her reins off to a young boy who came running from the stable. "We're about half a day from Osharia. We'll rest here and finalize the plan while we're in the city."

Ellisand slid off her horse. "I've never stayed at an inn before," she commented as she studied the ivy-covered stone walls. "Imagine the stories people staying here must have. I can't wait to see what it's like."

There's a bit of her personality returning. Saraht smiled and motioned toward the door. "Go on, I'll help Mother in. They should be expecting us."

Once she assisted her mother off her bay, the two walked arm in arm to the door. The main bar room was surprisingly busy for midday—and loud. Despite the sunlight filtering through a few windows, the atmosphere was dark and private, even with the enveloping noise. Benches with backs that climbed to the ceiling created private alcoves along the wall, and a few round tables occupied the open center of the floor adjacent to the fireplace. The center seats were congested with men and women dressed in bright colors, their laughter culminating into a great roar that drowned any other conversation.

Saraht guided Maylam to a seat at the bar and motioned for Ellisand to join them. "Jormand should be out soon," she said. "With this many guests, he's likely restocking the mead casks."

They didn't have to wait long before the innkeeper barged in through a curtain blocking the kitchen. He was just as she remembered him. Tall enough to tower over most men, he had broad shoulders that blocked out much of the mirror on the wall behind the bar. The auburn of his hair and beard was touched by more silver than the last time she'd visited, but his grey eyes were just as kind and friendly as they'd always been.

"Ahhaha!" He slapped a hand down on the bar, catching sight of her. "Pen told me you'd be arriving before the new moon. What a welcome sight you are, girl." Jormand looked over at Ellisand and Maylam. "Miss Maylam." He offered her a low bow. "And … ?"

Ellisand grabbed his hand and gave it a firm shake. "Ellisand," she said. "You're the innkeeper? Tell me, who are all those people dressed like wayfarers?"

Raising his eyebrows in amused surprise at her boldness, he motioned for her to lean in closer. "They *are* wayfarers," he whispered dramatically. "Stopping over before they head to the capital for their yearly performance. I hear some are talented acrobats, and one even has animals in her act."

"Incredible," Ellisand breathed back. "Is that a cat she has on her lap?'

"Indeed. Only cat I've ever seen that listens to a human's bidding."

"If you're done bewitching my companion, I think we have some rooms waiting for us," Saraht interjected. "There will be plenty of time to admire the performance troupe. I'd be surprised if they don't break out their instruments after last meal."

"Right, right." Jormand reached under the bar and fished out two keys. "Your usual room and the one across the hall. Did Mikel see to your horses? Boy's been harder to pin down than a greased goose on a feast day."

Saraht patted his shoulder. "All is well. These will do," she said, taking the keys. "We'll be down for last meal. Tell Pen I'm looking forward to her famous stew and homemade bread."

"She's been talking about it for days now. Go on. Give a holler if things are amiss."

Ellisand offered Maylam her arm, and Saraht watched the innkeeper disappear behind the curtain again. *The only man I'll ever love,* she thought affectionately. Just as she went to make her way toward the stairs, a large cat leaped up onto the bar and snagged her attention. Its green, jewel-like eyes held her stare with equal curiosity as it sat authoritatively on the bar edge.

"Cats," she muttered, shaking her head. "Ungovernable creatures."

The cat's eyes narrowed contentedly as if in response.

"Come." Saraht turned back toward her companions. "There are some things we need to discuss before we carry on with our journey."

The rooms of the Inn at Golinstone Fork were always cozier than Saraht felt inn rooms should be. The beds were large and the mattresses soft. There were more pillows than necessary, and great care had been given in selecting various paintings and decorations which added a sense of comfort. There was even a carpet—a luxury rarely used on strangers who could get to all manner of mischief behind their closed doors.

Letting Ellisand settle into the room across the hall, Saraht helped her mother lie down on the bed and cleared off the small table near the fireplace. She removed her copy of Raloria's grimoire from her saddle bags. Placing it gently on the table, she took a moment to appreciate the red leather flecked with gold, an outline of the goddess embossed on the cover.

The grimoire had been given to her when she was barely ten years old. An old priestess in red robes had been preaching Raloria's gospel one day in a town at the Faldean border. She'd spotted Saraht in the crowd and approached her, somehow knowing—or correctly guessing—the misery she'd been through.

The pitch had been irresistible. A world before the Cataclysm where women were rulers, scholars, and respected philosophers. They led nations, shared technologies, and used the powers of magic to control their more dangerous and volatile counterparts: men. It was all made possible through Raloria, Seventh Pillar of The Circle, who spoke to the people through her divine disciple, the warden Alyna.

But soon, other gods began influencing the world with the help of their wardens, enslaving or empowering different peoples, and the uprisings began. It was only a matter of time before women, who'd had no prior need to dedicate their lives to the mastery of battle, were overtaken by the savage nature and brute strength that was man.

Saraht was going to change all that. She was going to usher in a new age for the women of the world, one where they didn't have to walk down dark streets in fear or need a husband to prove their worth. With Ellisand on the throne as an ally and Orion's forces controlling the castle, she'd be free to search for the place the priestesses spoke of—the Sundered Gate.

It was time to fully involve Ellisand. The Wedminth heir was essential to the Faldean plan and Saraht's agenda to bring Raloria's rule back to the mortal realm.

She walked out and crossed the hall, knocking on the other room's door. Ellisand opened it without hesitation, her freshly scrubbed face gleaming and water droplets dripping from her hair.

"It's time to finalize our plans," Saraht said quietly. "Come speak with me in my room."

Ellisand followed her readily, which was relieving and unnerving at the same time. All of the young woman's mannerisms and behaviors suggested she was happy to follow Saraht's lead. Not a step was out of place, no hesitations present. Her expressions were genuine and friendly, even if subdued at times. Something almost too perfect about it all kept Saraht guarded. There was nothing Ellisand could do to harm her or her cause, but she remained uneasy. She didn't fully trust the Wedminth heir.

Inside her room, Saraht brought Ellisand over to the table. "You remember this?" she asked. "I showed you a copy of this book when we first met."

Ellisand nodded.

"Good. All that I do, all that I am, is because of this." She tapped the cover. "I'm sure you've been taught of the Deceivers, the goddesses who sought control over mortals through lies and manipulation." At Ellisand's hum of admission, Saraht said, "It's true, Raloria is considered one of those three goddesses—but she is no Deceiver. The truth is Raloria was a patron of women rulers before the Cataclysm, and when men overturned the matriarchy, they conveniently decided she—a Pillar, mind you, as she fought on Emblem's side—was as evil as the chaos goddesses Delvia and Fayla. They rewrote history against her to keep women subservient. I've seen the original scripts, Ellisand. They are kept in a temple in Faldea."

"How do you know the scripts are real?" Ellisand asked.

The question was innocent and expected, but Saraht couldn't help feeling scathed by its implication. "When you hold those ancient parchments in your hands, knowing they would turn to dust without the magic woven around them, you feel their authenticity as clearly as you feel the warmth of the sun on a winter day. I'll show you the temple one day, introduce you to the priestesses, and any doubts you have will vanish."

At the Wedminth heir's quiet acceptance, Saraht continued. "My spiritual commitments aside, you've known for some time now that I am an intricate part of Faldea's invasion process. Their king regent and my master, Prince Thiir, wants full control of Uhmeer. As Faldea's only neighbor sharing borders, Limnin is his first conquest."

She studied Ellisand's face. The other woman gave her full attention, listening politely. She sat on one of the chairs at the table, arms folded across one another.

Saraht continued. "The capital of Osharia is the heart of Limnin, and you're aware of my sworn oath against King Rothelian. Taking the capital and killing the king are both a part of Thiir's plan.

"You've proven yourself to be trustworthy and an asset, Ellisand. Rather than simply give you your birthright duchy, Thiir would offer you the throne, and I would offer you a part in a larger plan to liberate the women of Uhmeer in the name of Raloria."

She let the words hang between them, hiding the totality of her true intentions. Ellisand didn't need to know about the Gate or Saraht's reasons for seeking it. That part of the plan didn't involve her, and letting the Wedminth heir in on the details only increased the likelihood the plan might be spoiled. Saraht couldn't take the risk.

Ellisand stared at her for a long moment, seemingly warring with her own thoughts before asking in a hushed tone, "What are you suggesting?"

"Nothing unsavory on your part," Saraht assured her. "A minor role, really. You just need to arrange my entry into the castle. I'll take care of the rest, and Orion will use his magic to infiltrate and take control of the castle without directly engaging Rothelian's army in the city."

She looked at Ellisand pointedly. "The king has no male heirs. With him dead, the title will fall to you. Prince Thiir will support your claim on the condition that you swear fealty to him. With you on the throne, we can work together to see other women ascend to pinnacle positions of power in Limnin and throughout Uhmeer."

"I don't know what to say." Ellisand sat back, the color drained from her face. "I thought after what happened in Pardis, you'd never trust me again."

Saraht was pleased to hear Ellisand's remorse. Maybe her betrayal really had been just a desperate ploy rather than part of a larger scheme. "We chose you because we believe in you," she said carefully. "I *want* you to be there, Ellisand, at the head of the new world. The people will give you their full support. We can rebuild the world together without any major bloodshed."

Maylam let out a soft chuckle from her position on the bed and swung her legs over the side, wagging a finger. "My children, you are forgetting the most important part. You will be free, finally free, to be human. No more suitors, no more hours spent cinched into decorative dresses. No more silly refinement classes for skills you won't use. You won't have to open your legs for the sake of politics or push out babies until your body is used up. You'll never have to sit and listen to a man oversimplify an explanation ever again. What price can be put on such freedom?"

"The choice is yours," Saraht told Ellisand. "As a noblewoman, you know well where your fate lies under the rule of men like Rothelian."

Ellisand looked from Saraht to Maylam and to the book on the table. She reached out and gently let her fingertips trace the leather bindings. "Being queen doesn't sound all that bad," she said slyly.

Saraht smiled back. "Excellent." She pressed her palms to the table-top and leaned in for effect. "Now, let's go see about last meal."

The change in focus instantly banished the pervasive sense of apprehension and secrecy clouding the room, and Ellisand nodded enthusiastically, hopping to her feet while Maylam shuffled from her spot on the bed toward the door.

The dining area was congested with bodies and hot breath, pipe smoke, and steam from the kitchen. The colorful band of wayfarers still occupied the central tables, some guests so inebriated they slept in their spots. The orange cat from earlier was taking advantage of the troupe's distraction, stealthily sneaking away bites of food, indifferent to the occasional outcry when caught.

"Business looks good," Saraht said loudly to Jormand.

The innkeeper was hustling back and forth behind the bar, slamming draughts of ale and plates of food down for the serving girls to take to customers. He slid some mugs their way. "Been a right party here for days now." He gestured toward the wayfarers. "They seem to have bottomless coin for a profession rumored to be poor as salted farmland."

"Do they ever sleep?"

"Only if they've had too much to drink." He barked out orders to one of the girls on the floor. "The only one who ever leaves this room is that damned cat."

Almost as if it knew it had been mentioned, the cat emerged from beneath one of the tables and strolled over to them. It sat on its haunches, looking up at Jormand, and he sighed. "The furry beast knows I've a soft spot for it. They say he's some type of special cat. Does seem smarter than half the lads in here."

Ellisand knelt and extended her hand to the feline. "I won't hurt you." She rubbed her fingers together to catch its attention. The cat accepted her offering, brushing the side of its chin against her fingertips.

"Mother, what do you know about 'special' cats?" Saraht turned to Maylam.

Maylam shook her head. "There is nothing that I recall, dear one. If there were anything of note, the priestesses would have told you during your training. Faldea was good at keeping the old knowledge alive, if nothing else."

"Be careful using that name too loudly," Saraht cautioned in a low voice. "This close to the capital, people get opinionated."

Maylam squeezed her daughter's arm affectionately. "Forget the cat, and let's have some supper."

CHAPTER SEVENTEEN

It smells like horses. Raelyn partially opened her eyes. She expected to see the large animals surrounding her, the air fragrant with the smell of leather and the lather of horse sweat. As her vision adjusted to the brightness of day, she realized her hands and feet were bound. A mat made of woven grass protected her from the dampness of the dirt, and a tight bandage cinched her belly. She was a few feet from where she'd watched Mondek's final moments.

Laris. She twisted on the mat, scanning the camp frantically. There were other figures in the clearing. A few stood beside the body of the feyfolk lord, pointing up and talking amongst themselves. She couldn't tell if they were human. They stood with their backs to her, white robes and head garbs concealing any identifiable features. Beyond them, leaning against an old, fallen tree trunk, Laris met her questing gaze. He was bound, as well, and gagged. His shirt had been removed to treat his wound, now covered in heavy bandaging.

She let out a deep breath in relief. As long as he was alive, that was all that mattered.

"Do not shift around so." A white-robed figure approached her. "It was not easy to patch your wounds."

Raelyn studied the speaker silently, trying to determine who or what she was dealing with. Only the front of the man's face was visible within the white scarf coiled around his head and neck. At first glance, he appeared human, but the more intently she looked, the more his appearance felt *off*. His skin was taut and smooth, pale with a hue of autumn gold. Something was too sharp about his features, and his close-set eyes were piercing like those of a predatory bird.

"I am called Aetris," he said, kneeling next to her. "Are you in pain?"

She wasn't, to her surprise, aside from a dull ache at the back of her skull. She shook her head, distracted, condensing the void at her core into a tight ball. *I can't let them know what I am,* she thought, watching Aetris for any sign he'd recognized her power while she'd been unconscious.

"That is good," he replied, unfazed by the internal fluctuations in her control. "We did not expect to find you and your companion here. We had few medicines. Your name?"

Raelyn halfheartedly tried to tug her hands apart. "Are we captives?"

"Yes. The mage has killed a lord of the feyfolk and broken ancient law. He is dangerous and must be punished."

"Punished?" A wave of cold washed over her, and she continued to wiggle her wrists against the straps. "We were sent here by the *gonsidhe.* They told us Mondek was corrupted."

"Does that give you the right to take his life?"

Caught off guard by the brusque question, she let herself fall back onto the grass mat, unsure how to respond. At the time, the answer had been clear in the Moon Mother's garden. Mondek had been lost in hatred, killing indiscriminately—but did that give them the right to kill him? Faced with the reality that not all feyfolk shared the *gonsidhe*'s view, she couldn't answer the unexpected, accusing inquiry.

"We will take you to the roost and decide about you there. Do not worry. We like humans." He smirked. "Tell me your name."

The way he spoke made Raelyn's stomach turn, the unusual lilt to his tone suggesting a hidden meaning within the words. "Raelyn," she murmured. "My name is Raelyn."

Without warning, Aetris reached out and lifted a handful of her hair. He felt the strands between his fingertips before letting them fall with a soft, "How interesting, Raelyn."

Her stomach knotted again, and she shifted on the grass mat uncomfortably. Glancing over at his companions, Aetris straightened and left her without explanation. One of the robed strangers led a pack of stocky ponies into the clearing, their stout bodies boasting thick frames and muscled necks—clearly a breed accustomed to living in the demanding mountain landscape. Neither Laris nor Raelyn were in any condition to travel on foot, and their captors debated for a time about the best way to transport them.

They eventually helped Laris onto the back of one of the ponies, positioned between packs, and carried Raelyn to a makeshift sled hitched to a reddish-brown mare with four white socks. Nervous about being dragged along the rugged terrain, Raelyn tested her bonds again. She knew freedom wouldn't change their circumstances, but being restrained limited her ability to buffer the jostle of their journey. She gave Laris a small smile and nod of reassurance as he looked back at her, but she saw her doubt and worry mirrored in his eyes.

At Aetris's urging, she tentatively climbed onto the sled and settled back against the furs. Sending silent prayers to Genevive for a smooth ride, she gripped the saplings of the frame as best she could and braced for the first lurching movements of the pony. A warm sensation blossomed beneath her bandage as they staggered forward, and Raelyn tried to relax with the sway rather than resist it, knowing the tension was aggravating her wounds despite their numbness.

Traveling in the wobbly sled required patience. The ponies were surefooted, but with no road to speak of, Raelyn was forced to learn the art of shifting her weight to avoid toppling over. The group stopped often to reassess her transport, and she offered to ride astride rather than be dragged along the ground, but they refused her.

After a full day's slow meandering through the valley and foothills beyond Shattered Pass, the group finally reached their destination—what her captors referred to as "the roost." Sheltered within the tall, straight trunks of mountain pines, the fortress all but merged with the landscape, its walls and levels staggered like the crumbled boulders of a mountain. Built to incorporate the uneven terrain, the wooden structure was like nothing Raelyn had ever seen.

She rolled from one side to the other as the ponies walked through the gateway, staring up at level after level of intricately carved wood beams, staircases, and archways that framed the courtyard. When the group halted just past the entry, she was so caught up in her surroundings she barely noticed they'd stopped moving.

"Come," Aetris said, walking back to where she lay. "Rushlem is waiting."

Raelyn inhaled a sharp breath when she stood, surprised by the change in his appearance. Scarf pulled back, Aetris's angular face was framed by slender, brown feathers where she'd expected human hair. Longer feathers lay smooth down the back of his head and neck in a glossy cascade. And though the front of his open cloak revealed feathering partially covering his collar bones, his throat was bare.

"You did not know we are *vehsidhe*," he stated, scrutinizing her reaction. "You have never seen a griffin-born?"

She'd never even heard of a griffin-born. "No," she replied carefully. "This is my first time so far into the mountains."

"Prepare yourself then. You are about to meet many."

He firmly pushed her to walk in front of him toward another gate leading into the inner part of the roost. She stood with Laris while the giant doors slowly opened, finding comfort in his nearness. Still gagged and bound at the hands, he stood tall, shoulders back, as though his injuries were already long healed. She briefly wondered what medicine the *vehsidhe* had used on their wounds for such thorough relief. Her older injuries, though mostly healed, still held a lingering ache that was more bothersome than her more recent and severe wounds.

The interior of the wooden keep was no less grand than the entry courtyard. Everywhere Raelyn looked, detailed carvings embellished even the most unimportant furnishings. The air smelled of polished ancient lumber and velvet curtains, reminding her of the atmosphere in a well-loved library. Striking a sharp contrast to the dark wood floors and pillars, evenly spaced white wall panels livened up the hallway they walked through. As they passed other corridors and rooms, *vehsidhe* peered out in curiosity. Some intrigued, others concerned. Raelyn caught a few looks she felt were disapproving.

"We are not used to hosting strangers," Aetris said from behind her. "They look at you as you looked at me in the courtyard."

Feeling guilty about her earlier reaction of surprise, she nodded in response. Uneasiness coursed through her; their captors felt more hostile the deeper they went into the roost. The initial impartiality she'd sensed from Aetris was replaced with cloaked distaste, as if his time in their company was enough to sway his favor away from mankind.

The labyrinth of hallways ended at an arched entryway capped by the visage of a great griffin. Its mouth hung wide in a silent, endless shriek, and wooden feathers cascaded down the sides of the opening like giant wings. Beyond, stretched a long receiving hall with a high vaulted ceiling, its details lost in the dark shadows of the rafters.

At the far end of the room, a figure sat slouched upon an ornate throne. Coils of thick bramble vines decorated the glorified chair, though, if they were real or carved, Raelyn couldn't tell. The *vehsidhe* guards around the throne dais stood at attention, each holding an oversized spear. Armored up to their waists, they bared their chests, exposing unique patterns of feathers across human flesh. *So varied*, Raelyn thought, studying one guard's black feathers and dark skin and the other's vivid red feathers and pale complexion. *Just like the many different birds in the foothills of the Vast.* Were griffins so varied in their colors? She didn't know. The one she'd seen in person had been brown and white, just as the ones she'd seen depicted in books.

Aetris put one hand on Raelyn's back and the other on Laris's and ushered them down the center aisle toward the throne of thorns. A few feet from the raised platform, he pushed them to their knees and knelt between them. Arms raised into the air, he cried, "Divine Rushlem, Lord of the Skies, we bring you the slayers of Mondek!"

The slumped figure on the throne stirred. Like the other *vehsidhe*, Rushlem's face was notably human, though his skin lay in deep wrinkles, translucent with age. Pale-blue eyes, rimmed in red and framed by sagging skin, peered down at them. Weight sat oddly on his body, not concealed enough by his opulent, heavy robes.

"Humans," he said hoarsely and with disgust. "Only humans would dare to take such a life from this world. Tell me, what manner of death did Mondek meet?"

"Pierced by a godsbane blade, Divine One," Aetris replied. "Thrust into his chest with aid of the magic arts."

"This is the mage?"

"Yes, Divine One." Aetris gestured toward Laris. "We do not believe the woman has magic. She is his companion only."

Aetris can't sense what I am. The unintentional confirmation almost brought her to her feet, and she fought hard to maintain her composure and keep her gaze lowered. Her ability could be their advantage if they needed to fight their way to freedom. *Do any of the* vehsidhe *use magic?* None of the other griffin-born had gotten as near to her as Aetris, and with her improved control, any mages among them wouldn't have sensed her ability at a distance.

"Tell me, human, which god does your magic serve?" Rushlem asked.

His gag removed, Laris opened his mouth and stretched his jaw before answering. "I am a transcendent under the Holy King and a loyal servant to the will of Ute."

"*Tch.*" Rushlem waved his hand dismissively. "Transcendents, nadir—human words. You're all mages. All justifying your deeds in the service to your gods. Do you think the nadir who serve The Nameless God are any less devout?" A kissing sound escaped his lips as he sucked air through his teeth, eyes narrowed at Laris. "It was mages who created us during the Cataclysm, the Great War. The thought of winged soldiers able to attack from above was too tempting. Only they never quite got it right." He slumped back into the seat of the throne.

There was a long silence that followed, and then Rushlem looked at Raelyn. "We weren't the only things they created. Other instruments of destruction were wrought out of Man's ignorance."

She glanced up at him through her eyelashes, her face still turned toward the floor. He continued to watch her, brow furrowed in contemplation. "You are no mere companion to this man," he stated. To Aetris, he said, "The mage dies. I must think about the woman."

"No!" Raelyn sat up, her composure broken. "You can't! The Moon Mother of the *gonsidhe* sent us. We were acting for the benefit of all the mountain peoples."

"Convenient, don't you think," Rushlem countered loudly, "that she didn't do the act herself? Such a thing is a crime among our kind. We live and let live. That is our way. She saw an opportunity and took it, idiotic girl. Where is the Moon Mother now? Did you think she was your friend? You're disposable." He paused. "Well, at least one of you is." Rushlem motioned to two of the guards, and they hauled Laris and Raelyn to their feet. "Take the mage to the pit and put the other one under lock and key for now."

"No!" She struggled against the hold of the guard. "Let him go! Please!"

"Raelyn," Laris's voice was calm. "Worry about yourself for once. Do that for me."

Stunned into silence at his words, she adamantly shook her head. "No," she whispered, watching him be led away. "Please. Please don't do this."

Aetris moved into her line of sight. His expression was grim but not sympathetic. "It is a great honor to be allowed to live," he said, reaching his gloved, human hand to wipe away a tear on her cheek.

She recoiled from the attempted contact, rage boiling inside her. How dare he try to console her? "Don't touch me," she spat.

"Do not be so quick to make enemies. You may be here for a long time." He stepped back and waved at the guard to take her away. "Remember what I said."

Time felt frozen. Sitting on the edge of the bed, staring at the flickering candlelight from a sconce on the wall, Raelyn had no sense of how long she'd been confined. The room holding her was small. It reminded her of a servant's dormitory with enough room for a small cot and not much else. Since being locked in, she'd traced every line of the wooden walls three times over. There were no windows.

Tendrils of pain slowly returned to the wounds in her abdomen. The sharp pangs made her entire body ache, and she couldn't find peace. Lying flat was worse than sitting; standing made her lightheaded. So she sat, watching the flame of the candle flicker, the only evidence that life was moving on while she was forced to remain stationary.

After what must have been hours, the latch on the door clicked, and the bolt slid aside. Aetris entered, no longer clad in his light-colored robes. Like the guards she'd seen earlier, he was armored from the waist down, though a tunic and jerkin elevated his appearance.

She watched him but made no welcome. There was no reason to. They were enemies; Raelyn felt it intimately. The entire roost was against her, and she against it. They'd taken Laris and locked her away for a fate yet undecided. The loathing she felt was strangely empowering, even as beads of sweat broke out over her forehead from the pain throbbing in her core.

"You look unwell," Aetris declared. "The *ichtalmine* does not last indefinitely." At her continued silence, he sighed. "If you do not speak to me, this will be a very long night for you. I have questions, and they must be answered. Do not make me persuade you."

"Ask them," she replied curtly. "But I have questions, too."

"Your friend is yet alive if that is what you wish to know." He sat on the floor by the door, his back against the wall. "There will be a ceremony. His life will be taken as tribute to the greater life he took."

"When?"

"On the eve of the next day."

"Is there nothing I can do?"

Aetris shook his head slowly. "Your companion's fate is decided. But Rushlem is undecided about yours. It is not his way. Tell me why."

He still doesn't know. She decided to avoid the question as long as possible. "What happens to prisoners if they aren't sentenced to death?"

Her redirection didn't go unnoticed, and he frowned. "Human women are very rare here," he said at length, carefully choosing his words. "We are human enough that such novelties are highly prized."

A wave of nausea compounded the pain in her side. "A slave, then," she said softly.

He spread his arms out and shrugged. "Rushlem has not given permission. He has granted you immunity for now but will not declare why. He seems almost—" he leaned in, studying her "—afraid about you."

"I'm not a mage, and I'm not a skilled fighter. Or in any physical state to be a danger to you."

"This I know. But I can tell you are not being honest about who you are. I am not fool enough to think a lone mage coming to fight a feyfolk lord would bring a woman just for companionship."

Raelyn also wasn't a fool. If she'd been given immunity, just who was Aetris that he could come to her holding cell without escorts or worry of discovery? He wasn't being open about who he was, either.

"You're important here," she said, taking the gamble. "You're not just a member of a scouting party."

He grinned. The expression was unnerving, rapacious when paired with his intense gaze. "You have discovered me. Yes, I am son of Rushlem. When the Divine One sensed Mondek's demise, he tasked me to investigate." He pointed at her. "Now, who I am is known, but you remain a mystery. No more clever evasion. Tell me."

The roost lord knew she was a warden, Raelyn had no doubt. He'd alluded to it in the audience hall, and she suspected, like the Moon Mother, he had an innate ability that somehow sensed her secret. If Rushlem already knew, she couldn't devise a reason to continue hiding from his son. There might be a reason the knowledge wasn't openly shared, and Raelyn didn't want to miss the chance to cause discontent among her enemies. If nothing else, knowing she could negate magic might build fear and respect among her captors and buy her time.

"Where I come from, we are called wardens." She drew the last word out, watching for his reaction. "We are the counterparts to mages, able to use the influence of the void."

Disbelief flashed across his face, and he stared at her, the candlelight flickering wildly above him. In the long quiet that followed her words, Raelyn wondered if he would respond or if he was waiting for her to give some other grand revelation.

"I see," he finally said. "The Divine One's hesitation is warranted."

"Is it?"

"Wardens belong to the gods. You are fated. You should be freed to follow your path." Aetris leaned his head back against the wall, casting his gaze upward. "The *vehsidhe* do not allow mages to be born into our circle. The hatred of our creators runs deep in Rushlem. Children born with the gift are killed as soon as they show the signs. He will be coveting your power, desiring to add it to our ranks, but he knows it is wrong to hold you here. I do not know if he can resist."

"If you have no mages, what use would I be?"

He smiled again. "We could have mages if we could control them. Rushlem kills, but it hurts him to do so. You would be his solution, for now—a safeguard against the risk of magic. And," he added, "your children could be the answer for future generations."

The floor felt like it dropped from beneath her, and Raelyn clutched the sheet on the bed for stability. During passing moments since the fall of Albator, she'd wondered about the origin of her warden abilities and suspected there was some path of lineage involved. A latent ability that only manifested in select generations would explain why neither her father nor mother developed warden abilities—that she knew of.

"I see the thought is displeasing," he remarked, amused. "Be at peace knowing even Rushlem understands holding a warden against her will is to forsake the balance of this world. You will test his desire to help his people over his commitment to the good of Uhmeer. He knows he should set you free."

Despite his words, she could sense his deep sorrow and longing toward a future where *vehsidhe* children weren't put to the sword. Like his father, there was a part of Aetris that would sacrifice Raelyn's freedom and life for the sake of his people. He was warring with that same decision; she could see it written across his face.

"Is that all you wished to know?" she asked him. "I have no other secrets."

Rather than answering her, he let out a deep breath and resettled his position against the wall. His probing look reminded Raelyn he wasn't her ally. Their conversation didn't make them comrades or within one another's confidence. She was injured and alone in a room with a man still considered her enemy.

He must have sensed the shift in her thoughts because he chuckled.

Nodding to some unknown idea, Aetris stood. He kept the distance between them, a smile still on his face, and said, "Sleep. The night is growing late. We will speak again." Before closing the door behind him, he reached into a pocket of his jerkin and tossed a small vial to her. "It is called *ichtalmine*. It will numb your pain but does not speed healing. Take care to mind your wounds."

Unsettled by his amusement, she glanced down at the vial of blueish liquid, as silent in her farewell as she was in her greeting. Her awareness lingered on the door long after he'd left and she'd heard the bolt slide into place.

Rest was fleeting and broken, even after applying the *ichtalmine*. Raelyn had struggled to remove her bandages, and once they were off, the sight of her injuries had been shocking. She'd tenderly applied the viscous medicine to her red and purple skin but was unable to rewrap the wounds herself.

On the bed, with her shirt tied at her breasts, she propped herself up against the headboard, hoping the air would dry the solution in place.

She dozed on and off, too overcome with exhaustion to resist sleep fully. By the time a knock sounded on the door, the candle in the sconce had burned itself to snuff. She barely pulled her shirt down before a woman entered carrying a platter of food.

"If you care to end fast," the *vehsidhe* said, setting the tray on the floor. "The Divine Son sends his regards and recommends you break bread in reverence of this gracious meal."

Raelyn winced, sliding across the bed to stand. *Aetris.* What other Divine Son would send her a personal message? "Thank you," she mumbled, doing her best not to let her shirt brush against her wounds.

Hands on her hips, the *vehsidhe* woman watched with a guarded expression. Her feathers were silver, speckled with blue that accented the dark purple of her eyes. She looked to be older than

Raelyn by a handful of years. "You do not seem dangerous," she said matter-of-factly.

"I'm not dangerous." Raelyn reached for a cup of water on the platter.

With a sigh, the sliver-feathered woman stopped Raelyn's awkward bend with a gentle touch on her shoulder. She scooped up the tray and walked it over to the bed, setting it on the mattress. "Here." Her voice held a note of kindness. "I am called Laylia. If you need personal attention, you may ask for me."

Raelyn managed a meager smile. She was grateful for the offer and glad to see another woman. "Tell your Divine Son I am appreciative of the meal."

Laylia bowed her head slightly. "He was most insistent that you break bread. Perhaps it is wise to grant his request." She abruptly turned and opened the door, rushing out before Raelyn could thank her for the meal. The sound of Laylia's footsteps as she ran away echoed through the walls, and Raelyn stared at the door, puzzled by the hasty exit.

Taking the large piece of hard bread in her hand, she turned it over and back again. It was heavy and cold. It wouldn't have been appealing even if she'd had an appetite. Still, she knew better than to turn her nose up at free food. This could be her last meal for days to come.

She broke the bread apart using both hands and almost missed the hard lump that fell from its center and landed on the bed. Wrapped in layers of hide, the object was small enough to fit in her palm. She gently peeled back the outer covering to reveal a note written on the inside of the wrapping.

"Raelyn, it is not for me to decide your fate. The rock contained herein is all that remains of a communion statue to Volaris, Fourth Pillar of The Circle and once the patron of the vehsidhe. His name is no longer spoken in our roosts, and his temples are gone but for this stone. Perhaps he can aid you in some way."

She set the note down with shaking hands and let the stone fall back onto the bed, still covered in a second layer of tanned leather. Touching it might directly transport her into the void as it had with Genevive's altar. She could find herself face to face with a god she had no knowledge of. *He could kill me,* she thought, heart beating faster. *He could be the one who was hunting me.*

At the same time, she knew this might be the only way to save Laris. He was still alive somewhere in the roost. If morning fast was just broken, he had the better part of a day before the ceremony. She picked up the wrapped stone and rolled it within her hands. Maybe Hendrel would be waiting in the void with his counsel, as he had been with Genevive. With his guidance and the god's, there might be some hope. There was a risk, but if she didn't take the chance, Laris's life would surely be forfeit.

With a deep breath, she pulled apart the final layer of wrapping and let the bare stone fall into her open hand.

Just as it had been at the forest shrine, her journey into the void was instantaneous. The altar stone felt icy in her fist, mirroring the coolness of the space around her. Hendrel's familiar light was absent despite her hopes, but another light pulsed weakly nearby. She slowly walked toward it, and the pale glow shimmered into the shape of a tall man in tattered garments.

He faced away from her, staring up into the nothingness. Unlike Hendrel's hazy outline within the void, the man's details were clear to her, like a portrait done in watery white paint. His outline looked frosted, his light cold and dim. There was something ghostly and haunting about him.

"After all this time," he said as she approached, "the connection between the worlds is possible again."

Raelyn shivered, uncertain of how to proceed. "Are you looking for something?" she finally asked, peering into the dark with the specter.

His attention snapped down to her. "It is you who are looking for something, are you not?" Colorless eyes stared into hers, rooting her in place without the burden of touch. "Should I dare refuse communion after so many ages?"

She gasped when he darted, gliding around her quicker than she could follow with her eyes. He stopped abreast of her again, looming taller than when she'd first approached.

"What do you want of me, mortal?" His voice boomed around them. "What could a human like you want with the Fourth Pillar?"

"I need your help," she said more calmly than she felt. "My companion and I are being held captive by the *vehsidhe*, and this is the only way I might be able to save his life."

"Ah, the *vehsidhe*." The phantom stroked his pointed beard. "I tried to help them, you know. Poor things. The unwanted offspring of experimentation. I protected them, helped them defeat their creators."

"You're no longer their patron?"

The light around him sputtered, and Raelyn realized he was laughing. "Oh, not by choice! They cast me aside, destroyed my altars. They said I was, oh, what was the word—" he paused thoughtfully "—oppressive. You know, it *is* endlessly entertaining to see how much you can demand when you dangle people's desires in front of them. I guess my price just got too high." His broad smile narrowed his eyes menacingly. "People will do *anything* to survive."

She wanted to move away from him, realizing the magnitude of her error. Volaris knew she needed him; now she knew he would ask the impossible as payment. Before she could react, he enveloped her, trapping her inside his transparent form.

"I can help you, Raelyn." His voice echoed in her head. "You will let me have your body in the mortal world, and I will bring down the halls of your enemies. You gain your freedom, and I will once again walk in your realm. The void within you connects us, allows my existence, and you will carry me back to the mortal world."

"N ... o ..." she said weakly. It didn't matter what she wanted, she realized with dread. She could *feel* him seeping within her, into every part of her. The sensation was sickening, like being touched by a thousand icy fingers. It was intimate and intrusive, a violation of her mind and her body. She wanted to cry out, but her voice was no longer hers to command.

"Let's save your friend," Volaris said within her mind. *"Back to the mortal world, we go."*

CHAPTER EIGHTEEN

In a blink, Raelyn stood back in her holding room, staring at the altar stone in her hand. The transition was nothing like it had been in the past. She'd used no anchoring memories or thoughts to bring her back to the physical realm. The shift had been under Volaris's control, as was the rest of her. She was tucked away in her mind, a spectator—watching but unable to control any part of herself.

"Oh, it's so good to be back," he said out loud in her voice. "I've forgotten what it's like to touch and feel. All these sensations!" With unnatural strength, he crushed the altar stone into dust in her hand, giggling. "But this won't do." He poked her wounded side. "I forgot how fragile mortal flesh is."

Raelyn's connection to her senses was dulled, but she felt a tightening along her abdomen. Seeing her side while Volaris gazed at it, she watched in awe as the holes in her body knit together and the bruising vanished. A wave of relief washed over her; she felt vibrant and energetic, the fatigue of her journey complete erased. He'd fully healed her.

"Shall we begin?" Volaris lifted her arm toward the door, and the wood barrier splintered apart. "Now you will see what wardens are really for."

The guard in the hallway was quick to recover from the unexpected blast, but he'd barely stepped toward her when Volaris closed Raelyn's left hand into a fist, imploding the *vehsidhe* into a mound of bloody pulp.

She screamed into the silence of her subconscious, unable to look away because her gaze was not her own.

More guards rounded the corner of the corridor at the sound of the commotion. With a wave from Volaris, they erupted into flames as soon as they came into sight, writhing with otherworldly, blue fire so hot it melted skin from bone. The Fourth Pillar laughed gleefully as their shrieks reverberated through the roost. "More! More!" he called out. "Instead of oppression, I will give you annihilation!"

Arms out, he strode down the hallway, destruction in his wake. The walls trembled, caving in behind him. The beautiful wood caught fire, ignited by burning *vehsidhe* bodies and by flame trailing with his every footstep. Raelyn felt no heat from the blaze, only a persistent, crisp cold, like a frost on an early winter morning.

Volaris navigated the roost with familiarity, taking turns without hesitation. Some areas he left untouched while others he made impassible ruins, their structures collapsed and ablaze. He relished killing all the *vehsidhe* he encountered—she could feel it—burning most alive. Though, a few met their fates in more horrifying ways: collapsed inward or ripped apart when he harnessed the essence of their bodies. Raelyn tried desperately to shift her focus from what was happening, feeling the weight of the tragedy threatening to overwhelm her consciousness. She was truly helpless, more so than she'd ever been, once again the catalyst in an event that would claim countless lives.

The roost gave way to stone at the bottom of a long spiraling stairwell where a few deteriorating torches along the walls held the damp darkness at bay. Down the straight passage ahead, barred doorways appeared uniformly on either side.

"Your prison block," Volaris said, making a quick gesture to snap the neck of the guard rushing toward him. "Shall we see where your companion is?"

With a wave of his hand, the doors flung open simultaneously. The sound of the metal colliding with stone was deafening, and no prisoners came out to investigate the source of their newfound freedom.

Cell by cell, Volaris made his way down the corridor, eliminating *vehsidhe* prisoners as he went. Unlike those in the upper levels, the prisoners met quicker deaths, most never realizing their heads had been parted from their bodies.

Laris was in the second to last room, near where the guard had fallen. He sat on the floor, one knee bent, the other extended, bracing himself with his arm chained to the wall. The other arm hung limp at his side, the fingers of its hand purple and swollen, and Raelyn could see additional signs of mistreatment across his bare skin. His bandage was still in place, though barely, stained completely through with blood.

When he saw her, his expression ran a gamut of relief, confusion, and worry.

"Raelyn?" He stared at her in disbelief.

Volaris smiled. "Not quite," he answered. "A mage, hmmm? I like mages. Well, I'm a man of my word. You're free to go. And I would go quickly," he added, "if I were you."

If Raelyn could have cried, she would have. Seeing the pained expression on Laris's face was heart-wrenching. He knew, despite the fact it was her body and her voice, that the woman in front of him wasn't her.

"What have you done to her?" He struggled to his feet. "Who are you?"

"Do not test my patience, human. We've made a deal, your Raelyn and I, and I've upheld my part. Not that she actually agreed to anything." He chuckled. "Ah, it couldn't be helped. But maybe she'll be more cooperative this way. Now be gone."

They broke his hands so he couldn't form magic, she realized. It was amazing he managed to stand with his injuries.

"Heal him," she said to the god. *"He can't escape like this. Heal him."*

"Heal him?" Volaris responded out loud to her. "Why would I heal him?"

"Because I'm asking you to. Do this, and I won't resist. I can tell it takes energy to keep me locked down. Heal him, and I won't fight anymore."

It was a guess. Raelyn didn't know if Volaris had to actively maintain control over her free will or if she was too inconsequential. But the fact she still had a consciousness independent of his led her to believe he couldn't take her completely over.

The Fourth Pillar said nothing at first, and Raelyn took the opportunity to appreciate, perhaps one last time, the man before her. Even in his battered state, Laris carried himself with confidence and determination. He looked like what a god should be, she thought to herself sadly. Proud and capable, even in suffering. Not at all like the ghostly apparition that had taken over her body.

"Given that you may be my last warden, I'll grant this one boon,"

Volaris said, taking her from her focus. He stepped down into the cell and grabbed Laris by his injured arm. He cried out at the contact, and Raelyn wanted to cry out with him.

Out of the act of cruelty, she felt a heat build within their touch. Even with her dulled senses, she could feel the warmth washing over him, knitting together his injuries just as Volaris had done with hers. The experience was amazing and frightening at the same time. *This is the power of the gods.* It was extraordinary and limitless.

"Now, don't try anything foolish," Volaris said to Laris. "Raelyn is gone. Only I, Volaris, Champion of the Field, Lord of Fires, Destroyer of the Loches, remain. Death awaits you if you stay."

Laris nodded, pulling his arm away.

Leaving the mage standing in the cell, Volaris said to her, "We have one more important task." He strode back through the passage they'd come from.

Thick smoke, heavy in the air, made it difficult to see in the main corridors of the roost, but Raelyn could *feel* the adeptness of Volaris's movements as he navigated the passages with ease. She felt a growing cohesion with him, experiencing different sights, smells, and sounds from his perspective. Had she become complacent to his occupation of her body? Her words in the prison had been an empty promise to secure help for Laris, nothing more. But perhaps the part of her remaining intended to see the commitment through.

Out of the thick haze, Volaris stopped briefly at a closed pair of tall doors—the only ones in the upper roost Raelyn had seen fortified with metal. He placed a hand on the seam where the doors joined and slowly spread his fingers wide. The gesture was almost reverent and gentle, speaking of long-contained anticipation.

"You know," he said to her, "the *vehsidhe* murdered the last warden to host me after the Great War—your Cataclysm. You should want this as much as I do. Together, we will rule these weaker beings again. You are avenging the death of your brethren, Raelyn."

She didn't have to reply. They were one, and she knew he could sense her deep anguish, even if she wasn't being resistant. That he would even take the time to try and bring her to his cause felt pointless. He had complete control, regardless of what she wanted.

With no more words between them, a shockwave erupted from his hand on the doors, blowing them inward and off their hinges onto the floor of the next room. Stepping through the cloud of dust, Volaris stopped. He closed his eyes and inhaled a deep breath of the wood- and stone-scented air.

They were in a throne room, one far more extravagant than the audience hall where Raelyn first met Rushlem. The inner throne was designed to host only the most-trusted peers and advisors. With walls decorated with weapons of all types and banners of every color, it was small and intimate.

Rushlem stood at the back of the room, alone. Holding himself tall, he bore the weight of his robes proudly and more gracefully than before. It was pride and arrogance, Raelyn realized, that drew him up out of his hunched posture. It was as though he knew what he faced, and he considered himself equally matched.

"You," the *vehsidhe* lord ground out through his clenched teeth. "What treachery is this?"

"I should ask you the same," replied Volaris. "What type of ruler forbids magic when he himself is such a powerful being?"

"Change began with me," Rushlem said, lifting his chin. "I am the last. Not that you truly care. I know what you are. How did you get hold of the woman?"

"She came to me. She had an altar stone in her hand."

"Lies! They do not exist! They haven't existed in centuries!"

"You don't have to believe me," Volaris said calmly. "I'm here as proof. You know what will happen now, though."

Rushlem was prepared for an attack. Volaris's flames erupted around the *vehsidhe* lord but didn't touch him, unable to move past a protective barrier of swirling air. Raelyn could see the smug look of satisfaction on Rushlem's face, but she knew the god was holding back deliberately. Volaris wanted to exhaust his adversary first, creating the illusion that victory against him was possible. It was all too clear to Raelyn how tipped the scales were to the Pillar's favor.

Lifting both hands, palms upward, Volaris unleashed a rain of molten metal droplets. They melted through everything they hit, destroying and igniting the tables and chairs in the throne room, and sinking through the floorboards into the roost levels below. Again, Rushlem countered, using the stream of air protecting him to redirect the onslaught back toward Raelyn's body.

Instead of making contact, the drops collected, shaped by Volaris's hands into a long, black spear. Without touching it, he cast it toward Rushlem, driving the blade into the torrent of wind at the *vehsidhe*'s front. Raelyn felt the surplus of energy Volaris held back—a great reserve within reach, like the controlled power of a warhorse waiting to be unbridled. If he wanted to, he could have impaled the *vehsidhe* easily. He could have imploded or decapitated him from across the room as he'd done to so many others. Raelyn felt his joy at toying with the feyfolk lord, who still appeared confident he could match the god's power.

Volaris could have driven the spear home but let it deflect. Using his current of air, he added a breath of blue fire, creating a hellish tornado in the center of the room. He grew it out slowly, condensing the air until it contained the power of a summer storm, pulling the loose objects, debris, hot ash, and smoke around them into its spiral. From his position at the back wall, Rushlem fought the onslaught. He widened his stance and extended his arms, adding what little strength he had left to maintain his shield against the pull of the gale.

Raelyn watched with dismay, knowing the inevitable end. Rushlem was powerful; a *vehsidhe* lord, but he'd only been using air magic, when the Fourth Pillar had command over any magic he chose. She felt the innate power as if it were her own. What took human mages a lifetime to learn was effortless for the god, and he demonstrated his mastery over the wind as his final insult.

Little by little, the storm pushed forward, stealing air from the *vehsidhe*'s stream as it crept toward him. The moment it was about to break through the barrier, Volaris let the spiral dissipate. The air stilled, and remnants from the room crashed down to the floor. With a bored sigh, he made a snatching motion with Raelyn's hand, seizing Rushlem in an invisible grip, pulling at his essence.

"That was barely entertaining." He frowned. "I was hoping you'd put up more of a fight, old bird." Before Rushlem had a chance to respond, Volaris closed the grip, condensing the life magic and crushing the *vehsidhe* lord until blood seeped from his eyes, nose, and mouth. Entrails spilled out onto the floor from hidden fissures beneath his robes. Volaris let the body fall to the ground in an unrecognizable heap.

A feeling of exhilaration ran through Raelyn's body, offset by her disgust and dread. "I have missed the feeling of power in this world," Volaris said with pleasure. "No one exists who can oppose me."

He went to leave the room but stopped short. Standing in the doorway, Laris held his hands out, showing he was without a weapon. He kept the position, tilting his head in question when Volaris didn't react. "Raelyn?" he said tentatively. "Raelyn, I know you can hear me."

With a sound of disgust, Volaris glared at the mage. "You again? How foolish." He grabbed Laris's essence, pinning him in place, ready to rend him in two. "You should have run when I gave you the chance."

"No!" Raelyn's shout was desperate but commanding, fueled by fear and deep anger. It echoed within her, bounding off the walls of their joint consciousness. She'd just enabled and witnessed a massacre, her only shred of solace rooted in Laris's survival. If he were to die before her eyes, she'd be entirely lost.

Volaris hesitated, and Laris forced out a strained, "You have to fight him. It's your body, Raelyn," He grunted in pain as the hold on him tightened, but Raelyn was already mounting her offensive.

"You will not hurt him!" She screamed into her mind. *"I won't let you! I won't let you hurt anyone else!"*

"You dare challenge me?" The god's voice entered her head. *"You dare to resist? I will break your will like I will break every bone in his worthless body."*

The whole intent of the god pressed in on her, shrinking the space she occupied in their shared mind. She felt her senses deteriorate to nothing. She could no longer hear or see what was happening outside her body. His presence was a great weight, pushing her deeper into a pool of emptiness to drown her will.

Without any other recourse, Raelyn did the only thing she could think to do—the only thing she knew how to do. She latched on to the cold darkness ever-present in her core. The void was heavy and reluctant, held in its place by the connection to Volaris. But it was still *hers*—she felt it. With every ounce of strength she had, she heaved the boundaries of the void apart and spread her influence to its furthest reach.

Like a giant wave, the void surged, pushing away everything within Raelyn's mind. The cold nothingness severed her immediate thoughts and emotions. She felt nothing, saw nothing. All of her senses wiped clean. With its expansion, her sphere of influence cut the unbearable and intrusive presence of Volaris from her. His connection vanished, leaving her alone in the dark depths of her personal emptiness. The silence was deafening.

Darkness surrounded Raelyn, but she wasn't in the void. She was within herself, inside the black pit at her center that made her what she was. It was colder and darker than the seam of the world. Lonelier. Consuming. Fear gripped her. Was she trapped? Had she lost herself forever?

Laris. Had he survived? Her thoughts brought clarity, and with clarity, she felt her control returning, riding a budding wash of warmth. With renewed focus, she let the void shrink away, relinquishing her mind and settling back into its familiar ball of cold buried mysteriously within her core. She thought of Laris, envisioning his stoic expression; the rare smile he offered.

Slowly, the images gained substance, and she could see his face again in person, clouded by smoke and dust. In the brief moment before she collapsed onto the floor, relief and surprise replaced his imagined look of tranquility.

"Raelyn!" He dashed over to her, reclining her gently in his arms. "Raelyn, are you all right?"

She tried to muster the energy to speak but could only give a slight nod. Her body was uninjured, but fatigue wrapped her every muscle, and it was all she could do not to close her eyes and lapse into sleep amidst the chaos around them.

The roost was burning. Even though Volaris was gone, the aftermath of his rampage continued to unfold. Ablaze, the back of the throne room disappeared behind a wall of fire that licked upward along the rafters and spread across the ceiling. Without the shield of the god's presence, Raelyn felt the heat radiating against her skin, building a layer of sweat across her body.

"We've got to get out of here." Laris wiped her hair away from her face. "Can you walk?"

She didn't think she could, but she nodded anyway, willing to try so he wouldn't have to carry her to safety. *You* can *do this, Raelyn,* she told herself. *You will walk out of here with him.*

By some self-directed miracle and Laris's assistance, she shakily gained her feet. He looked at her in doubt. "I can manage," she said as firmly as she could. "I may need your arm."

Without hesitation, he tucked her hand into the crook of his elbow, leading her out the partially collapsed doorway and into the hall. Raelyn coughed, disoriented as the smoke in the corridor infiltrated her lungs and made her eyes burn. Laris stopped and motioned with his hands, and the flames and smoke nearest to them dissipated.

Raelyn looked at him in surprise, even though she immediately understood. Mastering threads of fire magic meant a mage could unravel them as well as create with them.

"I don't have the power to quell the entire blaze," he said, answering her unspoken question as he ushered her forward. "But I can get us through as long as the structure stays sound."

They pressed onward, their progression dictated by which passages remained open enough to pass through. Raelyn's strength improved with the urgency of escape, but she kept her hold on Laris. She followed his lead, trusting his senses completely as he took them through level after level of abandoned rooms and vacant halls.

"There!" he exclaimed as they stumbled out onto a balcony overlooking the entry courtyard.

The outdoor space was filled with *vehsidhe* frantically working to put out the flames and salvage the areas of the roost yet unaffected. Raelyn's attention immediately focused on Aetris calling out orders to a line of men and women passing water buckets from a large fountain near the stables. A hard lump of revulsion welled within her stomach. He'd given her the altar stone knowing the history between Volaris and the *vehsidhe*. He'd wanted this outcome, but why?

Laris pulled her toward the stairs descending to the levels below, and she dragged her gaze away from Aetris and focused on steadying her balance. She'd managed to keep her strength enough so far, but quickly running down stairs was more of a demand than her body was ready for. She relinquished Laris's support for that of the banister, doing her best to ignore the anxiety building at the thought of facing the *vehsidhe* below.

At the bottom of the stairs, they were met at spear point. A few onlookers paused in their fire-control efforts, but most survivors in the courtyard were too busy trying to thwart the flames to care what was happening.

Aetris greeted them with a smile. "Raelyn," he said, opening his arms as if to embrace her. "I am so glad to see you alive."

She glared at him, so disgusted she couldn't find words.

"Do not look at me like that. I am lord here now, after all."

Laris put a hand on Raelyn's shoulder. "They can't hurt us now. Don't let him provoke you," he warned her softly. "I can get us out of here."

She knew they were in no immediate danger. With Rushlem gone, Laris could get them out of the roost with more fire and blood if need be. But despite her loathing for Aetris, Raelyn had exceeded her fill of death and destruction. The thought of possibly having to battle their way to freedom made her stomach churn and wrapped her in a cloak of melancholy. She wanted to avoid more death at all costs.

Maybe there was hope. The new *vehsidhe* leader wasn't a fool. She was certain he also realized they couldn't stop Laris now that he was unbound and his hands were healed. Everyone present understood what the outcome of a confrontation would be, and the *vehsidhe* had already lost so much.

"You did this just to eliminate your father." Saying the truth out loud broke the tension but elevated her anger, and she shook her head in disbelief. "Why? There had to be another way. Why would you do that to your people?"

"Despite what you think, there was no other way." His smile faded. "It was not planned. But I could not pass up the opportunity that came with your capture. For years, we have watched our children perish. So many, even those who would never be talented enough for true magecraft. My children, Raelyn. My siblings.

"You know it is a crime amongst our people to take the life of a feyfolk lord. Had I moved against my father sooner, the people would not have followed me, and I had not the power to defeat him in combat."

"You sent me an altar stone under the guise of kindness, knowing the god attached to it was dangerous. You used Laris's life to lure me into killing your father for you." Raelyn clenched her hands into fists. "You knowingly unleashed a god on the world!"

"You put her life at risk for the sake of your rebellion?" Laris's voice filled with anger. "You could have killed all the people you claim to be trying to save. You did kill them, with your actions."

"A necessary risk and loss," Aetris countered. "What is the life of strangers when you have seen a hundred of your own put to the blade? Would you not do anything for your loved ones?" His look softened. "I did not understand," he said, "the totality of what might happen by giving you that stone. Too many ages have passed since the powers of the gods were witnessed. Too many people have forgotten. I only knew Volaris would seek Rushlem's death as the last of the true *vehsidhe* lords. I did not know he would consume everything and everyone in his path."

"You brought a god amongst your people with no true knowledge of Raelyn's abilities." Laris's voice rose. "What you did was beyond fool-hardy and not worthy behavior of any ruler."

"You have your crown now," said Raelyn sadly, looking out at the scrambling people in the courtyard.

"And from these ashes, we will rebuild." Aetris studied her intently and then looked at Laris. "I cannot hold you here anymore," he said with an edge of disappointment. "Not everything has worked out as expected."

"If you try to stop us, I'll burn what's left to the ground." Laris's threat hung in the air, and the guards shifted uncomfortably.

The tension faded with Aetris's laugh. "It will already burn to the ground soon enough. Go. Take your warden and be free. We will not stop you. If anything, I send you off in thanks." He motioned for the guards to lower their spears.

Taking her hand in his, Laris led Raelyn past Aetris and his men toward the open entry arch of the roost. All around them, *vehsidhe* rushed by, passing buckets of water and shoveling dirt to try and save their home. A child bumped into Raelyn, dumping the contents of a cup on the ground. The little girl looked up at her with tear-filled eyes and ran back toward the fountain to fill the meager container again.

Raelyn stopped walking. She knew she wasn't to blame for the evil and manipulation of others, but she couldn't ignore her role in the suffering around them. At the pull of her hand in his, Laris looked back. He sighed deeply at her pleading look, released her, and nodded.

"Wait," she called back to Aetris. "We want to help."

The *vehsidhe* leader didn't respond immediately. He looked at them in doubt but at length said, "Join the bucket line." Inclining his head toward the fountain, he and the guards left her and jogged toward the worst of the flames.

Raelyn ignored the fatigue creeping back into her body and turned to go where directed. She was stopped by Laris's touch on her arm. When she turned toward him, he caught her chin and gave her a quick, gentle kiss. "You're going to owe me for this," he said in a low voice. "They deserve to face the consequences of their actions, but I will do this for you." At her look of surprise, he smiled crookedly and then pushed her away. "Go," he said, heading toward the area engulfed by fire. "Do what you can, but don't push yourself."

She fought to regain her composure while he raced to the other side of the yard, wiping her cheeks as though she could erase the flush on them. Maybe someday he wouldn't rattle her so thoroughly with some words and a touch.

By the time the fire came under control, the sun was no longer visible in the sky above the mountains. Long shadows heralded the eventual night, made darker and longer by the cloud of smoke blanketing the upper aspect of the trees.

With Laris's help, the *vehsidhe* had saved a large part of the fortress, though, most of the eastern wing had been lost entirely. In the last hour of daylight, many survivors were resting—sitting or lying throughout the courtyard while a handful of guards and able-bodied men continued to cart buckets of water. Long past the point of exhaustion, Raelyn lay on a mound of straw at the front of the pony stalls, the pile soaked to prevent it from catching fire. After toiling in the heat of the blaze, the wet fodder was cooling, if nothing else. She let herself sink into it.

"It matches the color of your hair." Aetris approached her from the yard, covered in a film of black soot and a dusting of fine debris. His clothes were drenched in sweat and water. Beneath swollen eyelids, his sharp gaze was resigned, the threat around him diminished by fatigue and smothered by the dark shadows of the stable.

Too spent to summon her feelings of distain toward him, she nodded. "I doubt the ponies would notice the difference, either."

He gave a distracted smile, looking out at his people, and said, "I am here to acknowledge my debt to you. We would have lost everything if you had not helped."

"It wasn't me. Laris is the one who made the difference. You're lucky fire magic is his specialty and that his hands were healed." She could see Laris across the yard, splashing his face and washing his arms in a wooden basin.

"His kindness was not for our sake; that was made clear. He is not a man I would like to cross a second time."

Raelyn continued to watch her companion. "I thought that, too, when we first met. I still think that, to be honest."

"Somehow, I suspect we would be in different types of danger." He smirked at her confused expression. "Stay the night. With much of the roost destroyed, I regret there are not enough open rooms for all of us, but this stable is quiet, and we have blankets you may use. Tomorrow, I will send you off with some gifts to speed your journey."

He turned to leave right as Laris joined them. The two men shared a look of acknowledgment but said nothing, and Laris dropped down onto the straw next to Raelyn as Aetris walked away.

Eyes closed, he asked, "What did he want?"

"Just to thank us," she said. "He said to spend the night."

"And you trust him?"

"I'm too tired to decide," she answered honestly. "I'm not sure either of us can get up to leave right now, even if we wanted to."

He rolled closer and fixed her with a stern look. "Tell me honestly, Raelyn, you're unharmed? In all ways?"

Even in her tired state, his nearness was alerting, and her pulse quickened with his question. "It was the worst thing I've ever been through, aside from the death of my father," she admitted. "It was intrusive and … I won't deny that, but there's no lasting harm." With the words, an unexplainable urge to break down claimed her. Tears welled into her eyes, and she attempted to smile through them. "No, don't worry, I'm just overwhelmed a bit, remembering—that's all this is."

He pulled her into his arms. "When we've gotten through this, and you're ready, I want to know more about what happened."

Face buried in his chest, she mumbled her agreement. It felt good to let the tears flow, to let all the fear and uncertainty of the last days leave her. There was relief and immense comfort in his warmth. She let the sensations distract her and slow her tears until she was resting quietly against his chest, thinking of nothing else. When she went to shift away, he held her fast.

"Just stay," he said in a low voice. "You're not the only one who needs this right now."

The breath caught in her throat, but she let her body relax into his embrace. His arms tightened around her.

"When I saw you appear in my prison cell, I knew something terrible had happened." His breath warmed the top of her hair as he spoke.

"I was going to do everything in my power to get you back, even if I didn't understand what was happening."

His chest rose with a deep breath. "You saved yourself, though, Raelyn," he said. "You saved both of us on your own. You're stronger than you realize or give yourself credit for."

Unsure how to respond, she inhaled his warmth and lay in silence, listening to the growing sounds of conversation in the yard. After long moments of quiet, she tilted her face slightly and asked, "Does that mean we're even?"

"What do you mean?" He looked down at her, eyes heavy with fatigue.

"You said I'd owe you for helping the *vehsidhe*."

With a half-smile, he shook his head slowly. "No. We're not even."

"Saving us both doesn't count?"

"No." He shifted his hold, sliding a hand beneath the back of her shirt and splaying his fingers across her skin. "I'll let you know when all your debts have been paid." His eyes closed again, and he traced the line of her spine with his fingers. "That will have to wait for a time when magic hasn't exhausted me and we're safe with this journey behind us."

His touch sent a shiver through her, and she welcomed it. Pressed against his chest, enclosed within his arms, Raelyn reveled in the soothing contact of his skin against hers. It felt *right*, natural—a feeling of connectedness more powerful and enduring than any power of a god's over her body. *When we're safe.* The words circled in her thoughts. *When we're safe.* She pressed her forehead harder into Laris's chest.

"Am I interrupting?" someone asked from the stable gate. "We are preparing food. There is enough for everyone."

Raelyn recognized the voice and looked over. "Laylia?"

Stepping out of the shadows of the stalls, the female *vehsidhe* nodded, arms crossed at her chest. Despite the soot and ash on her dress, her skin and feathers glowed with the sheen of a fresh washing, and she stood proudly, shoulders back. Lines of weariness etched her face, emphasized by the dark circles around her eyelids.

"We meet again, human woman," she said flatly. "Though, you were far from harmless, as you promised."

"I would have told you to stay away if I had known."

Laylia didn't smile, but her eyes held a look of reluctant sympathy. "It is done now. I am not innocent, either," she said. "I knew about the altar stone. I delivered it. We will share the guilt of this day, as will few others." She looked away. "Come eat with us. The Divine One has asked."

The new Divine One. Raelyn shivered at the thought. The history of human civilization was no less bloody and treacherous, but seeing the consequences of rebellion up close was a far cry from reading about it in library manuscripts. Compared to the greater wars of Uhmeer, the incident with the *vehsidhe* was minor—a droplet in a timeless sea of battles and conquests. The realization that such devastation and destruction could be amplified across entire countries brought clarity to Raelyn's understanding of the world.

"We'll be there in a moment," Laris answered for her, and she realized she'd left the conversation hanging in silence.

Laylia left with a bow, her silver feathers catching the light of campfires out in the yard. Outside the stable, night drew across the fortress ruins, hiding the scars the fire left behind. There would be no stars, Raelyn knew, watching the smoke swirling through the air, but an alluring peace came from being surrounded by woodland quiet, even in the aftermath of chaos and disruption.

Laris pushed himself up from the pile of straw and offered his hand. "Let's not waste a meal. I doubt there will be much to spare for us on our journey come morning."

CHAPTER NINETEEN

Pale beams of dawn light stirred Raelyn awake, dancing across her eyelids and pulling her from slumber. She moved her head to the side and adjusted her position, nestling into the warmth of the blankets in one of the empty stalls. Growing increasingly awake, she realized the warmth wasn't just her own. At some point in the night, she'd draped herself across Laris, head on his chest, left arm and leg thrown over him while he slept on his back.

Embarrassed, she slowly added space between them, moving her leg off his thighs and her head onto his arm. Her left hand on the bare skin of his stomach she kept in place. His borrowed shirt had slipped above his waist in the night with their movement, allowing her to subconsciously seek the heat of his core, the comfort of his skin against hers. Afraid of waking him by pulling away the contact suddenly, she contemplated how to move before he saw how shamelessly she'd clung to him.

Raelyn adjusted the weight of her hand on his stomach, alleviating some of its pressure as she tried to ease away. Under her withdrawing touch, she felt a ridge of scar tissue running along the edge of her fingertips. *Such a severe injury,* she thought, noting the depth and thickness of the mark. Inching a little higher, she traced the scar with her first two fingers to test its breadth, careful not to lift her hand entirely.

"Are you doing that on purpose?" Laris asked, grabbing her hand to stop its motion.

Startled, she let out a gasp and attempted to pull away from him, but he held on to her fingers. "I was trying not to wake you!"

He pressed her hand back to her. "Raelyn, stay over there for a bit," he grumbled. "I can think of no faster way to wake a man up." He turned away from her.

She frowned and turned her attention to the ceiling. Staring up at the planks overhead, she wondered at the time. The courtyard outside was quiet, the only sound coming from the gentle chewing of ponies in the adjacent stalls.

"How did you get that scar?"

"A greatsword when I was ten and six" he said, still turned away from her. "I was a foot soldier riding along on a routine supply order. We were ambushed."

"You couldn't use your magic?"

"I wasn't skilled enough then or quick enough. It takes years to learn how to shape a particular type of magic. Like becoming proficient in a new language. Sometimes a lifetime isn't even enough."

"Does it hurt you still?"

He looked over his shoulder at her. "No. You didn't hurt me if that's on your mind."

She shook her head, still staring at the rafters. "It felt like it might be the type of injury that holds on to pain even after it's healed. Like old soldiers who complain of aches when cold weather sets in."

"It's barely daybreak." He changed the topic. "If you're done sleeping, we could make the most of an early start."

She was still tired; it sat heavily in her skull, putting pressure behind her eyes. It was silly to have worried about their entangled position to the point of ruining sleep. She'd panicked without reason. They were more than just companions; he'd made that clear. And with everything they'd endured together, the notion of decency and modesty between them was almost laughable. He'd seen her at her absolute worst, and she him.

"A little bit longer?" She pulled the blanket up over her shoulders.

Laris rolled to his back again. "A little bit longer. I'll wake you up. And not like you woke me up," he added.

She made a sound of acknowledgment, her eyes already closed. "You said it didn't hurt you."

"I'll explain it clearly to you one day," she heard him say with a sigh. "Get some more sleep."

Raelyn relaxed back into the darkness, letting early-morning sounds lull her to sleep.

At some point, tendrils of cold replaced the comforting embrace of natural slumber, and she opened her eyes to a painfully familiar, inhospitable, endless expanse of nothingness. Her heart sank when she realized where she was. Since gaining greater control over her powers, she hadn't slipped into the void unintentionally. Maybe she was more shaken from what had happened than she thought.

"Raelyn!" Hendrel floated over to her. "Are you all right? What were you thinking?"

Terror pushed away her joy from his unexpected company, and she looked around, panic swelling in her chest. "Volaris? Is he here?" She waited for the crushing intrusiveness of the god's presence, her eyes ripping apart the darkness for any sign of his approach.

The void was silent, empty of all but her and Hendrel.

Fear still holding her on edge, Raelyn wished she could embrace the wisp and say nothing, reveling in the comfort he brought just by being near. "It was the only thing I could do," she whispered once her heart stopped racing. Overcome by guilt, she sank to her knees. "I'm so sorry. I should have waited for you to come to me!"

His light flickered, and he took his boyish shape, a fleeting smile passing across his vague features. "No god can locate you easily without an altar stone to facilitate the connection. Volaris could roam the seam of the world for eternity and never find you again. You are safe, for now." He blinked brighter. "Some lessons must be learned through experience. Now you know the most dangerous part of being a warden, but you also know that you are your own master, and no one, not even a god, can take that power from you."

"It's a lesson I wish I'd been told instead," she replied solemnly. "So many lives are lost now, and all because of me."

"The consequences of leadership are always magnified, but you are not to blame for the evil within others. Had Volaris been benevolent, like Genevive, the outcome would have been very different, even if your actions had been the same. If you are to lead, you must stop doubting your worth."

"I'm not leading anyone. I wouldn't have even made it out of Albator without help."

"To be a warden is to be a leader, even if a reluctant one."

She took a deep breath, accepting the seed of understanding as it spread its tendrils through her mind. "Hendrel, tell me truly; were you sent to me by Emblem? You're the last Holy King, and I'm a warden when there is no warden in the Holy Citadel. Tell me the truth."

His outline flickered, and he floated next to her, a melancholy aura to his light. "I do not know why our connection came to be, Raelyn. I never communed with Emblem in life, and he does not speak to me in death. I only know that my spirit was pulled from this place and back to the mortal realm when you were born. You were an anchor for me, always there, your presence beckoning and known to me, no matter how far apart we were. If I left you for too long, the need to return would override all else."

He paused. "Is it the will of Emblem? Of Ute, his most ancient name? It is not my place to guess at his plan. But know this—there are no inescapable destinies. If Emblem wishes for you to reach the Holy Citadel, your journey and your decisions must take you down the right paths, and it is just one of many possible fates."

"More riddles." She frowned at him, feeling suddenly overwhelmed and exhausted again. If what she went through was what it meant to be the conduit for a god, she had no interest in ever doing it again, Lord of the Circle or not. The Holy Citadel was not where she saw her future. "I need to go back. I need to sleep. And ... I just can't be here right now. It's too much. Is it safe to re-enter the void if I need you?"

His form shifted back into its familiar flame. "Now that you know what you know, the risk is less, but Volaris was not the presence I sensed searching for you before. There is something else—someone else—using powerful essence magic to connect to the void. You may return, but only if I am with you in the mortal world. That's how you'll know it's safe."

She nodded.

"Rest, Raelyn." Hendrel flickered around her.

She closed her eyes and reached for the warmth of the stall and the prickle of straw on her skin. Gradually, the cold around her retreated and shrank back into the ball at her center, and she could hear the contented chewing sounds of ponies echoing nearby. With a deep breath, she cherished the packed rigidity of the stable bedding beneath her and the ache from lying on the ground, the discomforts welcome compared to the terror of the void. With her eyes closed, focused on the relief of being out of the seam, Raelyn let sleep claim her and take away her lingering uneasiness.

When she opened her eyes to Laris's firm nudging later in the morning, she felt more restored than during her first waking. Morning sun lit the stable and revealed fine dust particles, and a few of the ponies had left their stalls to wander outside. A film of smoke still hung in the air, but much had cleared out overnight, making it easier to take a full breath.

"Feel better?" asked Laris from where he sat on a barrel next to her.

She stretched and sat up. "Much. Though, I'd hoped to see Hendrel now that things have calmed down." She looked around, but the wisp hadn't returned despite their connection in the void. "I'm sorry I woke you so early."

"Don't worry about it." He smirked. "There are worse ways to wake up."

She studied him, wondering what he found entertaining, but it only made his smile wider. He leaned forward and plucked a few strands of straw from her hair. "Let's head out. Emblem knows how far we have to go, but we should make the most of each day's travel."

Vehsidhe crowded the courtyard, filling it with activity. With the fire out and the immediate danger passed, the slow process of recovering had begun. Many of the survivors sat focused on cooking and rationing or tending to the wounded. Some sifted through the remnants of the fortress, looking for anything that might prove useful. Others rested, taking the time necessary for their hearts to recover from individual losses.

Aetris stood in the center of a field of makeshift tents, helping direct those who were uncertain of where to put their energy. Across the courtyard, Laylia ladled food into bowls being passed out to those breaking fast.

"You look improved," the *vehsidhe* lord said as they approached. "The stable was comfortable enough?"

"Comfortable enough," Laris replied. "We will be on our way with direction to the nearest human settlement."

"I have promised the warden gifts before you go. They will be more helpful than any map or directions." Aetris waved to one of the guards, who brought over a long, wooden box. "Here," he said, opening it. "*Vehsidhe* talismans. They will grant you safe passage through most of the feyfolk lands. But most importantly, they will let you speak to the griffin of the mountain."

Raelyn took one of the two medallions offered. Hanging on a necklace, it was heavier than expected, made from a white stone with jagged streaks of gold. The feather-shaped pendant's edges were surprisingly sharp.

Would the Moon Mother have given us something similar had we returned? Raelyn watched the stone feather spin on its chain. She doubted she'd ever see Dar'Liha or the *gonsidhe* village again, but she hoped news of Mondek's defeat had made it back to the kind feyfolk.

"The griffin is not a friend of the *vehsidhe*," he went on. "Nor is he an enemy. We displease him because of our human blood, but at the same time, a part of him considers us kin. He is your best hope if you wish for a swift exit from the mountains."

"You're saying there's no guarantee he'll help us." Laris turned his identical talisman in his hand, looking it over. "It could be a waste of time."

"His aerie is on this mountain. If he is unmoved by your request, you lose only a day. Should that be the case, return here, and we will provide you with a guide."

Raelyn slid the necklace over her head, excitement coursing through her at the thought of meeting a griffin. For a moment, her elation chased away the wisps of numbness growing around her heart, a strange sense of disconnection she noticed with each passing battle and each day of the unknown. It was a dream of hers to see a griffin up close. If she got to speak with the majestic creature, no word of complaint would leave her lips, even if they had to crawl their entire way to the capital.

"How do we get there?" she asked.

"Behind the roost, there is a path up the mountain. It is steep and difficult but otherwise safe. It will take you directly to the griffin's aerie. Announce yourselves before you enter as friends of the Divine One and keep your talismans visible. Ah," he added, accepting two more items from one of the other guards. "Your weapons. Recovered from the Shattered Pass. We did not retrieve the godsbane blade, but your steel sword and glaive are here."

Famine felt warm in her hands, almost welcoming. A leather cover protected the blade, and a strap was added to the handle. She positioned it across her back and felt comforted by the weight.

"Now, eat," Aetris instructed. "The griffin is wise, but you will not find him bothered with the comforts of mortals." He motioned to Laylia who dished out two rations and headed toward them.

Raelyn and Laris ate in silence, steam climbing into the morning air from their bowls. The warm mash was simple but filling, and Raelyn was grateful for the energy as they left the roost and started up the mountain.

Narrow and slippery, the path took a winding and twisting course, its erratic route necessary to progress up the steep incline. A few sparse pine trees dotted the cliffsides and disappeared the higher they climbed into the peaks. Soon, only tufts of brown-green mountain grass poked out among the rocks.

Pausing in their ascent, Raelyn looked out across the Vast. From their position, endless mountains stretched away against the blue sky. A crisp breeze danced around her, and a wash of peacefulness rolled over her with it. *I could stay in this moment forever,* she thought wistfully, choosing to ignore, just for an instant, the thoughts of worry and fear always on her trail.

Somewhere out there was the Holy Citadel, and on the Holy King's throne, an imposter. Did he know about her? Was he the one searching for her? The fears and doubts sunk their claws in, and she shuddered, distracted by an imagined life more unyielding and confining than any she had ever expected. No destinies were inescapable, but what price would be demanded for her freedom? Staring out at the mountains, she wished for a reason to stay within their imposing shadows.

"Raelyn?"

Laris's voice summoned her from her thoughts, and she looked up at him on the ledge above with a smile of reassurance. "I'm coming," she answered. "I was just admiring the view."

With one last look out at the peaks in the distance, she steeled herself for the journey ahead. Hiding away wouldn't save Ellisand, and it wouldn't bring back Mengat, Lydantus, her father, or any of the lives lost in her wake. She owed it to all of them to carry on, to make it to the Sundered Gate and face Emblem's designs for her.

Laris waited not far ahead but already a level above her. "It looks as though we're close," he said when she turned back from her sight-seeing. "See the rock ledge and cave above?" He pointed.

Not far from where they stood, the path vanished where it met a wall of craggy stone. At the top, a large, flat ledge fanned out, and beyond it opened a wide maw in the mountainside. Raelyn waited anxiously to see the griffin emerge before them, but the aerie remained quiet.

"We'll have to climb," Laris said with resignation. "Again."

"It won't be any worse than when we were in the tunnels," she replied. "I thought my fingers would be worn to the bone back then."

"You did well," he said without looking back at her.

Pleased by his praise, she scrambled to catch up.

CHAPTER TWENTY

Climbing onto the ledge was less demanding than the trek up the mountain path. Staggered rocks, worn from use as steps at some point in the past, still provided access to the landing. Climbing over the lip of the rock, Raelyn was surprised to see how wide it stretched along the mountain before disappearing inside the large cave opening at its back. Unlike the caves in the foothills of the Vast, the entrance was tall and broad, allowing enough light to make long sections of the interior walls visible.

"Shall we announce ourselves?" Laris scanned the area. "Better to meet the griffin out in the open."

Shielding her eyes with a hand, Raelyn looked up at the sky. "What if more griffins come?"

"I think they are solitary. You're right to wonder, though. It's wise to be wary of the sky when dealing with creatures with wings." He walked to the cave opening and called out, "With the favor of the Divine One, we come seeking the great griffin of this mountain!"

The words echoed off the walls of the gigantic chamber, bouncing from one rock wall to another and back again. Her gaze pinned to the dark recesses where the light couldn't reach, Raelyn realized she was holding her breath in anticipation. Long moments crept by, but no answer came from within the cave.

"He could be out," he told her. "I don't know their habits. He might sleep deep within the cave during the day."

"I think the *vehsidhe* would have told us," she said, walking farther into the mountain cavity. "They said we'd only be gone for a few hours at best. Not that we have any reason to trust them, of course."

She placed a hand on the rough rock—pale, almost white in places, and small, shining flecks of mineral within reflected the daylight. The effect was more impressive when she gazed at the entirety of space; the walls sparkled as if made of tiny jewels.

"If you do not trust them, why do you invoke their name?" asked a loud, guttural voice from within a tunnel close to her. "It has been a long time since I have spoken the common tongue."

Raelyn froze and stared into the darkness. Scraping sounds from a large body brushing up against the rock carried out into the chamber, accompanied by the padding of slow, heavy footsteps. An eagle-like head appeared first within the shadows, soon followed by a feathered chest and folded wings that seemed too large for the space. Unlike the brown-and-white griffin Raelyn had seen once on an excursion from Castle Wedminth, his feathers were completely black, his feline back-side covered in tawny fur. Grey tufts flared out at each elbow, matched by long tendrils at the brow of his eyes and on the underside of his hooked beak. Once fully emerged before them, the massive cavern felt small.

"Humans," he said, disgusted. "Are you to blame for the smoke that chokes the base of my mountain?"

Raelyn opened her mouth, ready to claim responsibility, but Laris stepped to her side and said, "No. We are not to blame." He held up the talisman on his neck. "We were told this holds meaning for you."

The griffin lowered his head and peered at the dangling stone feather. Eyes narrowed, he blew a puff of breath at them through his nostrils. "Ancient, forgettable bonds. The *vehsidhe* of my domain are nothing to me now. They have become weak, spurned even among their kind."

"Things are changing," Raelyn said carefully. "There's a new Divine One. He wants change, and he'll allow magic again." The words were true, but they felt misleading. Saving the lives of future generations had come through plots of murder and at the cost of innocents. She wondered if the griffin cared about the morality of his near-kin.

"And does that please you, unraveller of magic? Do you not hate magekind?"

It didn't surprise her that the griffin recognized what she was. His presence was the most otherworldly and powerful of all the beings they'd encountered. "I don't hate mages," she answered. "I've seen magic do incredible good in the world. I think it's like anything else," she said, "steered by the person using it."

"And you?" He fixed Laris with a piercing, critical look. "Are you free of the sins of your kind? Or will you be seduced by power like so many before you?"

Laris met the griffin with his own, quieter intensity. "I have no grand ambitions," he said. "I swore an oath under the Holy King that as a transcendent, I would use magic for the betterment of mankind, not its destruction."

"The Holy King." The griffin snorted in amusement. "I hear Ute speaks no more. I hear," his voice boomed, "that the gods have abandoned you mortals."

"He's not silenced by choice," Raelyn interjected with a whisper. "His last warden was murdered. I've spoken with him."

As if she'd summoned him with her words, Hendrel's teardrop of flame sputtered into existence. It floated around her head and then darted in front of the griffin's face, hovering in his line of sight. He watched the light dance around, following it with his eyes but saying nothing, and a low sound of concession issued from his throat.

"Human woman, what is your name?"

"Raelyn," she answered with a bow of her head. "Raelyn Forthgrew."

The griffin sat upright. He shook out his feathers, sending a cascade of cave dust and wispy plumage into the air around them. "I am known as Braymorian. I was there, in the beginning of your age, when the gods warred. I am the oldest of my kind, and I do not concern myself with the lives of mortals." He held up a front claw, silencing Raelyn's attempted rebuttal. "Usually. However, I will listen to your request, as you undoubtedly came here with one. Though I have no love of gods or mortals, I respect the order Ute has bestowed upon this world. Now tell me, why have you and your mage sought me out?"

"We wish to leave the mountains. I've been given a task, a destination I must reach, and we were forced into the tunnels beneath the Vast during an attack." Raelyn stole a quick glance at Laris. He appeared deep in thought, watching the griffin warily. "The *vehsidhe* said you could help us."

"The nearest human settlements are many leagues away, with many obstacles between. Winter would have you deep within its grasp before you reached the foothills."

"Fly us out. There's no point in dancing around it." Laris crossed his arms. "Unless you have another way, we ask you to fly us out of the Vast."

Braymorian puffed another breath of air at them. "Why would I demean myself so?"

Laris shook his head and reached for Raelyn's hand. "Come," he said to her. "We'll go back and get a guide. We've made it this far; we'll get to the capital on our own."

"Wait." A wing extended to block their path. "Do not try my patience, mage. I will fly you, but not because I care to save you the months of toil it would take to climb over the mountains in your path. I will fly you because one day, you two may be all that stands between order and chaos, and I am too old to see this world start anew." He turned away from them, his bulky body knocking loose stone from the walls. "It is not easy for humans to travel through the air. You must ride within a harness, or the wind will steal your breath and force you from my body. Wait here, and I will retrieve it."

They listened to the scrape of feathers fade along with Braymorian's bulk down one of the tunnels. The griffin's black upper body melted into the shadows, leaving only his feline half visible as he went out of sight. When the gentle rasp of his movement against the rocks was no more, Raelyn turned to Laris excitedly.

"I've always dreamed of riding a griffin," she said, clasping her hands together. "I can't believe it's going to happen."

"Don't let your excitement get the better of you. It's not what you think. At least, not if the texts are accurate. The harness is more like a basket than a saddle, and it's off to the side, not over the back." At her crestfallen look, he added, "You'll still be flying on a griffin."

She watched Hendrel dance around the cavern. His light set the tiny minerals in the stone aglow as he darted around the space, each fleck glimmering in its own time, sending twinkling waves across the walls.

"Are you upset I didn't tell you about Hendrel being murdered?" she asked and gave Laris a regretful look.

"No." He sighed. "Surprised, but not upset. When the Holy King died, many transcendents suspected foul play even though the Citadel claimed a mysterious illness had taken him. The Holy Knights weren't forthcoming with details, and there was no way to learn the truth behind the story."

She felt relief wash over her. "I'm still trying to understand it all, honestly. Hendrel says I've only just learned what it really means to be a warden. But he speaks in riddles, always."

"Raelyn, deep down, you must know what it all means."

Wrapping her arms around herself, she looked at the rocks overhead and watched Hendrel's glimmering waves chase away the shadows. She did know what it could all mean, and the thought terrified her. The Holy Citadel was dark, with no warden to pass down the words or protection of Emblem. She was a warden bound to the last Holy King. It was not a stretch of her imagination to think of what for.

"It scares me," she admitted. "I can't even imagine being that person. I don't think I could go through connecting with a god again. Can a woman even be the Holy King?"

Laris walked over and took her hands in his. "If Emblem has chosen you, there'll be none who can deny you," he said in a low voice. "And anyone who would harm you would have me to face."

"I'm not the Holy King yet," she said with conviction. "No one has claimed that."

"You're right, but ignoring the possibility with all you know is foolish. Listen," he said, "there are no forks in the path right now. We have to get out of the mountains and to Osharia. Beyond that has yet to be decided."

She nodded. "I wonder how close we can get to the capital. I doubt Braymorian will be willing to fly us too far into human territory."

"If he could get us to the foothills, that would be enough."

"I can take you north and west," the griffin's voice echoed out of the passage, "to where the mountains seep into the edges of the Arn Hollow. It is the only place I can descend without tempting the wiles of Men. We will be unseen."

He emerged fully into the chamber and dropped a metal and leather contraption on the ground at their feet. "Behold," he said, unimpressed, "a relic from a time when griffins were allied with Men. To think I held on to it for all these centuries."

The harness was nothing like Raelyn imagined. From what she could gather by looking at the tangle of straps and braces, it would cinch around Braymorian like a wide belt just behind his wings. On either side were basket-like attachments, narrow but large enough to hold a person lying down. Metal plates, angled like arrow points, capped off each holder at the front, and a solid wood base helped the rest of the mesh tube keep its shape.

"We're to ride in those?" she asked in disbelief.

"It is the only way to protect you. Unless you are a mage with other solutions." He inclined his head toward Laris. "Come. Help me position it."

Braymorian used his front talons to sling the harness over his back. Sitting on his haunches, he pulled the ends of one strap together across the front of his chest and buckled them. "Mage, I will secure the buckle at my belly. Keep the holsters at the sides even."

"It's Laris," he replied while tugging the leather to position it. "They're even."

Braymorian tightened the central belt and stretched his body out. With a shake, he tested the harness's position and extended one wing and then the other. "It will do," he said. "You will climb into the holsters facing up or down; it is your choice. I recommend facing down so you may watch the land beneath us."

Raelyn puzzled for a moment, figuring out how the holster worked. Entry at the end with the pointed plates allowed her to crawl in feet first. Once lying on her stomach, she pulled the cap back into position and secured it with a bolt sunk into the wooden base. Leather straps supported the rest of her body and angled up to several anchor points along the central harness. Though she could easily let her arms dangle freely through holes in the lattice of straps, a handle cut from the wooden base on each side provided added security.

"Have people ever ridden on your back?" she asked, testing how much she could move her body.

"It is impractical," answered the griffin, "unless just above ground level and at slow speed. When we fly amongst the clouds, extend a hand and see how much force you must overcome." He turned his head to each side, making sure they were each secured. "Hold on until we are in the air."

Laris made an affirmative grunt, but Raelyn barely had time to grab the handles in her harness before Braymorian bounded out of the cave and across the landing. The motion was large and jarring; it was all Raelyn could do to keep her grip. Unable to see directly ahead, she felt his body leave the ground with a giant leap. Below, the landing disappeared from view, and the tops of the trees ahead swayed with downward wind from Braymorian's wings.

Despite not riding a griffin in the sense she'd always imagined, the feeling of being in the air sent exhilarating spikes of excitement through her. Air whipped around the metal cap to pull at her from the side, and through the openings in the leather straps, she could see the trees shrinking away. Small and tucked within the mountain valleys, they looked like blades of grass.

Braymorian continued to ascend, rising and dropping suddenly in his flight with the changing air currents. At times, Raelyn gripped the harness handles so tightly her knuckles went white. During times of steadiness, she relaxed her grip and took in the scenery below. Through it all, the mountains still loomed around them, and even though she knew they were traveling quickly, the stone peaks looked unchanging and immovable.

"The mountain of Tura Ley," Braymorian called back to them, flying near a dark peak jutting through the clouds. "Home to one of the last *montigrath* dragons in Uhmeer, Shedimyio the Husk. He sleeps, but you would have passed through his domain had you traveled by foot."

She couldn't yell a reply loud enough to overcome the wind, so she turned her attention to the mountain to their left. Unlike most of the others, it was barren from the base up; a tower of sheer rock cliffs with few ledges. Only near the top did the stone break apart into different levels. *An impenetrable fortress*, Raelyn thought, studying the severe cuts of rock. Precisely the place she would go if she wanted to be left alone by the world.

A gust of wind rattled through the holster, and she shivered. With the initial wonderment of being in the sky gone, other realities started to set in. She shivered with cold, and the constant wind across her lower half was numbing. She moved closer to Braymorian's side, but there was little warmth against his feathers. Fingers as numb as her legs, they ached when she tried to release them from their hold on the wooden handles.

As the hours passed, she closed her eyes and tucked herself out of the wind as much as possible. Part of her wanted to sleep the time away, but she was wary of becoming dislodged by an unexpected aerial maneuver. *Who would travel regularly like this?* she wondered. *Royalty?*

Assassins? She could think of only a few reasons for such a limited type of transportation.

"A time for rest, humans," Braymorian yelled. "We head down for landing!"

Raelyn was glad she hadn't tried to sleep. The sudden dip in their flight made her stomach twist. Clutching the holster handles, Raelyn felt her body lift in a brief state of weightlessness that vanished abruptly as Braymorian stopped his descent to ease onto the ground.

Hands shaking, she undid the latch on her holster and pulled herself out, unprepared for how her legs went weak when she tried to stand. Her butt hit the ground hard, and she winced without trying to get up again. Laris was in a similar state. From his hands and knees, he'd managed to roll to his back and was lying on the ground, arms and legs outstretched.

They were on a mountain ledge, far above any height Raelyn had climbed before. Barren rocks sheltered them from the wind, but the thin air and the cold hung heavy, icing their breath.

"We shall not delay long," the griffin told them. "I need only rest briefly."

"How far are we from the Arn Hollow?" Laris asked from where he lay.

"Another hour of flight, nothing more. I will leave you on the back side of the forest. A day of traveling inward will see you to settlements of Men."

Raelyn was familiar with the Arn Hollow, Limnin's oldest forest. Stretching along the country's northeastern mountain border, it wrapped into the northern territory where it was cut-through by the Endelaid, the source river for the east-flowing Ven and the west-flowing Quan. A wild place where no new trees had grown in centuries, its mysterious reputation gained clout through local superstitions. Raelyn's father once told her he'd taken shelter in the Arn Hollow in his foot-soldier days, but while it was a strange place, he'd felt safe beneath its canopy.

On his feet, Laris walked over and crouched next to her. "Well, was it everything you'd hoped for?"

She gave an exasperated laugh. "Not quite, but I don't regret it. Why would anyone choose to ride in one of those?"

"During the Great War, it was necessary to move delegates far distances in short amounts of time," replied Braymorian. "Important emissaries, mages—" he tilted his head and met her gaze "—wardens. All important pieces to be moved from one battlefield to the next."

"Did anyone ride dragons?" She let Laris help her up and smiled at his frown to her question.

"No. Dragons are unconcerned with the movements of lesser beings. They are beyond mortal influence, even when the gods waged battle in human bodies. They were here when your age began, and they will remain long after it is over."

"Take one flight on a griffin, and now you're thinking about dragons." Laris shook his head. "Only one dragon has ever been written into the history books as an ally of humans, and it was so long ago, I'm half convinced it was a myth."

"Old Hew of the Barrow." Braymorian nodded. "The tales are true. And he yet lives, though, his mountain is down in the southern range of Uhmeer. He is fond of the sea."

Raelyn eased close to Laris, seeking his warmth but too timid to force the contact. He caught her shy glance, pulled her in front of him, and wrapped his arms around her. Their shared warmth wasn't much, but it was enough to chase away the cold mountain air's bite. She couldn't help her smile and was glad he couldn't see her expression.

Braymorian watched them with interest. "You are mates?" he asked. "A strange pairing, mage and warden."

Raelyn knew he didn't mean mates solely in the intimate form of the word, but she blushed deeply and couldn't bring herself to confirm or deny the question.

The griffin narrowed his eyes in amusement, catching her embarrassment. "I had a mate once," he remarked. "A she-griffin the likes of which no longer exist. Feathers as red as the sun at dusk, fur the color of dark chestnut. Her name was Glavenia." He looked out into the mountains. "Her life was stilled in the Battle of the Grey, a great conflict between the griffins and the remaining forces of Ube after Ute's victory."

Compelled to comfort him, Raelyn left Laris's arms and did her best to embrace the griffin at his neck. She swallowed hard, feeling his sadness as if it were her own.

Braymorian gently nudged her with his head. "You are kind, Raelyn Forthgrew. Do not let the world change you. Come. Let us fly again. I would see you to the Arn Hollow before dark."

She stepped away sheepishly. "I need to be excused for a moment before we go," she said, eyeing the largest boulder at the far end of the ledge. The cold flight had successfully numbed her exterior to minor discomforts, but she desperately needed to relieve her bladder.

Braymorian huffed when he realized her meaning and shifted to face the opposite direction.

"I'll go as well, when you're done," Laris said, also turning away from her. "I'd rather not have the urge while we're locked in those leather holsters."

Raelyn didn't reply and hurried over to the rock.

The last hour of their flight was more enjoyable than the first part of the journey had been. The sun sank slowly in the sky, and the wind currents stilled as the bright sphere approached the horizon. They flew lower, still high above the treetops but close enough for Raelyn to catch passing glimpses of life. Fires dotted the valley floors, and every so often, a tall tower interrupted the sea of trees below. Skimming the edges of a stream clearing, she saw another band of *vehsidhe* who all stopped and watched them fly overhead.

Where the mountains rolled into hills, evidence of feyfolk vanished. Rocky knolls covered in tall grasses marked the foothills, and just as twilight embraced them fully, she saw the edges of a dark tree line.

Braymorian descended well before the forest edge, flying slowly above the ground. He eased them into the landing a few paces from the first trees in a shallow basin where a trickling spring bubbled out from the side of the natural earthen wall.

Not as shaken as she was after their first landing, Raelyn climbed out of her holster and stretched. "Would you like help taking the harness off?"

"There is no need," replied the griffin. "It will be easier to fly back with it in place, and I can undo the buckles without assistance."

"You'll fly back in the dark?"

"The dark is a griffin's preferred time to fly, but it becomes far too cold for human travelers."

Laris surveyed the area. "The water source is lucky, but this is too open to spend a night safely."

"You will not find many feyfolk in the foothills, and they have no love of the Arn Hollow. You would be safer here, at its edges, than too deep within the trees." Braymorian stretched his wings and sat back on his haunches. "There are wild creatures in the woods that are to be feared by feyfolk and Men alike. You are best served to travel by day."

"We're not so far from the forest that we'd be spared," Laris pointed out. "I would feel more comfortable with something at our backs."

"Are you not a mage?" The griffin raised an eyebrow. "A stone-skilled mage? Surely, you could erect yourself a shelter. There are plenty of rocks within the ground."

"I don't use my magic for trivial things. It demands strength—strength I might need if we are attacked."

"Bah, what nonsense. It would take nothing for you to create a basic hovel. I have never met a mage so recalcitrant to use his abilities. Why, when I last dealt with Men, there were mages who could manipulate the air, and that magic is not even visible."

"A lost art among humans," Laris said curtly. "But you're right. For our safety, a shelter tonight might be wise."

From where she sat on the bank by the spring, Raelyn watched her companions bicker with a sense of relief. With some semblance of control over her powers, Laris was free to use his. She wondered how many of their struggles would have been avoided if she'd been properly trained.

Hendrel blinked into existence next to her after being absent for their flight. He hovered momentarily before leaving to chase the spring on its journey toward the wood line.

"See?" she heard Braymorian say. "Your energy will be restored before the night is fully cast. You are too powerful to be concerned over such menial uses."

Laris's small three-sided shelter had a sloping roof that faced away from the Arn Hollow. Set into the ground with a stone floor that was slightly raised above dirt level, it looked far from comfortable, but it would be dry and protected from the wind. Raelyn pushed herself up and walked over.

"No fire tonight," Laris told her. "We can't risk the light drawing unwanted attention."

She nodded and turned to the griffin. "Are you sure you won't stay with us until the morning?"

"I am too long from my territory," he said, "and I would not linger in that of another. Though she rarely flies the skirt of the Vast, this is Ibinhet's realm."

Raelyn gave him another embrace. "It's always been my dream to fly with a griffin. Thank you for that. I will never forget it, or you."

"Perhaps someday we will meet again," he said. "Keep your talismans. They will mark you as a friend among all *vehsidhe*." He pulled away from her. "It has been enlightening, Raelyn Forthgrew. I wish you luck, wherever destiny may take you."

He leaped into the air, and Raelyn shielded her eyes from the sudden downward gust of wind. All too soon, Braymorian disappeared into the darkening night sky, leaving behind a sense of loss she felt deeply. In all her life, she'd never thought she'd meet a griffin, speak with a griffin, and fly with a griffin. It felt like a dream, and she stared into the sky long after he was gone.

"I'll keep watch." Laris inclined his head toward the stone shelter. "Try to get some sleep. It won't be comfortable, but we've slept on worse."

Instead of following his lead, she sat next to him. "Let me sit with you a while," she said, her voice soft. "I'm not ready to leave this moment just yet."

"I'm sorry you didn't get to ride astride like a fierce warrior maiden headed into battle. But we might be the only people to have spoken to a griffin in hundreds of years."

"How did you know that's what I imagined?" She smiled. "You knew why I asked about the dragons, too, didn't you?"

He nodded. "You're not the only one with such dreams. I think everyone with adventure in their blood has those thoughts."

Out in the darkness, Raelyn could see Hendrel's light bobbing up and down along the line of the forest. He'd told her she could enter the void as long as he was with her in the physical realm, and he was here with them now. Even though the thought of returning filled her with dread, she knew it was the only way she could continue learning.

"I have to go to the void tonight," she said, resolute. "Hendrel said it would be safe."

"Are you sure you're ready for that? You don't have to push yourself too soon."

"There's still too much I don't know. I can't wait any longer to get the answers." She turned and looked at him. "If I had known how to assert my control when Volaris took me over, I could have avoided everything that happened after. I know gods used wardens to walk the mortal world, but who was in control? Were the wardens just doing the bidding of the gods, or were the gods controlling the wardens? Where does my will end and theirs begin?"

He didn't say anything but held her gaze.

"What does Emblem want with me?" She could feel her frustration building. "I'm tired of feeling helpless and lost. We're journeying to the Sundered Gate, and I have no idea why."

"Because it's the only safe place." Laris ran a hand down her loose hair, smoothing it. "Hendrel knows the Holy Citadel isn't safe for you. He was murdered there by his knights. The Sundered Gate is the only place to commune with Emblem at an unsupervised altar. Once you two join ..." He sighed. "You will have the power to take the Holy Citadel back by force if need be."

"Have you known this all along?"

"When you spoke of the Sundered Gate after communing with Genevive, I was suspicious. If she wanted to claim you for herself, she could have at the mountain shrine, so why didn't she? But it wasn't until I learned the identity of your wisp that it all became clear. And then—" he cupped her face "—other events demanded our attention."

She could barely make out his features in the near dark, but she could sense his intention as keenly as if he'd spoken the words. Waiting until he was just a breath away before closing his eyes, he slowly leaned in and pressed his lips to hers.

A shot of warmth flooded her core at the contact. His kiss was slow and gentle, but after a moment, he broke away. Still holding her face, he softly said, "If you don't want this, I will respect your wish." He touched his forehead to hers. "I should have asked long before now."

Raelyn did want what was between them, more than she knew how to put into words, yet she was frightened at the same time. Ellisand was the one with extensive knowledge of passion and romance, having spent hours reading about it in secret and spying on servant liaisons. She'd described encounters she'd seen in great detail to Raelyn, but Raelyn had always tuned the embarrassing parts out. The fact was, she was beyond inexperienced—she was ignorant.

"Of course I … want this," she stammered. "But I don't know what I'm doing." Shame laced her words, and she looked down.

"Do you think I want you to be experienced?"

"Don't tease me," she whispered in embarrassment.

He stopped her attempt to shift away. "If you were experienced, it would mean you gained the knowledge elsewhere." He turned her face back to his. "And that is not a thought I care to entertain. I can kiss you?"

Still feeling humiliated by her ineptness, she nodded.

"Good." He traced his thumb across her lips before leaning in again.

Raelyn did her best to relax and let herself be kissed. She focused on his movements, caught between the sensations thrumming through her and trying to reciprocate the kiss in kind. One of his hands moved from her face to her back, drawing her body closer to his. Every inch of her felt on edge, ready for something that her mind and heart were not. His hand dropped from her face and traced the line of her neck. She subconsciously pressed into him, and at her gasp against his mouth, Laris stopped their kiss.

"Did I do something wrong?"

He let out a ragged breath. "No, you do all the right things," he said, adding space between them. "That's the problem." As if he could sense her confusion, he added, "The sounds you make, the way you move against me. You don't realize, Raelyn, the effect you have."

She felt the flutter in her abdomen intensify at his words.

"Any longer, and we'd be in danger of something I don't want until you're ready. And not on a cold stone slab, out in the wilderness, vulnerable to attack. You deserve better than that."

She understood, and feelings of inadequacy morphed into gratitude and a sense of safety. He cared for her, not just lusted after her; that much she knew. Without warning, she wrapped her arms around him, holding him tightly with her head on his chest. He returned the embrace in silence until her pressure around him eased.

"Go journey," he urged her. "I'll come sit and watch over you."

Hendrel was waiting for her in the void, already in his human form. He welcomed her with open arms and a wash of light that made the cold nothingness more bearable.

"You have returned," he said joyously. "And your abilities continue to grow, though, you need to practice them."

She offered a slight smile but didn't share his elation. "I didn't want to come," she admitted. "Everything is still very fresh in my mind."

"You learned the most valuable lesson as a warden, Raelyn. Some lessons are learned the hard way, but sometimes, that is the best way."

"People died," she said with bitterness. "How is that a lesson worth learning?"

Hendrel's light dimmed, and his tone became somber. "You understand now what's at stake. You felt it, experienced it in its worst version. Such things can't be explained in words alone."

"It all comes down to this, doesn't it? The true purpose of wardens. Will Emblem force me, too, one day?"

Her questions hung like heavy stones suspended in the nothingness around them. After a long pause, Hendrel shook his head. "Your destiny is your own, Raelyn, no matter how we steer you. Are you Emblem's intended? It seems clear. Will you be the next Holy King? That will depend on you and the choices you make. Just as we work to our ends, you will work toward yours and others to theirs. Nothing in life is certain. There are many possible outcomes. We cannot force you on our path."

"Before I go to the Sundered Gate, I need to know more about what happens when wardens embody gods."

"I will tell you what I can, though, I never experienced it in my short life." Hendrel clasped his hands behind him and rocked back and forth. "Wardens are like mages, born with a gift but individual capacity. Strong wardens can maintain their will against a god or others seeking to use their bodies. They can deny those beings from entry, regulate their actions in the physical world, and dispel them if need be.

"Weaker wardens are not as capable. They can be taken over against their will, sometimes by beings lesser than gods. For those poor souls, their will dissolves. They become puppets until the entity chooses to leave them.

"You are strong. The first time you came into the void, you pulled the spirits of the living and dead with you. In all my learning, I've never seen that ability attributed to another warden. To bring the life energy of a living mortal forcefully into the seam of the worlds is astonishing. And not only did you bring them, but you also took them with you when you left. Thankfully, too, because I had no way to instruct you on how to do it."

She sat down and leaned back, propped up by both arms. Part of her wanted to leave the void and come back when her mind felt less overwhelmed, but hearing Hendrel confirm her thoughts was empowering and reassuring, if not sobering.

"So *if* I commune with Emblem, I'll still be able to be me at the same time?"

He joined her in sitting, crossing his legs beneath him. "Emblem is not like the other gods. He is the most powerful, and Lord of The Circle. As strong as you are, I cannot say what will become of you."

"And what happens if I don't become the Holy King?"

"We cannot know." He shrugged. "Another may take your place, or the Citadel will continue to be dark. Without a Holy King, though, your world is in peril. The Holy King is the guardian of the physical realm, the conduit allowing Emblem to return if need be. His brother, Ube, is not dead, you know. Defeated in the Cataclysm, but not dead; he is a god. There are many who wish to replace Emblem and return chaos to the mortal realm."

"It's too much for me right now," she said, shaking her head and pressing her fingers against her closed eyes. After a long sigh, she looked up at him. "Tell me how to build my will. I will continue to practice everything else, but *that* I need to know if I'm going to the Gate."

"I cannot tell you." He shifted back into a flame. "Not because I don't want to, but because I do not know. Unlike abilities to manipulate the void, which can be taught, your will is shaped by your experience of the world. In some people it is broken, shattered by life's troubles. In others, it is a pillar of iron, forged by the same trials that broke some."

"So what am I to do? Just continue blindly?"

"Practice," he answered. "And ask for help in what you don't know. It's okay to seek knowledge in others."

"Riddles." She frowned at him and stood up. "I'll wait for you, then. I'm not angry at you, Hendrel, just so you know. If I seem ill-tempered, it's not you."

"I know." He did several spins around her. "I'm proud of you, Raelyn."

She smiled weakly at him, still feeling anxiousness and doubtful about her abilities and existence. She was trying to learn in months what wardens of the past took decades to master, and for all of his wisdom, Hendrel wasn't all-knowing. She realized that now. He could pass on to her what he'd learned during his lifetime, but details were hidden from him, as well.

I'll have to find my way somehow, she thought with forced conviction. No matter what it took, no matter how long or hard she had to train, she would never let anyone else control her will again. With a sense of grim determination, she set her focus on the cold, hard slab of Laris's shelter along the outskirts of the Arn Hollow.

CHAPTER TWENTY-ONE

araht decided she didn't like the cat. The orange feline took every opportunity to insert itself into their company but paid particular attention to Ellisand, sometimes staring at her intently until she returned its look. It was unnerving, but Saraht could find no reasonable cause to deny the creature their company.

"Ho, so you're heading out, then?" Jormand tossed a cleaning rag down on the bar. "Didn't think we'd be parting ways so soon."

"I have business in the capital," Saraht said. Across the room, Ellisand and the cat sat together at one of the tables. "The wayfarers have offered for us to join them on the road. As much as I'd rather travel alone, they can quickly pass through at the gate. And you know how I feel about Osharia guards."

"Might as well accept the good fortune," he said with a wink at Maylam. "Few travelers experience the benefit of being an honorary wayfarer."

"No, dear, not for me," Maylam said, dismissing the idea with a wave. "I have a mind to stay here if you'll humor an old woman."

"Ach, you don't even need to ask. I'll have the girls keep your room as it is." He disappeared into the back room with a shout.

Saraht knew her mother wouldn't venture into the capital. Not even as a dead woman, Maylam would have told her if asked. It was a kindness on Jormand's part to let her stay and an even greater kindness not to press the subject. The innkeeper knew their history—though, not in its entirety—and even after all these years, he spoke to them with great consideration.

"You're certain this is where you want to stay?" she asked her mother.

"What better place to witness a new beginning than the place where our journey truly began?" Maylam patted her on the arm. "Do not forget to check in with *him* once you're settled."

She nodded. Prince Thiir was the least of her worries at the moment, but she still had to handle him carefully. She was too close to her goal to let the plan fall apart now, and making an enemy of the Faldea ruler would immediately set Orion and his assassins on her trail.

Maylam's kiss on her cheek roused Saraht from deeper thoughts. She smiled. "Sorry, Mother, what did you say?"

"I was saying, dear, that I'm going to head upstairs." She hugged her daughter from behind as she went to walk past. "Be careful. Be wise. When the capital is ours, send word, and I'll come," she whispered close to Saraht's ear. "Make sure he suffers."

Too many words had already been said that should have been private, so Saraht nodded and reached her arms up around Maylam's at her chest. She felt her mother pull away. It was the first time they would be apart for more than a night in fifteen years. Though she was confident in her plan, she knew there was a chance they might never reunite. *As long as Rothelian dies,* she thought, *I can die with him if that's what it takes.*

The rest of her plan, the part no one other than her mother knew about, was motivated by more selfish interests. Somewhere in Osharia castle was the Sundered Gate, the only place left in where she could commune with—and bring back—Raloria. With the goddess back in the mortal realm, she'd restore the old ways and be free of Thiir and any other man who sought to use her for their gain.

"They're ready for you, ma'am," a voice from the door called over to her. Mickel gave an eager wave and a broad smile, and she waved back in acknowledgment.

"Jormand," she called loud enough to be heard behind the curtain, "we're taking our leave. Try to keep Mother out of trouble, will you?"

He threw the sheet of fabric wide and bounded around the end of the bar. "I'll tell Pen you said farewell." He smothered her in an embrace. "If you need anything," he said, "anything at all, stop by and see my cousin at the Hall of Lords. His inn is near the city center. Ask for Mollen. Oh, and watch your backs out there. Rumors are that Albator is nothing but dust and ash now. The duke is dead."

She pretended to be surprised. "Albator was attacked? That's a bold move. Faldea?"

He pursed his lips and shrugged. "No one knows. Not even the duchess who escaped could put a name to her attackers. Some say she speaks of penumbra and wretches."

Saraht felt a cold weight settle in her stomach. "The duchess?"

"Aye."

"She made it out alive?"

Jormand walked back behind the bar. "Arrived in the capital not long ago with some other survivors. One of the long patrolmen who stopped here yesterday said they were in poor shape."

Unaware of the turbulent feelings swirling within Saraht at what he'd said, Jormand smiled at Ellisand as she walked toward them holding the cat. "Wee thing's taken a liking to you," the innkeeper said thoughtfully. "Used to think I was his favorite till you came around."

"He likes everyone," Ellisand remarked and stroked the cat cradled in her arm. "The troupe calls him Chap, but I prefer Lydantus. It sounds more dignified."

"Lydantus?" Saraht steadied her composure and narrowed her eyes at the cat. "That's an uncommon name. Where did you come up with that?"

Ellisand smiled. "I'm not sure. Must be something I read at some point."

"Hmm, well, best go put him in the cart he's to travel in. I don't imagine he'd be fun to ride with on your horse's back."

Jormand nodded. "Aye. One scratch and your horse would leave you and the tiny lad in the mud. Here, hand him to me, and I'll put him in Bea's wagon. He's in her act, and I'm sure she'll be wanting to know he's safe."

Mickel was waiting with the horses out front amidst a handful of colorful wagons and mounts belonging to the wayfarers. Clouds of breath from people and horses alike filled the crisp morning air. Unlike their colorful clothes and carts, the wayfarers' steeds were solid black. With long manes and tails, they displayed abundant hair around their hooves called feathers. It was for luck, Saraht recalled, that only black horses were used by wayfarers. A tribute to a tale in their lore about a hero's midnight escape on a black stallion.

Saraht looked away to scan the rest of their traveling group but felt her gaze kidnapped by Lydantus peering at her from the back of a blue wagon with red trim. He watched her, unblinking, so still it made her shift uncomfortably in her saddle. *Damn cat. I usually like cats, too.* She turned her horse away from him.

A tall man on a large black gelding trotted over. "Ladies, welcome to Zeherit's Brigade. I, of course, am your host, the mighty Zeherit. We are honored to have you traveling with us." He bowed as low as he could in the saddle with a flourish of his arm and fixed Ellisand with a sultry look. "I hope you will enjoy your time with us."

Watching Ellisand offer him a flirtatious smile and tilt of her head in return, Saraht replied, "We are honored to join such a fine party." She turned her eyes to Zeherit. "We will follow your lead, master wayfarer."

With a hand signal, the carts and horses took to the road. Their path through Golinstone led past the center of town. Lanterns flickered to life in shop windows, and vendors walked the streets, propping up their booth flaps for the day's business. It was a small town but large enough to have a pleasing marketplace, and Saraht watched the morning activity with a sense of nostalgia. During the time she and her mother spent recovering at the inn, she'd often come to the market on errands for Jormand and Penelope. In another life, Golinstone was a place she saw herself settling in forever.

They passed through the archway at the far end of town in a long line. Zeherit and several other wayfarer men rode at the head of the group while the rest of the party filtered in alongside the wagons as they bumped along in single file. Many wayfarers rode their own horses, reserving the wagons for all of their living necessities and performance gear. A few faces of very young children peeked out of cart windows and flaps, but even older members of the company were on horseback.

Sounds of pleasant conversation were a dull murmur in the background of Saraht's thoughts. The duchess was alive. How that information had eluded them, she didn't know, but it would directly affect what happened next in Osharia. With the duchess alive, Ellisand was no longer the head of the Wedminth family, nor was she the direct heir to the throne. The duchess, not the duke, was directly related to the king. When he died, the elder Wedminth woman would claim her birthright.

All the effort Saraht and Maylam had put into grooming Ellisand as an ally might be for naught. Thiir wouldn't be pleased with the news; he likely knew already if word had reached outlying towns like Golinstone. *All that matters is that Ellisand gets me into the castle,* she told herself. After that, it didn't matter which Wedminth was on the throne.

Still, the news was disappointing. Saraht didn't like surprises, let alone this close to the completion of her plan. She would have to learn more about the duchess when they arrived in the capital. If there were a reason, the woman could always be eliminated.

She reined in her horse and waited for Ellisand's grey to catch up. Now was as good a time as any to break the news to her.

"Are you ready to be off the road for good?" Saraht asked as the pair paced forward.

"I'm not the adventurer I thought I was," Ellisand answered. "I much prefer the thought of it all to the actual journey." She drew a deep breath with a smile. "And honestly, I'm excited to test my skills at court. The court ladies are renowned for their schemes and their backstabbing. It sounds much more exciting than spying on castle servants for intrigue."

"I would have never thought, based on our first meeting, that you'd so take to the art of manipulation. I mean that as a compliment. You're not the frail girl I thought you were."

Ellisand's smile disappeared. "I had to leave that girl behind to survive, and I don't regret it. She had no place in the real world."

"Well, you may need your newfound strength in the coming days. I received word today, Ellisand. Your mother—she's alive."

The grey horse slowed as Ellisand's contact on the reins dropped. "What?"

Saraht circled back around to her. "She's alive. She arrived in the capital recently with a small group of survivors."

"A small group of survivors." The words were barely audible. "Was Raelyn with them?"

At the other warden's name, Saraht bristled inwardly. There was a good chance Raelyn was with them for all she knew. She'd received no information whatsoever on any survivors from Wedminth castle, a fact that was growing more irritating by the minute. "I don't know," she admitted. "Not many details were clear. Don't you want to know more about your mother?"

"What more is there to know?" Ellisand urged her horse into a faster stride. "I'm not surprised she's alive. She was always my strongest parent."

"It might change things for us."

"Queen or princess, it doesn't matter to me," Ellisand said flippantly. "I'm going to go visit Lydantus. Are you coming?"

"Ah, no. I'm very fond of solitude this time of day. I'll enjoy the morning sun. You go on." She watched the other woman spur her horse ahead toward the blue wagon. "Visit a cat," she muttered under her breath. "What nonsense."

Heavy fog lay over the foothills when Raelyn woke. She could see Hendrel's flame wandering toward the mountains, fading in and out of visibility within the curtain of thick vapor. At some point in the night, Laris had propped her head onto his folded jerkin. He was sitting next to her now, staring off into the same direction of the wisp.

"You didn't wake me again," she said sullenly.

"I keep telling you, I'm trained for this." He looked down at her. "You did manage to sleep?"

"Some. Thank you for this." She handed his jerkin back. "It's cold this morning."

"The seasons shift sooner in the mountains. This feels like the first step toward autumn."

She crawled out of the shelter and made her way over to the spring. The water was frigid, and her breath caught in her throat when she splashed her face. "Oh that's awful! My hands are like ice. Did you use this to wash this morning?"

"I thought it felt good. Are you sure you don't want to wash more than your face?"

Scowling at him, she shook her head. "No, thank you. What's one more day of being dirty? Maybe we'll find a stream in the forest in the warmer part of the day."

"I don't think you'll need to worry about it." He stood and pointed to the clouds gathering on the horizon. "We're bound to see rain later on. We should head into the forest and try to find food. If there are as many predators as the griffin says, there'll also be prey within."

Raelyn watch Laris dismantle their stone shelter while she positioned the glaive at her back. Using fluid movements and small, almost invisible shifts of his fingers, he dissolved the stone back into the ground as if it had never been there.

"Amazing," she breathed. "I'll never get used to seeing it."

He smiled at her genuine awe. "Just wait until you meet one of the masters someday. They make my abilities look pitiful. Come." He gestured for her hand. "Let's go."

Large, misshapen trees rose from the ground, their sickly grey trunks hidden beneath thick layers of wispy bluish moss. Raelyn was used to the old, gnarled trees between the duchy and the mountains, their dark groves, and their eerie quiet. She'd always thought those woods were mysterious and untamed, but the Arn Hollow felt unwelcoming. An impenetrable canopy of dark leaves blocked out the early-morning sun so thoroughly she felt as though they were walking in twilight. Aside from the crunch of their footsteps, all was utterly silent.

She knew it wasn't a time for conversation. Hendrel was gone again, and Laris was on alert. Content with the silence and warming her body up with steady movement, Hendrel's absence tugged at her awareness. His vanishing acts had become Raelyn's marker of potential peril. If the wisp was gone, they were in a place he didn't care to be.

He said to practice. I might as well take my mind off things. She focused on the void in her center, seeking the same feeling of compartmentalization she'd found during their battle with Mondek.

The process was slower, not fueled by necessity. Still, it came easier than before, and she picked different trees along their path as targets for her trial and error. Just as she successfully found a rhythm controlling two spheres of influence, she noticed Laris waiting ahead.

He pressed a finger to his lips as she approached and indicated the area just beyond. Careful with her steps, Raelyn looked past him and was surprised to a see a house. Made in the traditional style of wood beams and stone blocks, the large building seemed in good condition. Though touched by trees on every side, its walls were straight and intact, and she couldn't tell if the trees had grown around the house or if the house was built around the trees. Glass windowpanes revealed darkness within, but a tendril of smoke rose out of the chimney.

Laris took her hand and slowly walked a wide berth around the home. Raelyn watched for signs of activity. All remained dark and quiet until they skirted the front to head deeper into the forest.

When they turned away from the house and toward the shelter of the forest, the air filled with singing. Raelyn and Laris whipped around at the sound coming from inside the house. A few of the windows were newly illuminated, and the chimney churned out thick puffs of smoke. The singing continued, loud and clear and beautiful.

Looking at one another, they both breathed a sigh in relief. Releasing her hand, Laris unsheathed his sword and motioned for her to do the same with her weapon. Raelyn shifted the shoulder strap forward and unfastened Famine. If something ambushed them during their trek, she would have her weapon ready. The house in the woods had been a harmless reminder anything could lay in their path as they traveled onward.

A lack of undergrowth in the Arn Hollow was in striking contrast to the tangle of the duchy woods, and the giant trees' roots plunged into the ground close to their trunks. Walking was easy and quick, though, the light of day remained hidden above the canopy of leaves. Taking a break from her practice, Raelyn studied the ground while they pressed on. Brittle leaves beneath her feet cracked with dryness but weren't layered as thickly on the ground as she expected in a forest without sunlight. The farther they traveled, the more she felt like they were interrupting a moment in time when the Arn Hollow was trapped, forever unchanging.

Around midday, the welcome burble of a stream interrupted the silence. Wide with shallow and clear water, it carried on a flat path and gently cascaded down a short waterfall as the terrain sloped away. Raelyn spotted the overcast sky through the break above the streambed, framed by branches of the ancient trees reaching out into the space over the water.

Flecks of rain hit her cheeks. "Here it comes," she said, both disappointed and glad about the change in the weather. A soaking rain would do more for her than a spotty bath in the creek, but it meant spending the rest of their journey in wet clothing.

"Back into the forest," Laris called from halfway across the stream. "The canopy should shield us well enough unless it becomes a downpour."

He waited for her to find a path of rocks high enough above the water to cross. Making sure she was on her way, he turned and cleared the rest of the stream with two well-planned leaps.

Light rain peppered Raelyn's face, the fine spray settling across her skin in a cool, refreshing mist. She tentatively navigated the stones, not confident enough to follow Laris's lead to the opposite bank but pleased with her haphazard path. She jumped into the fullness of the Arn Hollow, and suddenly, pouring rain drowned out the sounds of the brook.

Within the cover of the trees, they watched the downpour hit the open area of the stream. Not a drop of water penetrated the thick mat of foliage overhead. Even the roar of the deluge seemed distant, coming only from the direction of the stream rather than from all around them.

"What is this place?" she said, turning to Laris. "Doesn't it seem like it's … I don't know, locked in place somehow? It's as if it isn't even raining here."

"I wish I had the answer," he told her. "The Arn Hollow is one of Uhmeer's great mysteries. Every little village has a tale to tell about it, yet none explain the forest itself or its strange features."

"My father once said he felt safe here." She looked into the shadowed depths. "I wouldn't say I feel safe, but I don't feel any immediate threat, either."

"Aye. I was wrong to assume there would be game here."

She offered a small smile and touched his arm in reassurance. "We've gone far longer without food before. Maybe we should have stopped at that house for provisions."

"Not with our luck," he said.

She laughed. "We haven't had the best, have we?"

"I'm amazed when I look back on it. We should both be dead several times over."

Raelyn looked at him fondly. It was all because of him they were alive. She would have never made it out of Albator without him. "I'm okay to keep going," she said. "We might as well get as far as we can. I feel like this place is very different after night falls."

"I agree. The griffin said we'd clear it in a day if we kept on, so let's put our faith in that. I don't think the stories about this place are purely myth."

Dreary trees claimed the horizon, all of similar size and spacing as they progressed. Between each trunk, fallen leaves painted different shades of grey along the ground like mottled skin. With no noticeable change in the amount of daylight seeping through the branches overhead, Raelyn found it difficult to track where they might be in the day. At her best guess, they'd been walking for hours, but the strange shadows and false twilight had her second-guessing.

She continued to practice compartmentalization, occasionally taking a break from it to shift around and expand her primary sphere of influence. Careful not to shift the sphere over Laris, she enjoyed using him as a barrier she couldn't cross but might be able to move *around*. A single sphere of void, she realized, could be any shape she wanted it to be, and it could flow and mold around an object she didn't want affected. It was easier than compartmentalizing two spheres, separate from one another, and achieved the same result from what she could determine. Maintaining and adapting the complex shape became too strenuous when she attempted to add multiple obstacles in its path.

Feeling somewhat accomplished in her discovery, she went back to adding the second sphere to her awareness. She could now form it readily, but controlling it as delicately as the first was too tricky. She had to maintain her control and focus on the unique shape of the first sphere while trying to create another unique formation with the second. She could see why keeping the shapes simple was advantageous. Circles could expand or elongate in various ways that wouldn't demand so much focus and control. She re-centered herself and tried to feel a third core of void within. Three circles might be easier to control than two odd shapes.

A high-pitched whine made her drop her concentration, and she stopped, scanning the forest with her glaive held out in front of her. "Did you hear that?" she whispered.

Laris nodded, his sword positioned at guard. It was the first sound they'd heard in the Arn Hollow not made by their passing.

Another long whine sounded off to their right and then another to the left. Like a chorus of melancholy voices, trees in all directions whistled and hummed. With creaks and groans in the absence of wind, their cries grew louder the longer they continued.

"What should we do?" She covered her ears as best she could while still holding her weapon.

"Stand with me," he called above the noise. "Best to face whatever's coming than have it catch our backs."

They came together, back to back, scanning the forest for any sign of movement or danger. The trees continued their siren's wail and then, all at once, stopped.

Heaviness built in the air around them and the forest shadows lengthened. Raelyn's feet felt anchored in place, weighted like they were stuck deep in thick mud. A large mass shifted at the edge of her sight within the trees, moving toward them steadily. She nudged Laris, afraid to speak out loud, and inclined her head toward the shape gaining ground on them.

At his sharp intake of breath she glanced at him over her shoulder. "Penumbra," he said in a low voice. "Like the one from Mengat's cabin. We won't be able to outrun it." He stepped in front of her. "I'll have to fight without magic. There's not enough stone here to pull from."

She clung to the back of his shirt, realization dawning on her. With all she'd learned about magic, she hadn't fully acknowledged it was something that had to be seen to be used. *Of course,* she scolded herself. *How can you create something new if you don't have something to work with from the start?* Laris had access to the few meager rocks dotting the forest floor, but it was nothing like being in the mountains, surrounded by a terrain of giant rock shards.

The penumbra was coming up on them slowly, taking extra strides side to side as if calculating its attack. Raelyn recognized the upright, wolf-like form shrouded in black smoke as the same type of creature that killed her father. Its eyes glowed like molten coals; their bright, orange-red light visible even at a distance. Deep loathing and the desire for retribution quelled her fear with each step the penumbra took toward them.

"Do they have magic?" she asked, eyes locked on their adversary. Maybe there was a chance she could keep the fight even.

"No magic. Just strength, speed, and hide thick enough to turn a sword edge."

The creature stopped ten strides away, tilting its head and shifting its gaze from Laris to Raelyn and back again. Black smoke around it swirled and shifted in a dense cloud and concealed its outline in the haze.

"Back away from me," Laris instructed. "Find cover."

Before she could object, he dashed forward, sword out at his side.

Expecting an attack, the penumbra received Laris's charge calmly. It darted aside at the last moment without retaliation and evaded his second strike similarly. Adjusting to the creature's sideways movement, Laris made to swing again but matched its step. His sword redirected into the center of its hind leg, and he drove forward with his upper body. The thrust was accurate, but the blade glanced off the creature's tough skin with barely a scratch.

From behind one of the giant trees, Raelyn watched with growing dismay. The penumbra was strong and intelligent. It seemed far more dangerous than any foe they'd encountered aside from Volaris. Without magic, it was invulnerable to anything she could do, and with its physical advantages, it seemed unconcerned with taking damage from their weapons. She recalled her terror of the penumbra during the battle at Albator; their smoke-concealed bodies lining the ramparts before she'd ruined everything.

Laris and the creature circled one another, but neither moved to attack. *It's toying with him.* She nervously clutched the pendant at her neck, feeling comforted by the touch of the cool stone, wishing it had the power to summon Braymorian to help them. She wished she knew how to use the weapon in her hand with more than just luck.

The *vehsidhe* talisman dug into her palm as her grip around it tightened in frustration. *Sharp edges.* Sharp edges. She had an idea.

Dropping to her hands and knees, she scooped the dried leaves around her into a pile and sat back onto her heels. With the glaive propped between her knees, blade facing out, she pulled the talisman over her head. Holding it like Laris had shown her, she struck it down along the weapon's edge. He'd told her any hard stone would do.

Sparks. She almost cried out with relief. Hands shaking, she repeated the motion, doing her best to pay attention to the technique. In a rush, she cut herself on the glaive on the third try. Along with her blood, tiny sparks floated down into the mound of dead leaves and a tendril of smoke rose from within.

Hunched over, she cradled her hands around the smoldering spark and blew lightly. It flared to bright orange with her ministrations and spread rapidly across its bed of leaves. It still wasn't a flame, just a line of glowing and spreading char; she needed something more than leaves. Without twigs or branches to add substance to her fire, she did the only thing she could think of—she ripped a strip of linen from the hem of her shirt. With it coiled around the spark bed, she blew again and felt a surge of hope with the fabric caught flame.

Pulling apart several more strips from her shirt, she used the glaive to make cuts in her sleeves for more fabric. One by one, she layered the remnants of her clothes into a loose pile around the struggling flame. Thick smoke threatened to extinguish her efforts, but orange tendrils grew around the cloth layers. She left the strengthening fire and hastily piled leaves again, this time in a wide track around the trees closest to Laris and the penumbra.

Raelyn watched the flame out of the corner of her eye, knowing there was no time to waste. Once the fire grew large enough, it would consume the leaves she'd gathered in moments even though she'd swept up enough to circle halfway around the battle. She needed to outpace the traveling fire with her leaf piling as best she could to give Laris enough magic to work with.

A ferocious roar startled her from her task, and she looked up. The penumbra lumbered toward her. Comprehension reflected in its eyes. Nostrils flaring, it leaped across the distance between them, and she dove toward the cover of a nearby tree. She stumbled hard to her knees and crawled forward toward the glaive laying on the ground. An arm's length away from her weapon, the creature bore down on her. Before it could grab her, a lance of fire collided with its side, sending it sprawling into a tree to her right.

"Get behind me!" Laris shouted to her.

She grabbed her weapon and ran to his side, watching him raise pillars of fire up around the nearby trees. *He's making the fire stronger, growing it,* she realized as the trees crackled and split with the heat. The penumbra pushed up, fur on its side burned away, skin red and blistered beneath the screen of smoke enshrouding its body. A resounding, rage-infused shriek issued from its throat, and it bounded through the line of burning trees and leaves, throwing itself up into a powerful jump. With an arc of his arm, Laris cast a wave of fire up to intercept the penumbra's motion. It connected, and the creature hit the ground hard, sliding to a stop just shy of where they were standing.

Breathing heavily, Laris extended his arms and slowly brought them inward, drawing the fire at the perimeter in with his movement.

Raelyn could tell he was pouring his strength into controlling the flames, preventing them from running rampant into the rest of the Arn Hollow.

Heat radiated and reddened her skin. Droplets of sweat left her hairline to travel down the sides of her face. She put a hand on Laris's back for comfort and to let him know where she was without demanding his attention. All around them, the trees burned; the fire reached into the sky as it climbed into the branches. Grievously injured, the penumbra staggered to its feet. Staring at them for a long moment, it turned its head to assess the burning forest.

"I have to kill it." Laris's voice was strained. "It will come for us again."

She didn't say anything in reply, too absorbed in the hateful way the penumbra watched them. It wanted them dead; she could tell, but it also sensed the battle was lost. It knew as well as she did that Laris wouldn't let it leave the forest.

Tucked within the center of Raelyn's hatred, a small seed of regret blossomed. She would never forgive the penumbra for what happened to her home, but watching the creature stand before them in agony, knowing death was imminent, felt unnecessarily cruel.

"Can you end it quickly, please?" she asked Laris over his shoulder.

"You know it wouldn't extend the same kindness to us."

"I know. Please."

With a deep breath and a nod, he gathered another lance of fire into the air above the penumbra. With a groan, it looked up at the flame and sagged to the ground in acceptance. Like dogs Raelyn remembered from Albator, it rested its head on its front feet and closed its eyes.

A pang shot through her chest. Something or someone was pushing these creatures. Aetris's words echoed in her mind. *Does that make it okay to take his life?* As each day passed, as they had to kill more and more, she wondered if she would ever feel complacent about it. She could justify it—kill or be killed—but she still felt remorse in the aftermath.

Laris brought the bolt down, and she buried her face in the back of his shirt. There was no scream, no death cry. The penumbra's last breath left in a long sigh, the black smoke around its form settling like dust on the ground. In the glow of the burning Arn Hollow, it looked peaceful.

Laris swept her up into a quick embrace. "I owe you more than this," he said, squeezing her tightly, "but I have to work quickly to put the fire out."

He released her and raced over to where the penumbra lay at the center of the burning circle, extending his arms once again to control the travel of the fire around them. With slow, deliberate movements, he pulled the flames in and away from their backs and condensed the fire into a tower of red, orange, and gold that threw itself into the sky as if trying to escape. His arms trembled with the effort to keep the blaze in check, a tremble that soon shook his entire body. He circled both arms in and then out in one powerful, quick movement, splaying his hands wide. The pillar of flame snuffed out like a candle, and Laris sank to one knee.

"Are you all right?" Raelyn rushed over to him. The smell of charred wood filtered in through her nostrils, and the air felt suddenly chilly. All around them, the trees were black and barren, the sky above clearly visible through the gap left behind by the fire. It was an eerie blemish in the uniformity of the Arn Hollow. *Like a scar*, she thought, looking at the damage.

"I'm fine, just fatigued," Laris answered. "Fire is one of the easiest magics to master because it's formless and fluid by nature, but that makes separating tendrils of its magic demanding. The larger the fire, the greater the difficulty. Give me a moment before we move on."

Laris's moment spanned an hour. They sat side by side on the ground near the body of the penumbra, silent. Though upright, his eyes were closed, his breaths deep and rhythmic. Raelyn worried about leaving the forest before dark, but she was more concerned about her companion. She didn't know how magic taxed the mind or the body. Was it painful? Was he injured? She studied his face, looking for signs of distress.

"I can always tell when you're looking at me," he said, opening his eyes slightly.

She didn't look away. "I was just wondering if you're really all right."

"I'm good enough." He straightened, took a breath, and pushed to his feet. "We should go even if I'm not. It's more important to find somewhere safer to spend the night. We've been attacked once, and I'm not fit for another fight."

"Do you think we have far to go?"

"We shouldn't if what the griffin said was true. Another hour, maybe, to the forest's edge."

Raelyn glanced at the charred remains of the trees no longer trapped in their perpetual, unchanging cycle. Their dark wood contrasted sharply with the grey of the world around them. "Do you think they'll grow back?" she asked.

"My guess is no. They say nothing new grows in the Arn Hollow."

Stepping across the burn line on the ground and into the untouched woods, Raelyn's regret flared again. *More death and destruction,* she thought sourly. Everywhere she went, it seemed, destruction followed in her footsteps. Compelled to look behind her before the black trunks were out of sight, she stopped mid-step.

A sea of grey trees cloaked in wispy moss stretched back as far as she could see. The Arn Hollow was just as it had always been, any evidence of their battle no longer visible.

"Laris," she called to him, searching behind them for the telltale burn scar in the landscape. "The trees…"

Was the burned section already out of sight? *Impossible,* she thought. *We've only just walked away.*

His silence was enough for Raelyn to know he shared her surprise at seeing the forest restored. She turned to look at him, and the clear sound of distant singing assailed their ears. Melancholic and haunting, the notes drifted around the trees, more consuming and enveloping than any fire or hard rain.

"Come," he whispered, grabbing her hand. "Let's not tempt our regrettable luck."

She nodded, and they picked up their pace, anxious to leave the forest truly behind them.

Dusk claimed the land fully just when they broke through the last line of trees and staggered out into a field of tall, golden grasses. Beyond, at the edge of the horizon, indiscernible shapes were clustered where land met sky, hinting at the presence of buildings, if not an entire town. A cool breeze sent the top of the grasses rolling and teased Raelyn of colder weather not far behind. Braymorian had warned them the journey from the mountains on foot would have seen them well into the depths of winter.

"The farther we can get from the forest, the better," Laris said, still holding her hand. Through the contact, she could feel the invisible tremors of fatigue that continued to wrack his body. "Those buildings are too far off, but let's press on until nightfall."

Meadowland morphed from wild grasses to one of cultivated grains as they picked their way carefully in the fading light. Wagon paths separated the tall reeds into neat patches of farmland, and the level footing allowed them to travel a bit farther even when darkness became absolute. They finally stopped at a collapsing storage shelter, its post-and-beam structure barely large enough for both of them to sit, the roof collapsed inward but still clinging to the supports.

Taking the position closest to the path, Laris sat down and lifted his arm for Raelyn to sit against him. She settled against his ribcage, more than ready to lose herself in the warmth and safety of his closeness. Leaning back, she hugged his arm draped across her front.

"That was smart, you know," he said quietly, voice laced with exhaustion. He rested his head against the top of hers. "Starting the fire in the Arn Hollow. Well done."

She pulled out the *vehsidhe* talisman from under what was left of her shirt. "It was luck. The good kind, for once."

His hand lifted slowly and touched the stone in the dark. "The feather? You used it like flint?"

"Just like you showed me."

"That's my girl," he murmured, twitching as sleep overcame him.

A surge of happiness welled up in her chest at his praise, chasing away the cool bite of the night air. She was glad for the safety that allowed him to rest and pleased by his easy affections. No matter what they'd gone through, he'd been steadfast and reliable, even when they were barely friends. The change in their relationship was as strange as it was welcome. She would have never guessed at their first meeting that he was capable of...

Of what? Love?

Even in her head, the word felt clumsy, like something out of a fairy story. To think that a powerful, renowned transcendent would fall in love with someone like her was almost laughable. Her pleasure from his claiming words dwindled, offset by a growing sense of doubt. If they hadn't been forced together through circumstance, would any of these feelings have emerged on their own? She knew it was unlikely. Lord Leofric would have left after courting Ellisand,

and Laris would have gone with him, still at odds with Raelyn based on their initial encounters.

Don't be silly. She drew a deep breath and closed her eyes. *There is no 'what could have been,' only what is. This did happen, and it is happening.*

The doubt retreated, and she pulled his arm tighter to her. She would stay up for the whole night, she decided. Even though it was probably safe for her to sleep, staying up on watch was good practice and good sense. He would have done the same for her.

Mind made up, she stared into the darkness, listening more than seeing, trying not to focus on Laris's breathing that threatened to lull her into slumber.

CHAPTER TWENTY-TWO

*L*ike concentric rings on a target, three perimeter walls around Osharia protected the heart of the city, with a fourth wall around the castle at its center. In each of the three outer walls, a set of gates served as a checkpoint where guards monitored activity in and out of the bustling capital.

Nestled within a wall of tarred wooden pikes and marking entry into the trade-and-labor district, the first gateway served as a filter. Most travelers heading to the city needed to go no farther; they were there for business. Guards directed the masses from the gate to different sections within the district: west for furs and textiles, east for exotic novelties, north for those looking for hirable services like guides, caravan leaders, and trackers. They were quick with their work, checking carts, wagons, and personal belongings where they saw fit but mostly unconcerned with whom they were letting in and why.

At the second gate, leading into the outer ring of the lower main city, the guards were more diligent. They asked questions and explored the details of travel stories. Anyone who seemed suspicious was pulled out of line and interrogated within the large stone towers on either side of the gate itself. Without the guard's approval, the stone wall dividing the lower city from the trade-and-labor district couldn't be passed.

Riding alongside the wayfarers, Saraht and Ellisand passed through the first two gates unimpeded. A few guards glanced their way out of general curiosity, but no one could be bothered to ask the same set of arrival questions to the entire troupe. They were waved on, one of the guards taking a brief moment to pet Lydantus as he lounged on the back of the slowest-moving cart.

Once through the final checkpoint, Saraht and Ellisand said their goodbyes to the wayfarers and made their way toward the city center and the Hall of Lords. Mollen was unfamiliar to Saraht, but she needed a safe place to hold up while Ellisand worked within the castle. With Jormand's name attached to her reputation, she felt confident she could come and go as she pleased without too much questioning. All she needed was a quiet room with a reliable lock on the door.

During their ride to the capital, she'd come to terms with the new information regarding the duchess. If anything, she'd realized, it might be a way to get Ellisand into the castle right away.

Nearing the city center, people crowded the streets. With residential areas on the outskirts along the wall, the business district made up a central hub in the city's middle. No tents and no open markets clogged the byways. This was the capital. There were rules about selling and buying goods. Dismounting to better maneuver through the crowd, Saraht and Ellisand headed toward a swinging sign bearing the comical drawing of a crowned man riding a pig.

A well-dressed young man at the door took their horses. Unlike Mickel, he greeted them formally and he kept his eyes downcast even when Saraht handed him a generous handful of coins.

"Shall we?" She turned to Ellisand, saddlebags over one shoulder, sword tucked beneath the top layer of her split skirt.

Ellisand nodded and offered a meager smile as she hoisted her belongings. Her eyes and posture conveyed an uncharacteristic nervousness. It was understandable, thought Saraht, given she was about to be reunited with her mother and introduced into the royal court all within the same few days—and all with the weight of a greater plan resting on her shoulders. While the duchess might have been granted some respite by the king when regarding social obligations, her young and vibrant daughter would almost certainly have much less private time once the two were reunited.

Stepping across the entry into the Hall of Lords, pungent incense stung their eyes and invaded their noses. Both Saraht and Ellisand raised their eyebrows in surprise and found ways to politely cover their noses while adjusting to the smell.

White walls with peeling gold trim did little to brighten the room, and imitation red velvet cushions covered every inch of seating, including the tops of the bar stools. Paintings hung over each booth along the walls, the images pinned within decorative gold-colored frames that looked like they hadn't been dusted since their creation. A handful of people sat in the space, talking quietly and sipping on tea or enjoying a late midday meal.

"Good afternoon." A very tall, lanky man behind the bar welcomed them. His eyes were almost entirely obscured by big, bushy black eyebrows that matched his long, but well-kept beard. Deep wrinkles lined his gaunt face. "What can I do for you today?"

Saraht leaned her elbows onto the bar. "I'm looking for Mollen, if you please," she said, watching his expression. "We've just come from the Inn at Golinstone Fork and were told this place would offer equal accommodations."

He picked up a glass and started to clean it. "I'm Mollen. From Golinstone, are you? It isn't often Jormand sends business my way." He gave them both a scrutinizing look. "One room or two?"

"Just one, actually." Saraht lowered her voice. "For me. The young lady here requires a guard escort to the palace. Could you contact the commander for this area?"

He set the glass down. "And who would I tell them they're escorting?"

"Ellisand Wedminth," Ellisand spoke up. "I escaped the attack on Albator, my father's duchy, and I heard my mother was just recently brought to the capital alive."

Saraht cringed. The story sounded rehearsed, but Mollen didn't appear concerned. He continued to stare at them and reached for another glass before saying, "I'll send one of the girls to the command office. Might take a few hours to arrange the escort. They'll assume you're lying."

"My mother can verify my identity," Ellisand said confidently. "That will have to be enough."

He nodded, still expressionless. "When they come, treat them like they're beneath you, and they'll have more a mind to believe your story. I take it you're not a part of this?" He glanced at Saraht and slid the two clean glasses over to them. He poured them a pale wine from an open bottle on the counter.

Saraht swirled the liquid and savored the aroma. "I'm just a traveler who helped her find her way. Now that she's here, there's no need for me to be in the picture anymore."

"Uh-huh." Hands on his hips, he waited for them to finish their drinks. "I'll give you the room on the top floor at the end of the hall. Looks out over the road. Convenient if you like to know when people are coming and going."

"Sounds like an excellent choice."

"The guards always ring the stable bell, even when Patrick is outside. Come down when you hear it and wait for them here," he directed the comment to Ellisand. "They won't think to ask who came with you if you're not hidden away in a room. Take these," he added, reaching for one of the keys hanging behind the bar. "I'll hang the spare, so no one notices the room is occupied."

Saraht took the keys with a slight bow of her head. "We'll listen for the bell."

With a grunt of acknowledgment, Mollen went back to cleaning glasses.

Osharia was well within the embrace of night by the time the sharp clang of the stable bell tolled throughout the inn. Saraht peered down at the road from the window of her room and saw three men standing on the Hall of Lords's doorstep while ten more waited on the road. They were tormenting Patrick, though, the stable boy appeared in good spirits and did his best to return the ribbing.

She grabbed Ellisand's cloak and held it out to her. "Be quick," she said quietly. "I'll go down first and wait in a booth. If anything unusual happens, I'll be ready to intervene."

The younger woman nodded and took Saraht's hand, clasping it. "I'll send word like we talked about. Two days' time."

Saraht nodded and quickly squeezed back in reassurance. "Remember, you're royalty," she whispered, dropping their contact and opening the door. "Command the common men. Save the feminine charms for the courtiers."

She brushed past Ellisand and hurried out the doorway and down the stairs. No soldiers were in the dining room; only a few patrons lingered to enjoy the evening inn atmosphere. Picking a booth near the corner of the room, far from the door, she slid in and sought to make eye contact with Mollen.

He was already walking toward her with a glass and a pitcher.

"Girls will bring some bread over," he said quietly. "Baked lamb if you're here long enough."

She smiled and thanked him, watching Ellisand enter the dining room and sit on a stool at the end of the bar. *She's learned well*, Saraht noted, pleased the young woman picked the seat closest to the stairs with the best visibility of the front door.

"Just in time," Mollen slid Ellisand a glass of clear liquid. "They'll get bored of Patrick soon enough. He's the son of one of the captains, so they have to raise his hackles a bit when they come."

Ellisand barely had time to nod before the front door flew open so hard it bounced off the stopper, flew back, and whacked the man coming through on the shoulder. He cursed and waved apologetically to Mollen. "Oi, Mollen, sorry. The lad's got us all out of sorts. You sent word a Lady Ellisand Wedminth was here seeking escort to the castle?"

"I am Lady Wedminth." Ellisand's tone was cool and commanding. "I demand to be taken to see my mother and the king."

Two more soldiers entered, along with a man wearing a hood. Saraht couldn't see the third man's features, but his posture and movement suggested he was more than a well-trained city guard. He stood just inside the doorway, letting the other men occupy the middle area of the bar.

"Lady Ellisand Wedminth." The first man offered a polite bow of his head. "Have you any proof of your identity? Or information about where you've been?"

"My mother can vouch for me," Ellisand replied, her voice steady but dismissive. She was doing well at remembering her station. She owed the guard obedience within the city walls but not respect; she was the king's direct relative.

"I can vouch for her," the man in the hood spoke up. The guard turned and looked at him, and he pulled away his covering to reveal a face with fine features and sandy-colored hair.

Ellisand's blustering act dropped. "Jackson?" She stood and stepped away from the bar stool. "Jackson, is it really you?"

Friends, Saraht realized, or lovers, perhaps. Though, she was fairly confident Ellisand was inexperienced with romance despite her inclination toward sexuality. The way she said his name was familiar, filled with an affection Saraht had only ever heard from one person in her life. Whoever this was, he wasn't an acquaintance or some trusted advisor. He was someone Ellisand truly cared about, someone who could catch her off guard.

"Yes, it's me, Lady Ellisand." His calm expression broke out into a wide grin. "By Emblem's Hand, I can't believe you're really here."

He stepped toward her, but Ellisand wasn't waiting. She ran the short distance between them, pushed through the bewildered soldiers, and threw herself into Jackson's arms. Sobbing, she clung to him while he did his best to comfort her. He let her hold on to him but didn't wrap her in an embrace. "We should get you to the castle," he said gently. "Duchess Wedminth wasn't informed because we didn't want to get her hopes up, but now that we know it's really you, we shouldn't keep her waiting."

"That's it?" Ellisand looked up at him with tears rolling down her face. "That's all you have to say to me?"

Jackson shifted awkwardly. "Lady, perhaps the castle would be a more fitting place for a reunion." He stepped back from her but offered his arm. "We've got a carriage outside. Is there anything from the inn you need to retrieve?"

Daggers in her gaze, she shunned his gesture and stepped away. She squared her shoulders and swallowed back her tears, lifting her chin. "Let's go see Mother."

Saraht watched them file out of the inn, intrigued by the interaction but unable to pin down the dynamic. It was clear Ellisand thought fondly of Jackson, and at first glance, it seemed clear he returned her sentiment. His commitment to decorum, however, suggested their relationship was either secret or neither had admitted their feelings.

Poor boy. Unless he's of noble birth, he may as well always keep those feelings to himself.

She watched out the booth window as the carriage pulled away and disappeared down a side street. Pulling at the lamb leg on her plate, Saraht chewed the morsel slowly, savoring the rush of spiced juices each time she bit down. She took her time. It wasn't often she had a moment of peace, but she knew it was a moment and nothing more. She had other responsibilities.

Handing off several coins to the serving girl, she headed to her room.

The rest is in your hands now, Saraht thought, glancing over her shoulder when she reached the top of the stairs. *Keep your focus, Ellisand, and you can have any man you want in the end.* She unlocked her door and entered the room, one hand on her sword.

All was quiet. Only the fading fire in the hearth stirred.

She tossed another log into the fireplace and sighed, trying to calm the apprehension squeezing her chest. Ellisand was clear on her goal within the castle over the next few days: become familiar with the layout and the people at court, play nice with the courtiers, and pick up on the current drama and gossip. In two days' time, send an update in the form of a thank you to Mollen for helping her get to the castle safely.

That part was out of Saraht's hands now, and she had more immediate concerns. Under her dress collar, the pendant felt heavy and cold, waiting. She could delay contacting Prince Thiir no longer. Orion kept the Faldea ruler informed about their progress through traditional communication routes, but waiting too long before contact from Saraht would put the prince in an ill temper. He knew she'd arrived in the capital. He was waiting to hear it directly from her.

She sat down on the edge of the bed and let herself fall backward onto the soft quilt. Like the Inn at Golinstone Fork, the Hall of Lords's room was more comfortable than most traveler accommodations. It was clean and freshly so. She could still smell the lavender used to perfume the blankets during laundering.

Shifting aside the cover on her pendant, she pressed a thumb to the anchor marble. For the first time in a long time, the sensation of entering the void unsettled her, and she shook her head to clear the feeling. The seam of the world felt exceptionally cold.

A pale flickering orb was waiting for her. It bobbed up and down lethargically as if its life were almost spent. It was possible, she guessed, that the poor soul could only be sustained for so long while its body hung in the balance between life and death in the mortal realm.

"Master?" Saraht watched the light for a reaction. "Master, I'm in the capital, and the girl is heading into position."

There was a long silence, and the orb's light stilled and sputtered brighter. "You've been neglectful of the goal." Thiir's tone was displeased. "Orion tells me you have started a crusade of righteousness with my precious time and resources."

"All for your glory, Master. When you declare regency, Limnin will be ready for a benevolent ruler. The common people want someone new to believe in. They'll abandon their nobles like their nobles abandoned them."

"Do not try to hide the truth of your actions. I know you, Saraht. I picked you myself, lifted you and your mother from the squalor the priestesses had you living in. No one knows you like I know you."

She shivered. Prince Thiir was beyond her ability to manipulate in mind and body, something she'd learned the hard way during their first years together. She couldn't fool him; she could only hope to plant seeds of suggestion so he would be lenient with her freedoms. "I know, Master," she whispered. "Nothing I do would ever work against your plans."

"This, too, I know to be true." The light dipped. "Though you forget yourself in my absence, you are where you should be. How long before you enter the castle?"

"I will have word in two days."

"And the other warden?"

"I've no news. Orion and I have not crossed paths as of late."

"Speak with him. What good are you both if you do not communicate? Two days, Saraht. Get me information."

"As you wish, Master," she replied.

"You may go."

Saraht knew he was no longer connected to her by how the orb blinked out and returned, its light dimmer than before. She watched it with a sense of sympathy. It was just another soul caught up in the power of a mad ruler. She wished a quick death to the host body trapped in Faldea. *May you find freedom before all of us, friend.*

CHAPTER TWENTY-THREE

"Wait a moment."

Raelyn stopped at Laris's request, pulling her eyes away from the buildings of the town just ahead. Fantasies of food and a warm bed preoccupied her, and she startled at the touch of his finger on a patch of exposed skin at her waist.

"This won't do," he said, moving his fingers to the frayed edges of her left sleeve. "Here. Put this on." He unbuttoned his jerkin and shrugged it off. "Or would you rather have my tunic?"

"This is fine, thank you," she said. "Keep your shirt. We can't both look ridiculous heading into town."

"*Haggard* is the better word for it." He looked at her swimming in the oversized jerkin, amused. "That's not much better, but at least it provides more coverage."

Following the wagon trail from the fields led them to a cluster of small barns with open sides and thatched roofs. Baskets and farming equipment clogged the interiors, except one which housed a handful of sheep. Just beyond the barns, houses and other buildings lined up, side by side, sharing walls in what looked like one continuous structure. The construction reminded Raelyn of a giant wall, and she wondered if it was a deliberate design that doubled as an exterior defense. They met no guards on the path into the town, and the few people who noticed Raelyn and Laris arrive nodded in welcome or looked away with disinterest.

"I may be able to pick up some work to get us lodging and food." Laris looked at their surroundings. "That looks like a smithy over there, and there's a carpentry stall. They always need willing workers."

"Are you sure you're up for that so soon?"

He nodded. "I slept the entire night, thanks to you. You're the one who needs the sleep right now."

He was right. Raelyn was exhausted, having passed the point of being sleepy hours ago. Fatigue weighed her down even as her mind trudged on, determined to stay awake. It was an odd sensation, as if she were moving through a dream. "I could see about working in a kitchen. There's likely an inn of some type here, don't you think?"

"It's a big enough town, but it doesn't seem to be a main thorough-fare. No gates, no guards. I doubt they get many travelers."

"I'll walk opposite where you're headed," she told him. "I know where to find you."

Laris touched her elbow as she stepped away. "I don't like the idea of separating. I'll come with you. We'll both see if there's work at the inn, if there is one."

Four streets over, on the opposite edge of the town, they found a small, single-story inn with an open-air dining area and corral with a pair of horses. Its carved sign over the front doorway named it an inn and nothing more. The door was gone, but sounds of laughter and singing from inside raised Raelyn's spirits. She would be grateful even if the innkeeper let them sleep out in the shed with the horses.

She went in first, ducking her head to avoid the low doorframe. As soon as she crossed into the dining area, the merriment within faded to quiet. Every face turned toward her, and she self-consciously tugged at the hem of her tunic. Laris's hand on her shoulder gave her confidence, and, taking a deep breath, she walked through the crowd and over to where a sweaty, burly woman rolled out dough near a clay oven.

"Excuse me." Raelyn leaned toward her. "Who can we speak to about work?"

"No work," the woman told her without looking up. "We don't do charity."

"We aren't looking for money," Laris said with a hint of annoyance. "We'll work off a few meals and a dry place to sleep, wherever it might be."

With a huff, the woman slapped the dough down on the table. Hands on her hips, she studied them both. "You two look like you've seen better days." She glanced at Raelyn's glaive and Laris's sword. "I don't want any trouble. Try the herbalist down the road. He needs help sometimes."

"I'll pay for them," someone said from the crowd. The man walked over and held out a coin purse. "Stay. Eat. I'll cover the costs."

Raelyn reached for the purse, but Laris stopped her. "We're looking for honest work," he said coldly.

"You misunderstand me," the man replied, a twinkle in his green eyes. "I'm not looking for anything unsavory in return. Just join me after you're settled for a few games of cards, and we'll call the debt repaid."

Laris ignored him and turned to Raelyn. "I'll go to the smithy. We'll pay our own way."

"Ezra." The man pushed his hand out in greeting. "My name, of course. Take the coins. I know what it's like not to have when you need. A gift." He winked at Raelyn. "The lady looks like she'll sleep right through till tomorrow."

Despite the strangeness of his generosity, the man offering to come to their rescue held a harmless charm. His voice was musical, like a bard, and boyish features gave him a friendly look. If it weren't for the rugged way he dressed and the sharp intelligence in his eyes, she would have placed him much younger than she knew he probably was.

Laris frowned, looked at Raelyn, and looked at the purse of coins. "I want your word, in front of the innkeeper, that there's no debt to be paid."

With a winsome smile, Ezra tossed the coin purse to the woman from the inn. "No debt," he said, pointing at her. "On my honor. That should be more than enough to cover their room and food."

"More than enough," the woman murmured, looking in the purse. "I'm not one to cheat anyone. There's enough here to get you some clothes, too. We don't have much in town, but there's a seamstress with readymade items, if you've a mind."

"I would be so grateful," Raelyn breathed. "I can go pick them up. Where is the seamstress?"

"Nonsense." Ezra sidled up and put an arm around her shoulders. "You clearly need rest, and I've got nothing better to do. Why don't you both relax, and I'll take the walk to the seamstress? I was on my way to the grocer next door as it was."

Alarms went off in Raelyn's head, and she eased out from beneath his touch and retreated to Laris's side. She nodded and looked away, suddenly uncomfortable but unsure why, and Laris stepped protectively in front of her.

The green-eyed man flashed his hands in apology and took a step back. "Ah, no offense meant—" he glanced at Laris "—to either of you. I can see you've been through a lot. Just accept this kindness for what it is. I'll return and send your clothes up with one of the girls."

He performed an unusual mixture of a bow and a salute and then turned and trotted out of the dining area, stopping outside to pet one of the horses standing near the gate.

"I'm no fancy innkeeper," the woman told them as she wiped her hands on her apron, "but this is my place. I keep a few rooms. You can take the last one down that hall. It has a tub and faucet. Door locks from the inside but poorly. I'd slide the dresser against it if you want privacy."

After their grueling travels, the room was more than Raelyn had hoped for, surprisingly large and well-lit by an octagon-shaped window in its exterior wall and two windows in the roof overhead. It was the first time she'd ever seen windows showcasing the sky. With one right above the bathtub, it seemed more luxurious than any place she'd been.

"You can bathe first." Laris grabbed the bucket by the fire and walked over to the faucet. "Once we wash, we'll go down and grab some food. The sooner you get to sleep, the better."

"I'm not even that tired," she said with a yawn and a laugh. "Well, maybe I am a bit. Are you sure you don't mind? You can go first."

Dumping the water into the tub, he said, "It's okay to think of yourself once in a while." At her crestfallen look, he set the bucket down and crossed his arms. "Or are we to bathe together, then?"

Heat shot up into Raelyn's face, and her eyes widened. She looked at the tub. It was large. Set on a metal base, copper tubing led back to the fireplace, where it spiraled into a coil for heating. The basin would easily fit two people. *Would we face one another?* she wondered. *Or would we sit on the same side?* She felt the color in her cheeks darken further.

"Raelyn." Laris pulled her attention back. "You should fight me at least a little on the idea."

"I'll go first," she said quickly and turned away from him, making herself busy by shrugging off Famine and inspecting it. She could hear his footsteps come across the wooden floor. "The tub's too small for both of us," she muttered.

"I think we'd find a way," he said from behind her.

A tingle raced up her spine with the thrill of the words. She could feel his closeness, his warmth already wrapping around her and drawing her in.

He brushed aside her hair and lightly kissed her neck. "I'll finish filling the tub." He suddenly grabbed her waist and pulled her back against him. "But don't play along with me too much," he cautioned. "I'm more serious than not."

One of his hands had slid beneath the looseness of the oversized jerkin, and heat pooled low within her hips as if spreading down directly from his touch. She instinctively brought her hand up and placed it overtop to ... what? She didn't know. To stop him or to entwine her hand in his, she couldn't decide.

"We're still not even," he whispered into her ear before stepping back.

She spun around to question him, but he was already walking toward the fireplace. "I'll get the bath going," he stated as if nothing had happened. "I think there were some towels on the stool." He knelt down and started piling wood within the copper coil.

Raelyn frowned, flustered. She went over to the stool and pulled a large towel off, letting it hang in her hand. She stared at it and chewed on her lower lip, replaying what had happened repeatedly in her mind. She listened to him pouring water into the tub, pumping the faucet, and pouring more water. With each clank of the faucet handle, her anger grew.

She whirled around and flung the towel at him. It hit him in the face, just where she'd intended, and he dropped the bucket. Water poured across the floor. He stared at her, a mixture of surprise and challenge written across his face.

"No more," she said sternly. "You can't do that anymore. You can't come over to me and ... and ... It's not fair."

"Not fair?" he said slowly, mulling the words over.

"Not fair. You never let me react. You just ..." She wanted to say "tease," but the word felt too accurate and inappropriate. "... make me feel flustered, and then you waltz away."

He leaned back against the tub and watched her, contemplative but not condescending. After thinking a moment, he replied, "I'm not doing it to torment you, Raelyn."

"I may be inexperienced, but I'm not a child." The flush across her face receded, embarrassment replaced by frustration. "I want to show you my feelings, too."

That was what it came down to, she realized. It wasn't the need to answer urges she felt physically; it was the need to express her affection. She wanted him to feel the same as he made her feel: safe, secure, cared for—wanted.

He covered his face with a hand and shook his head. "What would you have me do? I don't think you understand what you're asking."

"I do understand," she snapped. "I don't think *you* understand."

She sensed a change in him at her words. His demeanor shifted from mildly entertained to a dangerous state of calm. His dark eyes hooded, and he took a step toward her.

"No," he drew out the word, "you don't understand. I have to walk away from you because I know what happens when you do react to me. I'm selfish; I know. I can't help but touch you, hold you, kiss you, but what then?" He took a few steps closer. "Do you really want to find out?"

Heart hammering in her chest, she held her ground, staring at him defiantly.

He took the last step to her. "You have a habit of thinking of yourself last, and I wouldn't be happy if you did something too soon because you were thinking of me." He cupped her face in his hands and chuckled at her angry expression. "I would need your promise that you'll not go beyond your point of comfort."

Just what was her point of comfort? She couldn't say. She'd been told to save herself for marriage, that only the man who was her husband should get to know her on such an intimate level. That was a privilege nobles paid for in their brides. Laris had never mentioned marrying her. He hadn't said anything at all that might define their relationship. She didn't know how deep his feelings went.

But she did know how deep hers were. "I promise." She spoke the words grumpily but with conviction. "Maybe you should trust me a little."

He seemed amused by her retort. "Shall we put it to the test right now, then?" He scooped her up, and she let out a startled yelp. "Or did you want to wait until we're both clean and not starving? Tell me now—the bed or the bath?"

She swatted him on the shoulder. "Put me down. I'm being serious."

"So am I." Laris carried her over to the tub. "Maybe a bath will wash some of that ferociousness out of you."

She screeched and clung to him, laughing. "You wouldn't! Put me down. Put me down. I'll take the bath."

"Too late." He plopped her, clothes and all, into the tub.

Stunned for a second, she sat with her mouth agape, still holding on to one of his arms.

He laughed and looked at her smugly. "Is it warm?"

Raelyn pursed her lips and huffed out a laugh of disbelief. Without thinking it through, she reached over his shoulder and twisted her fingers around his shirt. Letting her body slide lower in the water, she used her leverage to topple him into the tub.

He pushed himself up almost instantly, but not before the water worked its way into every fiber of his clothing and saturated his hair.

Raelyn latched on to him again and dragged him back down. "Didn't you say the tub was big enough for both of us?" She splashed water at him when he sat back again. "Looks like you were right."

Both laughing, he fought her off, water splashing, Raelyn squealing when he accidentally tickled her. The tub clanked side to side with their war and rained its contents across the floorboards.

They both stopped abruptly when the door flew open, kicked inward with enough force to send the simple bolt flying across the room. Ezra jumped across the entrance, daggers in each of his hands. He looked at them both in the tub, trying to comprehend what he was seeing.

"Lady," he said hesitantly, scanning the room, "are you all right? I heard struggling."

Laris fixed him with a dark look and stood up. Without a word to their intruder, he offered Raelyn a hand and helped her up.

"We're fine," Raelyn said sheepishly and wiped strands of hair off her face. "I didn't realize we were being so loud."

Ezra cleared his throat, relaxed, and sheathed the blades. With a grimace, he said, "Apologies. I didn't mean to interrupt."

"You heard laughing and didn't mean to interrupt?" Laris asked coolly. He handed Raelyn a towel.

"A struggle," Ezra pointed out. "I heard a struggle. In my haste, I forgot not all couples' struggles should be interrupted." He grinned.

"Anyway, your clothes are out here in the hall. I dropped them when I thought I heard," he emphasized the word, "struggling."

Laris stalked past and picked up the garments. He brought them into the room and tossed them onto the bed. Without warning, he started removing his wet clothes.

Ezra looked at Raelyn awkwardly. "Uh, yes, enjoy the clothes." He bowed low and backed out, pulling the door shut behind him.

"Thank you," Raelyn called through the boards. She kept her face toward the door until she heard Laris move away from the area by the bed.

"Go ahead and take a proper bath," he told her. "I'll wait in the hall to make sure you have privacy."

She nodded. "Okay. I won't be long."

He stopped and kissed her on the forehead before opening the door. "You won that round," he said. "Enjoy it for now, because I won't lose next time."

Feeling pleased with herself, she stripped down with him guarding the outside and stepped into the tub. What little water remained was still warm, kept at a comfortable temperature by the heating coils sitting in the fireplace. She fished out the bar of soap they'd knocked into the bottom of the basin and scrubbed her hair and body. As tempting as it was to sit in the heated water, she didn't want Laris to have to wait for her indulgence. Thorough but efficient, she rinsed off and stepped out.

He has a good eye, she thought, holding up the dress Ezra had brought. Slipping it over her head, she toweled her hair dry a bit more and called to Laris that she was done. As he walked in, she curled up on the bed facing away and fought the temptation to invade his privacy and look over after she heard his clothes drop to the floor.

The softness of the bed threatened to swallow Raelyn completely. She lay on her side, staring out the window while Laris took his turn in the tub. The day was late but not ready to surrender to evening. Thick, white clouds peppered the sky, leftover from the rain the day before. Feeling clean and warm, she snuggled into the pillow and watched the random activities going on in the town outside. Behind her, the telltale splash of water let her know Laris exited the tub.

"Don't fall asleep just yet," he said, drying off. "Let's go have a decent meal, even if you aren't hungry."

She wasn't hungry. At some point in their travels, hunger had transitioned into a dull ache. When enough time passed, the ache eventually turned into a hard pit that sat in the space where her stomach should have been. She was well beyond feeling hunger but knew it was important to force something down.

A flicker of light at the window made her smile. Outside, Hendrel danced above the tall grass along the building's edge. He paused in front of the window in greeting and blinked back between the reeds. Barely visible out in the daylight, Raelyn doubted anyone else would notice him.

"Raelyn?"

"Mmm." She rolled over. "Do we have to?"

Tying the lacing at the top of his new tunic, he came over and stood above her at the edge of the bed. "Come. You'll feel stronger with some food, and it will make you sleep more soundly."

She sat up as he leaned down and picked something off the floor. It was the latch from the door. Laris looked at it, turning it over with a frown.

"So much for a lock." She inclined her head toward the dresser. "We can push that across the door tonight like the innkeeper suggested."

He set the broken latch down on the bed stand and nodded. "Not much that can be done about it now. Ready?"

She slid on the shoes from the seamstress and stood. Her dress skirt was a touch short, but she liked the lifted hemline and hoped it would be less inclined to soak up mud during the remainder of their journey. Straightening her bodice, she pulled the sleeves into place and tucked the *vehsidhe* talisman beneath the fabric at her neckline. "Ready," she confirmed.

Farmers and other day workers packed the dining area, enjoying drinks together before heading home and preparing for another long day of work tomorrow. Raelyn looked around for a seat. A waving hand in the crowd caught her attention, and she nudged Laris while acknowledging Ezra with a small smile.

"Is that the only open seating?" Laris looked around.

"Aye," said the innkeeper, overhearing as she pushed past with a tray of bowls and mugs. "Won't get any less packed in here, neither, not for another couple hours."

He sighed. "How convenient for him."

Raelyn could tell Laris wasn't impressed with Ezra's attention. She also felt uncomfortable with the way the stranger had attached himself to them. His initial impression of warmth and well-meaning was tainted by something she couldn't name. She'd felt it the moment he'd put his arm around her. Still, he hadn't done anything untoward—yet.

They wound through the crowd and over to Ezra's booth. He welcomed them with a smile and gestured to the empty bench across from him. "Just in time!" He pushed a basket of bread over. "Eat up. The girls are going to bring some boar soup and noodles. You like noodles?"

Raelyn took a piece of bread and nodded. "I don't think we're terribly picky today."

"You two clean up well." Ezra slapped the table, pleased. "I'm sorry about earlier. You should have heard what I heard from the other side of the door."

One of the serving girls brought two empty mugs for Raelyn and Laris, and Ezra filled them from the pitcher already at the table. "Wine. I'm not much of a mead drinker. So, how did you two end up in this little town off the beaten path?"

"We're just traveling the countryside," Laris lied. "Looking for a quiet place to settle."

"You must have had a rough trip. No horses, no packs, no money to start a life with." He gestured toward them with his hand holding the mug. "Sword and polearm, though, made it through your journey just fine. Nice choices, if I do say so."

"Is there something you want?" Laris's tone was annoyed. "I'd rather you get to the point."

Raelyn sipped her wine as a way to interrupt the tension. Across from her, Ezra smiled crookedly and reached for some bread.

"What could I want?" He spread his arms in a wide shrug. "I'm just a traveler, too."

Sitting in uncomfortable silence, they each reached for the boar soup when it came and ate without conversation. Finished first, Ezra watched them, a hint of a smile on his lips, his eyes unreadable but not warm. He topped off their wine glasses and leaned back, letting his gaze wander around the room.

"This is a small town to see so many patrons all at once," Laris remarked, bringing his cup to his lips. "Does this place even have a name?"

"Tordmend. I've been here for a few days now. That's what they call it."

Raelyn took another drink, letting Laris handle the conversation. She didn't want to give away details she shouldn't, and she could tell the green-eyed stranger was fishing for information. A wave of tiredness rolled through her, and she stared down into the red liquid of her mug, slumping into her seat. How long had they been sitting there?

"Were you waiting for something? Someone?" Laris asked. "Seems like a long time to remain in a town without cause."

"You're skeptical of me; that's fair. It's wise to watch out for strangers. Everyone has their agenda. I'm just a traveler caught up in the charms of the small-town lifestyle."

Clouds gathered at the edges of Raelyn's vision, and the sounds around her became muffled, indistinguishable echoes. Her head bobbed. She felt Laris slump forward against her arm and catch himself, straightening.

"You're not just a traveler," she heard him slur.

Ezra's smile of triumph gave his boyish features a menacing quality. "It seems I've been found out. They do say death recognizes death. I'm not surprised you caught on so quickly. I'd expect no less from a renowned Lomnir commander."

Raelyn could barely keep her eyes open. Through her hazy vision, she saw Ezra wave to one of the serving girls. Laris's head hit the table.

"These two have had too much to drink, I think," Ezra told the girl. "Someone should help them to their room."

It was dark when Raelyn opened her eyes, but she could feel a mattress beneath her. She was in their room, Laris beside her, unmoving, possibly sleeping. She couldn't lift her limbs or turn her head.

"Don't be alarmed if you can't move." Ezra's voice filled her head, unbearably loud. "The sedative does that." He crumbled something in his hands, and it started to glow. Placing the pieces in the lantern by the bed, he said, "Can't risk fire with a mage around. I'm glad you woke up so soon. I thought I'd be sitting here in the dark a bit longer."

"Why? *What* are you doing?" Having trouble moving her lips, Raelyn could barely raise her voice loud enough to hear. "We have nothing."

"Clearly." He stood and leaned over so she could see his face, its friendly features now concealed by a black mask and cowl. "It's not about that." His eyes studied her in the eerie light. "The people I work for want you. It's that simple. Dead or alive, they said."

Dread coursed through her immobilized body. "Did you kill him?"

"Who? The transcendent? No. Not yet, anyway. I gave him a larger dose of sedative to be safe, but I couldn't risk killing him in front of everyone. I will have to kill him before we go, though."

"I'm not going anywhere with you."

He patted her hair. "You are. It's not a choice. I can do whatever I want right now, and you can't stop me. You can't even turn your head." He sat down on the bed against her side. "Don't worry. I'm not the kind of monster who has my way with someone against their will."

She bit down on her tongue as he traced a finger along her jawline.

"I have been tempted from time to time, though," he said softly. "You looked so lovely last night, keeping watch in that farm shed; I admit some ungentlemanly thoughts came over me. But—" he sat back "—this was worth the wait. I'll get more for you alive, even though the original plan was to kill you both while the mage was exhausted."

"You deliberately set the penumbra on us first?"

He picked up each of her arms and laid them across her belly. "That's right. And well done killing that creature." He pulled a line of cord from a pocket on his black leather vest. "That surprised me, and I'm rarely surprised. What a trick. Creating fire for your lover to use. Impressive." He leaned his face in close to hers after tying her wrists. "I'm also rarely impressed."

In the eerie lantern light, Raelyn could see the madness in Ezra's eyes. Where there had only been veiled intelligence before, she saw fervor and obsession. He was enjoying his success, thriving on his complete control over them. She doubted he cared if she responded to his quibbling; he was reveling in the sound of his own voice detailing his accomplishments.

"I'll scream," she threatened, and he stared at her a moment.

"You can't scream. And if you try, I can always cut out your tongue." His expression sobered, and he moved over her, straddling her across the ribs. "'Alive' can mean many different things, Raelyn Forthgrew."

A light flared in front of Ezra's face, and he fell back, swatting at it and hopping away from the bed. Hendrel flickered wildly around the room, but once on his feet, Ezra ignored the wisp.

"I heard you had a wisp on your soul," he said, irritated. "Lucky for us, he's got no substance. I'd have to kill you if he could burn me." He walked back over. "If he gets too annoying with that light, I may have to anyway."

He climbed back onto the bed, standing over her and Laris with one of his daggers. "We should get on with it. Any last words for your mage?"

"I'll kill you," she said through clenched teeth. Tears welled up and streamed out of her eyes, down her temple. "If it's the last thing I do, I'll kill you for this."

"No, you won't, Raelyn. The only thing that can beat a killer like me is another killer, like me." His maniacal laugh filled the room, and Hendrel swooped down at him. Ezra brought a hand up to shield his eyes from the blinding light.

The mattress bounced hard, and something wet spattered across Raelyn's face. It was warm and dripped slowly down her cheek and chin. *Blood,* she thought, recognizing the smell. Above her, silhouetted by Hendrel's light, another man stood on the bed with Ezra. Ezra's body was rigid, and he clutched the other man's hand at his throat. Still unable to lift her head, it took Raelyn a second to realize the hand at Ezra's neck was holding a dagger embedded to the hilt.

"Or a killer like me," Laris growled, holding the weapon firm and easing Ezra's body down to its knees.

A gurgle issued from the assassin's throat. With a burp of blood, he rasped, "How?"

"Death recognizes death," Laris replied. With a swift arc of his arm, he pulled the dagger free and let Ezra slump down, face first, onto the bed. Hendrel floated back and forth over the body, and Laris slid off the mattress. He came around and picked Raelyn up, carrying her away from the bed to lean her gently against the wall by the fireplace.

She was still crying but couldn't lift her arms to reach for him.

He crouched next to her and pulled her head to his chest. "I'll explain later," he said softly. "We need to go."

He hurriedly gathered her old boots and glaive before returning to pick her up.

"How long before I can move?" she asked.

"I don't know. This might be uncomfortable, but it's the only way I can carry you right now." He positioned her over his shoulder.

Outside the room, the inn was dark and quiet. Laris slunk down the hall and through the dining area, guided by Hendrel's tempered light. Setting Raelyn down in a booth, he grabbed a cloth from the bar and filled it with leftover bread. He tied the makeshift satchel to his belt and retrieved her.

Raelyn expected Laris to head down the road and toward the town border, but once in the night air, he circled the inn and slipped into the stable at the back. With her propped up against hay bales, he hastily tacked two horses, Hendrel moving alongside to light his work.

"You'll ride with me for now," Laris whispered, doing his best to carefully sling her over the front of one of the saddles. He climbed up after and pulled her upright, positioning her upper body against his chest, legs to the side. "Speak up if you need me to adjust you."

"Yes," was all she could say.

With Hendrel blazing at the lead and the other horse in tow, they trotted out of the corral and back into the fields, away from the main road.

CHAPTER TWENTY-FOUR

A letter from Ellisand arrived precisely two days after she'd left for the castle. Mollen handed it to Saraht nonchalantly when she came down to break her morning fast. It was unopened, even though it was addressed to him. Without a word of greeting, the innkeeper handed her the letter, a warm cup of tea, and a plate of biscuits, then turned his back to her.

She didn't mind his silence. He was very different than Jormand, but they both had the same reliable, steadfast character that gained trust quickly. He didn't want to know what she was there for, but at the same time, he risked his safety to help her. *Maybe there is another good man in the world,* she thought.

She sat down in her usual booth by the back window. Morning sunlight, welcome after days of rain, scattered rainbows around the room as it streamed through sections of colored glass. She picked up a biscuit and added some jam and butter before dipping it into her tea. With care, she opened the seal on the letter.

Honorable Master Mollen,

I am writing to convey my deepest appreciation for the kindness and hospitality you showed me upon my arrival in Osharia. I want to extend an invitation to you and a guest to join me at the castle tomorrow evening for a formal expression of gratitude.

> *A carriage will come for you tomorrow at the eighth hour. The king and I eagerly await your presence for a royal commendation.*
>
> *With deepest admiration and thanks,*
>
> *Lady Ellisand Wedminth*

She set the paper down. Ellisand moved quickly. Saraht hadn't been expecting an opportunity to enter the castle so soon. Glancing at the bar, she watched Mollen aggressively move bottles and scrub the polished counters. He must already know about the invite; it was likely the cause of his surly attitude toward her. She finished her biscuit and tea and walked to the bar with the empty cup.

"Mollen?" she inquired. "Am I correct to assume you already know what was written in this letter?"

He grunted, staying turned away while he wiped down the counter along the back of the bar area. "Of course I do. Patrick came in here yammering on about it, waving the letter like an idiot."

"I will pay you. I don't expect you to do this task for naught."

He straightened, put his hands on the edge of the wood, and looked at her in the mirror. "You send that money to Jormand. I'm well enough off."

"Why are you going to this trouble for me, then?"

"I know who you are," he said bluntly. "Like a daughter to my cousin; he's talked about you often. And I think maybe you've had something to do with all the liberation efforts in black-light districts from Pardis up to the capital." She made a sound to protest, but he held up a hand. "Now, I'm just going off the general description and what I know of you from a family perspective. I don't need or want to know the truth of it." He turned to her. "I'll go to the castle tomorrow. If you need a dress, there's a shop on Isle Street."

He went back to scrubbing.

Saraht left a few coins on the counter before returning to her room. Ellisand's invite had been unexpected but ideal. Time was growing short; she was sure of it after her conversation with Orion yesterday. The transcendent had met her in the trade-and-labor district to discuss their plans. While always unfriendly toward her, he'd had an unusual air about him—a new confidence, as though whatever she had to say was no longer important. He'd been dismissive of her suggestions about infiltrating the castle, telling her his plan to tunnel with the wretches under the castle into the sewers was ironclad and she needn't worry. The wretches were unparalleled excavators, and his magic would further speed the process. She was worried, however. Orion and his forces needed to be in place if her plan was to work—and if it failed, she'd need his help to escape.

Something about his behavior during their meeting had been unsettling. She wouldn't be surprised if he and Thiir had developed their own plan for taking the throne. The Faldean prince's patience with her had its limits, and she'd sensed his irritation in their last conversation. She was sure plans beyond her were at work. Thiir's scheming was boundless.

The time was now or never. Tomorrow, she would kill the king. Whether Orion and his forces successfully infiltrated and seized command during the chaos was unimportant. She didn't need them. She just needed to get to the Gate.

Soon, she would be free for the first time in her entire life.

A night and a day on horseback brought them to Osharia. By the time Raelyn and Laris approached the first gates of the capital, she was ready to be out of the saddle and on solid ground. Raelyn always loved horseback riding, but the effects of the sedative were slow to wear off, and once she'd moved to her own mount, the sway of the horse's movement made her stomach and head ache. She felt sluggish and dimwitted, hungry and still exhausted. If the city was impressive, she was too disinterested to notice. Even Hendrel had disappeared once the walls of civilization came into view.

Riding next to her, Laris reached over and pulled the reins of her horse, halting them both. "Are you feeling better? I'll speak with the guards here to see if anyone else from Albator has arrived."

She shook her head. "I'm not feeling well at all."

"Your movement?"

"Better," she admitted. "I still feel slow."

"As long as you're improving." He dismounted. "Better food and sleep would help, if we could ever manage to secure them."

She slid off the saddle with his help and clung to it briefly to gain her balance. "I'll wait with the horses over there." She pointed to a toppled stone. "It'll be a relief to sit on something stationary for a bit."

"Don't forget about the bread," he reminded her as he walked toward the guards at the gate.

Stumbling drunkenly over to the stone, she did her best to pick her feet up and managed not to fall on her face. Detaching all but one side of the reins, she let the horses graze before grabbing a roll of bread for herself from Laris's saddle. With an awkward plop, she sat down on the pillar and lifted the roll of bread to her mouth. Like the rest of her abilities, swallowing felt delayed, and she was careful to keep her bites small so she wouldn't choke.

By the time Laris returned, she'd barely made it through half the roll.

"Raelyn—" he knelt next to her "—they say the duchess and others have arrived safely. They offered to have a captain take us to the main gate to speak with the guards at the castle."

"Did you tell them who we were?"

"I told them who I was." He put a hand on her knee. "I wasn't sure if you wanted to be known."

He was being kind to her, she knew. It wasn't just about protecting her from more assassination attempts; it was about protecting her from the duchess and anyone else who might blame her for what had happened in Albator. She suddenly wasn't sure she wanted to go to the castle so overtly. Why should she? Maybe there was another way for her to enter without being recognized. Hidden as a servant, she might be able to find the Sundered Gate without much risk.

She met Laris's watchful gaze. He had no other choice. He was a Lomnirian commander, and if Lord Leofric was in the castle, Laris was obligated to return to his side. There was no hiding his identity.

"What if they try to imprison me?" she whispered.

"I'll protect you. I promise. And if there's no home for you in Limnin, we'll return with Lord Leofric … to Lomnir."

Too much was crashing in on her at once. There'd been no time to have discuss the little details between her and Laris. They'd always been on the run, battling for their lives, focused on getting to safety and surviving. Now, the realities were pushing in. He had a home and a life in Lomnir. Would he stay with her? Would his title and position allow him to? Where would she end up, with no kin and hundreds of deaths on her conscience?

"Easy, easy." Laris could see the look of panic on her face. "We're almost there, Raelyn. This is the most direct way to get you to the Gate, and then you can claim your power. Nothing else matters—not the opinion of the duchess or the will of the king."

She looked over at the guards. They were pointing toward her, speaking to a pair of men in different-style armor. The two newcomers clasped forearms with the gatekeepers and started walking toward Raelyn and Laris.

"Commander," the taller of the two said with a salute. "I'm Lieutenant Brekk; this is Captain Warrant. We're here to escort you through the city."

Laris returned the salute. "Lieutenant. Captain. This is Raelyn, a fellow Albator survivor and one of the personal attendants of the duchess's daughter."

The men bowed to Raelyn, their expressions void of any recognition. With a deep breath and a strained smile, she dipped her head in greeting. Laris's description wasn't untruthful, but it hid enough details to make her forgettable.

"Your lord is still at the castle," Brekk told Laris. "We've sent word to have him meet you at the gate to verify your identity. I'm sure you understand."

"Of course. Lead on." Reattaching the reins, he helped Raelyn up and onto her horse but remained on the ground to walk with the guards.

She hooked her fingers into the saddle and let her body relax. The sway was less bothersome than before, and she could take in more of her surroundings.

Osharia was just as her father had always described it many times— too large and too wild. Riding above the heads of the crowd, she could see where that impression came from. There was infinite chaos within the loose order in the trade-and-labor district. Nothing seemed simple; even the men haggling at the fish market discreetly swapped coins under the bins. Children in rags raced through the streets, and one flashed a knife and a smile when he caught Raelyn watching.

As they passed through the next two city gateways, she found the interior sections of the main city cleaner, but disarray was still beneath the surface. Shops and businesses of all types boasted open doors and friendly faces, yet in the shadowed corners, Raelyn could see the whispered conversations and deals taking place. Just because the people in the city itself were wealthier and wore nicer clothes did not mean they were of better moral ilk. She suspected the secrets here were far darker than those of the trade-and-labor district.

When they finally arrived at the castle's perimeter wall in the city's center, a pair of guards opened the iron gates to allow entry. Raelyn, Laris, and their escorts filed through, crossing an empty cobblestone square and passing into a garden area. Clumps of blue flowers created a sea of petals, filling the area with waves of different blues and greens. Dangling, thin tree branches lining the path reached down at Raelyn, their small teardrop leaves and yellow flowers brushing against the top of her head. *Beesbane*, she recalled. Beautiful but deadly when powdered, Ebest had told her. The tunnel of spun gold stretched to a set of decorative gates where a group of men were waiting.

Raelyn immediately recognized Lord Leofric, who strode toward them and clapped Laris's back with a forceful embrace. Her stomach rolled when he looked over at her.

"Lady Raelyn!" Leofric grabbed her horse's bridle, shaking his head in disbelief. "Thank Emblem. What a miraculous few days it has been here."

The huge smile on his face confused her, but she met it in kind. He seemed genuinely pleased to see her, which gave her hope and bolstered her spirits.

"Has much been happening in the capital?" Laris asked him.

"Astounding happenings, truly," Leofric said with a laugh. "Our own arrival was slow and uneventful, but Lady Ellisand returned just a few days ago, and now you've been restored to us, as well."

Raelyn slid out of the saddle so fast she fell forward when her feet hit the ground. "What did you say?" she demanded, forgetting all propriety.

Lord Leofric reached to steady her, unbothered by the lack of decorum. "Yes, Lady Raelyn, she's here, and uninjured. Though, she has been through quite an ordeal. Come." He motioned them toward the castle. "There's no sense in talking about it now. You're safe. Let's get you inside and seen to. We have all the time in the world to discuss the details."

They hadn't gotten far across the castle courtyard when Raelyn heard someone scream her name. She looked up the veranda to her right at two figures leaning over the railing. A woman in a scarlet dress waved vigorously, leaning so far forward the man with her had to pull her back.

The world around Raelyn ground to a complete halt. *Jackson. Ellisand.*

Was she dreaming?

Ellisand pushed Jackson away. She lifted her skirts and ran down the stairs from the veranda to the courtyard, calling Raelyn's name over and over. Raelyn forgot everything else and staggered forward, willing her still-heavy legs into a run. She and Ellisand collided together with such force they knocked each other off their feet.

"Rae! Rae!" Ellisand half laughed, half cried. "I never thought I'd see you again."

Tears of happiness and relief flooded Raelyn's eyes. "I'm so sorry," she sobbed. "I'm so sorry I couldn't save you. Are you hurt? Did they hurt you?" They rolled around in the dirt, crying and clinging to one another.

Ellisand and Raelyn sat up together, holding hands, laughing and sobbing all at once when Jackson caught up.

"Come now, Lady Ellisand, don't keep her all to yourself." He swooped Raelyn up and gave her a firm but short embrace. "By The Circle, Rae, I should have known you'd be just fine."

Still sitting on the ground, Ellisand laughed and wiped her face. "I never gave up, Rae," she said. "I never gave up. I thought of you and what you would do." She started to cry again.

Laris walked over and clasped hands with Jackson. "Well met, lieutenant. Nice work getting everyone here safe."

"Sir Laris, you were true to your word. We are forever in your debt." Jackson glanced at Lord Leofric as he joined them. "Lord Leofric was right when he said no one was more capable of tracking our runaway."

"In the end, I don't think she needed me." Laris shrugged at Jackson's look of surprise. "She's strong and capable. I owe her my life."

Jackson let out a whoosh of breath and ran a hand through his hair. "She's always been a fighter," he said, carefully studying Laris's face. "It sounds like you two went through more than we did."

"It's an unbelievable tale."

"I'd like to hear it. You'll not return to Lomnir too soon, I hope."

Laris caught Raelyn's sorrowful look. "That depends on Lady Raelyn," he proclaimed loudly. "I don't intend to leave her. My apologies, my lord." He turned to Leofric. "I will honor my duties, but I won't be parted from her, even if it means she returns with us."

The group fell into a stunned silence, waiting for Leofric's response. He chuckled. "Laris, rest easy. I would not dishonor my most trusted friend and advisor by parting him from his lady. But we must speak on it—all of us. I have no need to rush back to Lomnir. We are all still recovering. I'd rather not step back onto the road again for a bit, truthfully."

Ellisand jabbed Raelyn in the ribs. "What is going on here?" she asked accusingly, her voice quiet enough for only Raelyn to hear. "Don't tell me you've fallen in love?" She grabbed her friend's arm and tugged on it playfully.

Unable to control the smile on her face, Raelyn nudged her back. "Shhhh. Nothing's happened. We've just grown close."

"Oh bother, as if I believe you. I expect details eventually."

"I have a story to tell, that's for certain. But your mother?" Raelyn whispered to Ellisand. "Will she permit me to stay?"

"I will handle Mother," Ellisand assured her. "Though, Rae—" she leaned in close "—we need to speak about something important. Soon and in private. Tonight. It can't wait."

The seriousness in Ellisand's voice stole away some of Raelyn's elation, and she nodded. "Come to my room?"

"I'll come late. You know the knock."

The four-beat knock on her door sounded well past the middle of night. Raelyn lay in bed, staring at the ceiling, marveling at the silkiness of the night dress against her skin and the size of the bed. Alone in her room since their arrival, she'd eaten well, and a deep, short-lived sleep had claimed her soon after she'd lain down.

The room was too quiet and empty for the slumber to last, and even with Hendrel's reappearance, she was lonely and found herself watching shadows in the corners for sinister movement. Famine rested under the frame of her bed and within reach but brought little comfort. She wondered if Laris had managed to fall asleep.

The knock sounded again, and Raelyn hopped to her feet. She eased open the door, and something brushed by her legs in a flash. Before she could look for it, Ellisand slipped in, holding a candle, and quickly hugged her.

"Did you just see something?" Raelyn muttered, looking around the floor.

Ellisand giggled and pointed to the bed where a large orange cat was bounding across the sheets chasing Hendrel.

"Oh!" Raelyn pressed her hands to her chest. "Oh, he looks just like this cat I met on our journey. Can I pet him?"

Her friend nodded. "He's very friendly. I met him at an inn near the capital where he was traveling with a troupe of wayfarers. They sent him here for me after we parted. His name is Lydantus."

"What?" Raelyn grabbed her arm. "What's his name?"

"Lydantus. Rae?"

"Is it possible?" she whispered. "That's the name of the cat I also met."

The orange feline stopped his play and sat down on the bed, looking at them. He blinked slowly at Raelyn, the gentle hum of his purr chasing away the cold silence of the room.

"This is what I need to talk to you about," Ellisand told her. "Come, under the covers like we did when we were little."

They climbed onto the bed and pulled the top quilt over their heads, anchoring it with pillows to create a tented space. When they were girls, they'd tell each other scary stories and tales of the Vast. As they grew older, the late-night conversations steered toward secrets Ellisand learned spying on servants and her frustration with Jackson's lack of attention. This conversation felt too serious for their nostalgic talks, but the memories provided a sense of security and comfort.

"Rae, I know you're a warden," Ellisand blurted, taking Raelyn's hand. "When I was captured, I was taken to meet a Faldean soldier who was also a warden."

"Ell, wait, what—"

"I know, I know." Ellisand squeezed her hand. "It seems unbelievable, but it's true. Her name is Saraht. She's a commander for Faldea, but she was born here."

"She didn't hurt you, did she?"

"No, not at all. I … I came to respect her. The things she told me made sense, you know? Like how women shouldn't have to be pawns or playthings for powerful men. That women are capable of greatness. I believed her. I still do. The future she paints is—" she paused "—better. Better than marrying some oaf who only wants me for my bloodline."

"You have to slow down. I can't follow." Raelyn was lost trying to piece together the fragmented story. "What future?"

At his meow outside of the covers, Raelyn lifted the quilt and let Lydantus in. He lay down between them and stretched out, cleaning his paws.

"One where we are finally the queens we always dreamed of being!" Ellisand continued excitedly. "I need you to meet her, Rae. She's coming to the castle tomorrow night, secretly. I want you to hear what she has to say. She's wise and admirable. She's saved so many people, and she wants to save more. *I* want to help her save more. Will you do this for me? I need my best friend at my side."

Raelyn's eyes scanned her friend's face. There was a maturity to Ellisand that had not been there before their parting, a look in her eyes borne of hardship. Raelyn's heart ached to think of what her friend might have endured. If it was anything like her own journey, there were scars that might never heal hidden beneath Ellisand's beautiful exterior.

"Okay," Raelyn said with a sigh. "I'm with you. Of course, I'm with you. I don't really understand, but what is it you want me to do?"

"Just meet her tomorrow when she arrives. Listen to what she has to say. She's a warden, too. She was trying to help me find you." She leaned over and planted a friendly kiss on the top of Raelyn's head. "I should go. I'm watched more closely here than I was at home. We can talk more tomorrow. Try to sleep, yes?"

Raelyn nodded with a smile she didn't feel and watched Ellisand slide out from their makeshift tent. Lydantus bumped her hand with his head for a final pat before he, too, slunk out from under the quilt. Still beneath the covers, at the sound of the door click, Raelyn rolled over and hugged one of the pillows so tightly a puff of feathers burst from the seam.

Something about what Ellisand had said was deeply unsettling. Saraht had been searching for her, but with good or ill intentions?

Could she be the one behind the assassin and the penumbra? She was Ellisand's kidnapper, a Limnin enemy commander. Just what had she done to sway Ellisand so confidently to her cause?

Throwing off the covers, Raelyn padded to the door and opened it, creeping out into the hall. "Hendrel, please," she whispered to the wisp, "can you help me find Laris's room? But dim your light a bit or we'll draw attention."

The guards of Osharia castle were no different in their routines than those at Albator. Raelyn knew there was a tempo to the patrols, but she didn't know the range each pair of guards covered during their rounds. It was easy enough to stay hidden in the dark crooks of the halls, but if she stepped out at the wrong time, she risked encountering a second or third pair of patrolmen.

Hendrel blinked in and out of existence while they snuck from shadow to shadow, leading Raelyn down corridors and several flights of stairs. He eventually settled in front of a split set of wooden doors painted the same dark blue as the ones of her room.

With a silent prayer, she gently tapped on the door. Long, agonizing moments passed with no response, and Hendrel spun around in a quick whirl and disappeared through the wooden barrier.

A few moments later, the door creaked open. "Raelyn? What in the world are you doing?" Without waiting for her reply, Laris grabbed her wrist and pulled her inside, closing the door behind them.

Chamber lights still lit, fire blazing in the hearth; it was clear he hadn't been sleeping.

He ripped a sheet from the bed and covered her shoulders. "Here." He tugged it snug. "You're in your nightdress."

Furrowing her brows, Raelyn protested. "I don't need to cover up. You've seen more of me than this."

He stopped her with a knowing look and gently faced her toward the center of the room.

"Raelyn," Jackson greeted her from a seat by the fire, looking extremely uncomfortable.

Warmth spread in her cheeks. "I couldn't sleep. I didn't know you'd be here."

He barked a laugh. "I don't know if that makes it better or not. I mean, I'm sorry. I just ... Well, you two ... it's just unexpected, that's all. I guess I didn't think you were already, well, you know …" With a big sigh, he shook his head and motioned to one of the chairs by the fire. "Just don't mind me. Come, sit. Laris and I were discussing your journey."

She drew the sheet closer and stepped around to the chair, mortified but unable to think of any way to make the situation less awkward. There was no point denying anything about her intentions. Jackson wouldn't believe her, not when she'd shown up in a flimsy nightdress in the middle hours of the night.

Laris handed her a glass of warm wine. "I was telling Jackson about the assassin we met near the city."

"You were poisoned, Rae? Laris was saying it took hours for you to be able to move?"

"Sedated." She looked down at the red liquid, remembering. "He must have slipped it into our drinks during dinner." She turned to Laris. "But it didn't affect you as much? How did you recover before me?"

"I didn't drink the wine. I was suspicious of Ezra from the moment we met him, and when he burst into our room with enough force to break the door lock, I suspected he was setting us up for something that evening."

"You were faking the whole time?" She stared at him in awe. "But you were so believable!"

With a soft chuckle, he refilled his cup and sat in the chair next to her. "It doesn't take too much acting to let your head hit the table. I could tell by how the wine affected you that it was drugged. I just had to play along."

"Incredible," she said into her cup. "I can't believe it."

"You have no idea who he was working for?"

They both looked at Jackson and shook their heads.

"Wait." Raelyn did have an idea. "There is someone. Just this evening, I had a conversation with Ellisand about her captors. She told me the woman was looking for me—on Ellisand's behalf, to be fair—but it could be something."

Jackson rubbed his chin. "The Faldeans? I can understand attacking if you were pursuing them, but you two were leagues away, in the depths of the mountains. That's a lot of effort to hunt you down."

She didn't reply. Jackson would understand if he knew of her connection to the Holy King. For whatever reason, Laris hadn't told him, and Raelyn wouldn't break the news, either. It was difficult enough to have him assume she was sneaking around in the night for a lover's tryst without adding that she might be the world's next spiritual leader to his thoughts. He was like a brother; she didn't want to completely shatter his perception of her. At least not until it was necessary.

"Raelyn is a threat to any mage," Laris pointed out. "Without knowing anything about her, they were likely worried she'd thwart their bigger plans. One of the men who captured Ellisand in Albator was a mage. He and Raelyn had an altercation in the city, and he wanted her dead then, as well."

"How did Ell escape?" Raelyn asked suddenly. "She didn't tell me. We didn't get to speak for long."

"They were attacked in the night, she said, by some animal while camping on the edges of the Pardis territory. She used the commotion to slip away and steal a horse." Jackson smiled with pride. "Something you would have done, Rae, I think. It's a good thing your survival instincts rubbed off on her."

Raelyn nodded absently. "Yes. Good thing." She wasn't convinced. Ellisand said she'd met Lydantus in an inn near the capital, and she spoke highly of Saraht not as a captor but as a companion—she'd invited her to the castle. Why was she being deceptive with her story?

"You're getting into the bad habit of not sleeping," Laris said, watching her. "You still look exhausted."

Jackson stood. "I can see you back to your room. We're all due for some sleep, and I've accepted a captain's position here. No one will think it improper if I escort you."

She bit her lip and avoided his gaze. "I was hoping I could sleep here tonight. Is that all right?"

For a second, he stared at her, dumbfounded, and then stammered, "I … don't ask me! Why wouldn't it be okay? You're a grown woman, Rae." He looked helplessly at Laris.

Raelyn wanted to box his ears like she had when they were young. "I wasn't asking *you*."

The color drained from Jackson's complexion, and he looked back and forth between them, shaking his head. "I'll take my leave then." He hurriedly drank the rest of his wine and set the cup down, fumbling it as it touched the table. "Daft thing," he mumbled, setting it upright. At the door, he turned around with one hand on the handle. "I will have to kill you if you hurt her, you know."

"I know," Laris replied, unconcerned. "I would expect no less, captain."

Jackson gave Raelyn a terse nod and left the room, shutting the door softly behind him.

"He's a good man and loyal friend, but I think he believes I've got you under some sort of spell."

"He's always been like a protective big brother. But I think he knows he can't protect me from you even if he needed to." Her eyes were growing heavy, and she turned in the chair, pulling her legs over the armrest. With her head against the upholstered back, she added, "It felt strange in my room without you."

He walked over and gently picked her up. "You need proper sleep."

Her eyes were already closing. "Soldiers don't need to sleep," she murmured.

He made a sound of amusement and tossed her onto the bed. The bounce snapped her out of her drowsiness, and she gasped, letting go of the sheet.

"I couldn't resist," he said with a warm smile, then shook his head. "Did you really walk through the castle in that silk shift?"

Suddenly self-conscious, she reached for the blankets. "It's the middle of the night. No one was going to see me."

"I was going to see you."

"I'm fully covered. It's not like I'm naked!"

"It leaves nothing to the imagination," he remarked dryly. "You might as well be naked. I should make you put one of my shirts over that for the night."

"You're being ridiculous. This is what everyone sleeps in."

He sighed and crawled onto the bed beside her, propping his head up with his elbow as his eyes traced her face. With his other hand, he reached out and stroked the length of her hair splayed across the pillow.

"You talk to me about not being fair, and here you are lying in my bed, silk pressed to your every curve, wanting to sleep." With a growl of frustrated resignation, he flopped to his back. "You are my greatest challenge, Raelyn Forthgrew, I swear it."

She smiled and placed a hand on his chest. Slowly, she inched over to him, waiting for him to demand space, but he lifted his arm instead and allowed her to rest against his side.

"Go to sleep."

He tensed as she wiggled closer and stretched her arm across his torso, nestling her head on his chest. She was too content to care about what was proper. He was warm and smelled of fire and wine, and she let herself melt against him. Despite her fatigue, her prior sleepiness evaded her. The heat from Laris's hand resting at her hip was all she could focus on. He was right; the fabric of her nightgown was inconsequential and a poor shield against his touch. Guided by some subconscious longing, she discretely shifted, allowing his hand to fall just below her belly button.

"You're playing a dangerous game," he mumbled into her hair, fanning his fingers out and sending jolts of heat between her legs and down her inner thighs. "Go to sleep."

"I don't want to sleep," she said quietly, tilting her head up to plant a light kiss on his neck. It was meant to be playful and innocent, but her lips lingered on his skin a moment too long, and the hand at her belly pulled away as he rolled and shifted her onto her back.

"If you wanted to take things slow, this isn't the way," he said, staring down at her.

Raelyn turned her face away, the wanton feelings coursing through her offset by a sudden, gripping embarrassment. What *exactly* was she doing?

Laris gently turned her face back toward him. He settled his weight over the top of her, one leg between hers, and kissed her softly, pausing to whisper against her lips. "I'm not denying you this time, but remember your promise to me. Not a moment more than you're comfortable with."

She nodded, the sensations rippling through her, overwhelming her ability to speak. She could feel *him* pressed against her, resting at the same spot his hand had been moments before. The realization of his need for her was intoxicating, pulling the thump of her heart down into the mound between her legs. He kissed her again, and she reciprocated in kind, ignoring the uncertainty of innocence and letting her body take over.

His lips shifted to her neck, and she gasped, trying to pull away from the tickling licks of pleasure, but he held her firm and shifted his weight fully over her, lying between her legs. She bucked beneath him as his kisses moved from her neck to her ear, his breath on her skin as enflaming as his lips. She needed to feel more of him. Sliding a hand beneath his shirt, she drew it up along his chest, reveling in the hotness and sweat of his skin. Aiming to rest her hand over his heart, she brushed his nipple, and he groaned against her throat. Pleased with his reaction, she ran her fingertips over it again.

"Two can play that game," he grumbled in warning before cupping her breast and lightly flicking her nipple with his thumb. He stifled her soft cry of pleasure and surprise with a kiss, caressing and pinching until she felt a blossom of moisture accompany the heartbeat between her thighs. When he took her breast with his mouth, teasing her nipple with his tongue over the silk shift, she lost all coherent thought.

"You're too much." He sat back and pulled his tunic off.

Raelyn followed the line of his scar with her gaze, marveling at how it thrilled her and enhanced his muscles already highlighted in shadows from the fireplace behind them. The feel of his hands drawing up the hem of her nightgown interrupted her pleasure-filled haze, and she sobered, nervous to be so exposed.

"I want to see more of you." He stooped and kissed her lightly. "You're beautiful, Raelyn. Let me worship you."

Face burning and body aflame with a different fire, she relaxed and let him slide his hands up her body, pulling her gown up as he did so. She sat up to aid him, and he held her close while tugging the fabric over her arms and head. Laris wrapped her in his arms, bare skin to bare skin, for a long moment before he wordlessly trailed a line of kisses down her neck and along her collarbone.

Falling back against the bed, she briefly closed her eyes, enjoying his attentions and giggling when his kisses tickled her stomach. He looked up at her, fingertips curling around the waist of her undergarment. "If this is where we stop, tell me now." His voice was thick with the effort of his pause. "Once I taste you, I'll want all of you."

Raelyn didn't know what he meant, but his words and tone quickened her pulse and sent a tingle through her core. "Don't stop," she mumbled, closing her eyes again. *He's already seen most of me,* she thought as he removed her last piece of clothing.

He kissed her belly, drawing out a contented sigh and smile from her, but her eyes snapped open when she felt his breath between her legs. Before she could object, he kissed her at the heart of her heat and desire, lapping her moisture with his tongue, and she almost leaped off the bed.

"Try to relax," he gently advised, holding her thighs still with his hands. "I'll go slower."

Emblem's Hand, she didn't need him to go slower. She needed him to stop just as much as she needed him to continue. Her body was aching, throbbing. Each movement of his mouth fueled waves of pleasure crashing through her core. She felt powerless to stop whatever was coming.

Laris held her against his mouth when the storm unleashed inside her. She cried out, wrapping her fingers in his hair as her body shook and her back arched. She felt giddy and euphoric, laughing and gasping all at once as the climax took her.

When she quieted, he eased his hold on her thighs and reached down to slide off his trousers. Still caught in a surreal haze, she smiled when he climbed back up to kiss her face, easing his nakedness between her thighs. She could tell, despite his desire, he was worried she wasn't ready.

To alleviate his unspoken concern, she initiated another kiss and drew her knees up higher, another flare of yearning pooling in her at the feel of him against her most sensitive skin.

He caressed her face and touched his forehead to hers. "This may be uncomfortable at first."

She swallowed the lump in her throat and nodded. Raelyn knew the details of lovemaking and what happened the first time a woman lay with a partner. Such information was readily available to young girls growing up in a castle. Though wisps of nervousness existed in her thoughts, her body still lounged in the hold of euphoria, and more than anything, she wanted to see the same ecstasy on Laris's face.

Relaxing as best she could as he entered her, she clung to his shoulders in anticipation and clenched her jaw with his initial thrust. A sharp pang shot through her, but he stilled, and slowly, the pain faded to a dull ache. She leaned back against the mattress, accepting his kisses as he slowly began to move inside her again.

It was uncomfortable but not unbearable, and the headiness she saw in Laris's eyes ignited her desire again. She watched his pleasure build, and felt the rhythm of his movement match the lust in his gaze. When he gripped her hips and issued a deep groan, she felt a surge of satisfaction and contentment and lifted her hips to meet him more.

The dull ache between her legs vanished, replaced by blooms of pleasure that radiated through her with each of his thrusts. Barely aware of what she was doing, she tightened her legs around him, needing to feel more of him, needing to feel him deeper inside her.

He issued a soft grunt as her thighs sought to keep him from pulling away.

"Careful," he forced out. "I can only control myself so much." He sat back to loosen her grip but didn't resume his motion. Remaining deep within her, he took a moment's pause and leaned in for a kiss. The stillness was almost too much for Raelyn to bear; the kiss a poor distraction. The length of him inside her summoned hot licks of pleasure, and she ground against him, pleading with her hips, her soft whimpers muffled by his mouth on hers.

At her insistence, he broke off the kiss and tenderly brushed away the locks of hair across her forehead

"You win," he whispered against her lips.

Laris slowly and deliberately drew out from within her, but before she could utter a sound of protest, he plunged inside again, burying himself as he lifted her hips. She gasped, suddenly aflame as he moved relentlessly, purposefully, stroke after powerful stroke.

He'd been holding back. The realization left her as quickly as it appeared, banished by a rising tide of ecstasy. It engulfed her, and she cried out as before, lost in the sensations coursing through her.

She clung to the bedsheets, unable to stop the tremors of pleasure. In a moment of breathlessness, Raelyn locked eyes with Laris and watched as his head tilted back with the yell of his own release. She smiled broadly, overjoyed as she watched him, feeling him throb inside her.

Breathing hard, he collapsed on top of her and lazily brought his hand up, running his fingers through her blonde tresses. "I didn't hurt you too much, did I?"

"No," she said quietly, stroking his head as he lay against her chest. "You didn't hurt me."

"It will get better each time."

She chuckled, and he looked up at her. "I don't know if I can handle that," she admitted. "I think my soul left my body at least twice."

"The greatest compliment any man could receive." He eased his weight off to her side and took her hand in his. They lay in companionable silence, the dwindling firelight throwing long, bobbing shadows throughout the room.

"I meant what I said earlier," Laris commented after a while. "I won't be parted from you, Raelyn. Wherever you call home is where I'll call home."

With her heart feeling as though it would burst with joy, she snuggled closer to rest her head on his shoulder. "Even if I wish to live in the Vast with the feyfolk and griffins?"

He laughed and pulled her into his arms. "Even if you surrounded yourself with wretches and penumbra, there's nowhere else I'd rather be."

CHAPTER TWENTY-FIVE

Warmth scattered across Raelyn's face, and she opened her eyes to a bright sunbeam slipping through the curtained windows across from the bed. With a stretch, she splayed her arms and legs over the soft covers, relishing the transition of the fabric from warm to cold the farther she reached from her nest of blankets. With a sigh and soft mew of contentedness, she wiggled down into the plush mattress, a smile on her face.

"There's tea and fruit if you want some." Laris was sitting at a table near the bed, watching her.

She beamed at him. "I haven't slept that soundly in ages. Did you sleep well?"

"Aye. Though, I enjoyed your morning antics just now even more."

She buried her face in her hands with a laugh. "It was just so comfortable. I wasn't thinking about much else."

"You can make those happy sounds anytime you'd like, as far as I'm concerned." He set his cup down and walked over to the bed to sit beside her. "I think we should make the most of our time today searching for the Gate. If nothing else, just so you know where it's at before our time gets committed elsewhere. The longer we're here, the more notice we'll draw and the more we'll find ourselves beset with duties at court."

Raelyn's contentedness dimmed with the weight of his words, and she felt the cold press of reality tighten around her. After a long pause, she said hesitantly, "What if I don't want to use the Gate? Maybe I don't want to be the Holy King."

"That's your decision to make," he told her gently. "But finding the Gate is why we're here. It's at the heart of everything we've been through."

"You're right. No matter what I decide, we've come too far to leave it unfinished."

He leaned over, a big smile on his face, and pulled at the fabric of her nightdress. "Are you to leave my room this late in the morning wearing only this? You didn't think that far ahead last night, did you? Not that I mind."

"I didn't think about it at all," she admitted with a groan. "Imagine running into Jackson again. I don't think he could stand the indecency."

"I doubt he'd mind as much as you think, Raelyn. I wonder that you never considered your old friend would eventually ask for your hand." He waved away her attempt to disagree. "I know his heart lies elsewhere, but friendship is a good foundation for love. Did you think he'd never marry once Lady Ellisand was betrothed? He's a young man."

"Impossible." She shoved him lightly. "Don't speak of it. It makes my stomach turn a bit."

Grabbing her hand, he planted a kiss on the palm. "He's too late now anyway. Come, enjoy the fruit and the tea, and I'll see about getting clothes from your room. I'm sure your maid is beside herself wondering where you are."

He kissed her hand again, and her smile faltered. "Before you go," she said, "there's something I need to tell you. When I spoke with Ellisand last night, that woman I mentioned was looking for me." She took a deep breath. "Ell says she's a warden."

"A warden? That seems unlikely."

Raelyn shook her head. "I don't know the truth of it, but Ell's invited her to the castle tonight. This woman, Saraht, is arriving in secret, and I don't really know why Ell is bringing her. I feel unsure about it, but ... maybe she could help me. I know Faldea is our enemy, but Genevive once told me to learn to see friend from foe. Maybe this is what she was talking about."

Laris looked at her, his expression grim. "I don't like it. Sneaking a Faldean officer into the castle would be high treason, even for the king's niece. If Lady Ellisand is caught, her life will be forfeit. You should tell Captain Jackson immediately. He's someone you already trust, and he hasn't been here long enough to be corrupted by bribes."

"I know you're right, and I don't like it either, but ..."

"But?"

"But what if Saraht knows something that could help me? I've been so alone in trying to figure out what it means to be a warden. Even if I speak to her briefly, it might unlock something important for me."

He let himself fall back onto the bed. "What are you asking of me, Raelyn? To ignore this possible threat to your safety and the safety of your king?"

"No." She shifted position to see his face better. "That's not what I'm asking. You can tell Jackson, but wait until I can speak with Saraht. You can alert him as soon as we're done if you want. What could she do in that short time just by talking with me?"

"If she's a soldier, a lot. She could kill you, or take you hostage. I can't let you do it."

"You can be as nearby as you need to be," she coaxed. "It's in the grand ballroom. She won't be able to sneak anyone else in, and there will be a dozen guards at least. Please, Laris … for me?"

His defeated look told her she'd won, and he sat up with a frown. "You do know you'll owe me for this," he pointed out. "When all this is over, it might be time to call in my debts."

Elation at his support didn't dull the fire behind his words, and she threw her arms around him. "I think I can find a way to repay you," she said coyly. "Thank you."

He laughed and pulled her off the bed and onto her feet. "I'll remember you said that. Now, let me go see about those clothes."

He left her with a kiss, and Raelyn watched him go before heading to the table to break her fast. Her hunger surprised her after the first bite of food, leaping out of its hiding place for the first time in weeks. With Hendrel floating over different fruits to guide her choices, she ate ravenously and drank four glasses of tea. The fruit wasn't filling, and she emptied several plates before feeling satisfied.

Grapes in hand, she wandered over to one of the windows and pulled the thick, taupe curtains aside. Lake Osharia glittered just beyond the edges of the lawn. The capital's water supply, fed by run-off, had been dammed by transcendents ages ago to provide a reliable water source for a city grown too large to be supported by the river systems. The large body of water curved with the landscape around the castle, its shores empty stretches of grass, sand, and rocks where trees didn't obscure the view. As the capital's primary water resource, the lake was off-limits to commoners and heavily guarded inside the castle grounds, walled behind the same exterior stone barricade that separated them from the rest of the city.

She popped a grape into her mouth, contemplating what would happen come evening. Another warden in the capital was astounding. According to what Hendrel had told her, with his death, they were the only two in all of Uhmeer.

Maybe Saraht could become the Holy King.

Raelyn ate another grape. Did it matter which warden was Emblem's conduit, as long as the world had that connection? Maybe Saraht would be a better choice as a warrior and a warden with greater grasp of her skills. Maybe she would relish the opportunity to take the position of the Holy King; Raelyn surely didn't.

If nothing else, Raelyn wanted to know she was on the right path. Speaking with Saraht could help her understand her place in the world. There had to be a reason why the only other warden had chosen to align herself with Faldea and walk the warrior's path.

I wonder if she's looking for the Gate, too. It would make sense. Forces were guiding Raelyn, but maybe that didn't mean she was undeniably the chosen one. Perhaps Emblem was leading both wardens to his communion altar so that at least one could succeed in the journey.

But searching for the Gate didn't explain Saraht's role in the Faldean attacks or the kidnapping of Ellisand. Raelyn pondered the other warden's motivations. Perhaps it was as simple as accessing the Gate was easier as a Faldean commander if Faldea were in control. Yet, if Saraht was originally Limninian, why would she have left the country? Too many questions swirled through Raelyn's mind to feel confident in the evening meeting. Laris might very well be correct; the situation could quickly turn dangerous.

Slipping off her heeled shoes, Raelyn wiggled her toes against the red carpet of the hall. Casual dress in the royal castle was more extravagant than the most formal attire in Albator, and taking off her pinching shoes offered small respite. The rest of her remained confined by the multitude of layers beneath her green gown; her bodice was cinched so tightly she could barely draw a breath. Not even a single strand of her hair had escaped the ministrations of the maids; her elaborate braid was so finely and intricately crafted that it rested just above her collarbone instead of down her back.

With her shoes dangling from one hand, she strolled down the long hallway, smiling politely at the servants and doing her best to remember the proper curtsy for each lord and lady. They were all faces in a sea of bodies moving around her. She had no interest in polite conversations or presenting herself to the high-ranking courtiers who might expect it. Finding the library was priority.

Earlier in the day, she and Laris had agreed to divide their efforts to find the Sundered Gate. Since its exact location was a secret guarded by the Holy King, only the general location—the capital city—was recorded in public history tomes. Osharia's libraries seemed like reasonable places to begin their search, not necessarily as a direct way into the Gate itself but for clues that might indicate its whereabouts. Once the seat of the Holy King before the construction of the Holy Citadel, Osharia had a long and rich history. It wasn't unreasonable to think there might be some written accounts that preceded all mention of the Gate being wiped from modern documents.

Raelyn had already visited the small library on the floor by her quarters. More of a parlor, it was designed for sitting and quiet socializing, with game boards and a few large bookshelves. The books within were common classics, ones she would enjoy if her life ever settled back down with time for reading.

This wing of the castle was more challenging to navigate, and she was reluctant to ask the guards for help. They watched her, some with open curiosity, but none spoke, and their scrutiny lacked any friendliness to put her at ease. Hallways led into more hallways, and they all boasted multiple doors, some locked, some open. After wandering and trying door after door with no success, she rounded a corner in the hall and saw a room filled with books behind an open archway.

Lifting the hem of her skirts off the floor, she hurried in and breathed a sigh of relief even as her heart sunk in her chest. It was an actual library; books lined every wall, floor to ceiling. Free-standing bookcases, stacked in rows four deep on either side of the room, divided the area into sections. Dusty display cases capped off the ends of each row and abutted the long tables where scrolls could be rolled out for examination.

Where do I even start? She walked the room perimeter, running her fingers lightly along the shelves. *History books?* That was her best guess. Hopefully, in some forgotten manuscript, there was more than a general mention of the Gate or something linked to the Gate that might narrow down the search.

Hendrel's light flickered into existence over Raelyn's hand trailing along the bookcases. She smiled, instantly comforted by his presence and glad he could join her now they were alone. She'd spoken to him briefly before parting with Laris to see if Hendrel, as the last Holy King, could provide guidance, but he'd had nothing to add to what they already knew. His life had been taken too soon for him to learn many of the secrets from past Holy Kings.

She stopped at a stack of oversized, thick books, all uniform in color and ascending in number. "Here we are," she said quietly. "Let's go to the very beginning." She pulled out the first book and had to wrap her arms around it to carry it to the table.

As soon as she opened it, she knew it wouldn't have what she was looking for. Its historical accounts started with the first Limnin royal line, not with the early Holy Kings. What she needed to know was already generations in the past. She flipped through the pages, scanning for keywords or phrases, just to be certain.

"I wonder how Laris is faring." She looked to Hendrel bobbing at the top of the page she was on. "Down in the catacombs, searching for hidden doors. Sounds more appealing, doesn't it?"

She put the book back on the shelf and pulled out the next. "We might as well go through them all. I'm not sure where else to look."

By the eighth volume, Raelyn's stomach growled, and she straightened, tilting her neck back to stretch out the tension radiating through her shoulders. A few hours of scanning and reading, and she had nothing to show for it. She wracked her mind for other places where relevant information might be hidden. History books were too obvious; likely, the first place details of the Gate had been erased.

She walked the room again and studied the different sections. *Biographies? Maybe,* she thought. Though, they weren't much different than general history books. *Economics?* She didn't believe the Gate had any ties to the capital economy. *Architecture?* She paused. If Osharia had been built on the site of the Sundered Gate, maybe the altars would have been referenced in one of the notable architectural feats, like the castle itself or the Hall of Transcendence in the city. It was worth a try.

She pulled a stack off the shelf and carried them to one of the cushioned chairs at the back of the room. Opening the first, she scanned the words but found it difficult to skim the architectural details. Though the examination took longer, like all the other books, no mention of the Gate or anything that might represent the Gate jumped off the pages at her.

She closed the book with a loud clap and sighed. How was she supposed to find something hidden away by the most powerful mages hundreds of years ago? *Better minds than mine have tried, I bet,* she thought. *If they couldn't uncover it, how can I do it?*

She left the stack of books by the chair and took a turn around the room. Under the heavy layers of her dress, she craved movement to ward off the feeling of being stuck in place forever. With Hendrel dancing around at her side, she pulled her mind off detective work and focused on enjoying the artistry of the books around her.

There was something pleasant about old books. She'd always thought so, even as a child. Their different sizes and colors, the thickness of their bindings, were features that told a story about the book itself.

She bent down at a short cabinet built into the wall to peer through its glass doors. The bottom shelf was empty, and the top only half full. Small, thin books with colorful covers leaned against one another, their cover pictures vibrant even behind the clouded glass of the cabinet.

"Children's books?" she said to herself. "How strange."

King Rothelian remained unmarried, and even though he was reported to have illegitimate children spread around the country, he didn't recognize his bastards and was known for not being fond of children. To find a child's books in the castle wasn't completely out of the question; many other kings had resided in Osharia, and all of them except Rothelian had had legitimate heirs. Still, finding such books in one of the main libraries was unexpected; a nursery was the more likely place for them.

She opened the cabinet and pulled out one with a bright purple cover. She knew the story; it was one of her childhood favorites about a tree and its many gifts to the world. Seeing the familiar pictures revived her spirit, and she wrapped the feelings of nostalgia and contentedness around her heart like a cloak.

Hendrel floating at her shoulder, she went through the little books one by one, seated on the floor with her legs crossed beneath the formidable skirts of the green dress. Some stories she knew, and others were unfamiliar. There were tales about real people and animals and fairy stories about places and magic she'd never heard of.

She slid the last book out carefully. It was familiar to her, so much so that her chest constricted when she touched the cover. Her mother's favorite book. The one with the lake. She opened the cover reverently, just as mesmerized by the artwork inside as she'd been as a child. Brushing the image with her fingertips, she took in all the familiar colors and lines. *How I longed for this lake as a child*, she thought. It had become such a fascination of hers, she'd spent hours poring over her father's maps, just to locate the large bodies of water that speckled Uhmeer, charting imaginary routes so she could go visit them. Flipping through the pages, the urge threatened to clutch her again, and she chalked it up to the grief that still sat in her core.

"Find anything of use?"

She looked up to see Laris walking toward her from the entryway. "No, sadly," she answered. "Not unless you have use for some old children's books."

"Not yet." He knelt and kissed the top of her head. "I was also unsuccessful. The open catacombs are barren and well-maintained, and the old passages are locked behind heavy iron gates. They're simple locks; any mage skilled in metal could undo them. It seems unlikely they're protecting anything more than the dead."

"At this point, the Gate could be anywhere. We have no real clues to go on."

He gently took the book from her hands. "This has seen better days."

"It's a wonderful story about a brave little boy who saves a town. Strange, though, don't you think, to find children's books here?"

"Maybe His Majesty had the royal nurseries converted to something else. One of the maids might have felt it a shame to throw them away." He slid the book back on its shelf. "Ready for a midday meal? In private, or do you want to attend the dining hall?"

She frowned. "Private, please. I'm putting off seeing the duchess as long as possible. I can't imagine her feelings toward me have changed."

"No, but I am surprised she hasn't put out the alarm about you being a warden." He helped her to her feet. "No one has approached you since you've been here, have they?"

"I haven't seen anyone other than the guards, and they haven't come into the room. No one has been in here for hours."

Holding the crook of Laris's arm, her shoes in her other hand, Raelyn let him lead while she appreciated the library one last time. The midday light was less forgiving, highlighting layers of dust that servants couldn't be bothered to clean, fading the colors of the books with its universal brightness. Outside, the lake peeked through the window, its waters calm and its shoreline empty.

Hendrel disappeared as they left the room, and Raelyn continued taking in the serenity of the calm water through the glass. Floor-to-ceiling windowpanes in the hallway were set close enough to provide an almost unbroken image of the entire body of water. Manicured flower beds and decorative trees ate up the ground, connecting the castle to the eastern shore. Heading into the adjoining hall, Raelyn could finally see the long waterfall along the south end of the lake, where the dam held back most of the water from the aqueducts below.

At the last window before the hall turned a corner, she paused. "Wait a moment." Staring out at the lake, a vague sense of familiarity pulled at her, and she searched the edges of the shoreline, trying to decipher what was calling her attention.

She turned back to Laris and grabbed his elbows. "The Holy Kings," she whispered, "were they all children? Like Hendrel?"

"Some, from what I know," he answered in a low voice. "Why?"

"The lake. It's the same as the lake from the little book in the library. That's the image I saw." She pointed out the window. "The trees are in the same places, just bigger. That boulder with the unusual shape—it was there, in the illustration."

Laris looked at her, puzzled. "Just a local artist pulling from life. What are you suggesting?"

"I don't know, but—" she looked around to see if anyone was within earshot "—what if *that's* where the Gate is? What if those books were used to teach the Holy King even as a child? Hendrel told me he wasn't raised like other children. He was being trained from his earliest memories."

"Did the book mention the Gate?"

"No, but think about it; it's the perfect location to hide a place you don't want just anyone to stumble across. In the lake, only a mage could access it. It *feels* right, Laris. That lake has been calling to me my entire life."

"I don't know, Raelyn." He looked out to the calm water. "There's no proof of that. A clever idea, but a stretch, I think. Wait, what are you doing?"

She was hurrying away from him, heading toward a door to the balcony overlooking the gardens. "I need to get a closer look," she called back over her shoulder.

With a firm push, she lurched through the doorway and let her shoes tumble to the stone floor. A warm wind grabbed stray pieces of her hair and whipped them about, instantly threatening the ability of the braid to hold the hairstyle together. Skirts gathered up in her fists, she jogged over to the balustrade and peered below. It was a drop, but she didn't think it was too dangerous, and she swung a leg over the side.

Laris grabbed her upper arm. "What in Emblem's Hand do you think you're about to do?"

"Help me drop down?" she implored him. "Or make me some steps?"

"You know I can't alter the castle with magic. They'd have my head."

"Then help me ease down." She extended her arms out at him, pleading. "Help me, or I'll come back later and do it myself."

He narrowed his eyes at her but took her by the hands. "You don't need to threaten me. I well know what you're capable of."

She offered him a quick smile. "Hurry, before someone sees us."

With Laris's help, she managed to land on her feet, pitching forward with momentum but not causing any harm. He dropped behind her while she adjusted her skirts, landing softly even without assistance.

He pulled her behind the cover of a conical shrub and took stock of their surroundings. "We should have done this at dark," he whispered. "Out in the daylight like this, anyone could spot us from the castle, not to mention the guards patrolling the grounds."

"There were shadows in the image of the lake in the book. They would have been up from that small grove of trees. Those could hide us well enough, couldn't they?"

"Perhaps. You're not exactly the image of speed and stealth in that boat of a dress."

"I agree." She started pulling at the loops, securing the layers around her waist and connecting the skirt to her bodice. "I've just about had enough of it, too."

He reached over and stopped her frantic unbuttoning. "Raelyn, no. You're not stripping down to run across the castle gardens to the lake. Be reasonable. If someone catches us, it will be difficult to pretend we're just lost guests."

She disengaged from his grip and kept undoing the clasps. The outer layers dropped, and she stepped out from them. "I'm taking the chance. I have to know if my hunch is correct."

"You're not going to be able to see into the bottom of the lake." He stilled her again. "Even if the Gate is there, it's beyond our sight and reach now."

"There may be signs, though," she countered. Urgency built inside her. She *needed* to get to the lake. "Maybe clues in the water's edge. I'm not leaving until I see."

"I could carry you out of here," he warned at her defiant look.

"You'll have to catch me first."

She took off at a dead run. Arrowing toward the small cluster of trees that blocked a patch of the lake's edge, she felt like a little girl again, out in the fields of the duchy woods, chasing Ellisand and Jackson with a wooden sword. The wind pulled large sections of her braid free and brought a burning sensation to her chest with the labor of her breath. While she felt the best she had in weeks, fatigue quickly claimed her, but she forced herself to keep running until she crossed into the wooded area.

Laris was not far behind. She knew he could have caught her but intentionally hadn't; stopping her during her dash would have paused them out in the open for too long.

He fixed her with a withering look and shook his head. "My greatest challenge," he groused.

Raelyn smiled at his gripe, glad for his company and appreciative. She could always count on him. Through everything, Laris had always been there for her, and he continued to watch over her, even when she tested his limits.

From the safety of the trees, she scanned for any sign they'd been seen. Osharia's lake was inaccessible to the public and protected, but most of the guards were positioned by the dam. The body of water was too large to patrol constantly, but there was sure to be at least a pair of men on horseback keeping watch on the shoreline.

Content with no one else in sight, she started undoing the last layer of her skirts. It wouldn't do to have unnecessary fabric dragging her down once she was in the water.

"With that little clothing on, we'd best tell people we're here for a lovers' outing," Laris said from where he leaned against one of the trees. "I'm serious, Raelyn. It will be the most believable story with us both dressed down."

"You're coming?"

"Of course I'm coming. You obviously don't want to just dip your toes in. We might as well both look for evidence of the Gate." He pulled his shirt over his head and bent down to remove his boots.

She walked over and turned her back to him. "Help me with my laces? The maids tie them so they're impossible to undo alone."

Without a word, he brushed her messy braid aside and pulled at the bindings. Halfway down her back, the snap of a branch made them look up at the edge of the grove.

"Unbelievable," Jackson said with an exasperated sigh. "You two have private quarters for this sort of … of … recreation." He sheathed his sword. "In what world did you think you would just leap off a balcony and not be seen by someone?"

Raelyn stayed where she was, Laris methodically working to retie her bodice laces. "We're sorry, Jackson. I wanted to see the lake. It looked so beautiful."

His mouth sank into a deep frown. "You don't look like you're here to see the lake, Rae. I don't think seeing the lake would have required you both to undress."

"We were about to swim," Laris remarked calmly. "You could join us if you want, Captain, or are you here to take us back inside?"

"I'm here to investigate a report of two intruders on the castle grounds. There are four other men with me, spread out within the gardens and the water's edge. I don't think now is the time for us to all go for a swim."

Raelyn could tell by the strain in Jackson's voice he was doing his best to control his anger. She'd never seen him lose his temper, but she'd always known when he was close. "Are we to be punished?" she asked, moving to gather her skirts.

"I dare say you should be," he snapped, "but a one-time transgression for voyeurism might be forgivable. I think even the palace commander would take pity with what you've been through, but don't push your luck. Get those on and follow me. I can't protect you from the walk of shame you're about to do, so may that be a lesson for you both."

Alone in her room, Raelyn took a bite of biscuit and stared up at the decorative molding around the ceiling in thought. Maybe Laris was right. Perhaps the book was only the effort of a local artist to create a remarkable illustration for a beloved children's story. To place any importance on it beyond that was silly. She'd gotten them in trouble for nothing.

Picking at the food, she slouched in her chair, recalling Jackson's words when he'd left her. *"At least marry him, Rae,"* he'd said. *"If he's ruined you for another, at least marry him."* He'd been hinting at the loss of her virginity before vows, she knew, but his choice of words still annoyed her.

Ruined me. She scoffed out loud at the thought. As if her choice to love someone out of wedlock wiped away other worthy qualities she had. It was up to her who she gave herself to and when; her virginity wasn't some prize awarded because of a proposal. Ellisand's tales of a women-empowered world sounded more appealing by the second.

Appetite gone, she went over to the bed and flopped down on her stomach, head on her folded arms. Closing her eyes, she sought out the void and let it grow rapidly around her. The transition was becoming easier; her hesitation was almost gone.

Already weaving about the emptiness, Hendrel's teardrop form steadied when she opened her eyes. "Raelyn," he welcomed her. "How develops your search?"

"Not well, I'm afraid."

"I am sorry, but I can be of no help. I was never told about the location of the Gate. But I was pleased to see some of those old stories in the library."

Hope flashed in her chest. "You recognized those? Am I right to think they were used for the Holy Kings?"

His child form materialized, and he shrugged. "I was raised in the Citadel, not Osharia. Those are not my books, but I had many of the same stories."

"So, it's possible, then," she mused. "Maybe they *were* tools to help with early teachings. Hendrel, that book about the little boy, the one I was reading last, did you have that one at the Citadel?"

He nodded.

"And were the pictures in it the same?"

He nodded again.

So, the same image was in that book at the Citadel. Her hope expanded into excitement. "Do you think those children's books could hold hidden clues to the Gate? Would the Holy Knights have used them that way?"

"I cannot know," Hendrel replied. "I can tell you that nothing was without purpose in my life, Raelyn. If I was read a book, it was for a reason, be it to teach morality, perhaps, or to one day pass on a divine secret—who can say? Children's books are often used to impart ethics and conduct in the very young, especially for those who would rule others."

"Yes, that does make sense." The hope within her faded. "I was so certain the Gate was at the bottom of the lake. I feel foolish."

"Do not feel foolish for what can't be disproven. Even if the book is not a clue, that might still be the Gate's location. But if so, how would you access it? You would need a powerful mage skilled in water magic."

She nodded, thinking. "Yes, and I know of no such person, though, Laris may."

Hendrel shifted back into his familiar flame. "I do not believe you would be given an impossible task, Raelyn, so think to that. If you have been sent to the Gate, there will be a way for you to enter, with or without help."

"I'll keep looking," she assured him. "And I'll get back to my practicing, I promise. I just have to make it through this banquet tonight."

"I will remain absent in the presence of so many. Osharia is not like Albator, where you were known since birth. There are always political factions at odds and schemes for personal gain in any capital, and until we can determine friend from foe, I will remain hidden."

"I understand," she said, "and I will see you back in the physical realm when you can return."

Clearing her mind, she recalled the details of her room and the feel of the bed beneath her. As with her transition into the void, leaving was becoming less demanding. She needed fewer details to call herself back, and the transition was no longer disorienting.

At a knock on her door, she rolled over. "Who is it?"

"Your maids, m'lady, come to prepare you for this evening's events."

Already? Raelyn slunk off the bed and over to the door. There were at least a handful of hours before she was expected in the grand ballroom. She groaned inwardly and opened the door. The servants hurried in, toting piles of skirts and a sparkling blue dress.

"Are we to start so soon?" she asked, distraught.

"Oh, yes, m'lady. The time will be gone before you realize. Miss Helena has to re-plait your hair. You cannot wear it in the same style as you did for the day."

"Ah, of course." Raelyn forced a smile. "I wouldn't dare to think so."

CHAPTER TWENTY-SIX

*S*cents reminiscent of seasonal change hung heavy in the night air. Even inside of their carriage, Saraht could feel the shift from summer to fall in everything from the temperature drop at dark to the subtle changes in color she saw on trees they passed by. Torches lighting their path up to the castle added to the autumn ambiance, casting an orange glow that barely illuminated the cobblestones.

"All right," Mollen said gruffly from the seat across from her. "I'll introduce you as my intended. We've been courting for a little more than a year, let's say. After that, you'll be on your own. Don't involve me in anything beyond accepting the king's gratitude."

"Not to worry, dear friend. I don't require anything else beyond that." She looked back out the window as the coach pulled to a stop. "No matter what happens, Mollen, do not wait for me."

He stared at her without inquiring after more details but nodded as the door opened.

The young man receiving them was familiar; Ellisand's friend, Saraht recalled. Dressed in the formal uniform of the castle guard, he greeted her with a bow and his hand to step forth from the carriage, then turned his attention to Mollen. Saraht moved off to the side. Tonight wasn't about her. She was nothing more than Mollen's companion; it was natural that the focus and conversation fell to him.

"Master Mollen," Jackson greeted him. "We are honored to receive you and your lady for the banquet tonight. Lady Ellisand awaits you just inside." He gestured for them to walk with him. "His Majesty and the Duchess Wedminth welcome you."

Mollen returned the bow and offered his arm to Saraht. "My intended," he introduced her to Jackson. "Lady Saraht Pellistar."

She curtsied to Jackson, pleased with the noble ring to the fake surname Mollen had chosen.

"Well met, lady." He smiled. "Doubly blessed you are, Mollen, to have both the favor of Lady Ellisand and your equally lovely bride-to-be."

Saraht kept her polite smile, though, the sincerity of Jackson's compliment and his winsome grin stirred a swell of pride. It had been a long time since she'd felt beautiful in the eyes of a man who wasn't viewing her as a means to an end. She could see why Ellisand harbored affection for him.

At the top of a long staircase, two guards opened the castle's exterior ornate doors leading to a small vestibule. After a few moments inside the entry space, another set of doors pulled open into the castle's interior. As expected, Ellisand was there waiting, her hands clasped together in anticipation, her face radiating happiness to see them. She rushed to greet Mollen, as was proper, ignoring Saraht to fawn over the man everyone thought had been instrumental in her return to the castle.

Tuning out the pointless small talk and formalities, Saraht moved her attention from Ellisand's pristine purple gown and white fur mantle to the young woman standing just behind her. Watching Saraht with big blue eyes framed with dark lashes, the woman looked similar in age to Ellisand, if not a few years her senior. Long blonde hair cascaded down her back in a mass of curls and small bejeweled braids. She was striking in an ethereal way, unlike the worldly beauty of Ellisand.

Their eyes locked, and Saraht felt unmasked, rocked by a sense of vulnerability. She offered a cordial curtsey and received the same in return. Though the other woman didn't smile, her expression suggested an openness; not welcoming, but not hostile. If anything, she looked considerate, trying to decide on Saraht from her first impression.

"Lady Saraht." Ellisand caught her attention by grasping her hand. "It is so good of you to join us this evening. Welcome." Her eyes conveyed a more profound, warmer greeting than the generic words, and she gave Saraht's hand an imperceptible squeeze. "I would like to introduce you both to a dear friend who also just returned to us from the ashes of Albator, Lady Raelyn Forthgrew."

A sword straight into her chest would have been less staggering. Saraht forced her body to remain stone-still and recovered her thoughts when Ellisand squeezed her hand again. She looked down to hide the surprise she knew reflected in her eyes. *The warden is in Osharia. With Ellisand. When? How?* Orion's report had said the penumbra was dead, but he felt Ezramoris would tie up the loose ends. His assassin had clearly failed.

"Lady Raelyn," Mollen was saying, "a pleasure. A friend of Lady Ellisand's is always a friend of ours."

With a big smile, Raelyn stepped forward and took Mollen's hand. "I am so grateful for your kindness. You will forever have my gratitude for helping Lady Ellisand find her way back to us safely." She turned to Saraht and reissued the polite curtsey. "My lady."

Another glaring difference between the two women, Saraht noted. Ellisand was naturally skilled at masking her true feelings, so much so that adding a bit of Maylam's wisdom had made her intentions almost unreadable. Raelyn, in comparison, made no effort to hide behind a façade of pleasantries. Her distrust and wariness were evident, revealed by the slight furrow in her brow and smile that lacked substance. Her eyes spoke even louder; she looked at Saraht *knowingly.* They were both wardens, and they both knew it.

"My mother won't be able to join us this evening," Ellisand said regretfully. "She's remained ill since her arrival in the capital and is not feeling well enough to experience the crowd. She sends her apologies as well as her deepest thanks."

"Weren't a need for any of this," Mollen said. "I didn't do anything other than call for the guards."

"A noble deed, though, it might not seem that way." Jackson stepped over to them. "Men of lesser morals would have considered selling our lady to one of the criminal organizations in Osharia for a ransom bid or worse. You did the right thing, and that's not so common anymore."

Saraht cursed to herself. Jackson was more endearing than expected. Like a white knight from a fairy story, he seemed to embody all the noble and righteous qualities men could possess but none of the repulsive ones. At the thought of his likely death this evening, she felt a pang of remorse.

"Come," Jackson carried on. "You'll receive a formal introduction into the grand ballroom, and I'll escort you up to the king. It's appropriate to thank His Majesty when he dubs you with his sword, but beyond that, do not speak. Lady Saraht, as we enter, please follow Lady Ellisand and Lady Raelyn to stand behind your seats."

Watching Mollen and Jackson walk ahead, Saraht felt Ellisand fall in by her side, Raelyn a few steps behind them. She slowed her pace, allowing the men to get beyond earshot of her whisper. "She knows who I am?"

Ellisand leaned closer. "She knows you're a warden and my friend. She's an ally, Saraht. Please speak with her. We could win her to the cause, and I know she has questions about what you two have in common. Will you speak with her? Please?"

Time was not a luxury Saraht could expend indefinitely. Somewhere beneath them, Orion and his team of wretches and penumbra were finishing their tunnels underneath the castle. At the first toll of the middle-night bell, they'd emerge into the sewers and infiltrate the castle, taking out the guard barracks on the perimeter first and working inward toward the king's chambers. For her to have enough time to exact her revenge, Saraht had to be ready whenever the king excused himself from the ballroom.

But her curiosity about Raelyn was an itch that needed to be scratched. What Ellisand said rang true; if Raelyn could be won to their side, the possibilities were endless. No one would be able to stand against them. It was also possible she'd discovered something about the Gate—that, Saraht needed above all else.

"I'll speak with her," she said softly. "Can you take us somewhere private?"

Ellisand nodded. "After Mollen's recognition, there will be time for guests to mingle. We can step outside onto one of the balconies."

Giant crystalline chandeliers hung down from the ceiling centerline of the grand ballroom, coating the room in golden illumination. Tall candelabras banished any remaining shadows, and large decorative lanterns lit the way to the ballroom's attached balconies on the western wall.

Saraht waited patiently as the event herald announced Mollen and read through his accolades for helping Ellisand. Her heart thrummed in her chest, and a cool dampness rose up in her palms. She was more nervous to talk with Raelyn than she was to execute the rest of her plan for the evening.

She followed Ellisand to their seats dutifully, playing the role of attentive fiancée while studying the room's layout, number and position of the guards, and the complicating factor of the guests. None of the rich, pompous fools there were of any real threat, but too many people between her and the king meant she had to be strategic about her positioning during the evening. As expected, King Rothelian was on a stage above the rest of the attendees, surrounded only by his current mistress, personal guard, and the royal Master Transcendent.

The three women stopped at their seats and waited for the dubbing ceremony to conclude. It was brief; Saraht doubted the king cared to be there. It was likely at the wishes of his sister, the duchess, that any banquet was being had at all. Keeping her face turned toward Mollen and the king, Saraht glanced at the man who had joined Raelyn and taken a seat on her right. A mage, she guessed. She could tell by his posture and easy, confident demeanor. Only a set of deadly skills would allow him to be so unbothered by meaningless social obligations and a room full of strangers. His poise was common to all those who could manipulate parts of the world to their will. The man looked up at Raelyn, and she squeezed his shoulder discretely.

A mage and a warden. Saraht puzzled over the strange combination. *It will be more difficult to win her to the cause if she loves a man.*

She switched her attention back to Mollen as the orchestra picked up a tune, signifying the end of the ceremony. King Rothelian returned to his table and chair and waved to officially allow his guests social freedom for the evening. Sitting within his pile of purple and golden robes, he looked every inch the villain Saraht knew him to be, pale eyes staring out into the crowd while he stroked the hair of his red beard.

Ellisand linked her arm with Raelyn's and turned to Saraht. "Would you care to join us, Lady Saraht? We'll take in the evening air before it gets too chilly."

"If it pleases you, Lady Ellisand, the offer of fresh air sounds lovely." Saraht turned to follow her host, noting how tightly her former ward held onto Raelyn's arm.

They walked through the sea of people dispersed across the dance floor and assembled around the long tables for food, stopping occasionally for Ellisand to share a greeting or a quick word of idle conversation with the gathered nobility. Just before they reached the balcony doorway, a group of young girls stalled Ellisand indefinitely, giggling and begging her to tell them about her ordeal.

"You two go on," she told Raelyn and Saraht. "I'll join you soon."

Was that deliberate? Saraht wouldn't put it past her protégé to have orchestrated the interruption. Seeing Ellisand in her full royal glory reinforced the suspicion there was more to her than she'd ever fully let on.

"I hope you won't be too cold."

Almost as if Raelyn had commanded it, a blast of cool air assailed Saraht's face when they stepped out onto the balcony. "I've been colder," she answered lightheartedly. They were alone. The guard remained inside the doorway, watching the guests in the ballroom.

"Lady Ellisand has told me a lot about you," Raelyn said carefully.

"Yes, it seems she has. Come, Raelyn," she lowered her voice and stepped closer. "Let us not dance around what we both know. I hear you're a warden, as am I. You've only just come into your powers, it would seem?"

Relief shot across Raelyn's face, and she nodded, her whole body visibly relaxing. "I know next to nothing. I've only just learned the fullest extent of what wardens were used for."

Does she mean communion? "A great and terrible ability," Saraht replied, unwilling to relinquish the information if Raelyn spoke of something else. "Born from the experimentation of mages hundreds of years ago."

"Have … have you ever?"

"Have I ever what?"

They stared at each other, silence and distrust between them.

Anxiousness bloomed within Saraht; time was precious. She couldn't waste too many words deciphering what Raelyn knew and what she didn't. She had to take her chance. It was now or never to get the information and test the other woman's ideals.

"I know it must seem strange to have me, an enemy, here as your friend's guest tonight, but let me assuage some of your fears. Yes, I was part of Ellisand's kidnapping, but it wasn't for any reason you might think. She's an important part of the change that's coming. I want all highborn women—all women—to take back their autonomy and power in this world, regardless of their country of allegiance." She leaned on the railing, looking out into the darkness at the city lights beyond. "Have you heard of the goddess Raloria?"

Raelyn shook her head.

"I am her acolyte. Long before the Cataclysm, she supported and upheld women seated in stations of power across Uhmeer. She fought for them through her warden, Alyna, creating a golden era without wars and strife.

"I recruited Ellisand because the ruler of Faldea has promised Limnin can be restored to that matriarchy under his greater rule. Ellisand, you, the women in the castle—you'll all be free to live life as you please, not be shackled in some arranged marriage where you wither in the shadows of inequity."

"Ellisand said you had a beautiful dream, but that doesn't explain why you're here tonight, if we're speaking so plainly." Raelyn joined her in looking out into the darkness.

"I'm here at your friend's invitation, nothing more. We've grown close. I'm the one who helped her escape. She thought you might want to join us in saving the women of Uhmeer."

"Are you sure you aren't here because you're looking for something?"

Saraht's breath caught in her throat, but she swallowed it and did her best to keep her expression neutral. Raelyn was bold, and Saraht wasn't sure if it was deliberate tact or simple inexperience. "I'm sure you know Osharia holds appeal for wardens," she responded slowly. "But that's not why I'm here tonight."

Raelyn sighed. "A shame. I was hoping you might be able to point me in the right direction."

She doesn't know where the Gate is yet, either, Saraht realized, mildly disappointed. "I'm here tonight just to visit with someone who has become dear to me, but I'm willing to help us both find what we're looking for. Being wardens makes us closer than kin, despite where our loyalties lie. I think all wardens would like to uncover Osharia's secret."

"Yes, but it was silly to ask. I always feel so uncertain." Raelyn stared up and breathed into the night sky. With a laugh, she added, "I almost swam to the bottom of the lake because of a picture I saw in a children's book, if that tells you how much I know."

"The lake?" A chill ran up Saraht's spine.

It was the perfect location. Hidden and inaccessible to most, the Gate could be left in its original state, submerged within the depths of Osharia's waters. "It seems a big ask," Saraht redirected. "The lake is necessary to the city. You'd have to drain it, break the dam, or use magic, and doing away with the water would be devastating. Have you any other ideas?"

"No. I don't even know where to begin. I was hoping some greater power had sent you here, as well. It just seemed unusual that we'd both find ourselves in the capital at the same time."

It was inexperience, Saraht now knew, that made Raelyn so forthcoming with her words. Without saying specifics, she was giving away important details, details Saraht wasn't going to gloss over. If the other warden's words were true, she'd been in contact with a god or spirit guiding her to the castle. Was a Pillar seeking to use Raelyn as a conduit? *Could it be Raloria?* She bit down the spike of jealousy. Raelyn hadn't reacted when they'd spoken of the goddess moments before. Something else was trying to get her to the Gate.

She caught herself staring out into the growing darkness, eyes hunting for a glimmer of the lake water even though she knew it was on the other side of the castle. As soon as Raelyn had said the words, Saraht had known. She'd *felt* it. The Gate might as well be calling to her now.

"Have you two become friends yet?" Ellisand sauntered toward them from inside. "I should have prepared you both better, I think. What do you say, Rae? Isn't Saraht's idea of the future appealing?"

"It is. I'm just not clear how it comes to pass, Ell."

"That's for powers greater than us to decide." Ellisand put an arm around Raelyn's shoulders and gave a squeeze. "But I want to support that vision, Rae—peacefully, of course—from my new position at the royal court. Saraht and I believe I can advocate for change. Maybe even delay Faldea's plans for war, if I can make enough of a difference."

"But why is Faldea so invested in establishing a matriarchy?" Raelyn asked them. "What is there to gain from that?"

"It's not Faldea," Saraht answered honestly. "It's my plan—our plan. A way to unite Uhmeer again like it was in the golden days of Raloria. Faldea was a way to get me close enough with the female next of kin to Limnin's king."

She left much unsaid. Raelyn's naïveté made her disarming; Saraht found she *wanted* to give up all her personal plans and details. She sensed the capacity for deep empathy within the other woman, and she could tell Raelyn was driven by a desire to do what was morally right. Those sensibilities would undoubtedly respond to Saraht's personal mission for revenge—and the allure of that was dangerous. It compelled her to share more secrets to win Raelyn to the cause, but Saraht was already vulnerable as a representative of Faldea behind enemy lines. If her full intentions were known and Raelyn couldn't be swayed in loyalty, Saraht would be marked an enemy of both countries.

They all fell silent, sensing another presence approaching from the ballroom. Raelyn's dark-haired mage stopped just inside the balcony threshold, his features hidden by the contrast of the light behind him and the dark of the evening.

"Lady Ellisand, Lady Raelyn, I require your attention for a moment." He issued a bow to Saraht. "I will return them promptly to you, lady." His tone was cool and controlled, his posture relaxed. His simple request held an air of disinterest.

Surprised, Ellisand turned to her. "Sir Laris is not one to waste words," she said in good humor. "Please excuse us, Saraht. We'll return in just a moment. Come inside if you're too cold."

Saraht felt the tension melt from her body as they left. Alone on the balcony with just the darkness and the stars, she could momentarily escape the overbearing burden of being so close to King Rothelian— the man she despised most in the world.

This was the place where her mother had endured unspeakable torture before being shipped off to even darker circumstances. The evil of the castle was palpable, and she sucked in a deep breath of cool air.

"You know," said Jackson, stepping out to join her, "I saw you at the inn when we came to retrieve Lady Ellisand. I didn't think much of it then; you were seated in the back, watching like the other patrons, but something about you stood out." He stopped in the center of the terrace. "It was the intensity of your stare. I understand it now, sadly."

With a wave of his hand, six guards filed out onto the balcony behind him, sealing Saraht off from the door to the ballroom. "To think you would be so bold as to try to enter the castle. I expected more sense from Faldea's military leaders."

The coiled ball of initial shock nestled in her core exploded into an inferno of anger, and she clenched her fists so tightly her arms trembled up to her shoulders. Had she been betrayed? Had Ellisand set her up, lured her to the castle under the guise of their plan? Saraht's glare burned into Ellisand through the glass panes of the balcony window. They locked eyes.

She dares to feign astonishment still? She looked away from her protégé's stunned countenance, her stare filled with what appeared to be disbelief. If Saraht hadn't known what a talented actress the young woman was, she would have believed Ellisand didn't know about the unfolding events.

"You'll come with me peacefully, or we'll be forced to kill you here," Jackson told her.

No doubt the king had already been removed from the area, and they would have no qualms with killing her in front of the Limnin nobility. She'd make for the best kind of gossip for the lords and ladies, the kind that had put them in distant danger. They'd use her story to drive attention and sympathy toward themselves even though none had been in harm's way.

She took a steadying breath and folded her hands at her front. There was no point in fighting. Even at her best, Saraht was not a match for so many skilled soldiers and at least a pair of powerful mages. She'd let them take her to a cell where she'd wait for Orion and his war party to come and release her. It was already drawing close to the middle of night. A few more hours, and phase two of the plan would be underway.

Raelyn pulled Laris aside as Jackson and his men led Saraht away. "Why?" she asked, taken aback. "Why would you not wait for me to come to you first?"

"It was the only way," he said, keeping his voice down, "to assure she was away from the guests and you both. This way, Lady Ellisand escapes any blame. The king doesn't need to know she was involved. It can be portrayed as a bungled espionage attempt."

"But now she's going to blame *me*. Ellisand will think I've betrayed her."

"Raelyn, you *have* betrayed her," he said harshly. "But for her good and the good of your king and country. Who knows what could have happened here if we hadn't intervened? Or if Lady Ellisand was found out and declared a traitor? You knew this would happen even if we had waited."

She pulled away from him, shaking her head, and turned back toward Ellisand.

Her friend stood still as stone, skin pale, eyes glimmering with the sparkle of unshed tears. She stared at the ballroom exit where they'd led Saraht, and Raelyn could see her trembling. Stepping toward her, arm outstretched, she froze in place when Ellisand acknowledged her with a look that made Raelyn's blood chill.

"I didn't…" she whispered. "I didn't mean—"

"Do not speak to me," she said so only Raelyn could hear. With a slow, deliberate turn away, Ellisand cleared her throat. "I can't stand the sight of you right now." She lifted the hem of her skirts and strode purposefully out of the banquet room, a pair of guards filing into line behind her.

CHAPTER TWENTY-SEVEN

"For Raloria's will. For Raloria's will," Saraht whispered the words to herself repeatedly while staring at the solid iron door of her cell within the bowels of Osharia Castle.

Formed by natural stone, the pocket of her prison had been carved out of the bedrock itself. An ancient design, she suspected, and a clever one requiring no magical fortifications. Even the lock at the door was wrought of ordinary metal. Simple but effective against someone with her particular talents. The hinges of the door were another matter. Forged from magic-made steel, they must have been an oversight at some point in the door's past maintenance. When she willed it so, they would be easily dismantled. She'd been biding her time, waiting for some indication Orion and his war party were moving freely within the castle.

As the hours crawled by, Saraht's initial anger at Ellisand's treachery was replaced by a deeper, darker hatred born from the realization she'd been doubly betrayed. Even within her cell, she'd heard a toll of the bell for the middle of night, but the uninterrupted patrol of the guard outside told her nothing of major concern was happening. If Orion had breached the castle, every soldier would have been called to task, including the guards in the dungeon. The prisoners, locked behind their doors of iron, became inconsequential when a large threat loomed.

Orion wasn't coming. Prince Thiir had abandoned her.

She had no choice now but to make her escape and fight her way to the king. She'd come this far; there was no escaping into the night to fight another day. She would have her revenge or die trying. The time had come.

Saraht extended her sphere of influence to the door and neutralized the hinges. The heavy iron barricade stayed in position, held in place by its weight and the metal framing on the outside. She walked over to it and pulled to test its resistance. It was firm but moveable; she needed to correctly time her exit.

During the hours she'd sat waiting, the guard had passed by her door sixteen times. His patrol route was short, and she could tell by his footsteps he was alone. She worked a shard of broken hinge from where it stuck, wedged in the stone, and pressed against the iron door. Eyes closed, she listened for the chink of his metal boots on the stone floor.

At the sound of distant footsteps, Saraht spread her influence far enough to reach the guard—but no farther. She couldn't risk altering other magic structures and alerting more soldiers, yet she needed to make sure he had no powers to use against her. It wasn't unheard of for a foot soldier to have some proclivity for magic. Many people were born able to see the tendrils of power; they just lacked the talent or the dedication to become proficient with it.

Chink. Chink. She waited until he was two steps past her cell before heaving the door inward and leaping into the corridor. The iron square crashed down and sent its echoes bouncing down the passages. Momentarily stunned, the guard stared at her wide-eyed before pulling his sword.

His brief hesitation was all she needed. Dropping low, Saraht closed the distance between them. She lunged forward with her knee between the man's legs and drove her shoulder into his sternum, her arms breaking his posture at the knees. An awkward, ill-timed sword swing in the tight space added to his imbalance, and he landed on his back, his arms flailing.

With practiced speed, she moved over him and pushed her weight down through her knee on his stomach. He groaned and reached for her, and she plunged the hinge fragment as deep into the socket of his eye as it would go. She held it there through the last twitches of his body, emptiness and calm tempering the hatred in her heart. She'd been lucky; guards in more important positions had more armor. Against plate mail, she would need other strategies.

Picking up the guard's sword, she rifled through his belongings and tucked a set of keys and a matchbook into her bodice. Cuts in the sides of her skirts freed her movement, and she stepped over the body and headed out the way they'd brought her into the dungeon. No doubt other guards were coming, alerted by the crash of the iron door when it had fallen.

She hurried down the corridor, listening intently, ignoring the calls from other prisoners behind their impenetrable barriers. One of those prisoners was likely Mollen, locked away for his unknown association with a Faldean commander. There was no time for sympathy or charity. She needed to get outside if she wanted her revenge.

At the end of the corridor, the stone stairwell leading up to the castle basement disappeared behind the hulking forms of three descending guards. Better armored and holding their swords aloft, they walked cautiously toward her, unable to pass one another due to the narrow passage.

Saraht pulled at them with her sphere of influence. The man in the lead's armor cracked, and he stopped, looking down in confusion.

"Soldiers shouldn't rely on magic items," she chastised. "It creates an area of liability."

Feinting to test his reaction, she noted he brought his sword up on his centerline to block. She feinted again and added a searching thrust. The guard stepped back and parried her blade, but his movement was excessive, and his sword clanged off the stone wall with a shower of sparks.

Saraht pressured him with a series of nagging cuts and slashes and used him to drive his companions back toward the uneven footing of the stairs. As it was, she felt confident. Her speed and technical mastery were superior in close quarters, where small, precise movements bullied fighters who relied on their brawn alone.

Reaching the stairs and the end of their backpedaling, the other guards pushed their leader forward, and he jabbed at Saraht with a thrust to her chest followed by a chop at her thigh. She riposted, slashing upward and catching the man across the exposed skin of his throat. He slumped to his knees, blood pouring down his neck onto the white linen of his vestment.

The other guards pushed in together as their comrade fell, lunging at Saraht in turns, able to face her side by side but not with enough room to fight effectively. She slipped on the blood-slicked floor and pitched forward. The end of a sword grazed her cheek and sliced into her ear. On one knee, she deflected the left guard's blade and pinned it against the wall with her body. He went to pull away, and she pivoted onto her other knee to thrust her sword up under the rib cage of the man on her right. During her step up to regain her feet, she grabbed one of the fallen weapons on the floor and spun back around, decapitating her final opponent as his blade cut into her hip.

Hastily, she searched the bodies, gaining a dagger and another set of keys. All around her, the passages were quiet; was it possible the last three guards hadn't sounded a castle-wide alarm? *They must not have thought the noise was serious,* she mused. The first man she'd killed hadn't had a chance to scream.

Holding her sword at the ready, she crept up the stairs and into the castle's cellar. Divided into four large sections, the stone-and-dirt space served as a melting pot of storage for all the castle's factions. Giant casks of wine lined the walls, hemmed in by tall stacks of cloth and linen. Saraht knew the layout by heart. Memorizing architectural plans was important when planning an invasion, but she'd committed the castle rooms and corridors to memory long ago when first tending the seed of vengeance growing inside her.

She slunk along the wall and wove through the small spaces between crates and boxes until she saw the grate. Round and rusted, it hung on one hinge over an oval opening in the wall. The sewer entrance. The exact place Orion should have emerged from hours ago to start the invasion. She peered into the dark tunnel behind. It was still her saving grace and would lead her to the exact place she needed to be.

The bite of the night air felt deserved, chilling Raelyn's bare skin just enough to make her regret stepping outside onto the terrace of Laris's room. She embraced the discomfort like a shroud of atonement, hoping it could overpower the misery and guilt she felt dragging her into exhaustion. In the distance, the torches along the lake edge flickered without interruption, and Raelyn wondered if Hendrel was out adding his light to their dance. She could see the lake's outline in the moonlight, a peaceful image in chaotic circumstances.

"Raelyn," Laris called after her from inside. "Raelyn!"

She ignored his summons and strode to the railing to lean over the edge, wishing for a split second she would fall into the night and disappear. "Please," she said, her voice hoarse but firm. "Please just let me be alone right now."

She could feel his presence in the doorway, but he didn't pursue her or try to argue. In the first few hours after Saraht had been arrested, she couldn't speak to him. At first, it was because she was angry. Not because he'd involved Jackson sooner than anticipated but because he hadn't told her his plan.

No secrets. That's how it was supposed to be between them.

He wasn't wrong for what he'd done; she knew it had been the wise and correct decision. Not letting her know, though, made her feel powerless and unimportant.

She was also frustrated by her own failure as a friend and by how the night's events had gone into disarray. She hadn't learned anything definitive other than Saraht's greater vision for the world, and there was a good chance her closest friend would never trust her again.

It wasn't all for naught, she reminded herself. During her brief interaction with Saraht, Raelyn hadn't missed the other warden's reaction regarding the Gate's whereabouts. At the mention of the lake, she'd seen the same certainty in Saraht's eyes that she felt in her own heart.

They both felt it—the call of the Gate. Whether it was a true call or intuition, it was an experience they shared.

Is she here to claim the station of Holy King? It seemed unlikely. Saraht had spoken of a goddess named Raloria.

A sigh caught in her chest, and she was seized by sudden rage at the confining corset preventing her from taking a full breath even in a moment of despair. Pulling at the laces, buttons, and clasps, she ripped the layers of her dress off, relishing every tear of fabric giving way. Free of the top, she stepped out of the skirts and stood in her undergarments, finally liberated. She drew a deep breath and held it, ignoring the goosebumps across her exposed arms and midsection.

The weight of a blanket over her shoulders made her let the air out, and she pulled the quilt close. "Thank you," she mumbled, staring into the distance.

"I'm sorry for speaking so harshly in the ballroom." Laris joined her to lean on the railing. "Will you allow me to explain?"

"I understand why you told Jackson when you did," she replied. "It was just unexpected, and I thought you'd let me know your plans."

"I didn't plan anything. It was an opportunity that we couldn't let pass by. That woman is dangerous, Raelyn. You know it as well as I do, no matter what her motivations were for coming to the castle."

She was quiet for a long moment. "Do you think Ellisand will forgive me?"

"I think she's been manipulated into believing some dangerous ideals, and she has to let go of those first before she can return to the person you used to know." He placed his hand over hers. "You can help her do that by being her friend, but it will take time, and your friendship might not be reciprocated along the way."

Her response was interrupted by a brief knock before the room's door opened, and a pair of guards stepped in.

"Apologies, sir," one said. "A prisoner has escaped. We have orders to secure everyone in their rooms."

"Escaped?" Laris squeezed Raelyn's hand before letting go. "Which prisoner?"

"The Faldean spy from this evening, sir. She's killed several men, and we believe she escaped into the sewers."

"She's heading out of the aqueduct system, then. Your men have sent reinforcements to the waterway entering the city?"

The aqueduct. Their words fell away, background noise to a puzzle aligning in Raelyn's mind. *The lake drains into the aqueducts.* She gripped the blanket edges so tightly her knuckles turned white. *You'd have to break the dam.* Saraht's words echoed in her head. *You'd have to break the dam.* Break the dam—an easy task when it was built with magic.

She stepped behind Laris and whispered to him, "I know where she's going. We have to get word to Jackson. Quickly!"

Forearm pressed against the gash in her hip, using her sword as a walking stick, Saraht limped through the damp grass toward Osharia's lake. Her progress was painfully slow. The agony of injuries weighed down her every move, and the tip of the sword sank into the ground with the press of her body weight, forcing her to continually tug it free as she trekked onward.

She had no logical reason to believe Raelyn's theory was correct, but she *felt* it—a deep certainty telling her the lake was the answer. Raelyn must have felt it, too, to have been so compelled by an illustration in a child's book. The Gate was calling to them, to the void within them. Injured and outnumbered, Saraht knew this was either her end or her salvation. If she wanted Rothelian dead, the lake was her one chance, no matter how farfetched.

"That's far enough," a familiar voice commanded her from the top of the dam spillway. Jackson stared down, a hundred men at his back along the crest of the structure, the light of their torches blending with the flames of the larger signal fires. She could make out the outlines of archers with their bows drawn and ready.

Stopping immediately, she pushed her sword tip into the ground for support. Off to her right and down a steep embankment, the controlled overflow of the dam raced in a waterfall down the cutoff barrier. From there, it ran in a channel through grates in the inner city wall and meandered a lazy path around Osharia before joining up with the Ven. The water was deep and the current fast. She might survive it if she made the jump, but her energy was spent, and there was no guarantee she'd be able to swim past the wide bars of the grates and into the city.

"I have no need to go any farther," she yelled to him over the roar of the water. "I surrender." She steadied herself and spread her arms wide. "I know defeat when I see it."

Jackson motioned with his hand, and the archers let down. He and six other men started walking toward the steps at the side of the dam.

Arms still wide, Saraht locked eyes on him. Acknowledging the shame of watching an honorable man die an unworthy death, she hesitated a moment, fortifying her resolve, before she expanded her sphere of influence to its maximum.

The dam shuddered, and the ground shook with its sudden instability.

"No!" Jackson cried out to her. "Don't!" He turned back to his men. "Get off the dam! Go!"

It was too late. Any regret or hesitation was gone. *Sacrifices are always necessary for the greater good,* she assured herself. With a slow smile, Saraht watched Jackson and the other men scramble to get off the dam walls.

They weren't fast enough.

She manipulated her influence, focusing it on the ends of the mage-made structure, crumbling them first to trap the soldiers. Water raged through the openings and cut away chunks of the embankment.

An arrow clipped her shoulder, and she faltered, dropping to a knee. With a growl, she clasped her hand over the wound and ripped apart the rest of the magic holding the dam together. The walls around the spillway disintegrated, and Jackson and every man with him fell into the torrent below.

The water thundered as it left the lake, filling the air with the deafening sound of its escape. Thick mist rose up in a cloud around the breakpoint. From her position, Saraht watched, spellbound, taken by the ferocity and power behind the surge. It overcame the entry aqueducts with ease, hammering at the grates in the wall between the castle grounds and the inner city. In mere moments, the grates and the wall holding them were gone, swept into the city with the current. The rapidly rising water engulfed the buildings closest to the gap in the barrier wall, crumbling the structures at their foundations and carrying large remnants into the heart of the city with deadly force. Water raced out in every direction, gaining speed and power as it funneled through areas that didn't immediately give way.

Saraht pushed to her feet. She hobbled up the incline toward the lake shore. Even with the gaping hole flooding water into the city, the current would slow as the water level dropped, and it was unlikely the basin would drain completely until morning at best. She needed to find a place to hide nearby but out of danger of discovery. By dawn, countless soldiers would be hunting the grounds for her. If she dared travel the shoreline now, she'd be picked off by reinforcements responding to the dam's collapse. She looked behind her at the buildings disappearing in the distance. The soldiers would have to split forces between finding her and saving people in the city.

So much death.

Her warrior's heart cracked as she watched the muddy, debris-filled rapids churn on their path of destruction. *The greater good,* she repeated to herself, pushing away resurfacing thoughts of doubt and guilt. There were times in life where innocent people had to die so that more innocent people could live. She was doing this for them, for the common folk. Their future freedoms came with a price.

At least Mollen was safe in a prison cell. With Raloria on her side, she could liberate him after she killed the king.

Scanning the lake edge under the moonlight, her gaze settled on a large, fallen tree jutting out into the water, partially submerged. Its trunk was wide and long, and gnarled branches twisted out into the water, leaves long rotted away. She trotted over to the shoreline as quickly as her broken body would allow. Positioning herself far enough away where her blood trail wouldn't sabotage her location, she cut the rest of her skirts away and tossed them into the current before easing into the water. Saraht swam up to the tree and pulled herself out to the top of the longest branch. Wedging her arms and legs within the limbs, she braced against the increasing current. The water was cold but still held enough of late summer's warmth to keep her body temperature from dropping dangerously. Debris trapped within the branches concealed the portion of her head above the water.

In time, she knew she'd have to adjust her position with the dropping waterline; she just needed to hold out long enough for search parties to pass by. In the darkness, torchlight wouldn't reach the end of the branches, and the moonlight wasn't strong enough to define more than the tree's outline. With any luck, initial patrols would declare the area cleared and send more men to handle the disaster happening in the city. By morning light, she might have a window of opportunity to find and reach the Gate.

From her position on the terrace, Raelyn looked out helplessly over the aftermath of the dam break. She hadn't witnessed the moment of the disaster, but the deep, melancholy ringing of the castle alarm bells had roused her shortly after she'd fallen asleep in a chair by the fire. Not much had been visible during those last hours of darkness, but the twilight of dawn revealed more devastation with each moment of its growing light. Much of the inner city was destroyed, a wasteland of slowly draining water. Elevation had saved some of the buildings, and many structures farther away from the castle had managed to withstand the force of the water after it slowed down. Like islands, they dotted the temporary sea, last bastions of life for people caught in the flood.

She felt the massive loss of life deeply.

Nausea gnawed at her insides; she had no idea what might have happened. The guard at the door wouldn't let her or Laris leave, though, he'd been quick to relay her message to Jackson about where Saraht might be headed.

Did the dam break mean the Faldean warden had succeeded? Had Jackson and his soldiers defeated her? Was Jackson safe? The unknowns lay as heavy on her as the sense of death in the air. She wanted to send Hendrel to find out what might be happening, but he was nowhere to be found. If Saraht was the one behind the assassination attempts, entering the void with her in the capital might not be safe. Raelyn had yet to learn what other abilities or connections Saraht had at her disposal.

Trapped in Laris's quarters, the feeling of futility was unbearable.

Raelyn returned to the chamber door and opened it to the hall. "Please," she asked the guard, "is there nothing you can tell me? No updates? Any word from Captain Jackson?"

"Lady, return to your room. I cannot give you any information."

She nodded but didn't retreat. "I've known him my whole life. Please, it's very important. You would want to know if someone you cared about was injured." He kept his eyes forward, but she noticed his long blink, and he shifted position awkwardly.

"I'm under orders not to discuss the details of the fugitive search."

"So they haven't found her yet?"

He finally looked at her, annoyed. "Please go back inside, lady."

"Just tell me something, anything," she begged. "I'll leave you alone, then, I promise."

More than irritation drifted through his gaze, and dread washed over her. "What's happened?" she whispered. "Something's happened?"

The guard sighed. "Lady, please do not ask me to tell you the details."

"You will tell me, or I will stand here with you for the rest of your shift." She lowered her voice. "Is it Captain Jackson? Tell me."

"A hundred score of men and then some, washed away." He looked back out at the hall, a hitch to his voice. "No word or fresh sign of the fugitive. They believe she may have escaped into the current."

It took her a moment to register the impact of his words. *A hundred men washed away?* Raelyn's knees buckled, and she slid to the floor.

"Lady!"

She couldn't speak and held up a hand to stop the guard as he reached for her. Everything swirled. She closed her eyes against the surge of lightheadedness. *Jackson? Dead?* It was impossible. She refused to believe it. "Not possible," she whispered. "Not possible."

"Raelyn!" Laris appeared at the doorway and knelt next to her. "Are you all right? Are you hurt?" He looked at the guard.

"I asked her not to force it out of me," the man said with a panicked frown.

She clung to Laris, to the comfort he always brought her. His warmth and support unveiled her vulnerability, and tears began pouring down her face. "It's not possible." She cried into his shoulder. "I've sent him to his death. Jackson. I've sent him to his death."

"The new captain and two regiments were washed away by the dam break," the guard told Laris solemnly. "I should not have told her. I'm under orders."

"You've done no wrong," Laris told him, running a hand down Raelyn's hair. "There's no good way to relay such grim news. Come, Raelyn, let's go back inside." He pulled her arm over his shoulders to help her stand. "Maybe more answers will come soon."

He led her over to one of the chairs by the fire. It was the same chair she'd sat in the night of their arrival at the castle, laughing and talking with Jackson after their joyful reunion. Staring at the empty seat across from her, Raelyn couldn't stop the wave of fresh tears, and she sobbed so hard her chest ached. How many more people she loved would die because of her? She shouldn't have involved Jackson last night; she should have sent word to someone else, anyone else. It was her blind faith in him that had guided her actions, the certainty that he could accomplish anything because he was Jackson, her reliable, unshakeable, unbeatable childhood friend. She'd sent the word to him because she *knew* he would take care of things, just as he always had. In truth, she'd sent him to his death.

Saraht. The name burned in her mind. She repeated it over and over, channeling her grief into anger. Another mistake. Another moment of selfishness. She should have never agreed to let that woman into the castle, should have never spoken with her.

Ellisand. She would blame Raelyn for Jackson's death, too. But Ellisand had changed; she'd put them all in danger.

"Raelyn," Laris said from where he looked out the window. "I think you need to come see this."

The last thing she wanted to do was move from the chair, but the intensity of Laris's gaze out the window gave her hope. Maybe, by some miracle of The Circle, survivors were being discovered as the water level stabilized. She pushed herself up and walked over, wiping her face on the sleeve of the black jerkin she'd borrowed from Laris hours before.

Large swaths of the once-manicured lawn were gone, cut away by the torrent of water escaping its prison. A steady stream continued from where the dam once stood, but the broader level of the lake was too low to produce much volume or current. Within the shallow waters, almost at the lake's center, exposed stones peaked out in a large circle, interrupting the smooth surface. Through the glass, they were unidentifiable—nothing more than unusual rock formations—but Raelyn knew beyond a doubt what she was looking at.

"The Sundered Gate." She pressed her palms to the windowpane. "It really was in the lake. Emblem's Hand." She grabbed Laris's arm. "She broke the dam to expose the Gate. She didn't escape, don't you see? You have to help me get there!"

He firmly took her by the arms. "Raelyn, we'll inform the guard and send the soldiers. There's nothing for us to do on our own."

"Yes, there is," she said, adamant. "Laris, she's going to touch an altar stone. She's going to bring a god into this world, and then no number of soldiers will be enough to stop her. I'm the only one. You have to let me go. I'm the only one who can stop her if it goes that far."

He stared at her for a long moment before touching his forehead to hers with a sigh. "When we reach the ground, just run," he told her, quietly. "I'll keep the soldiers away from you as best I can, but I won't be able to stop an arrow while we're on the move. They don't know you, Raelyn, and they'll be ready to kill anyone suspicious on sight."

She nodded, her heartbeat a loud backdrop to his instructions.

"Swim as much as you can when you get to the lake. It might be too shallow in places, but if the statues are life-sized, you still have some depth to work with. You feel comfortable in this?" He touched her sleeve. "It might be too large."

"I'll shed it in the water if I have to. Off the terrace?"

He looked at her thoughtfully. "Off the terrace."

Raelyn pulled her hair back and cinched it into place as she followed him outside. Ensuring her sphere of influence was close, she watched Laris extend his hands toward the stone railing. The stones parted, and new steps spiraling down to the ground grew from the terrace edge.

"Raelyn." He grabbed her before she started her descent and spun her into a kiss. "Be careful," he said after breaking the contact.

She grabbed him and initiated a brief kiss of her own. "I love you," she said and pulled away. Her heart couldn't bear to hear his response. She ran toward the newly formed stairs, leaving Laris stunned on the terrace.

CHAPTER TWENTY-EIGHT

hen Raelyn's feet touched grass, she started running, her eyes fixed on the dark-brown line marking the lake's receding shore. By the time her lungs began to burn, shouts were ringing out, and she caught a glimpse of soldiers pointing and approaching from the top of a grassy knoll. Stone barriers sprung out of the ground between her and the men. *Laris.* She didn't dare take the time to look back to see where he was. More shouts. More stone walls erupting on each side of her. Eyes watering, chest heaving with each breath, she kept running.

With a leap, she left the edge of the grass and landed on the sand of the newly uncovered lake bottom. Soupy and thick, it held her fast, and she pitched forward with the momentum. On her hands and knees in the muck, rock walls rose around her as a shield, creating a protected corridor between her and the remaining water pooled in the deepest parts of the basin.

Her relief and respite were short-lived. Out in the water, a log bobbing on the surface caught her attention. From a distance, it looked like a pile of floating debris stirred loose by the shifts in the lake current. This close to the water's edge, she could tell it was far less innocent. Someone was swimming toward the circle of statues, cleverly hidden.

Saraht. Anger refreshed her energy, and she clawed down the rocks, sand, and silt to the remnants of the lake. Throwing herself into the water, she propelled forward with desperate kicks, reaching as far as she could with her hands to paddle. Ahead, Saraht paused and looked back. Realizing she was being followed, she abandoned the log and sticks in favor of the speed of open swimming.

Through their splashes, Raelyn could see the newly revealed faces of the statues. Saraht would reach them before her, but she might have enough time to make communion before the other warden returned possessing a Pillar.

Pain suddenly lanced through her arm, and she sucked in a mouthful of water, her swimming interrupted. An arrow. She surfaced with a cry and snapped the shaft, casting it away. Another arrow hit the water close by, and she took stock of the soldiers gathering on the distant shoreline. *Keep moving!* she commanded herself. Diving under, she swam as far as she could with the air in her lungs, surfaced, looked at the statues, breathed, and dove under again.

Along the shoreline, she caught a glimpse of soldiers pushing boats into the water, but Raelyn was more concerned about Saraht. The other warden's telltale splashes vanished, and the lake surface stilled. Swimming into the center of the Gate, Raelyn twisted around in the water, trying to find her adversary. *She's already communing.* Panic made Raelyn's heart jump and threatened to choke her. *Which one is it?*

She didn't know which statue was Emblem.

Eight stone heads protruded from the lake's surface, none set apart from the others. She'd expected Emblem's altar to be unique; he was Lord of The Circle. Yet all the statues were of equal positioning.

"Hendrel!" she screamed. "Hendrel, please!"

She needed him now, more than ever, but no friendly flame appeared, and precious moments dragged by. She raked through the memories of childhood lectures about The Circle. It was all a blur. She couldn't even recall half the names. Her gaze searched the altars and settled on a familiar visage with long, braided hair.

Genevive. She was Raelyn's only hope. Communing with any other god was too dangerous. She'd been guided by Genevive before. The goddess was the safest choice.

Boats of soldiers sped toward her. Time was up. With a deep breath, Raelyn dove under the water again and swam toward the statue of the Second Pillar. Arm outstretched, she moved blindly, the murk of the water too thick and painful to keep her eyes open for long. She peeled them wide underwater for a split second, and her hand made contact with the stone.

Like blinking from one world to another, the cold of the water was replaced by the cold of the void. Raelyn's breath came in heavy gasps, and she dropped down to sit in the emptiness.

She'd made it. There might still be time to save everyone.

"Raelyn." Genevive's voice echoed around her. "You have summoned me again. This time from the Sundered Gate. Why have you touched my altar?"

"I need your help, lady. I … I didn't know which was Emblem's statue. I had no other choice."

"So you were seeking Ute. You have come to take your place as the Holy King?"

Raelyn shook her head. "No. No, not exactly. I was ready to accept my fate as Holy King to save everyone, but I found you instead."

Pinpoints of light, like fireflies, gathered in the darkness, and the image of the goddess materialized. Despite her beautiful appearance, Genevive's ghost-like transparency reminded Raelyn of Volaris, and she shuddered involuntarily.

"You can go back," Genevive told her. "I will show Emblem's face so you might find him."

"If I go back now, the soldiers will capture me, or Saraht will return and kill me before I can make it to the altar. You are my only choice."

"You are asking to be my conduit? Such a thing is forbidden by Ute's law. We are not allowed to influence the mortal realm any longer."

"There is no Holy King." Raelyn wanted to shout with urgency, but her voice cracked with the threat of tears. "There's no warden in the Citadel to act as a conduit for Emblem to come and protect the people. If Saraht brings Raloria into the mortal realm, there will be no one to stop her. I will be the first one she kills."

"Raloria?" Genevive smirked, amused. "Are her priestesses still haunting the mortal realm? How interesting. She would, indeed, be willing to break Ute's law without fear of reprimand. This speaks of plans beyond what we know."

Raelyn had no interest in intrigue. "I'm asking you to help me, lady, please!"

"There is no love lost between Raloria and me. Even as a Pillar, she has always sought dominion over mankind. We have battled as adversaries during other ages of this world, long before the Cataclysm united us as allies under Emblem's will." The goddess floated over to

Raelyn and placed a weightless hand on her shoulder. "I will help you, Daughter of the Void, but many may still perish. The gods are beings of magic. We do not need to pull magic from the world to create it. Our powers are devastating in your realm."

Raelyn bit her lip, recalling how Volaris had incinerated the *vehsidhe* and had torn their bodies apart on a whim. She knew better than most just how devastating the powers of the gods truly were.

"If it's a choice between certainty and possibility, what choice is there to make?" Raelyn held out her hand. "Help me. Help me save Uhmeer."

Genevive bowed graciously and reached to accept Raelyn's hand. "May Ute forgive us."

Raelyn's eyes opened, finding she was level with the lake's surface. She felt effortlessly weightless in the water—beyond buoyant. No wetness registered on her skin; the cold was gone. Only the enveloping, healing presence of Genevive tingling throughout her body stirred her senses.

"Raelyn," Genevive said out loud through Raelyn's voice. "Allow me full control."

Raelyn instinctively gripped the void within, holding it like a shield. She relaxed and let the pit of cold settle down into her core. Terror clouded her thoughts the moment she let go of her point of control. But this was what she'd asked for, and she needed to trust the goddess. She allowed the void to retreat from her grasp, calm, small, and quiet.

A boat of soldiers coasted into the center water of the Gate, circling Raelyn. They yelled at her and pointed, but their words were muffled and indistinct. She watched them from the distant part of her consciousness, where she sat as a link between worlds. She was a bystander, nothing more. The woman floating in the water was not her. It was Genevive, the Second Pillar of The Circle.

"She's coming," Genevive warned.

Her arms extended, and the remaining water in the lake exploded outward, carrying the boats and soldiers away with it. The sky disappeared behind a cloud of vapor as the droplets evaporated with the force of her shockwave. Men and boats rained down onto the shoreline in piles. Dazed, the soldiers slowly got to their feet and clustered together, uncertain what to make of the lone woman standing at the center of the enormous, fully revealed Sundered Gate.

Genevive knelt and pressed a hand against the marble floor of the raised altar platform. "It has been many ages since I've been here." She stood and squared her shoulders. "I'm sure you can say the same, Raloria."

"How dare you come to defy me, you snake! To think that I'd finally come back to the mortal world just to see your ugly face."

Genevive smiled and turned to look at the goddess in Saraht's body. "I see your priestesses finally snagged a warden for you after all this time," she said. "A pity all of your other altar stones were destroyed."

"Yes, a pity." Raloria lifted a hand, and the volley of arrows dropping toward them from the lake edge fell apart into dust. "These pathetic mortals would have learned their place a lot sooner. I should take care of them first."

She stepped off the marble and walked up the lakebed, unimpeded by the mud and silt. The soldiers shot another round of arrows, and she batted them away with ease.

Power surged through Raelyn, vibrating her body, and the ground around Raloria rolled and buckled. Towers of dirt rose, dragging bedrock from the depths. The summoned columns of land climbed toward the sky and crashed down on top of the other goddess, encasing her in a mountain of soil and gravel tall enough to be level with the grassy lawn at the lake's edge.

Without pause, Genevive called forth a circle of storm wind. She stood in its calm center while the currents danced around her. With a wave of her arm, an identical sphere formed around the soldiers still recovering from their expulsion from the lake. No sooner were the protective winds in place, Raloria burst forth from her burial spot, shooting rocks and debris in all directions.

"I see you can't wait," she snarled at Genevive. "Why, sister? Why not join me? There is no one to stop us. This world would be ours."

"I am loyal to Ute and his law. No good can come of gods toying with mortal lives. In his absence, you will face me." Dark clouds gathered over the lake. "I am the Second Pillar, surpassed in power only by Hestran, First Pillar, and Ute himself. I will remind you of your place."

During her time joined with Volaris, Raelyn had felt awed by the god's reserves of power. It had reminded her of sitting on a trained warhorse as a child, feeling the strength and power under her and knowing there was no way she could control it once the horse started running. With Genevive, the feeling was vastly different. Instead of sitting on a warhorse, Raelyn was on a boat in the ocean, paddling but completely at the mercy of the tides and waves. The goddess's power was unfathomable, deeper than the ocean itself, but it didn't evoke terror or dread. The power wrapped Raelyn in a cloak of comfort, replacing her doubts with absolute confidence and assuredness. It was soothing, empowering—nothing like the lack of control she'd felt with Volaris.

Dark clouds collided overhead, shooting lightning bolts, accompanied by loud claps of thunder.

Raloria slid back down the lakebed to the Gate and stepped onto the slab across from Genevive. With a wave of her arms, creatures of flame sprang to life around her: knights on hellish steeds built from fire. She yelled a battle cry and pointed, sending her minions at full gallop across the marble expanse.

Genevive looked up at the sky through her shield of wind, and the clouds let loose with a deluge of rain. Raloria's fire creatures dissipated into steam and ash. The rain droplets froze, turning into sharp projectiles and encasing the statues and surrounding lakebed in ice. On the other end of the Gate, Raloria waved her hands above her head and met the icy shards with a barrier of flame.

Genevive watched calmly from under the shelter of rock she'd constructed.

"You always did like fire," she called to Raloria. "Such easy magic. You don't have to reform it; you just have to redirect it."

"I can make it hotter, if you'd like." The Seventh Pillar knelt and touched the ground.

A crack split the lakebed, and molten rock seeped up and surrounded the Gate platform. It filled the low areas around them, creating a pool of orange and red with slow-forming bubbles and waves of heat that cast currents through the air. Raloria turned her palms up and lifted darts of red-hot rock from the molten lake. With a flick of her hands, she hurled them at Genevive, one after another.

Lightning flashed above Genevive, and she shot one arm out. Another soaking rain poured down, cooling the molten rock around them and hardening the pieces sailing through the air. With a wave, the airborne rocks scattered, clattering against the marble slab and its altars. A lightning bolt struck the ground at Raloria's feet, knocking her backward.

"Raelyn," Genevive spoke within their shared mind. *"It is time to end this. Matching Raloria's strength is futile, and the battle will be eternal. But if I unleash more of my power, the remaining mortals in this area will likely perish."*

Raelyn hesitated. The thought of so many more innocent lives lost weighed heavy on her, but how many more would die if she didn't allow this sacrifice? *"What other choice do we have?"* she asked grimly, watching as the goddess continued to battle.

"There may be another way, but it is risky. You are a warden, Raelyn, exceptionally powerful." Genevive hastily erected stone shields against a barrage of ground spikes. *"I believe you can cast Raloria back to our realm without killing her conduit, but you cannot use the void without casting me back, as well. It is the only way to end this without more death."*

"I can't. I barely know how to control our connection. Saraht would kill me in an instant."

Genevive ignored her protest. *"An instant is all you may have to save everyone. I can get you as close to her physical body as possible to reduce how far you must extend your influence."*

"What if I'm not strong enough?"

"I can feel your power, Raelyn. I believe, of all the wardens across the ages, you have the ability to do this. It is why Ute has chosen you. But there remains a great risk. Do you feel compelled to spare the life of this woman? Sometimes, death is a kindness when the heart is filled with hatred."

Raelyn searched her own heart. Saraht was responsible for the death of her father, the destruction of her home, and the loss of Jackson. All the pain in Raelyn's world laid at the feet of the woman standing across the Gate. But, despite the anger and outrage she felt, Raelyn didn't want anyone to die. More than anything, she just wanted to understand.

"I'll do it," she said, resolute. *"I don't know how, but I'll do it."*

"When we are close to one another, reach for the void and focus every bit of your power on Raloria. We do not know if this will work. No warden has ever cast a god out from another. Are you sure you wish to chance unleashing the Seventh Pillar on the world?"

"No," she answered, and it was true. She wasn't certain at all. It sounded like the wrong choice. Her father had always said sacrifices were necessary and acceptable if they were for the greater good. A part of her knew the logic in that, but she couldn't condemn the lives of innocent people—people she loved—when there was a chance she could save everyone. For once, she had the opportunity to protect those she cared about. *"I'm not certain, and I'm terrified, but let's take the chance."*

It was an all-or-nothing gamble, a desperate reach for salvation from the depths of destruction. Raelyn steeled herself. She would either save everyone, or she would die alongside them at the dawn of a new age.

"Raloria!" Genevive called across the marble battleground. "Let us end this with honor and as equals. Will you cross swords with me, sister?" Swords appeared in her hands, their blades white and glowing like the lightning she commanded. "For old times' sake."

Raloria sneered. "You were never very good with weapons, Genevive. I wonder that you'd limit yourself so."

"I grow bored deflecting your weak magic," she replied. "Perhaps this will be more entertaining."

Pride stung by the insult, Raloria summoned a spear of fire. "I'll show you who deserves to be the ruler of this world!" She ran to meet Genevive's purposeful stride toward the center of the Gate.

Hanging on the edge of anticipation, Raelyn watched the goddesses trade blow for blow. She kept her awareness on the fragment of void resting quietly inside her, carefully contained. She couldn't afford any doubts, any hesitations. There was no room for error.

A double slash by Genevive brought Raloria's spear up in defense. The Second Pillar pushed in against the Seventh. Her pressure slid Raloria back a step, and the goddesses shared a heated glare over their weapons.

Like plucking a fish out of water, Raelyn grabbed control of the void at her core. She placed all her focus into the pit of emptiness and expanded it just as she'd practiced. Instead of maintaining awareness of what was happening outside her body, she fully gave herself to the black center of nothingness. She was the void, expanding outward, bringing oblivion to everything around her.

Genevive's presence vanished, and once again, as when Volaris left her, the emptiness remaining was enveloping. It was *her* darkness, the part of her that was the void and the part of her that was grief and loss. The sense of disconnection, of drifting in her own mind, locked her in place. This time, there was nothing to draw her back out. She accepted the prison of nothingness as her deserved end and closed her eyes, focusing on the sensation of floating.

A shockwave rippled through her; something disrupted the darkness. She jolted, registering pain. The void receded as another twinge of hurt spread through her. More pain. Her consciousness pulled back from the emptiness, and she became aware of her surroundings; the void was once again just a pit at her center.

"Die! Die!"

Hands gripped Raelyn's neck, and she looked through hazy vision at Saraht on top of her. Bloodied and battered, the Faldean commander let go of the choke and hit Raelyn in the face. The blunt pain brought her back to full consciousness, and she reached up to defend herself.

"I'll kill you!" Saraht repeated over and over, bearing down on her.

Raelyn clawed at her attacker's face, desperate to get up and away. Saraht hit her again, dropping her elbow onto Raelyn's cheek, splitting it open. Dazed, she stopped struggling, and Saraht reached for her neck again.

Pulling at the hands around her throat, the edges of Raelyn's vision faded in and out of focus. She felt weak. Her arms wouldn't listen. They were heavy and slow. *No!* she thought. *I can't die here. I can't let her get to another altar stone.*

With a cry, she mustered her strength and let go of the hands at her throat to reach up. She pushed her thumbs into Saraht's eyes, forcing the other woman to sit back and relinquish her hold. Momentarily free, Raelyn rolled to her side and dragged herself away, senses still swimming from asphyxiation.

Saraht growled in rage. She grabbed at Raelyn's kicking legs.

The air around them whistled. When the sound stopped, Saraht went still, and both women looked down at the point of an arrow protruding from her chest.

Raelyn flinched when another arrow landed next to the first, and blood spread a slick sheen across the remnants of Saraht's sullied dress. Raelyn looked up at the top of the lake shore, studying the silhouettes of the soldiers still watching the battle. Following the line of a dark trail down the gravel and dirt to the edge of Raloria's hardened molten lake, she saw a figure walking toward them, bow in hand.

His face scraped and bruised, Jackson nocked another arrow and took aim. He let it loose, and it landed between the others, the three shafts lined up like flags across Saraht's back. She looked at Raelyn, eyes wide, a mixture of disbelief and despair across her features. Her mouth opened, but no words came out, and she slumped forward onto the marble.

Raelyn fell onto her back next to the body. Dark clouds from Genevive's magic lingered overhead, and a water droplet landed in the middle of Raelyn's forehead. She stared up at the sky, mind and body overexerted. She felt everything all at once, the emotions rushing through her but none staying long enough to settle. Staring up at the clouds, she simply *was*—grateful for the peace that came just from existing, for one moment, without expectation, duty, or responsibility.

Warm hands lifted her. Jackson was alive. There would be time to decide which path of fate she wanted to walk. The Sundered Gate had been revealed, and she was the only warden left. Eyes closed, she thought of Laris and his likely capture. Jackson would see him released from detainment for helping her; she had no doubt. And Hendrel—she wondered where he'd gone in her moment of need. She let out a deep sigh.

There would be time to figure it out. She had lots of time.

"Easy now, Mother, easy," Ellisand said, propping the duchess up with another pillow. "There's no need to worry. The guards say the threat has been eliminated. King Rothelian has dispatched aid to the city and opened the royal warehouses in the trade district to be used as shelters. I'm sure the soldiers have already started bringing in survivors."

With a cough, Duchess Wedminth nodded and leaned back into the softness of the bed. Ellisand smoothed her mother's hair away from her pale, damp skin and patted her hand affectionately.

"I'll go get you some more tea. They say you'll be better in no time."

"You know they'll come for her now," Altha rasped. "Now that they know what she is."

Ellisand paused at the dresser, hand extended toward the white pitcher flecked with gold. "Who will come, Mother?" she asked, watching steam rise from the spout in a long curl.

"The Holy Knights. They'll take her away and lock her up." The duchess cackled gleefully but was stopped short by another fit of coughing. "Stupid girl," she mumbled when her breath returned. "We were doing her a favor all these years. Now she belongs to them. They'll already be on their way."

"Raelyn's resourceful." Ellisand dropped a lump of sugar into the cup. "I'm sure she'll be fine, even in the Holy Citadel." *And with her gone, I won't have to worry about her interfering again.*

Ellisand would have the throne. Saraht was dead, but her dream of a matriarchy was as alive as ever. As queen, Ellisand would never again need to sit silently while others made decisions on her behalf. She'd have the power to do whatever she wanted, and she could continue in the quest to save and elevate women around Limnin.

But Raelyn was more powerful than Ellisand could ever be, even as a queen. She could cause trouble, bring everything to a halt—she'd already shown a willingness to be disloyal to Ellisand if she saw fit. No, Raelyn couldn't be allowed to stay in Osharia.

Ellisand let out a deep breath, recentering her thoughts. There was no need to get worked up. Raelyn would be leaving Osharia, that much was for certain. The Holy Knights would see to it. A surge of satisfaction swelled in her chest at the thought, and she smiled. Raelyn had to pay for betraying her confidence, anyway. Maybe some time under lock and key would humble her.

Pulling a small, hidden vial from her bodice, she tapped its contents into the steaming cup of tea, just as she had every day since reuniting with her mother. The yellow powder dissolved quickly, aided by a stir with the spoon.

Ellisand had always paid attention to Ebest's ramblings. The old alchemist would have demanded they be uprooted if she'd seen how many beesbane trees decorated the capital gardens.

"Make sure you drink it all," she said sweetly, taking the cup to the bed.

Nothing was going to stand in her way.

On the windowsill adjacent to the duchess's bed, Lydantus stretched and arched his back before settling and sprawling out on his side. Quiet but alert, he studied Ellisand as she handed the cup to her mother, his emerald eyes unblinking, always watching.

ACKNOWLEDGEMENTS

This book would not have been possible without the support of many extraordinary people, most especially my husband, who has always championed my writing dreams and shared my passion for all things fantasy.

I am eternally grateful to my nieces and my siblings-in-law, who took the time to read and provide feedback during the final drafting process. Special gratitude is due to my friend and fellow author, Lizzi, who reignited my drive to write creatively and offered valuable insight on the entire journey.

To my wonderful editor, Morgan at Glasswing Editing, and Nicole and Kyera at Golden Scales Publishing, thank you for believing in this book — and in me — and for putting the shine on a work I can be truly proud of.

ABOUT THE AUTHOR

A Pennsylvania native, H.R. Cole grew up `immersed in fantasy books and completed her first novel (handwritten) when she was twelve. Her love of reading and writing fantasy continued through a career in the veterinary field, where she managed a four-doctor hospital, and later set her up for a successful writing career in medical journalism.

In her creative writing, Cole addresses common inner dialogues related to self-worth and insecurity. She loves to forge her characters through hardship while representing inner growth in a realistic way.

Cole lives with her husband, dogs, and cats in the mountains of Upstate New York.

Photo by P. W. Cole